"Cassandra, that's Vayl's front door. And you've just described the kid who was ringing the bell."

Did he answer?"

"I don't—"

A shot rang out, tearing my heart in two. Jack growled menacingly, already on his way down the final set of steps. I glanced into the well made by the turn of the stairs from second to first floor. Yeah, I could jump it. So I did, landing on another one of Vayl's overstuffed sofas. The impact sent me rolling into the walnut coffee table fronting it, knocking it across the hall into a case full of antique knives. I raised my arm, protecting my face from the shattering glass.

Not knowing how far the glass had scattered, I protected my bare feet by jumping back onto the couch. Then I took half a second to assess the situation.

Twenty feet from me, at the other end of the hall in front of the open door, Vayl lay in a spreading pool of blood, the bloody hole in his forehead a result of the .38 Special lying on the floor. There were two reasons the young man kneeling over him still wasn't holding it. He needed both hands for the hammer and stake he now held poised over Vayl's chest.

Praise for the Jaz Parks series

"The humor really shines as Rardin's kick-ass heroine guides readers through her insane life."

—*Romantic Times*

JAZ PARKS NOVELS

Once Bitten, Twice Shy

Another One Bites the Dust

Biting the Bullet

Bitten to Death

One More Bite

Bite Marks

Bitten in Two

The Deadliest Bite

THE DEADLIEST BITE

A JAZ PARKS NOVEL

Jennifer Rardin

orbit

www.orbitbooks.net

Orbit
Hachette Book Group
237 Park Avenue, New York, NY 10017
www.HachetteBookGroup.com

First Edition: June 2011

Orbit is an imprint of Hachette Book Group, Inc. The Orbit name and logo are trademarks of Little, Brown Book Group Limited.

Library of Congress Cataloging-in-Publication Data

Rardin, Jennifer.
The deadliest bite / Jennifer Rardin. — 1st ed.
p. cm.
ISBN 978-0-316-04381-6
1. Parks, Jaz (Fictitious character)—Fiction. 2. Vampires—Fiction.
3.Assassins—Fiction. 4. Hell—Fiction. I. Title.
PS3618.A74D43 2011
813'.6—dc22
2010046446

10 9 8 7 6 5 4 3 2 1

Printed in the United States of America

"The Deadliest Bite is not the one you get from the nest of vipers striking at you from the top of an angry gorgon's head. It comes from the demon that's sunk its teeth into your soul, the one that refuses to let go because, oh baby, your blood is like red, red wine."

—Jaz Parks interview with Jennifer Rardin, August 2007

Chapter One

Wednesday, June 13, midnight

I'll say one thing about walking around with a rubber band up your asscrack—it helps train you for torture.

"They call them thongs," the girl at Victoria's Secret had told me, doing her best not to look at me like I'd experienced major brain damage sometime between high school and college.

"I know what they call them," I'd said as I picked at the flimsy material and tried not to wince. "I just don't understand why..." I'd looked around the store. They were everywhere, like fluffy pink bunnies that multiply while you aren't looking and then blow your foot off the second you step on them.

The girl had blinked her silver-lined eyelids and shrugged. "They're sexy."

"Uh-huh. Are they comfortable too? Like, am I gonna come home from work all tired and grumpy and say to my dog, 'I'm crapped out. Time for a warm bath, flannel pj's, and my thong?'"

"It could happen." She'd smiled, faintly, just one corner of her mouth rising, which had reminded me of why I was standing in the middle of lingerie paradise in the first place. Vayl. Who was, even now, counting to one hundred, giving me a chance to find a new cubbyhole to hide in before he began hunting the halls of the red brick monstrosity he called home.

As I padded through neatly arranged rooms full of expensive furniture and beautifully displayed antiques, it struck me as hilarious that the vampire who owned them all chose to spend his free time playing strip hide-and-seek with his sorta-human girlfriend. I caught sight of myself in the gilt-framed mirror over the fireplace and smiled. Because I was more than that. Vayl called me his *avhar*—a Vampere word that described better than any other the infinite number of ties that bound me to him. I also smiled because, after sixteen days of rest and relaxation from a series of missions that had nearly killed both of us, I had to admit I was looking better. Eating three meals a day had filled out the hollows. Now I couldn't count each rib just by looking. My fingernails had stopped flaking. My eyes had brightened until sometimes they reminded me eerily of my father's snapping green orbs as they cut through us the first day he got home from a tour, inspecting the troops to see how we'd grown in his absence. Even my curls seemed bouncier and redder except, of course, for the white-streaked one that curved into my right cheek like a familiar friend. I didn't let my glance linger on it. No point in reminding myself of my first trip to hell when this game, like all the others Vayl and I had played, was designed to make the most of the time we had left until I had to go back.

"Fee fi fo fum! My senses are tingling with huuu-man!" Vayl called.

"Crap!" Just one in Vayl's awesome bag-o-tricks was the ability to pick up on strong emotions. My little detour down Vanity Lane had given away my position.

One last glance in the mirror. We'd been playing the game for a while. All he'd left me wearing was a watch, the blue lace Victoria's Secret underwire I'd bought, which gave me such incredible lift I had actual cleavage (yeah, baby!), the matching dungeons-r-us thong, and a pair of three-inch black heels that made sneaking damn near impossible but did wonders for my legs. Of course Vayl was down to a pair of red silk boxers, so our next encounter promised to be mondo fun. Especially if I made the hunt interesting.

I snapped the band of my watch. My super-genius buddy Bergman had invented it for me, wiring it to use the kinetic energy it had stored from my movements to shield their sound. Sometimes being an assassin for the CIA comes in handy. Especially when you get to use cool spy gadgets to play sneak-n-peek with your lover.

I was on the main floor, looking for a decent place to tuck in, listening for sounds of movement above and hearing none. Geez, the guy lived in a ninety-year-old Victorian! Shouldn't one floorboard squeak? Then I'd know which staircase he was descending, at least. The main one connected the second, third, and fourth floors to the front door. The rear stairs, darker and much narrower because snobs didn't think servants deserved elbow room back when, only went from the kitchen to the second floor, where all the bedrooms were located, and the basement, where all the creepy, clanky junk had been installed.

Though I wasn't sure I had time, I paused for a second, reached out, and *sniffed*. My nostrils flared, though the scent that wafted into my brain stem had nothing to do with true odor. It was all mental, and never before had I been so pleased to have had this Sensitivity to *others* (as in nonhumans) dumped on me. The price, dying twice and then being brought back by a mind-blowing Power with a soft spot for model trains, and me, had always seemed too high. Even though I'd gotten to know Raoul well enough to think of him as both my Spirit Guide and my friend, it still did. But if I could finally get some fun out of the deal, maybe...there! Vayl was definitely sneaking down the servants' stairs.

I tiptoed toward the front of the house and slipped into a room he liked to call the conservatory. Although when I told him Miss Scarlet did it in there with the candlestick he just looked at me blankly and said, "Was the candlestick sitting on the pianoforte?" In some ways the dude is permanently stuck in the eighteenth century.

Some of that showed in the choices he'd made for the room, as well. A huge window seat spanned the whole length of the front wall. Covered with lace-edged cushions, it gave the lazy lounger a spectacular view of Ohio's countryside. Because Vayl didn't live in Cleveland, but had bought a house about twenty minutes outside the city, where if you stood still long enough you could hear cows mooing across the cornfields.

He hadn't bothered draping that window, although he had thrown Bergman at it, which meant it was covered by a UV shield that kept perverts (and the worst rays of the sun) from peeping inside. It was also (along with the rest of the house) protected by the most sophisticated alarm system known to man.

Which was probably why when Vayl did chill out in the room, he could feel extra-relaxed in the high-backed white sofa that sat perpendicular to the fireplace. Tall gold tassel-shaded lamps stood at each end of the couch, though he could see in the dark, so they had to be more for looks than practicality. I hadn't figured out yet if he preferred the couch or the overstuffed blue chair across from it, its round, tufted footstool reminding me of a foofy dog set permanently into begging position. After all, that would give him a better view of the gleaming white instrument sitting at a diagonal in the corner opposite the widely arched entryway. It was, in a fact, a real antique pianoforte. Vayl had played it for me the night before, some classical piece that would be great to fall asleep to. I'd matured enough, in the time I'd known him, not to say what I was thinking out loud. But as soon as I got a chance I'd be taking that guy to a Killers concert. He had no idea what he was missing.

I lifted up the window seat, expecting to find boxes of puzzles and old toys like the ones my Granny May had stored in hers. But either Vayl wasn't into storage or his house was big enough to display all his goodies, because the cabinet under the bench was empty. A perfect hiding place for one five-foot-five twenty-six-year-old who badly wanted to see her vamp shed his shorts.

Unless she had a touch of the Claustrophobia.

I stared at the dark, empty space. Three seconds later I decided it had shrunk in the three seconds I'd considered it. While my competitive streak warred with my fear, I looked around for an alternative.

A round table covered with a floor-length blue satin cloth stood in the corner next to another blue chair, this one less comfy but more elegant than its fireside cousin. *Under the table?* Less confining, since the cover was flexible. But no. It held too much glass; both an old-fashioned globe lamp embossed with blooming roses, and a figurine of a hummingbird tasting nectar from a red petunia. However, behind the chair…*yup, that'll work*. I'd shucked my shoes and swung one leg over the back of the chair when the doorbell. Fucking. Rang.

Vayl skidded around the corner. "Jasmine!"

Shit, damn, shit, shit, shit, shit! I tried to think of a less graceful position for a woman who'd deliberately set out to look sexy to be caught in. But I couldn't imagine anything worse than straddling a wing chair with one hand on the wall for balance, one foot on the armrest, and my mostly bare ass stuck halfway between. So I yelled, "Get out!"

The screen door slammed. Moments later a car peeled away.

"I think I scared off your visitor," I said.

"It is midnight in the middle of nowhere. Either he had no business being here in the first place. Or his business would have proved a maddening distraction from *my* business, which is much more important." Vayl leaned against the door frame, crossing his hands behind his back so I'd be sure to get a great view of his broad, curl-covered chest. He grinned, his fangs giving him the look of a hungry lion. "But I have a feeling you were not speaking to him to begin with."

"Well…no. I mean—" I motioned to myself. "This isn't how I figured you'd find me. In fact, you weren't supposed to— Oh shit, there's no way to get out of this position without looking even more ridiculous. Turn around."

"I will do no such thing."

"But—"

"Jasmine, your body is more delectable than melted chocolate on a sea of sugar candies. And the fact that you wore that lovely confection for me—"

"It's coming right off," I warned him as I reclaimed my leg from the no-girl's-land between the chair and the wall. "Stupid piece of crack-grinding—urf!" Whatever I'd meant to say got lost in the spin as Vayl swept me off the chair and twirled us around the room in a spontaneous waltz. His laugh, a deep-throated sound of such genuine mirth that I always ended up joining him, accompanied us even better than the clinking keys of the pianoforte would have. Which was where I ended up sitting, my hands on the lid beside my hips, pinned there as his arms wrapped around me and he covered my lips, my neck, my shoulders with kisses that grew more passionate with each brush of his lips as they crossed my skin, leaving trails of fire that grew with every indrawn breath.

And just before my claustrophobia kicked in, he loosened his arms so he could feather his fingers up my spine and down my shoulder blades. I shivered.

"Cold?" he murmured into my left breast.

"Nnng." I laced my fingers through his and brought them up to my mouth, smiling triumphantly as he moaned.

"We need cushions," he said.

I wrapped my legs around Vayl's hips and locked my elbows around his neck, which was corded with muscle that had been packed on in the days when heavy lifting meant cutting wood for the family's fire and hammering horseshoes out of raw iron. I ran my fingers through his jet-black hair, his soft curls springing around my nails playfully like they, too, realized what little time we had left to just enjoy each other.

We were halfway to the couch when I whispered, as I nuzzled his earlobe, "All *I* need is a flat surface. Baby, it doesn't even need to be horizontal."

Low growl rumbling from his chest into mine as he veered off couch-course. We slammed into the wall, knocking a gasp from me that blew into his ear, making him shiver with delight. His fangs scraped down my neck and suddenly I couldn't touch him, kiss him, love him enough. I wanted to become a part of him, dive through him and leave the finest part of me inside his heart. And the best part was knowing, by the urgency in his touch, in his moans, that he felt exactly the same way.

Afterward we lay in the doorway, tangled around each other because, finally, we didn't have to let go. Vayl ran his finger across my collarbone. It stung enough that I looked down, saw the trail his teeth had left. Just scrapes; he hadn't drunk from me this time.

"Jasmine, I cannot decide how to feel about these." His finger traced the marks again, a sweet irritation. I looked into his eyes and realized how much I depended on their color to clue me into his thoughts and emotions. They'd faded from passion-bright emerald to stormy blue.

"What are you worried about?" I asked.

His finger came under my chin, lifted it up so he could plant a gentle kiss on my lips. "The temptation to taste of you fully rises higher each time we make love," he said. "You feel it as well."

It wasn't a question. He'd had a special insight to my emotions since I'd offered my neck to him the first time, during a mission to Miami when his personal blood supply had been tainted.

I said, "Yeah. Resisting has been...tough."

"And yet we must."

I brought my hand up to his wrist and squeezed. "You never stop surprising me, you know that? Not two months ago you were suggesting you should turn me. And now—"

"You know I was not myself then. Besides, I have had time to consider, and so have you. Think what happens to us each time I drink of you. We are becoming more powerful, and yet unlike any other man and woman on earth."

"Well. We did start out kinda unique."

His nod gave me that. After all, the guy was a Wraith, which meant he could freeze his enemies from the inside out. Even among the Vampere that talent was rare. And people who knew me hesitated to even call me human anymore. Being able to walk in Vayl's memories had made me wonder sometimes myself, although I thought I'd proven that I still had it where it counted.

Vayl said, "I have mentioned couples like us to you before. You do remember the reason that *sverhamin* and *avhar* are so deeply respected among my people."

"Yeah," I said. "I remember."

His hand went to my hair. Dove into my curls and brought a bundle up to his lips, as if only they could resuscitate him. His eyes closed as he inhaled my scent. "Woman, you have no idea how close we walk to the edge of disaster."

"You mean, besides the fact that we assassinate national security threats for a living? Or did until our goddamn Oversight Committee shut us down."

"Never fear about that," Vayl reassured me. "The circle always turns. And I believe Martha knows exactly how to spin this particular wheel."

I had to agree. After learning that our old secretary had actually been running the department all along, I was more certain than ever that nothing could stop the bullet train that was Martha Evans from getting exactly what she wanted. And since, currently, her two priorities were to reopen our department and catch the clawed killer of Pete, the man who'd believed in me when no one else had, who'd hired me into the department and paired me with Vayl, I was cheering her on with both fists in the air.

I shook my head. Leave it to me and Vayl to turn a forced vacation, not to mention a beautiful relationship, into an even more potentially lethal situation than offing monsters for a living! I said, "Okay, so what's so bad about you taking a sip from me every once in a while? Why is it something that should keep me looking over my shoulder?"

He buried his face against my neck, speaking so quietly that I had to strain to hear.

Maybe he hoped that, if I didn't, none of it would be true. "I have told you something of the world that parallels yours, the one in which we *others* walk without pretense but, perhaps sometimes, with even more fear. The Whence runs according to a set of rules you would find both brutal and baffling. And its Council enforces those rules always with its bottom line in mind—whatever happens, do not attract the ire of humanity."

"What does that have to do with you and me?" I asked.

Vayl's hold tightened, becoming almost painful as his breath caught. "I believe because we are *avhar* and *sverhamin* we are changing with every exchange of blood and power, but not into anything this world or the Whence has ever seen. Because I am Vampere and you are Eldhayr the eventual outcome will not be that you become a vampire, but that we both transform into new creatures. Different, powerful species who began our lives as killers. Who are, in fact, the most effective assassins on the planet. Do you think the Whence, or even our own people, will wait around to see if we decide to be friends or foes?"

I couldn't answer. He'd sealed my lips at the word "species."

He went on. "I believe this is why every *avhar/sverhamin* couple has disappeared within a year of their bonding. Either they realized their own danger and melted into the night of their own volition, or they were erased out of fear of what they were becoming together." He drew his face back, showing me eyes that had gone orange around the edges. "This is why we must hold back, though every desire in us calls for the exchange. Your blood, my power. We must never taste of one another in that way again. It is too dangerous for us now."

"How do you know we're not already doomed?" I whispered.

He smiled then, his dimple appearing just long enough to charm me into a stress-releasing breath. "Because we have not yet been visited by a Blank."

"A Blank? Who's that?"

"One of our counterparts in the Whence," Vayl answered. "Except instead of eliminating the monsters who threaten to destroy humanity, they kill *others* whom the Council fears will make humanity want to destroy them."

The doorbell rang. And, yeah, I'll admit I jumped inside the circle of Vayl's arms. As he chuckled I said, "Speak of the devil."

"If we ever have to deal with a Blank, believe me, he will not announce his presence at the front door."

"So who the hell is it?"

Vayl's eyebrow raised a tick. "I suspect it might be the visitor you frightened off before."

"Who shows up at a vampire's door at"—I checked my watch—"one in the morning?

"Perhaps he is an encyclopedia salesman."

"Vayl." I hid a grin. Such a charming trait, this tendency to get stuck in the past. *As long as it's just little bits of him and not the whole enchilada.* The thought sent stabbing pains through my chest every time I remembered our most recent trip abroad, which had ended with his nearly losing all sense of the present in Marrakech. I said, "Nobody buys encyclopedia sets from door-to-door salesmen anymore, because they can get all the information they need from the Internet."

His lips pressed together so tightly I'd almost call his expression a glower. "How can you trust an entity everyone willingly refers to as a Web? If it is as large as they say, you must know the spider that spun it is mountainous."

The doorbell rang again. I said, "I'd like nothing better than to discuss what weapons people use to protect themselves against netbugs. But it sounds like your guest really wants in."

He pulled me close. "Do not worry. It is probably a motorist who has lost his way. People who threaten me never ring the doorbell first. Besides, I saw him on the second-floor security cameras the first time he was here. He is an innocent."

"How could you tell?" I demanded.

"It is one of my gifts."

"Fine." I started grabbing underwear. "But I'm not really prepared to entertain. Where's my shirt?"

"I think we left it in the guest bedroom."

Okay, that meant a run upstairs. But where were my pants? Oh yeah, the library. I'd probably never find my heels again.

"Do you know where your clothes are?" I asked.

"My pants are in the kitchen. And I believe you dropped my shirt in the billiard room," Vayl answered as he slipped back into his boxers, his eyes sparkling like newly polished gems at the memory of our latest game.

"Okay, that leaves you to deal with the dude at the door." I checked the monitor beside the light switch. "He looks nervous. Also tired."

"He has probably been driving in circles all night. I suggest you take the back stairs. I will get rid of him as soon as possible, and then let us go shopping for dinner supplies, shall we? Tonight I think we should try cooking spaghetti again. Perhaps this time I can teach you how to boil pasta without clumping it."

"Good luck with that. Although I'm sure Jack would appreciate a decent meal. He's probably sick of Purina," I said as we walked toward the back of the house, the doorbell insisting that we both move our asses because young-and-nervous needed to find his way back home!

"Wait a moment," Vayl said as he opened the kitchen entrance to the newly fenced backyard. "Jack wants to go with you." My enormous gray-and-white malamute stepped inside and brushed past him, nodding his thanks. (Yes, I'm serious. He's überpolite. Even poops in the same spot so you don't have to go "treasure hunting" every afternoon.) I hadn't yet turned toward the servants' stairs, but Jack divined my intentions and trotted up to the second floor before stopping at the top, grinning at me from white-toothed doggy chops as if to say, *See what good shape I'm in? You should never leave me home during a mission again.*

I ran up after him, patting his head affectionately as I passed him on the way to the guest bedroom. "You're right. I missed you like crazy too. I'll try to keep you close from now on, okay?"

The door I wanted had been thrown wide during Vayl's hunt, the puffy pink duvet still pulled up to reveal the spot where I'd hidden under the four-poster bed. I crossed to the freestanding mirror where he'd tossed my tailored white shirt over the support structure. I threw it on over my bra. Stepped across the hall to the big, elegant room I shared with him to grab a pair of cheek-covering panties to slip on. And, of course, the pet that had preceded Jack had to come with me too, so on went the shoulder holster I'd left sitting on the mahogany dresser. Inside it rested a Walther PPK that had once shot only regular ammo. Then Bergman got ahold of it. Now, with the flick of a button, it transformed into a vamp-smacking crossbow.

Jack had spent the time sniffing hopefully at the sofa that sat at the foot of the bed, its soft gold leather inviting him to jump up and make himself at home. "Don't even think about it," I told him. "There's a reason your bed's downstairs. Now let's bolt before you get into real trouble. I think I hear my pants ringing."

We ran up the main stairs to the third floor, where I found my jeans crumpled beside the cozy brown suede chair where I liked to curl up every afternoon with a book and a can of Diet Coke. I pulled my phone out of the back pocket and stuck it between my ear and shoulder while I shoved my legs into my Levi's.

"Hello?"

"Jaz? Where's Vayl?"

"Hi, Cassandra. He's with me."

"He's all right then?"

"What?" I felt my fingers go numb. Usually I reacted faster. It was my job to make sure my emotions didn't cloud my judgment. Even for the two seconds it took me to realize my psychic friend was freaking out about my lover. "What did you See?"

"There was a mix-up in Australia. I accidentally packed one of your T-shirts in my suitcase. So I was folding it back into my luggage because Dave and I are coming up to visit you and Evie. It was supposed to be a surprise—" She swallowed a sob.

"Tell me now, Cassandra." I tried to keep my voice calm. No sense in shouting at the woman who'd already saved my brother's life with one of her visions. But if she'd been in the room I'd have shaken her till her teeth rattled.

"When I touched your shirt I saw you, leaning over Vayl's body. He had a stake through his heart. The blood—oh, Jaz, the blood." She started to cry for real now.

"Anything else? Come on, Cassandra, I need to know everything you Saw." I'd zipped into my pants. Run to the stairs. Managed to make it to the second floor without breaking my neck. Jack was way ahead of me.

"I don't know. There's this explosion, but not like the kind you see in movies. It's more…ripply. And at the middle is a young man. Younger than you. Taller, even, than Vayl, with full brown hair that keeps falling onto his forehead. He's snarling, which makes two deep dimples appear on his cheeks. He's standing in front of a tall oak door above which is hanging—"

"A pike with a gold tassel," I finished.

"Yes!"

"Shit! Cassandra, that's Vayl's front door. And you've just described the kid who was ringing the bell."

"Did he answer?"

"I don't—"

A shot rang out, tearing my heart in two. Jack growled menacingly, already on his way down the final set of steps. I glanced into the well made by the turn of the stairs from second to first floor. Yeah, I could jump it. So I did, landing on another one of Vayl's overstuffed sofas. The impact sent me rolling into the walnut coffee table fronting it, knocking it across the hall into a case full of antique knives. I raised my arm, protecting my face from the shattering glass.

Not knowing how far the glass had scattered, I protected my bare feet by jumping back onto the couch. Then I took half a second to assess the situation.

Twenty feet from me, at the other end of the hall in front of the open door, Vayl lay in a spreading pool of blood, the bloody hole in his forehead a result of the .38 Special lying on the floor. There were two reasons the young man kneeling over him wasn't still holding it. He needed both hands for the hammer and stake he now held poised over Vayl's chest. And Jack's teeth had sunk deep enough into his right wrist that by now he'd have been forced to drop it anyway.

Only a guy as big as this one wouldn't have been thrown completely off balance by a full-on attack via 120-pound malamute. Despite the fact that a hundred pounds of the guy was weight he didn't need, his size had kept him off his back, though it hadn't allowed him to recover his balance enough to counter with the stake in his free hand. That would change if I didn't reach the scene in time.

I jumped to the outer part of the stairs, holding the rail to keep from falling as I cleared the fallout from the display case. Another jump took me to the floor. Five running steps gave me a good start for a spin kick that should've caught the intruder on the temple, breaking his glasses in at least two places and taking him down so hard he'd be dreaming before his head bounced. But unless they're drugged, people don't just sit and wait for the blow.

He pulled back, catching my heel on his nose. It broke, spraying blood all over his shirt and Jack. His glasses flew off, hitting the wall, but remaining miraculously intact. And it didn't take him down. In fact, it seemed to motivate him. Desperation filled his eyes. He ripped his hammer hand out of Jack's grip, though the bloody rips in his forearm would hurt like a son of a bitch when his adrenaline rush faded.

Afraid his next move would be a blow to my dog, I lunged at him. I was wrong. He threw the hammer at me, forcing me to hit the floor. I rolled when I felt his shadow loom, knowing the worst scenario was me pinned under all that weight. But it never fell on me. I jumped to my feet and began to unholster Grief, though the last thing I wanted was to kill the bastard before I found out who'd sent him.

Still, I was too late. The intruder had retrieved his revolver and was aiming the barrel at my chest. He'd probably hit me too if he squinted hard enough and held his breath long enough to stop shaking. The only positive I could see was that I stood between him and Vayl. For now.

Jack growled menacingly and began to approach the man, his fur standing on end so that he looked like the miniature bear he sounded most like when he vocalized.

The gun wavered as the man said, "You tell that dog to stop, or I will shoot it."

"No, Jack," I said. "Sit."

He came to an unhappy stop beside me. Once again I stood staring at my ultimate end. Because my Spirit Guide had informed me that my body couldn't take another rise to life. If this scumbag capped me, I'd be done. And I *so* wasn't ready.

I said, "I don't know you. And I thought I'd pegged all of our enemies. You're not a werewolf. You're not Vampere. You're definitely no pro."

His eyebrows went up. So. He hadn't been told about our work. Baffling. Still, whoever picked him had chosen well. Amateurs occasionally succeeded where professionals failed because they were unpredictable. And motivated. This one definitely had his reasons for being here. I could see it in the way his eyebrows kept twitching down toward his nose. He was a time bomb ready to blow everyone in the room to bloody bits.

He raised the gun. Uh-oh. While I'd been thinking, so had he. And it looked like he'd made a decision. "You need to walk away from that vampire," he said.

"No."

He pushed the revolver toward me, to make sure I understood he could pull the trigger. "I'm not playing. I will kill you if that's what it takes to smoke him."

"Doesn't matter. I'll die if you do that anyway."

The remark confused him. Upset him. *This isn't a bad man, but damn, something has pushed him way past his limit.* I watched his finger tighten on the trigger. I said, "Don't. Dude, you'll be killing a federal agent. They put you in jail forever for that kind of shit."

"Jail?" He laughed, his voice rising into girl-land as he said, "I'm already in hell." Which was when I knew there was nothing I could say to divert him. I looked down at Jack, touched the soft fur on the top of his head in farewell. Glanced over my shoulder at Vayl, only long enough for the pain to lance through my heart.

I could pull on him, make my final moments an epic shootout. But Jack could get hurt in the crossfire, and I'd never forgive myself if that happened. "Get it over with then."

"NOT SO FAST!!"

I slammed my hands over my ears, though I was pretty sure the voice came from inside my head until I saw that the intruder was wincing and wiping blood from his earlobes as well.

The floor started to shake. Jack yelped and tried to hide between my legs as the polished pine floorboards between me and the intruder began to splinter and the fiery outline of an arched doorway pushed itself up from the basement below.

"Well," I whispered to my dog. "This is new."

I was pretty sure the intruder couldn't see the plane portal rising to stand between us. Most humans never did. But he did get a load of the five-by-six-foot gap developing in the floor. And when Raoul seemed to step out of thin air, I didn't blame him for needing to sit down. Which he did. On a plush, round-cushioned chair that was currently covered with wood chips.

My Spirit Guide recovered Vayl's attacker's weapon so easily I felt a little stupid that I'd ever been paralyzed by it. Maybe I was getting soft in my old age. Maybe seeing Vayl halfway dead had freaked me out more than I should've let it.

Raoul reversed the gun and lightly tapped the intruder on the forehead with it. "Wrong choice, Aaron. And I thought you knew better." He lifted the back of his jungle camouflage jacket and stuck the .38 in the waistband of his matching pants as Aaron tried to get his face to stop twitching. Raoul regarded him quietly for a while and then turned to face me. "Stop trying to get yourself killed. Even the Eminent agreed with me on this one. It isn't your time yet."

"I wasn't *trying*—it's not? Cool!" Nice to think that the folks who called the shots upstairs had actually approved of Raoul's helping me for once. Especially since it had involved saving my neck again.

"So what do you and the other Eldhayr think about this dude? What did you call him, Aaron?" I asked, pointing my chin toward the failed assassin.

Raoul pulled me aside. "I'm not allowed to interfere there." He looked hard into my eyes, trying to communicate information I hadn't known him long enough to decipher. He said, "All I can say is that it's good, really good, that you didn't kill him. Keep doing that."

"What about Vayl?" I asked. "What can you say about him?"

"Do you really need to hear that he's going to be okay? You already know that, Jaz. A bullet to the head can't kill a vampire as powerful as him."

I shrugged. It's one thing to understand something intellectually. It's something completely different to see your lover looking fully dead from a head wound. So I reminded myself again, *He's just been knocked out. If you lifted his head you'd see the back of his skull has probably already re-formed. You shouldn't be trying to figure out how your stomach can manage to clench itself that tight. You should be patting yourself on the back for hooking up with a guy who's that tough to kill.*

"Jasmine? Jaz? Is it over? What happened?"

The voice, small and tinny, could've been mistaken for one of my inner girls, the various parts of my personality that I chat with when I'm überstressed or strapped for choices. But it was real. And hysterically worried. I suddenly realized I'd dropped my phone during the fight and now Jack was trying to dial China with his nose.

"Cut it out," I murmured as I picked it up. "You don't even like rice." I laid the receiver against my ear. "Cassandra? I can't believe you're still there."

"He's important!"

"Of course he is. But he'll be fine. Vampires are—"

"No! I mean, yes, of course. But I'm talking about the young man."

"WHAT? You can't be on Raoul's side in this. This guy Aaron nearly killed us both!" I glared at the would-be murderer. He stared straight at me. Raised his chin slightly. But his lower lip was sending out an SOS I figured his mom could hear from inside her local beauty shop's hair dryer.

Cassandra yelled, "Jasmine Elaine Parks, you listen to your future sister-in-law, dammit! Something is making me tingle like I'm electrified. Let me talk to Aaron!"

I held the phone out to him. "You have a call."

He looked away. "I'm busy."

"Either you talk to the nice lady or I punch your lights out." His eyes, suddenly round and uncertain, went to Raoul, so I added, "Oh, don't look to him for help. He's like the UN. He'll bitch and whine about my behavior, but he'll sit back and let me do the dirty work because, in the end, he knows I'm the one who's gonna save the world."

Raoul growled, "That was a low blow."

I shrugged. "I'm sorry. I know the Eminent is always tying your hands. I just tend to get pissy when people try to kill the guy I love." I looked up at him. "But I do appreciate you coming when you did. Stellar timing, as usual."

I shoved the phone toward Aaron. "The threat still stands, mainly because I'm still highly ticked off and I wanna hit something. It'd be so great if you gave me an excuse."

Aaron took the phone, staring at me suspiciously as he said, "Hello? Yes. No." He listened for a while before his face puckered. But he managed to master the emotion Cassandra had eked out of him before he said another word. Which was "Thanks."

He handed the phone back to me. "Well?" I asked the woman on the other end, who deserved a respectful ear, both because she'd survived nearly a thousand years on this Earth and because she'd chosen to spend the next fifty or so with my brother.

Cassandra took a deep breath. "I can't be sure without touching the boy, but I consulted the tarot while he and I were speaking. It points to the same signs the Enkyklios has been showing me. I have to do more research, but—"

"What are you trying to tell me?"

"Whatever you do, don't hurt him," she repeated, this time in such a sober tone that I looked at him with less anger and more curiosity. Which was why I didn't shove his head into the wall like I'd been planning to when she said, "I believe that, in another life, he was Vayl's son."

I stared at the guy, who looked so much younger than me that it was hard not to think of him as a kid. He glared back. And then, all at once, his face crumpled. It was like he'd only brought enough adrenaline with him to get him through fifteen minutes of action. After that the bravado shattered like an old piece of glass. I said, "You're lucky to be alive."

He tried to answer. I could tell he wanted to say something smart-ass and slightly witty. Instead his jaw dropped and he keeled over, his head hitting the floor with a satisfying *clunk*.

I looked at Raoul. "Cassandra says that's Vayl's son."

Raoul studied the unconscious young man. Then he said, "We should break it to him gently."

Chapter Two

Wednesday, June 13, 1:30 a.m.

I sat next to Raoul on the second-to-last step of the main stairs, watching the boy who would be killer sponge up Vayl's blood and squeeze it into a bucket of bleach water between bouts of gagging that never quite turned into a pukefest. Soooo satisfying to see him gross out on an aftermath he hadn't planned for. But not quite enough to leash the urge to impale him on the lance artfully displayed in the corner next to the front-door topiary and the chair Aaron had previously sat down in before he'd fallen and given himself a goose egg right in the middle of his forehead. Frankly, I couldn't wait for him to look in the mirror. I felt it would be the big blue bow on a gift that just kept giving.

So, for now, I kept one hand buried in Jack's soft fur, and when the rage rose to heights that felt a little too violent for Aaron's personal safety, I reminded myself to imagine that goose egg at about three times its current size. I also glanced at Raoul every thirty seconds or so. In life he'd been a Ranger, so at his core he was a fierce fighting man. That was why he'd chosen to battle on into the afterlife. Still, around that core existed a serenity that calmed me. So just rubbing shoulders with him helped me remember that now was the time to live up to the nickname our department's warlock, Sterling, had dumped on me, and Chill.

"What's he going to do to me?" Aaron asked, trying not to look down the hall but darting his eyes in that direction anyway. He couldn't see the kitchen door from where he crouched because you had to go through the dining room to get there. Which was a good thing. Better to spook him with his own wild imagination. Let him think Vayl was sharpening up a set of butcher knives, or calling in a whole slew of slavering revenants to tear into Aaron like a Christmas turkey. Unless, of course, he spilled his employer's name, address, and current Facebook status.

So Raoul and I just mustered up our most baleful expressions and kept silent on the news that Vayl had taken his massive headache back to the fridge, where he'd found some prepackaged, government-distributed blood to nuke in his favorite coffee cup. Though it would speed healing, what he needed most was a good day's sleep. Knowing him like I did, I figured that while he ate he'd probably take the servants' stairs to our room, which had a connecting bath the size of my entire first apartment, where he'd clean up before he came back down. It wasn't just that he didn't care to walk around with blood caked behind his ears. Like me, he needed some time to decompress or he would, without even thinking, tear a hole in Aaron's throat that you could drive a remote-control car through.

I could feel my *avhar*'s fury even now, burning like the flames I'd seen in the sky the night Raoul and I had traveled to hell. Then it had blazed through anyone who dared to raise their eyes from the ground. Yeah, them and their fifty closest pals. Vayl was just as capable as Raoul of dishing out that kind of damage. Luckily he'd figured out a long time ago the danger he posed to anyone in his vicinity if he let his inner predator take the reins. So as soon as he'd regained consciousness he'd put a hand to his head, taken a long look at the blood on his fingertips, and then raised his icy blue eyes to mine. For a moment they flickered over my shoulder, acknowledged Raoul standing guard over Aaron, then returned to me where I still knelt beside him, holding tight to his other hand.

If I'd just met him I'd have thought he was some kind of sociopath, his face was such a hardened mask. But by now I knew the blank stare meant he was struggling to keep his feelings from erupting into violence. Cirilai, the ring his grandfather had crafted at his mother's request and that had, as she'd predicted, once again saved his soul, sent hot stabbing pains through my fingers. I jerked my hand out of his, staring at the golden knots twisting lovingly around each exquisite ruby that sparkled on my finger, wondering which one had zapped me.

"What happened?" asked Vayl.

"Cirilai hurt me. I think that means *you're* about to blow," I said.

He nodded, his eyes fading rapidly to black. "Deal with that," he said, his finger-flick indicating that if I didn't do something with Aaron, he'd have to. And it wouldn't be pretty.

"Absolutely."

He'd been gone about twenty minutes when Aaron began to show concern. Which was when I told him, "Whatever the vampire plans for you will be relatively painless compared to what *I'm* gonna do."

He paused in his scrubbing to stare me down. "You don't look that scary." The dude couldn't quite get the tremble out of his throat, but he still managed to meet my eyes. I gave him half a point for effort.

Raoul laughed. "Do you want to know how her friend Cole describes her?"

Aaron dropped his head to one side, which was all the encouragement my Spirit Guide needed. He said, "Cole says she may be a skinny white chick, but she'll kick your ass so fast you'll wonder why your butt cheeks are dented."

I hid a smirk and reminded myself to call my buddy, and former recruit, as soon as I had a free minute. Our last mission had been a bitch to him and he wasn't adapting well to the downtime. In fact, this situation would probably cheer him up immensely. Give him something to take his mind off the fact that he'd nearly become a demon in Marrakech, and part of him had liked it. I sent a mental message to Teen Me to try to remember where I'd left my phone in all the chaos, while I went on with the task at hand. Which was to get as much information as I could out of the prisoner while Vayl was still pissed at him. Because as soon as he found out they'd once been as close as two men ever managed to get, that'd be the end of it.

I said, "Raoul here says your first name is Aaron. What's your last name?" I asked.

"How does he know that?" Aaron demanded.

"It's his job. Now. You got a last name?"

I watched him consider stubbornness. And then realize it didn't really matter. We had him cold. He said, "Sullivan."

I sat forward just enough to cause Jack to readjust his head where it lay on my lap. He moved it to my knees, blinking his eyes from me to Aaron and back again like he truly understood our conversation. "They sent you in blind, didn't they? I'd almost guess someone wanted *you* dead, except you nearly succeeded in killing Vayl, so I have to believe whoever hired you really wanted him out of the picture. Would you like to fork over any names before your lips get too puffy for me to understand you perfectly and you have to keep repeating yourself?"

Raoul said, "Jaz. Do we have to threaten him with violence already? He hasn't even stopped cooperating."

I glared at my Spirit Guide. "I'm itching for an excuse to punch this little creep. Would you stop being so damn nice?"

I turned to Aaron, waiting for his answer. But apparently Raoul's soft heart had made his decision for him. He sealed his lips shut, shook his head, and went back to cleaning.

I said, "You should know it's not just me and Vayl you have to worry about. After we're done with you I'll be calling a very select group of government agents who, after hearing you've nearly smoked one of the most valuable public servants this country has ever known, will be only too happy to make sure you disappear forever. But not before you learn how to scream like a little girl. That is, unless you cooperate. You got me?"

Aaron didn't bother to look up as he said, "I have nothing to tell you besides the fact that I tried to kill a filthy vampire and I failed. Now I'm going to get my blood sucked dry. In fact, by morning I'll probably be one of those leeches with legs myself." He shook his head, spat with disgust, then wiped it up with a rag I'd be burning shortly.

Rip out his hair and feed it to him, Jaz! It was my Inner Bimbo, teetering on her bar stool because she was balancing a cigarette between two fingers and a rum and Coke in the same hand, and rummaging through her big, black bag with the other hand. I had to chime in, even if it was only in my mind.

Why do you care? He's so not your type I'm surprised you're actually able to see him. So far the only upside to his personality I've found is that he's discovered the single kernel of bravery inside his core and he's hanging on to it for dear life—what the hell are you doing?

After what just happened with Vayl, you have to ask why that piece of shit deserves battery clips and a strong current? As for what I'm doing, I thought I had a book on self-defense in here, you know, just in case one of my lovers gets a little too frisky. When I find it I'm going to read you all kinds of suggestions for how to deepen his dimples. She paused to imitate a bellows, sucking in and blowing out enough cigarette smoke to give the entire bar the feel of a foggy Halloween night. *Remember, I'm the one who knows best how to make you lose control.*

Pull in the claws, Sheba. This one gets to live. Although if I decide to slap him around a little you can be my cheerleader.

Stellar! I even have the outfit!

Why am I not surprised?

I'd been silent enough to make Aaron-boy nervous. Still concentrating on his cleaning he asked, "What're you going to do with me?"

Fuck if I know. So I answered his question with a question. "How many vampires have you met?"

"Including yours?"

"Yeah."

"None. I wouldn't say we'd been properly introduced, would you?"

I stood up and, surprisingly, Raoul didn't hold me back. He didn't even protest when I grabbed Aaron's .38 Special out of his waistband and shoved it against the little prick's skull. "I've had enough of your attitude. Normally I enjoy smartasses. But not when they've just tried to murder the man I love."

"He's not a man. He's a parasite!"

I pushed down on the barrel hard enough to leave a nice round imprint if I ever decided to back off, and Aaron figured out it was my turn to talk. "That *vampire* has been working for the United States government for eighty years. He's saved our country from decimation more times than I care to recount. In fact, dumbass, you just nearly destroyed a national treasure."

He looked up at me then, his cheeks jiggling slightly with the nerve it took to meet my eyes. I found myself respecting him slightly more as he managed a firm, "No."

"In some circles he's considered to be more important than the president."

Aaron scrubbed for a while in silence. When he had nothing left but clean floor to stare at he threw the rag in the bucket and sat back on his heels. "I don't believe you." Stubborn. I should have expected as much from Vayl's spawn, even this many generations removed from his direct influence.

"Astral," I called.

I'd left the robokitty Bergman had invented for me upstairs with orders to stay in my room until she heard from me again. Hopefully she'd function properly now that I really needed her to pull through for me.

She streaked down the stairs, a sleek black missile on four legs with twitchy ears, a lashing tail, and a tendency to burst into inappropriate songs that had developed only after Jack had surprised her during a reconnaissance, causing her to blow her own head off. The repairs had been more, and less, than a complete success. Considering the latest eccentricity to appear in what had become the quirkiest personality I'd ever seen in a homemade cat, I was voting for less.

Jack greeted Astral by sitting up straight at Raoul's knee. He knew better than to jump her now. In fact, most of the time he was willing to wait until she approached him or called him over to play. I watched her just as carefully, and let out a breath I hadn't realized I was holding when all she did was bob her head at me and say, "Hello!"

I nodded at her, though I understood that I was acknowledging a mobilized supercomputer, and said, "Show me Vayl's file. Keep the top secret parts to yourself."

Astral's mouth ratcheted open and a light clicked on, movie-theater style. At the same time a hologram of Vayl's papers appeared in front of my face even as I heard a velvety-voiced woman reading them. "Vasil Nicu Brâncoveanu. Born in what is now Mogosoaia, Romania, on November 18, 1713, though at the time the area was called Wallachia. Became a vampire in 1751. Current assignment: Agent for Antiterrorism Division of the Central Intelligence Agency commonly known as ATD. Division is temporarily shut down at the request of its Oversight Committee due to the murder of one of its agents, Ethan Mreck, and its director, Peter Huttin."

Of course that wasn't the whole truth. Our division existed as a subsidiary of the ATD, its name so secret only a few people in government had ever even heard it. And my boss, Pete, had actually been following his "secretary" Martha's orders all along. But the rest—way more truth than I'd wanted to deal with today. Damn Aaron Sullivan.

He said, "Why are you letting me see this?" The whites of his eyes had begun to show. "This really isn't a bluff, is it? It doesn't matter what I know if you've already decided to kill me." He shoved his thumb into his mouth, started to chew the nail, then quickly wrapped his arm around his back with a guilty look, like he'd been caught raiding the cookie jar. I wondered, suddenly, how many times his parents had cracked his knuckles for biting his nails as a kid.

Hiding a sudden rush of sympathy, I pulled the gun away from his head. "You have pissed me off more deeply than anyone I've met in the past six months and you're still alive. That reads well for your future. The fact that I'm explaining Vayl to you at all should give you even more hope."

"But why?"

"Yes." Vayl had come through the dining room door. He held a bag of frozen peas to the wound on his forehead. "Why do you give this young man my secrets?"

I felt Aaron do a big swallow beside me. It's one thing to attack an unsuspecting victim inside his front door. Especially when you're rushing in with your head full of preconceived notions. It's a whole other story to mop up the blood you spilled and then watch your target saunter down the hall, all cleaned up and pissed as hell that you interrupted a fabulous evening, ruined his favorite shirt, and gave him a pounding headache.

I savored the moment, knowing how quickly it was about to change. Dreading the possibilities ahead of me. Vayl's two sons had been murdered when he was still human. He had made it his quest to find their re-embodied souls ever since. And now that the reality was staring me in the face, I wanted to annihilate it. So typical.

I stepped back, shoving Aaron's revolver into the waistband of my jeans to make sure it was well out of the way when I told Vayl, "Cassandra called to warn me about the shooting just before it happened. Obviously I was too late to stop it, and I sure as hell wanted to follow through with the retribution after I'd seen what this dude had done. But she wouldn't let me."

"Why not?" Vayl asked, his icy blue eyes tracking every stray hair, every bruise and hollow of his attacker, cataloguing what he saw for future reference.

I cleared my throat. "She believes he's your son."

Vayl went still. His eyes broke to mine, hope blooming in them like wild daffodils. "Is she sure?"

"Not without touching him, but she spoke to him. She ran the tarot. And the Enkyklios is confirming. She says this guy Aaron is the reincarnation of your boy Badu."

I glanced at Raoul. He was watching Vayl intently, his hands buried in Jack's fur. I realized he was hoping Vayl wouldn't be crushed when Aaron rejected him. That, despite his personal problems with vamps, he was quietly supporting the creature he'd tried to boot out of my life a few months ago.

After a minute I realized Vayl hadn't responded. I looked back up at him and tried to decide if he'd changed in that moment, or if I'd suddenly been given leave to see him more clearly. His hair, still glistening with droplets from the shower, curled riotously all over his head. His jet-black eyebrows slanted like wings over eyes that had softened to gold with brown flecks dancing in their depths. They contrasted startlingly with the hard lines of his cheekbones and jaw, although when I saw the dimple appear in his right cheek I knew his feelings ran deep to the hopeful side of the bank.

"I cannot believe it."

"Okay." *And yet, you want to, so damn desperately. Oh, Vayl. I won't be able to stand it if this little fuckhead breaks your heart.* I glared at Aaron, showing him with my eyes exactly what I would do to him if he hurt my *sverhamin*, in any way, ever again.

Vayl stepped closer to the young man, the intensity of his stare making the boy look nervously for an exit. Like he'd make it that far. Vayl grasped him by the shoulders and raised him to his feet, looking so deeply into his eyes that Aaron winced as he asked shakily, "What do you want?" Then, realizing he might not like the answer, added, "I'm a really rare blood type. It's probably all bitter and tangy."

"Undoubtedly," said Vayl. He glanced at me. "How sure is she?"

"I'd guess about eighty percent."

His eyes went back to his would-be assassin. "It is more than any other Sister of the Second Sight has given me in all these decades." He switched to a different language—Romanian, if I had my dialects right—speaking almost urgently as he pressed his hands into Aaron's shoulders.

"I don't know what you're saying." Aaron looked to me desperately. "I don't *know*! But I swear, my dad is—was—Aaron Sullivan,

Sr. He worked for the power company until he died. And if I don't kill this vampire"—he lifted his forearm so he could point at Vayl while he talked—"he's never going to stop haunting me and I'm never going to pass the bar and I'm going to spend the rest of my life clerking for Schmidt, Glesser, and Roflower at a desk the size of a DVD player!"

"Look, kid." I checked myself. I couldn't be more than a year or two older than the guy. Even if I'd already survived more than his grandma, maybe I should avoid talking like her. I tried again: "Your ghost infestation is not our problem. Go bag yourself another vamp before we shred you like last year's bills."

"Jasmine." I turned my whole body toward Vayl as warning bells clanged so loud in my head that for a second I felt like I'd been transported into a church steeple.

"What?"

Vayl patted Aaron on the arm and said, "Excuse us." He came over to me. "May I speak with you at the end of the hall for a moment?"

"Sure." I walked up to Aaron and began to frisk him.

"Jasmine," Vayl protested. "You have done a remarkable job. Now that we all know he is my son I am sure that is not necessary. Especially with Raoul right here—"

I held up the vial I'd just retrieved from the inside of his calf. "Holy water, no doubt." I stood. Folded my right arm around Aaron's neck, forcing him to stoop to my level. He gasped, all the blood rushing to his face, his eyes bulging in shock as he realized a girl half his size had taken complete physical control of him and he hadn't even thought to resist.

I said, "Look at us closely, Vayl. One of us just inspired you to ram into the wall so hard the chandelier dropped half of its diamondy doodads on the floor. The other shot you in the head. You'd better make sure, right now, that you're clear whose side you're on."

The sides of his lips drooped. "This is not about loyalty."

"It sure as shit is. Don't you dare make the same mistakes you made with Badu three hundred years ago. This little fucker—" I looked at Aaron as I spoke, noted his size, and said, "Okay, this *big* fucker just tried to *kill* you. He may be the walking incarnation of your murdered boy, but that doesn't change the facts. And you have to face those facts. All of them. *Now!*"

Vayl's chin dropped a centimeter. Not an agreement. Just an acknowledgment that he'd think about it as he motioned to the end of the hall. I threw the holy water to Raoul and watched resentfully as Vayl moved away, the muscles bunching and releasing in his perfect ass. An hour ago I'd had my hands wrapped around that work of art, and my brain had been so deeply steeped in ecstasy it was practically rose-colored. Now I wanted to take that same rear and pinch it until the annoyance forced him to realize he couldn't just instantly forgive the guy who'd tried to kill him, never mind who he'd been two hundred and some years ago.

I took a deep breath. Vayl wasn't the only one who had to work to contain his violent tendencies. I slipped my feet into a spare pair of shoes I'd left beside the front door yesterday and followed him to the end of the hall. We crunched through the glass of the cabinet he barely glanced at and ended up facing each other in front of his grandfather clock between two doorways, one leading left to the dining room, the opposite opening to the guest bathroom.

He said, "I have not lost my mind."

I realized I'd crossed my arms when I dropped them in disbelief. "Oh?"

"Aaron needs to think that I trust him implicitly."

"Why?"

"So that he will believe just as deeply that you do not."

His dimple made another appearance and I clasped my hands behind my back so I wouldn't be tempted to grab him. I turned my back so Junior wouldn't be able to read my lips as I whispered, "Are you suggesting we pull a little good cop, bad cop scenario on him? And you're even letting me be the bad cop?"

He bowed his head. "That, my *pretera*, is how much I love you."

"You have never been sexier than at this very moment."

"It is a shame we have so much company," he agreed quietly.

I cleared my throat. "Okay. So you're not buying the I'm-being-haunted story either?"

"Certainly not. Those issues are easily taken care of through mediums. The boy has been weaponized. And until we discover by whom, we cannot help ourselves, or him."

I lifted my chin. "So you still wanna help him?"

"Jasmine, I cannot discount the fact that he may be my son. But my hopes have been lifted too many times for me to embrace him completely until I know for certain. Still, I cannot let him flounder knowing the chance exists."

I nodded. "Okay." I rubbed my hands together. "Damn, I wish I had a doughnut to throw at him."

Vayl smirked. "You enjoy our games, yes?"

I smiled up at him. "You bet I do."

"Then let us finish this one quickly, because I have just thought of another. And it is definitely limited to two players."

I let him see the fire in my eyes before I pulled myself together. When I turned around I'd adopted the expression I'd seen almost every morning at the breakfast table during my childhood. Pissed-off mom is only a half step away from bad cop. As soon as I started talking, I'd be there. A little tidbit for you future operatives. Write it down.

Chapter Three

Wednesday, June 13, 1:45 a.m.

Under Raoul's direction Aaron had dumped his red-tinged bucket of water outside and dried the floor, and was sweeping up wood chips by the time we returned to the front entryway. I had to work to hide my relief, and it didn't help to recall why. The last time I'd seen my lover's blood spill beneath his body, it had been because my fiancé, Matt, had taken a knife meant for me. Though he'd been gone for over a year and a half now, I missed him every day. I never wanted to feel that way about my vampire.

Raoul still sat on the stairs, scratching Jack under the chin just the way he liked it while Astral oversaw all the action from the top of a four-legged humidor that bridged the gap between the front door and the entry to the billiard room to its right. Vayl had once kept a large fern there, but after the cat had planted herself in the middle of it for the third time, he'd taken her hint and moved it. Since then she'd commandeered four other spots in the house. The fact that they gave her excellent views of the entire floor was, we decided, no accident. Bergman took his security far past the bounds of paranoia, and we had no doubt he'd programmed safety measures into Astral that had yet to be tapped.

Vayl and I approached Aaron with the same purpose, but with polar-opposite attitudes. I reminded myself to keep all my fun on the inside.

"We need to ask you a few questions," Vayl began. "Please join us in the conservatory." He motioned to the music room, where several glittering bits of light fixture still lay scattered on the Persian rug. As Aaron walked into the room he looked at them, glanced up at the chandelier, and back down at the mess Vayl and I had caused.

I pointed to the dropped glass and said, "*This* is what happens when we're having fun. Just think what I'm gonna break if you piss me off again."

He stopped just as he reached the sofa and turned to me, his eyes shuttling nervously between me and Astral, who'd provided the perfect soundtrack for me as she came into the room. Drowning Pool's song "Bodies" pounded into Aaron's ears—"Let the bodies hit the floor/Let the bodies hit the floor"—making him shiver as the robokitty sauntered past him, blinking sleepily as she went. She jumped onto the fireplace mantel, placing herself so close to the middle she could've been confused for a figurine if she hadn't chosen that moment to do a test cycle, which made her click like the dial of a washing machine.

"Can't you make her stop?" Aaron demanded.

I shrugged. "She's programmed to respond to my mood," I lied. "And right now..." I let myself trail away, smiling dreamily as the song howled through the room and Aaron hunched his shoulders like he thought somebody was about to jump him. All the girls inside my head shrieked with laughter.

Raoul was having no problem keeping it serious. He'd stayed at the edge of the conservatory, leaning against the archway, while Jack sat at his feet, both of them content to observe first and judge later.

Aaron had noticed my attention wandering. He asked, "Is that your dog?"

"Why?"

"You don't seem like the type who'd like dogs. Or...anything...really."

"You got that right. The mutt belongs to my boyfriend." I patted Vayl on the back and said, "He's such a softy," as he crossed to

Aaron's side and motioned that they should sit on the couch beside each other. I stood behind the chair opposite them. At my height it's tough to loom, but I did my best to seem as if I were the kind of person who, having already broken a light fixture and a display cabinet today, wouldn't hesitate to toss an easy chair into his lap.

Vayl settled into the corner of the sofa, making himself comfortable with his arm across the back and one ankle propped on the other knee as he asked, "This haunting you spoke of. I do not understand why my death would end it. Most ghosts simply need closure. Some require a gifted person, such as a medium, to help them fully cross over. I have never heard of one demanding a sacrifice in order to—" He stopped, grimacing at me as I pulled Aaron's .38 Special out and laid it on the top cushion of the chair. "Must you?" he asked.

"Oh, yeah," I said, nodding grimly. "Because you and I both know that Junior here is lying through his teeth." I waved him off as he started to protest that Aaron was probably under a lot of pressure. I stroked the gun lovingly. "Whoever sent him should've told him he's got the lamest cover story since my brother told my parents he was going waterskiing with his buddies and not one of them owned a boat. Lucky for him our dad wasn't able to track him down until he'd already enlisted."

Aaron stared, predictably thrown off by my detour into family history. He finally responded by saying, "I don't have a brother."

"Yes, you do," Vayl said.

"No," Aaron insisted. "My sister—" He stopped, gulping slightly when Vayl set both feet on the floor and leaned forward, elbows on his knees, hands clasped between them. I felt the familiar cold caress of his power as it swirled away from him. He could've rammed it down Aaron's throat, made him tell us every detail of his life right down to the brand of popcorn he preferred. But the possibility of Badu floated over all our heads, and he'd never mind-blast his own son. So he simply told the truth and backed it up with a press of magical assurance so that Aaron would know in his heart that Vayl's words were genuine.

He said, "The fact that you are alive and here now proves that your brother's soul may also be present in this world. The fact that you, of all people, have been sent to kill me, bodes ill for whoever Hanzi is in this lifetime. Because if you fail, your handler will most certainly send him to complete your work. This puts him in terrible danger, both from the people who have trapped you, and from us." He glanced at me. "We are trained to act first and think second. We may kill him in self-defense before we have the chance to save him."

"You're crazy," Aaron muttered. "Talking about me like I was actually alive hundreds of years ago. I'm a lawyer. Almost. I deal with facts. Case histories. Precedents. I could never buy some wacko theory like that."

"Bullshit," I said. "You're the one who thinks he needs to kill a vampire to stop a haunting."

"Nobody needs an excuse to smoke vampires!" Aaron exclaimed. "Ask around! I'd be applauded in the streets for flicking another parasite off the ass of humankind!" Then, as if realizing that he was sitting right next to one of the parasites he'd just insulted and maybe he should've just kept his big fat mouth shut, Aaron pressed his lips together so hard they looked like a single entity. But not soon enough for me.

I picked up the revolver in one smooth motion and took a shot. Boom! Aaron screamed as the pillow under his arm jumped and a couple of feathers fluttered into the air. I found myself wishing he'd brought a shotgun. Now that would've made a big splash!

"Jasmine! You shot my couch!"

"You're looking at it all wrong, as usual, Vayl. What happened was that I didn't shoot your kid. Now, be honest, which means more to you?"

Vayl motioned to Aaron.

"That's what I thought. So I'll buy you a new couch, which will, I promise, be a lot more comfortable than that stiff old backbreaker. I also promise, if this little shit doesn't start talking I will start taking chunks out of him." I chambered another round.

"Don't tell her, Aaron!" The demand didn't come from any voice I was familiar with. But Aaron knew it well. He spun in his seat.

Aaron gasped. "Dad!"

I let the .38 drop to the floor and risked a look over my shoulder. A man, or rather what was left of him, floated in the corner behind the pianoforte stool, Vayl's framed collection of Picasso pencil drawings showing clearly through his brown business suit. He held his emaciated hands out, his entire expression echoing the pleading gesture.

"What's he doing here?" I asked Vayl and Raoul. "Ghosts are supposed to be rooted to their homeplaces." I put a hand to my eye, trying to shove back the pain that suddenly exploded there. "Something's wrong," I whispered, just as a gout of blood gushed from my right nostril.

My knees buckled. Vayl caught me and pulled me upright before I could hit the floor. Raoul, only a step behind, had pulled a length of gauze from a first-aid kit I never even knew he carried. He pressed it under my nose and nodded for me to hold it there as I forced my eyes back up to the ghost, who was continuously scratching his forearms like he couldn't stand the feel of his own skin. I looked up at Vayl as he wrapped his arm around me. "It's Brude. I can feel him, beating his fists on the walls of my mind. We weren't supposed to know that he's done something to the Thin. He's made it so ghosts can walk. So they can travel long distances. Of course. If he's going to defeat Lucifer and crown himself king of New Hell he's gotta be able to transport his armies. He must be behind this. If he kills you, he paralyzes me—" I moaned, not so much from fear of that happening. We'd survived this long for a reason. But because my head felt like Brude had ripped it off and rolled it down Vayl's stairs.

"That is not going to happen," he said.

"Just because it hasn't so far—" I put my fingers to my temples and rubbed. It didn't help. Then Raoul shoved my hands away and took over. The pain began to subside.

"What do you know about Brude?" Aaron had risen from the

couch. He held the pillow in front of him. Aw. Now I was going to have to put it in Vayl's third-floor armory along with a little plaque with the inscription MOST PATHETIC SHIELD EVER.

Vayl said, "He is the king of a realm called the Thin. It is a nightmare world where souls sometimes travel, or are trapped, on their way to their final destination."

"My dad's there?" Aaron whispered.

Vayl answered, "It seems so. We believe that Brude has engineered this entire scene, except for my survival, of course. Because he wants to render Jasmine helpless, at least for the length of time it would take for him to kill her from the inside out."

That word "helpless" galvanized me. I stepped away from my nurses, my headache bearable now that Raoul had massaged the worst of it away, my nosebleed on temporary hiatus. *It's gonna take more than that to put me down, suckah.* In support, Teen Me did a couple of painfully lame front kicks toward the locked door in my mind behind which Brude paced.

Please stop, I told her. *You may think you're pulling off Jackie Chan, but the only person you're reminding me of is that skinny dude from* Nacho Libre.

Aaron's nose wrinkled as he stared at me, his lawyer's mind ticking off new facts that were making his mouth twist with disgust. "He's inside you?"

"He tried to possess me," I admitted. "It didn't work, but I couldn't boot him out of my psyche either. So I've got him trapped. For now. I know how to vanquish him. I was just waiting for this guy to find me the best route into the place." I nodded to Raoul, who managed to look more anxious than he had just seconds before. As if I needed another reason to worry. Hadn't his scouts had any success at all?

"If you beat Brude, what happens to my dad?" asked Aaron. He winced as Senior wailed in the background.

"The Thin existed before Brude and it will continue after him," said Raoul. "But once his hold over your father ends, I can save him."

"You?" Aaron looked Raoul over doubtfully. Now I was doubly insulted. First he dissed my vamp. Then he questioned my Spirit Guide. That kind of ignorance only came from years of hard work. And I had no patience for such bigotry.

I kept my voice low, which should've been a warning to him, as I said, "The fact that you took Vayl down before? That was what we call a rookie run. It happens to all newbies. Once. Then most of them get cocky and die. You are in the presence of masters, you little shit. All you have to figure out is whether you want to be standing in the crossfire or watching from the roof when we get down to business."

While I waited for him to decide I wondered if I'd gone too far. If, maybe, the ghost of Aaron Senior, and Junior's shocked blue eyes, would cause Vayl to launch into an "Aw, come on, be nice to my wittle boy" lecture. But when I looked up at him, he leaned down and brushed a kiss onto my cheek. "Have I told you lately what a magnificent woman you are?" he whispered, his breath tickling the lobe of my ear.

I shook my head, not trusting my voice to stay steady at that precise moment. I cut my gaze to Raoul, who'd been studying the moaning ghost of Senior thoughtfully. When he realized I was watching, he said, "If you needed any more proof that you've got Brude scraping the barrel to save his sorry hide, there it is." He motioned first to the ghost and then to his son. "My scouts still haven't found a clear path to any of hell's gates for you yet. But I promise, it'll be soon." He pointed to my head. "How much does it hurt and how often?"

I tried to shrug it off, but a new, piercing pain forced me to grimace instead. I felt Vayl's arm slide around my waist as I said, "It's intense when it comes, which is about every other day now."

"How long does it last?"

"A few hours. Usually I can sleep it off."

"And the nosebleeds?"

I wadded the gauze up in my fist, as if to make it disappear would prevent me from having to answer the question. But when I looked up at my Spirit Guide, he stared steadily into my eyes, waiting, demanding a reply. "Small ones every twelve hours or so. Big ones every thirty-six." We both knew it meant my time had wound down from weeks to days. If I didn't destroy Brude soon, not even Raoul could save me.

I didn't like his frown. It looked a little too…sympathetic. "I'll be fine. Just find us a way in that won't get us shredded before we're even halfway there."

He held up his hands. "All the citizens of hell know you have the Rocenz. When Vayl jumped through the plane portal and cut it from the demoness's grip, he made what you would call 'big news' in the netherworld." He didn't add that Vayl had been forced to literally chop Kyphas's hands off to retrieve the tool that would save my life. The grisly memory still woke me up some nights just short of a scream. Raoul went on. "Hell wants it back."

"Of course it does!" I hissed. "It only turns people into fucking demons!" His eyes narrowed, reminding me to watch my mouth and my temper. Now was no time to lose it, not when actual parts of me were unraveling. I took a breath, tucking in the part of me that still raged at the memory of Cole, his eyes flashing red, fighting the change as Kyphas carved his name into her heartstone with the Rocenz.

If only she hadn't clapped the hammer and chisel back into a single fused tool before Vayl set off that grenade. That was the big black raincloud neither Raoul nor Vayl nor I wanted to admit we stood under. Even if Raoul's scouts found us an unguarded path to one of the gates, we still didn't know how to separate the two parts of the Rocenz. Until we did we couldn't carve Brude's name on those gates. And it had to be stricken into that blasted metal, because with each blow of the hammer onto the chisel, the magic of the Rocenz, imbued by Torledge, the Demon Lord of Lessening, would reduce Brude to his essence. When we were done with the son of a bitch he would be taken down to the dust from which he'd come. And then, maybe…well, I hadn't said anything to Vayl yet. But we'd done some research and figured out that the Rocenz could also separate Roldan,

Vayl's worst enemy, from the gorgon who kept him alive. Split those two, they die, and then you have some sweet revenge on the Were who killed our boss, Pete. But I had to survive first.

I took a breath. "So how much time do you figure I have left?"

He hesitated, his eyes darting to Vayl before they came back to me. "You're strong. Anyone else would have surrendered by now. As it is, I'd guess you have four, maybe five days left. Seven at the most."

I nodded. Crept my hand around Vayl's arm and slid it down toward his hand until I felt his fingers wrap around mine. I felt better instantly. "Okay, then. Here's what I think."

"Um, excuse me?" Aaron was holding up his hand. Geez, did he still think he was in high school?

"Yes, Aaron?" said Vayl.

"I don't know if this'll help your plans or not, but I wasn't just supposed to kill you."

We stared at him so long that he checked to make sure his fly was zipped. Finally Vayl said, "You were given further orders?"

"Yeah."

"Noooo, Aaron!" wailed Senior from the corner of the room. Raoul waved at him and the sound muted so quickly you'd have thought he was holding a TV remote.

"Oh, that's cool," I said. "You've gotta teach me that one."

"If you survive this ordeal, I will," Raoul promised.

"Deal." I gestured to Junior. "What were you supposed to do after you'd offed Vayl?"

"They told me to put his, uh, remains in a bag and bring them to their boss."

"How could you do that? He's a freaking ghost!"

Aaron shook his head. "No. Look, you keep thinking this guy, Brude, was telling me what to do. But I only heard my dad mention him once. The same way you'd say, I don't know, Kim Jong-il. Or Bernie Madoff. But he's not the one who gave me the orders. You know, the one who said, 'Do this or your dad will never stop haunting you.' That was a different guy."

"Did he tell you his name?" Vayl asked.

"Yeah. In fact, he said it a few times. I got the feeling he wanted me to drop it before I killed you. But that seemed kind of melodramatic. So I didn't." He paused. And then when he realized we were waiting for it he said, "Oh! You wanna know—yeah, his name was Roldan."

Chapter Four

Wednesday, June 13, 2:15 a.m.

Once Aaron had dropped the name of the werewolf who'd become Vayl's worst enemy (I would've said nemesis, but that's so Sherlock Holmesian), Aaron Senior gave up the fight and faded away. So did my headache. Most likely a sign that Brude had just fallen back to find a better position from which to attempt a stroke-inducing attack the next time I seemed even remotely vulnerable.

Vayl had looked down at me. "You need food. And I could use another bite as well." He smirked at his pun. "Let us take this discussion to the kitchen, shall we?"

So we'd ended up crowded around his table for two, using chairs he'd brought in from the dining room to make up the difference, staring out the window into the backyard, where Jack had decided he needed more running time.

Astral had taken her customary perch on the mantel of yet another fireplace that sat between the door and the hall that led to the utility room. Between it and the kitchen sink on the opposite wall sat a wide maple butcher-block table with a built-in knife rack along the edge. The rest of the kitchen had been designed in a horseshoe shape around the table, with the refrigerator to its right as you entered the room. It had been covered to match the stained pine cabinets. The gas stove had been designed to look like something out of a pioneer kitchen with its cast-iron shell, though it had modern guts. My second-favorite item in the kitchen, it charmed me only slightly less than the brick floor, which must've cost a fortune to lay, but made me feel cozy every time I came into the room.

Aaron's comment, as usual, kind of pissed me off. "This room doesn't really fit the rest of the house. You should have it redone."

I pressed my lips together. If Junior really was Vayl's son, I'd have to find a way to get along with him. And snapping his head off every ten minutes probably wasn't a good place to start. So I kept quiet and let Vayl answer. "I suppose an interior decorator would find it clashes," he said. "But I am not so concerned about these matters as I am about surrounding myself with fond memories."

That was all he said, so I didn't know if the kitchen he'd had such happy times in had belonged to a woman he'd loved. Or if he'd just enjoyed meals from a cook who'd had a similar setup. And right now—I didn't wanna know.

So I dug into the bowl of cookie dough ice cream that Vayl had dipped for me and grooved on the grossed-out expression that passed over Aaron's face as he watched his former target sip a second helping of government blood from his favorite mug.

Raoul was the one who finally spoke up. "Does knowing that Roldan ordered the young man who may be the incarnation of Badu to kill you really change anything? As far as I'm concerned, my mission remains unchanged."

Vayl's chin dropped slightly. "I agree that you should continue." It seemed like he was about to say something more, but he let it go.

I said, "In four days, if your people haven't met with any success, we'll take the path you think will most likely get us there successfully. If you can recruit fighters for that journey, we'd appreciate it. But be straight with them, okay? We want them to understand it'll be a battle the whole way in." I stopped there. No sense adding that we'd be lucky if any of us made it back out.

"What about the Rocenz?" Raoul asked.

I glanced at Vayl. Then I said, "We found out on our last mission that Roldan's people had been guarding its resting place for a while. I imagine they know the spell that separates the parts, don't you?"

"How do you plan to get that information?"

"Our psychic is still working her resources," Vayl said. "But tonight's event confirms that Roldan has anticipated our next move. And that he fears its success to such a degree that he is trying to kill us"—he pointed to himself—"or cripple us to the point that we can no longer act." He pointed to me. "What I am saying is that Roldan knows that we must come after him, because we believe he knows how to separate the pieces of the Rocenz. It is inevitable that we should meet one more time. And he is terrified of the outcome."

"So's Brude," I murmured, rubbing my forehead even though it didn't hurt anymore. "They both have so much to gain from our failure that their partnership couldn't be tighter if it was forged at an anvil. That means we can't play them off each other. And Brude's been in my head long enough that, even though he can't hear my thoughts, he can definitely sense what's going on in the world beyond my eyeballs. Plus we know, somehow, he's able to communicate with Roldan."

"Yes, but how?" wondered Vayl.

"It has to be the gorgon," said Raoul.

"The who? The what?" Aaron backed his chair up an entire foot as he asked, pushing hard against the table as if he wanted nothing more than to flush his life, once and for all, of a group of people who spoke so casually of werewolves and demons, and who might actually put him face-to-face with a demigod who could transform him into a pigeon perch.

Vayl, kind and loving father that he was, patiently explained. "Roldan once attempted to turn a ward of mine named Helena because he felt they were destined to become lifemates. I wounded him fatally during that fight, but I did not wait to see him die. Instead I threw him into the gutter where he was rescued by a gorgon and her retinue. She offered him eternity—he accepted. Even now, I do not think he understood the price he would have to pay, because gorgons eat death. In a way, she has been consuming him since the day his natural life ended."

"How can anything be that powerful?" Aaron whispered. To give him credit, he didn't sound one bit envious.

"There's a Balance," Raoul said, somewhat cryptically. "However, I believe that the gorgon's power allows her to stimulate communication between Roldan and Brude. Maybe she's woven a psychic connection between them, I don't know."

"She's a damn demigod. She can do pretty much what she pleases," I muttered.

"So we agree that the gorgon is the mediator between Jaz's enemy and mine, bringing them into a partnership designed to destroy us both," Vayl said.

Raoul grimaced. "So much for the element of surprise."

Aaron had crossed his arms over his chest like he needed a big hug and sure as shit nobody else was gonna give him one. Now he said, "Well, that's just great. Your enemies have the inside scoop. Which means they probably already know I didn't kill Vayl. So when I show up at Roldan's door with a bag full of dirt and rags, he's going to kill me. Then *I'm* going to end up in that freakshow you call the Thin for the rest of eternity! Because you know that's exactly where that Brude son of a bitch threatened to send me if I failed!"

I smiled at him. "I like you better when you swear."

His jaw dropped.

Vayl *tch*ed. "Jasmine. Do not encourage him." He set his empty mug on the table. Which reminded me to take a couple more spoonfuls of ice cream. Then he said, "First of all, Brude would have brought you to the Thin regardless of whether or not you succeeded in killing me. He is raising an army. He needs bodies. But, while you are alive, you really should have more confidence in our abilities. Very well-respected officials pay us to keep people just like you alive and happy every single day."

"Not lately," I muttered, thinking darkly of the three senators on our Oversight Committee.

Vayl's lip twitched as he went on. "So, while we understand that Roldan is expecting us, of course we are not going to appear on his doorstep with a gift basket."

"I'd like to send a gift basket to—"

Raoul frowned at me. "Jaz, seriously, eat your frozen cookie dough."

I licked some ice cream off my spoon, which might or might not have been interpreted as sticking my tongue out at my Spirit Guide, as Vayl finished. "Roldan has no idea I am still alive and will not hear from Brude because we know a psychic who will help Jasmine block his emanations completely."

He nodded to me, giving me leave to call Cassandra, who sure as hell did know the trick. I might've been surprised to learn that once, but this chick had ducked a deal she'd made with a demon for five hundred years. Of course she'd studied up on the lore. She gave me a prayer that I memorized within thirty seconds, told me exactly where to splash the holy water (behind the ears, really?), and I knew it had worked when Brude wailed like a lottery winner who's just watched his ticket go sailing overboard.

When I came back to the table, grinning widely at my success, Vayl paused in his explanation to say, "I was just telling Aaron and Raoul that we will make a public production of my murder and tomorrow we will send Aaron to Roldan's lair with the remains of a vampire in hand, as he requested. That will get him, and us, through the front door, so to speak. After which point he will hide in a very sturdy closet until we are finished with my old nemesis." *Hmmm, maybe I should've used that word. It sounded pretty cool when Vayl said it just now.* He turned to Aaron. "Surely you find that plan preferable to an eternity in the Thin?"

"Where are you going to get vampire remains?" Junior and I asked at almost the same time.

Vayl sat back in his chair almost triumphantly. "A Rogue has entered my territory. I have given him several days to move on because, ah, I have been otherwise occupied." He didn't look at me, which was a good thing, because he'd have seen me shoveling Edy's Slow Churned into my gullet so fast that I gave myself brain freeze.

"Ahh!" I smacked my hand against my forehead.

"Jaz!" Raoul grabbed my shoulder. "Are you all right?"

Vayl lunged forward and half-lifted me from my chair. "What is it? What do you need?"

"Freaking ice cream. God*damn* that's cold!" Then I realized what I'd just done. "Oh. Sorry, guys. No, I'm fine. I was just... yeah, eating too greedily. Won't do it again, I promise."

They sank into their chairs, obviously debating whether or not to clonk me over the head with Vayl's ice cream scoop.

I smiled weakly. "So, we're going to smoke a Rogue vamp? That could be fun."

Chapter Five

Wednesday, June 13, 2:30 a.m.

I've traveled all over the world. But as I stood outside Vayl's house in the wee hours of that mid-June morning, my dog sitting quietly at my side, I decided nothing felt quite as peaceful as rural Ohio by moonlight. The smell of growing corn and recent rain cleared my lungs and my head. I turned my back to the neatly trimmed lawn that separated Vayl's property from the surrounding woods and fields, and studied the three men who stood in the shadow of my *sverhamin*'s stately old house. Vayl stood talking quietly to Aaron, their dark hair almost melding into one picture. But while Vayl held himself tall and proud, one hand resting comfortably on his jewel-topped cane while the other twirled an old-fashioned wooden stake and managed not to snag it in the pocket of his black jeans or on his long-sleeved black button-down, Aaron slouched. It wasn't even a comfortable I'm-chillin'-with-the-beats kind of shoulder hump. It was an I'm-out-of-my-league-but-I'm-plowing-through-anyway kind of hunch. And it didn't ease from talking to the vampire, so whatever Vayl was saying provided no comfort. Raoul couldn't help himself, he probably had a soldier's bearing even in true Eldhayr form. As it was, the erectness of his posture could only have been copied by a straight, strong oak tree. And he sure didn't look like he'd be comfortable if we invited him to rest on the come-and-sit-a-spell front porch that marched all the way around the perimeter of the house, stopping only at its fairy-tale turret that somehow made me feel underdressed.

Like Vayl, I'd changed into darker clothes. I wore a navy blue runner's pullover with long sleeves, and even darker blue cargo pants. I felt a little guilty for not using every single pocket, but I carried what I needed up top. Grief was fully loaded with vamp-killing arrows. And I'd strapped my vial of holy water to my right arm.

Knowing that Vayl and Raoul were also properly armed, and that between us we'd manage to make sure Junior didn't become vamp-toast, I let my gaze wander. To the right of the house sat the brick garage, which didn't seem attached when you looked at it from the outside. But when it was storming, or you just didn't want whoever was outdoors to see you access the house from the car shelter, there were underground passageways. Since we didn't trust Aaron to keep information about Vayl's secret tunnels, doors, and bookcases to himself, we'd brought him to the party the old-fashioned way. Raoul, however, had just assumed the invitation covered him as well. Which was why I said, "Look. You don't have to come. In fact, killing Rogue vamps couldn't have been on your to-do list today. Why don't you—"

"You're not getting rid of me," Raoul said flatly. "My job is to keep you alive as long as possible. I'd never forgive myself if some random *other* killed you when you were so close to freedom."

"See?" said Aaron. "Even he thinks vampires are monsters!"

"That's not what I said," Raoul corrected him. "Stop trying your lawyer talk on me, boy. I have no patience for half-truths and hidden lies."

As I quietly admired the way Raoul had put the little bigot in his place, Vayl spoke in a quiet voice that demanded the kind of attention that even the crickets had to respect. "Aaron, when you were Rom and your name was Badu, it used to infuriate you when people called you a gypsy. They did not mean the word kindly. And you did not understand why the accident of your birth should pin such hatred upon you that you were once arrested for walking down the street in the company of a local girl." He paused, looked down at the cane that had accompanied him through much of the past two centuries. The tigers that stalked down its length kept their judgments to themselves as he said, "The boy you were would spit on the man you have become."

Aaron's head reared back as if he'd been hit. But he didn't say anything as Vayl took his remote from his pocket. A small black keypad programmed to respond only to his touch, it allowed no one into the house or the garage from the outside once they'd been locked down unless he keyed the entry on the pad, or opened the doors from the inside. Now he pressed a series of buttons and the garage door began to rise.

Jack, realizing a car ride had just entered his future, ran for the garage with his tail wagging wildly. I looked around for Astral. In this light she was nearly invisible, and I'd learned she liked it that way. Suddenly I saw her eyes shining from the front of one of Vayl's flower beds. I didn't know what was weirder, that a dude who slept all day surrounded his house with geraniums and marigolds, or that my robokitty's eyes were silver in the moonlight. Then I saw the sweep of double high beams cross the porch.

I spun back toward the road at the same time that Vayl said, "What have we here?"

The car was crawling down the gravel road that led to his drive, hesitating and then jerking forward like the driver had just learned how to shift it into first. It swerved onto the shoulder, nearly hit the ditch, corrected itself, and then trundled into the drive.

By that time we were on our way.

Vayl had released the sheath from his cane's handle, revealing the handcrafted sword that rode beneath.

I'd pulled Grief, though I left the safety on for now.

Raoul carried no weapons that I could see. But the Eldhayr had once healed my broken neck with a word and a touch. I figured he had other hidden talents.

Jack and Astral came along too. Maybe someday I'd own cute, fluffy pets without the capacity to harm a butterfly. But probably not, which was why even my cat carried a couple of grenades around in her digestive tract, and my dog knew exactly how to use his teeth to greatest effect.

The car, a rusty white Lumina, made a graceful right turn and came to a stop in a drive-blocking maneuver that I would've suspected was the beginning of a full-out assault on the house. Except that the driver's side door opened and a man tumbled out, falling to his hands and knees on the dew-drenched grass.

Vayl was the first to reach him. Already he'd sheathed his sword. He looked up at me. The tone in his voice chilled me when he said, "Jasmine. Come quickly."

I holstered Grief and ran to his side, Raoul, the animals, and Aaron right behind me.

The man, practically curled up in a ball, wore a filthy gray sweatshirt and cutoff shorts. He could've been anybody. Except for the red high-tops that made my heart twist inside my chest.

"Cole?" I whispered.

He raised his head and blinked his blood-red eyes. "Help me, Jaz."

I slapped my hand over my mouth to hold back the moan as I dropped to my knees beside him. Jack, understanding only that something had just gone terribly wrong in Happysville, pressed his nose against Cole's cheek. Cole reached out blindly, wrapped his hand in my dog's fur, and then buried his face in it.

I swung to Raoul. "What happened? Kyphas only had him half-demonized when we saved him. And Sterling purified him afterward."

"Didn't the warlock tell you to keep Cole close?"

"Yeah, and we did until he decided to go to Florida to visit his family."

Raoul frowned down at the man who'd once loved me. "Obviously he never left. It's important after a purification for the victim to stay close to friends and family until he or she has worked through all the guilt and anger. I'm guessing Cole felt so much of both that he thought it best to isolate himself before he hurt someone else when, in fact, that was the worst thing he could've done."

"But he didn't hurt anyone back in Marrakech," I protested.

"I doubt he sees it that way."

Vayl had knelt beside me by now. He put a hand on Cole's shoulder and pulled him back. "Talk to us, son."

The gentleness in his voice brought tears to my eyes, because it meant Cole was doing even worse than I'd feared.

Cole pulled away from Jack. When he ran his hands through his wild surfer-boy hair I thought I saw the nubs of two horns shoving their way through his skull. "She's pulling me back," he said, his voice hoarse and dire.

"Kyphas is dead," I reminded him. "Vayl blew her to bits—"

He shook his head. "No. No. No. I can feel her." He thumped his hand against his chest. "And I want it." His crimson eyes bored into mine. "Make it stop. One way or another. Jaz, I'm counting on you. Don't let me go over."

I shared a doubtful look with Vayl. "You killed Kyphas. Right?"

He shrugged. "I could not imagine her surviving that blast. However, Cole is telling us differently. Perhaps the sea creature that was attacking her at the time took more of the damage than I anticipated it would. Or maybe hell pieced her back together just so it could have the pleasure of torturing her."

I wanted to deny the possibilities, but bizarre was pretty much Lucifer's domain. And I had Cole to worry about right now. I looked up at Raoul. "Please. There must be something you can do."

I could tell he wanted to leap back through the nearest plane portal by the way he held himself, stiff with denial, reminding me with his eyes that his office stationery had NONINTERFERENCE imbedded within the weave of the paper itself. "I'm not his Spirit Guide, Jasmine—"

I said, "No. Maybe you could've jumped and run back in January, when you were just a scary buzz followed by an earsplitting voice in my head. But not now. You're my friend. And he's my friend. Which makes you his friend by default. And friends save each other's souls." There was a lot I didn't say that I let him read in my eyes. That if he let Cole slip away I'd never fight for him, or the Eldhayr, again. And that there was every chance I'd come after them for letting him down—providing I survived the massive revenge I'd attempt to visit on the demon who'd broken my pal in the first place.

Raoul swiped off his hat and threw it on the ground. "You owe me."

"Absolutely. We both will."

He glared at Vayl, like he'd had something to do with my uppity attitude. "Guard us."

The request struck me as weird, until he grabbed my arm and wrapped the fingers of his free hand around the back of Cole's neck. "Oh," I whispered, dizzy with the rush of separation as he swept me out of my body.

Chapter Six

Wednesday, June 13, 2:45 a.m.

I immediately relaxed. Never had I broken from my physical self so willingly, even though I knew the return trip would feel like a fall into thorn-covered bushes inhabited by army ants and killer bees.

I flew up and up, the rush of flight so extreme I nearly forgot why I'd forced Raoul to yank me off this edge to begin with. He obviously hadn't, his spirit form even more forbidding than his physical one as he pulled Cole and me toward a distant star.

I looked back, reassuring myself that, yes, the golden cords that signified every relationship binding me to life still stretched from the world to my spirit. Dave was safe, wherever he wandered. Albert, too, along with Evie and baby E.J. I savored every connection, but most especially Vayl's, because it meant he hadn't given up everything, or maybe that he'd earned something back, by creating a relationship with me.

I couldn't see Cole's cords, which wouldn't have been alarming, except that he seemed to show no interest in them either. "Raoul? Has he lost everything?" I asked, motioning to my own lifelines.

"They're fading," Raoul said shortly. When I realized he was done talking, I slipped my hand into Cole's, such as they were, and whispered, "I'm here."

He didn't look at me. Only nodded and kept his eyes glued to that star, which was growing brighter as we approached it. Soon we could see it was a plane portal, similar in shape to the ones that seemed to appear near me wherever I went. But instead of being wreathed in flames and black at the center, this one shone with light so brilliant that human eyes would've been blinded by it.

Raoul began to chant as we jetted toward the light. Everything in me said to turn away before my brain fried, but the light had begun to *sing*. And I'd spent enough time with Sterling, who wanted nothing more than to become a bard, to realize I was staring into the source of the old guild's power.

We burst through the doorway accompanied by a chorus of voices so utterly beautiful that tears would've streamed from my eyes if I'd had them. Cole and I looked at each other. And smiled. How could we not? We stood in a meadow of wildflowers beside a stream so clear we could see the fishes' shadows. Music still echoed in our ears and now we knew the source—it was the combined orchestra of all the cords that touched our souls to those of the people we loved.

Raoul said, "Cole Levon Bemont, hear me and know the truth of my words. Your futures lie before you." He picked a ripened dandelion and blew the white seeds into the air. Suddenly we saw Cole in twenty different places. But all of them shared one common denominator. A flame-swept sky covering a landscape of mutilated creatures who'd once been human.

Cole staggered backward, shaking his head. "No. No. There has to be another way."

Raoul came to me and whispered in my ear. I jerked my head away from his. "Are you serious?"

"You asked for this," he said.

I hesitated, watching the man who had taken beating after beating for me, who'd followed me into this career after his business had been burned to the ground because of me, fall to his knees as his eyes darted from one hell-scene to the next, searching, searching, and always finding the demon he would become marching among the forsaken, a blood-drenched whip clutched in his hand. And I did as Raoul asked.

I strode to the newest golden cord to be added to my collection. It was only four months old, but its beauty outshone that of the others in this place like a rose among the clover. I strummed E.J.'s cord, playing the song my niece had begun to sing for me, and with me, since the moment she was born. I'd heard it before, when I battled a demon called the Magistrate. Then it had sounded out pure and fine as a fresh snowfall. Now, in this place of wonder, her song had changed. Become full of interesting harmonies interspersed with drumbeats so intense I half expected an army to take the field. Instead the cord began to vibrate against my non-hand so painfully that I backed away. "Raoul?"

"Behold," Raoul said to Cole.

He turned away from the nightmare spread out before him just as the cord seemed to separate and rebraid itself into a new shape, that of a woman whose dark brown hair swept in ringlets down her back. When she looked up, as if in amazement that a sky so blue could exist anywhere in the universe, the sun glinted off her red highlights.

"I've never seen eyes so green," Cole whispered. His hands had dropped, palms up, into his lap, as if he were a beggar pleading for her mercy. "What's her name?"

Raoul looked at me. "Her name is Ezri..."

I finished it for him. "Ezri Jasmine. E.J. for short. She's my niece in, what, twenty years?"

"Twenty-three," Raoul told me.

Cole didn't seem to have heard. His jaw had dropped slightly, as if he'd been hit by an armored truck. He whispered, "She's an angel."

"You could say that," Raoul agreed.

I riveted my eyes to his. But he avoided my gaze. Suddenly random events in my life clicked together in new ways. I understood why the Magistrate had gone after E.J. during that battle back in Tehran. Why the part of her that connected to the cosmos was able to resist his attack so well for so long. And maybe even why her father did his best to avoid me during those rare times that Evie blackmailed me into attending a family event.

Cole stretched out his hand as if he wanted to touch her but knew the museum guards would kick his ass if they saw him defiling the fine art. He said, "Ezri? She's—"

"Your destiny, if you choose to embrace it," said Raoul. "You won't seem old to her when you finally meet, because having most of your name chiseled to the demon's heartstone has slowed your aging process by decades. But be warned. Even if you decide to wait for her, you'll have to endure tortures in the space between. As I said, the Rocenz has changed you. But its marks aren't clean and precise, like a carpenter's tool. They leave the scars of a brand. For some the dark fire becomes so alluring that they choose it despite the fact that it burns away everything that made them human."

Cole touched the horns that had almost completely receded back into his skull. "She's just a baby now? How do I fight it for twenty years?"

"Twenty-three," Raoul corrected.

Cole's eyes drank her in. He knew he wouldn't see her again for decades, and I could see him trying to memorize every feature, right down to the beauty mark high on her right cheekbone. Finally he said, "You saw how well I made it through the first couple of weeks. How am I going to pull off years?"

Raoul reached into his pocket as he said, "Soon Vayl will decide that you need to travel to Romania, which has just recently embraced its roots as the country that birthed vampirism. Perhaps you will find a use for these?"

I couldn't see what he held at first. He did a little turning motion with one hand, set the object down with the other, then stepped back and watched with us. A pair of ruby-red lips smiled up at us as its blinding white wind-up vampire teeth chopped up and down so fast they looked to be stuck in the middle of the Antarctic without a hat or scarf to keep them toasty warm. The vamp mouth walked around in circles with the help of a pair of pointy-toed black dress shoes.

Cole's chuckle started somewhere near his belt buckle and by the time it emerged from his throat he was doubled over and slapping his thigh. Which isn't easy when you're mostly spirit. "Excellent! I can just see Vayl looking down his nose at those, going, 'Those are not in the least bit amusing. Also, you cannot get a good anchor into your victim when you are gnawing at him like some kind of jackal.' I'll take two!"

Raoul handed him the teeth. "They'll take form for you as soon as you reenter your body."

"Magical!"

Raoul smirked. "Just don't lose them." His eyes sent the bigger message, *or your sense of humor*.

Cole nodded. "Gotcha. Thanks."

Raoul clasped his hands behind his back. "Anytime," he said, his faint Spanish accent suddenly a little easier to detect. *By damn, he is getting attached to us!* "We must leave soon," he said, nodding to the golden cords that surrounded us. They were beginning to fade. "Perhaps you'd like to say goodbye?"

"Can she hear me?" Cole asked.

"At some level."

Cole went up to E.J. Wow, she was tall! Her eyes were nearly at the same level as his. I felt tears prick my eyelids. To see the child I'd give anything to or for standing, all grown up, beautiful and healthy, blew me away. The man who'd decided to spend the next chunk of his life hoping she'd save his soul walked to within a few inches of her. Her gaze, uplifted and thoughtful, flew far past his tired blue eyes. But he didn't seem to mind.

"Ezri, it's Cole Bemont. Remember that name, okay? It's going to be a big deal to you someday." My hand flew to my mouth when his you-really-should-hug-me grin appeared. I hadn't seen it in so long I'd almost forgotten how happy it made me when it came out to play. "I'm not the man that you're going to need me to be yet. But I've got a while to get myself straight. And, I promise, by the time you're ready for me, I'll be set to sweep you off your feet." He leaned forward to murmur into her ear. Her eyes came to his face, sparkling as they found a new focus. When he pulled back she was smiling straight at him. The breath left him in a long sigh. He blew her a kiss. And then he turned to Raoul.

"Okay, dude. Take me back to my so-called life. I've got work to do."

Chapter Seven

Wednesday, June 13, 3:15 a.m.

Raoul dropped us into our bodies so fast it felt like falling from a plane without a parachute. And the pain of reuniting sum and substance—well, my brother, Dave, wrestled in high school. One Saturday morning, somewhat miraculously, I didn't have to work. So I went to his tournament, where I saw one of his teammates throw a guy onto the mat. Happens all the time, but this snowy day in January the kid tried to catch himself—and failed. His arm broke so severely that I could see the bone shove the skin out of place. His shocked scream reminded me of the sounds Cole and I made now as every one of our nerve endings fused back to the source of their existence.

"I wish you would stop doing that," Vayl said as he helped me to my feet. His lips pressed into a straight line as he continued, so quietly I thought only I could hear. "Every time you leave I am more certain than ever that you will not be returning."

I realized I was wrong about how the sound carried into the velvety black countryside when Aaron said, "Roldan told me you were a badass." He stood on the gravel drive with his fists stuck deep in the pockets of his bleach-stained jeans, most likely so we couldn't see his hands shaking. When he realized he had Vayl's attention he went on. "He warned me to kill you quick, otherwise you'd shred me like grass clippings. But there you are, kissing up to some chick who's been impersonating a blackout drunk for the past half hour. How am I supposed to believe you're going to save my skin when you're just another whipped—" He gasped, stopped in mid-sentence by the whirlwind of movement and coiled violence that ended with Vayl dangling him in the air by the throat.

My *sverhamin*'s voice seemed to rise from a place guarded by iron bars and rusted chains as he said, "You are still the same sharp-tongued coward who let your brother take the blame for every foolhardy escapade you ever attempted, including the theft of the wagon that led to your deaths over two hundred and fifty years ago. But *I* have changed. I will no longer countenance disrespect from you." He set Aaron back on his feet. Dropped his hand and watched him rub the red spots away from his neck. I couldn't find a single speck of regret on Vayl's hard-lined face. Just twin flares of rage flying out of his deep black pupils as he said, "I have had a great deal of time to think of how I might put right what went wrong during our lives together. Do not tempt me to turn you so that I might have eternity to teach you how to behave like a decent man. Because my first lesson will be to teach you that only the strongest can truly, deeply love. And if you have no woman in your life, you will understand the reason why." Vayl was at least kind enough to turn away, so the stark and sudden pain in Aaron's eyes was an emotion he didn't have to hide or, later, be ashamed of.

But if the son had been stricken, the father was pained as well. I could detect a note of longing in his voice, the kind I'd heard before when he'd suggested we could be a great Vampere couple. I'd refused then, and now I saw the same terrified denial on Junior's face. But suddenly it was like I'd stepped up on a platform where I could observe Vayl from a totally new angle. And I realized how lonely he'd been all those years with no family to get him through the empty days or share the laughter with. Not that he'd found much to call humorous, much less entertaining, in his early years as a Rogue. Even less so when he'd entered into a Vampere Trust. In fact, when we'd first started working together I'd become convinced pretty quickly that the dude had completely forgotten how to have fun.

I stepped up and slipped my hand into his. When his eyes dropped to mine I put all the love I felt for him in my smile. The black bled from his pupils like a healing bruise, replaced almost instantly by honey gold with flecks of the warmest amber. "I'm so proud of you," I whispered.

"Way to represent," agreed Cole. He still sat at Raoul's knee, his hands flopped between his legs like he didn't even have the strength to cross them. He winked at Vayl. "We attached guys gotta stick together."

Vayl's eyebrows practically shot off his forehead. "What happened up there?" He took a threatening step forward.

Suddenly Cole found the energy to raise his arms in protest. "I promise you, I am over your girl forever. Although she's awesome, I've got my eye on the prize now." He nodded so definitely that Vayl instantly checked himself. Cole's eyes danced. "Hey, Jaz. I just realized. Someday, if it all works out, I'm gonna be your nephew. You know what that means, right? Magicians at my birthday parties, and trips to the zoo, and—"

"Stop!" *Holy crap! He's back—and here I am without my beat-them-off umbrella!* I thought fast and then said, "You might jinx it."

"Right. You're absolutely right." He made the zippy-lippy motion. However, he pointed from me to him and back again a couple of times and then mouthed the word "relatives" before subsiding into happy-grin land.

Oh. Man. Could I deal with Cole at Thanksgiving? Giving Albert shit over the turkey and making veiled references to the "adventure" we'd shared in Scotland while Evie sat in barely concealed shock at his impudence, E.J. looking around the table in absolute confusion, while I tried desperately to think of an appropriate lie to explain how very well I knew him? Or would they all be so flipped out that I'd brought a vampire to dinner that it wouldn't matter?

I was suddenly readier than ever to go kill the Rogue Vayl had targeted. Still under the assumption that we'd only encountered a slight detour in our original plan, I asked Cole to move his car to one side of the drive so I could back mine out.

"Where are you going?" he asked as he grabbed the open door to help himself to his feet. As Raoul filled him in, I strode toward the garage, assuming Vayl would follow with the rest of the group trotting more or less cooperatively behind. That was usually how it worked. Except I'd taken half a dozen steps when I realized nobody was following me. Not even Jack. I turned around.

"Jasmine," Vayl said tiredly. "She is doing it again."

The four men had gathered in a circle at the front of Cole's Lumina. All of them had riveted their attention to the ground at their feet, as if they couldn't believe Kentucky bluegrass managed to thrive this far north of the state line. Jack trotted around them, occasionally sticking his nose between their legs, but he didn't like what he saw enough to stay in one place for long. He'd pull his head back, sometimes jumping like he'd been startled, and begin his rounds again.

Dammit. We do not need this right now. And the worst part is, it's all my fault. Or, more specifically, Jack's fault. Which makes it mine. Dammit!

I joined the circle, Vayl and Raoul moving back to give me room. As expected, Astral lay in the middle, flat on her back, waving her feet in the air while she cackled like a drunken hen. "Cluck, cluck, hic-cluck." From the mini-projector in the back of her throat a startlingly realistic hologram replayed a series of images just like the ones we'd seen the last time she'd pulled this stunt. I'd come in in the middle, so I missed the skier flying off the cliff and the painter falling from the ladder. But I did make it in time for skateboard-crashing-off-the-garage-roof guy and hang-glider-dumping-into-the-ocean dude.

"Cluck, cluck, hic-cluck," said Astral.

"Do you think it's worse?" I asked.

Vayl crouched for a closer look. "It seems about the same to me.

But then, this has been going on for two days now. How did she get so much footage?" he asked as six kids went tumbling off a toboggan.

"Well, she does have access to all the FBI, CIA, and Homeland Security databases. Plus she's an Enkyklios, and who knows what those Sisters of the Second Sight have recorded while they were globetrotting, trying to get all the info they could on the world of *others*. Or, now that I know, I should say the world of the Whence."

"So that's what it's called," murmured Aaron as he watched a figure skater blow a triple axle.

"But..." Raoul motioned to Astral, whose clucking was so convincing I wouldn't have been surprised if she'd laid an egg. "Why?"

Vayl glanced up. "I think perhaps Bergman missed a wire or two the last time he reattached her head."

They all looked at me. I raised my hands. "Hey, I feel terrible about that incident. But honestly, Bergman shouldn't have made her self-destruct button so sensitive."

They gave me the point and went back to Astral watch. Finally Vayl said, "We cannot let this continue. What if she chose to emit some vital intelligence in her video feed instead of some fool slipping off his roof while trying to anchor his Christmas lights?"

"I agree," said Cole. "You should call Bergman."

All eyes came to me. Again. "Yeah, but he's..." I sighed. "Fine. But if he cries, I'm handing the phone to one of *you*."

I left the circle as I dug out my cell and dialed his number. The series of clicks that preceded the ring lasted for at least thirty seconds, signaling the fact that even though he was still staying in Morocco with his new girlfriend, Bergman's paranoia hadn't slipped a notch. Our call would be encrypted as thoroughly as if the President of the United States were sharing the line.

I thought Bergman had probably been born with a suspicious nature, but it had been sharpened to its current razor edge in college when a classmate had stolen his research and tried to use it to create a brand-new energy source. The fact that he'd blown himself to smithereens instead hadn't given Bergman much comfort. After that he'd put five deadbolts on the door to his room and informed the rest of us that if we entered without permission there was every chance that we'd be impaled by a jungle spear.

I wasn't sure what it said about me that I continued to share an apartment with him until I graduated from college, or that he remained one of my closest friends to this day. Except that his mind unfolded before me like a work of art. And his inventions gave me happy tingles right down to my toes. Before Matt, and then again before Vayl, hardly anything else in life had done that for me.

Finally Bergman answered the phone, which was when I thought to check my watch. Had I just woken him? Naw, it was already about nine-thirty in the morning over there. He said, "Jaz! It's you!"

"Yes. Hello." *Oh man, how do you tell an inventor his cat is on the fritz? Is this a good news/bad news scenario? Wait, I can't think of any good news. See, this is what Evie means when she tells me I need to work on my attitude. Something good has to have happened lately. I mean, besides the mind-blowing sex with Vayl. And all the other fabulous moments in between, which you can't really explain to your old buddy. And that's not* his *good news anyway.*

"Jaz? Are you still there?"

"Yeah! Hey, Miles, how are you?"

"Great!"

Did that sound fake, or was it just the thousands of miles standing between our cell towers? "Excellent! How's Monique?"

"Great!"

Huh. "Super. That's good news." *Hey! That's the good news! Now for the bad news.* "Uh, Miles, why I'm calling... Astral's kind of acting up."

"What's she doing?" Total professionalism in his tone now, except for that thread of frantic worry he was trying hard to suppress.

I described the problem. He wanted every detail. I had to go watch her some more so I could describe what era I thought the stuntman had been living in when he tried, and failed, to jump a canyon the size of Rhode Island. "What do you think?" I finally asked him.

"Her self-recalibrations may have jogged something loose," he said. "I'll need to do some tinkering to be sure, but I think I can fix her."

"So I should, what, shut her down? Box her up and mail her to you?"

"God, no! She's a member of your team! You can't function without her!"

"Well, I wouldn't—"

"She needs to be repaired immediately, Jaz. I'll be on the next plane out of Marrakech!"

"Bergman! Seriously, I can—"

"I won't hear of it! I'm booking my ticket online right now."

"Miles. What's happening?"

"What do you mean?"

I let a few seconds of silence stretch between us. Then I said, "When Vayl, Cole, and I left Morocco, you and Monique were so lost in Cuddleland you barely said goodbye. Now you can't wait to leave her?"

"It's not her, exactly. It's her kids. They came to visit. And, well, one of them is only a year younger than me!"

"So?"

I could almost hear Bergman's gears turning as he considered and rejected reasons he knew I wouldn't buy in the first place. Finally he said, "I guess I knew it couldn't last. She's twenty-three years older than me and—"

"Stop." This couldn't be a coincidence. I turned to Aaron. "You're twenty-three, right?"

"Yeah, how did you guess?"

I didn't answer him. I was too busy trying to keep up with my racing mind. Raoul had said that E.J. would be twenty-three when she and Cole finally met for the first time. And now Bergman had let slip that Monique was exactly the same number of years older than him.

Somebody was trying to send me a message. And considering the sources of the numbers, I had to think that same somebody wanted me to survive this ordeal. I tucked the idea away until I could bounce it off Vayl and went back to my call.

"Listen, Miles. You're my best friend. I'll back your play, no matter what you decide. But I'm just saying that's a pretty ridiculous reason to dump the only woman I've ever met who will cheerfully put up with your bullshit. If it's something else that you can't get past, fine. But if all you're worried about is the age difference, then grab on to this—Vayl is two hundred and sixty-eight years older than me."

"Damn."

"Yuh-huh."

Long silence. "I need to come there. Just for a little while. To think."

My throat closed. More than I wanted my own happiness, I wanted the people I loved to find peace and love in their own lives. Eventually maybe I'd accept my startling lack of control over their decisions and just let it be. But I knew that at some point I'd probably try to talk him into going back. The French innkeeper was too good a fit for him, dammit! For now I said, "Okay. Text me the details of your flight and I'll pick you up at the airport."

"Make sure it's an unmarked car."

"Holy shit, Miles! What, did you think I'd be riding up in a parade float?"

"Is Cole with you?"

"Yeah."

"Possibly."

I promised him to keep it on the down low and we hung up. At which point Astral ran out of disaster video, rolled over on her side, and farted out one of her grenades.

"Take cover!" Vayl bellowed as he snatched up the explosive and hefted it as hard as he could into the field that fronted his house. He grabbed Aaron's arm, I whistled to Jack, and Raoul slapped Cole on the back of the head to snap him out of his bemused daze. We booked to the back of the garage, making it just in time for the explosion, which sounded so much like a fouled firework that Aaron checked out the sky.

Then he looked at Vayl. "Does this kind of stuff happen to you all the time?"

Vayl considered his question. "Only since I met Jasmine." He smiled at me. "She makes life incredibly exciting."

"But you're not alive...are you?" Aaron asked. For once he just sounded curious. Was he finally learning?

Vayl leaned his shoulder against the rough brick of the garage wall. In the dim light of the moon the shadows covered his entire face, so that all we could see was the glitter of his eyes when he lifted his head. "I have watched humans move through their entire existence without ever truly testing the limits imposed upon them by their families, their cultures, and their own minds. They have willingly traded love, risk, adventure, and knowledge for a safe haven from pain. If those humans can choose undeath, I can choose life."

"Hello."

Aaron shrieked as Astral joined us, sitting quietly beside Jack, who panted over her happily, both of them acting as if nothing potentially deadly had just happened. Animals. So charming of them to poop and forget.

Chapter Eight

Wednesday, June 13, 3:45 a.m.

We wandered around to the front of the garage, though only Vayl and I could see the devastation the grenade had caused to the cornfield. He could probably read a map in the dark, and my sight had radically improved each time he'd taken my blood, to the point where I barely needed to use Bergman's see-in-the-dark contact lenses. Which, I could tell, Cole wasn't wearing tonight.

"So," he said. "You guys were already outside when I got here, and the garage door was up. Jaz sure seemed eager to take off just now, so where were you headed?"

Vayl had been checking his watch. He slid it back into his pocket and said regretfully, "We did have plans. But now it is too late for us to make a round-trip to Cleveland and be assured of completing our mission successfully before dawn. We will have to wait until tomorrow to smoke the Rogue."

Cole held up a hand. "Wait a second. Your Trust stretches all the way to the city?"

Vayl said, "Our Trust includes the city." He stared hard into Cole's eyes. "And you, as well, if you would like to rejoin us."

I held my breath as Cole considered his offer. I'd only observed the inner workings of a single Vampere Trust—the one Vayl was attached to for most of the 1800s. So it had been pretty twisted. Plus, he hadn't given me a lot of detail as to how ours should work since it was still mostly a show-car organization, put together for the sake of certain observers inside the Whence. Formed to protect those of us who were most obviously attached to Vayl from his enemies, who'd flout human law but would never risk trial in *other* courts, our Trust didn't even have its own letterhead. I mean, if you're gonna be official, shouldn't you at least have a logo or something? So, while I wasn't sure what a nod from Cole would provide him specifically, I knew that when he'd left Vayl's protection in Marrakech he'd opened himself to attack from Kyphas. Which meant that if he accepted Vayl's offer he'd be taking a solid step away from her.

Cole ran a hand through his sun-drenched hair, pulling it back from a face that could easily have taken him into the spotlight, onto the big screen along with the rest of America's pretty people. Instead he'd chosen dark shadows and cold rooftops. "I stand by the demand I made in Australia," he said, his old charm lighting up his face as he reminded Vayl. "I want to be the secretary of social events."

"Of course."

"Then I'm in." *Aaaahhh!* Inside my head, Teen Me was jumping up and down, screaming at the top of her lungs, and trading high fives with Granny May, who'd taken a break from some new project she'd started at the dining room table. For once I agreed with my inner adolescent. This was worthy of major mental celebration. Especially when Cole said, "I'm gonna need a party fund."

Vayl sighed. "Fine."

"So tell me, how far does our territory really run? And if it includes Cleveland like you said, what happened to the three nests I heard about last time I was in town?"

"I will show you a map," Vayl said. "We are responsible for the city, its suburbs, and several miles of surrounding countryside. As for the nests"—he looked at me—"Jasmine and I have been busy."

Cole stared at us. But he didn't say anything as we led him, Raoul, and Aaron into the house. We'd decided Astral couldn't be trusted near people until Bergman fixed her, so I'd ordered her to secure the perimeter until further notice. As a result Jack seemed slightly bummed. So I took him to the kitchen. To my surprise, all the other guys followed as well.

"What do you want?" I asked my dog as I opened the fridge. "Cottage cheese? Baking soda? Oh, I know." I pulled out a covered dish and, when I noticed him looking up at me suspiciously, said reassuringly, "Don't worry. Vayl cooked it."

I pulled out a couple of brats and set them in his dog dish. "Don't get used to this," I warned him as he dove into them with the snorting noises that signaled deep satisfaction. "You're back to that hard square stuff for your next meal."

The guys had settled around the tiny table, Vayl and Aaron on one side opposite Raoul and Cole. They all looked pretty wasted. But I could tell Vayl had more to lay on them. He motioned for me to join them, so I pulled the desk chair over and sat at the end of the table. Then he said, "I have a bad feeling. It is near to making me ill. Hanzi—or rather the man he is today—is in terrible trouble. The longer I think on it, the more certain I am that Roldan will have cornered him just as he did Aaron here. We cannot wait for him to make his move. We must find him first."

Cole, Raoul, and I traded helpless looks. They left it for me to say, "But, Vayl. You've been searching for him for…ever. What makes you think we'll have any better luck now?"

Vayl leaned his head toward Aaron. "My younger boy is with me now. I believe it is inevitable that I will be rejoined with the elder. But fate seems determined to reunite us in violence. If there is any way we can stop that from happening, we must try."

"What do you suggest?" asked Raoul. "And don't look at me. This is one area where I absolutely can't step in for you."

"Cassandra," said Cole.

"She has read me before, and failed," Vayl said.

"Yeah. But you said yourself times have changed. You have to bring her here. The sooner the better, I think. Let her touch you and Aaron. I'm betting she'll have a mega-vision that'll head you straight to Hanzi."

Vayl turned to me, his eyebrows raised a notch. "She's coming this way anyhow. Family visit before Dave's leave ends," I explained.

"Call her," he said. "Tell her I will charter her and David a plane if they will agree to come tomorrow."

And just like that I knew my crew was going to be whole again by the time the sun set on the following day.

Raoul had agreed to take the first watch over Aaron, who protested that it was ridiculous to imprison him until we reminded him that he was, according to his own law, an attempted murderer. At which point he quietly followed my Spirit Guide to the guest bedroom, his head clearly so full of new thoughts to ponder that he didn't even protest the company of Jack, who still felt like being social after his last trip to the backyard. Cole, who was just as exhausted as Vayl's attempted assassin, took the green room, which also contained a guest bed and bath in addition to an indoor sauna that made our newest Trust member fall to his knees and pretend to kiss Vayl dramatically on his nonexistent ring.

"I will be your vassal forevermore, me lord," he said in a horrible Cockney accent, bucking his front teeth so far over his bottom lip as he talked that it completely disappeared. He rolled onto his back. "Do you want to rub my tummy to make it official?"

"Would you get up?"

"Okay, but I'm warning you, I may have slightly obscene thoughts about you while I'm sitting in your sauna. I'll try not to, but it's probably inevitable, I'm just that grateful."

I grabbed him by the cheeks, reminding myself forcefully not to pinch as I pulled him forward and kissed his scar-free forehead. "Just get some sleep, you doof. We're going to need you fresh tomorrow."

He brought his hands up to wrap around my wrists so he could pull my hands down and kiss the back of each one. His eyes held depths I never would've imagined the day we first met in a ladies' bathroom in the house of a terrorist sympathizer. "Thank you," he said. "For everything." A light seemed to go on from his heart, and I had no doubt whom he was talking about when he said, "You'll take good care of her for me?"

"Of course."

He nodded and dropped my hands. "Then I'll be in your debt forever. Anything you want, anytime, you just have to ask. Except for right now, when I suggest you run, don't walk, out the door, because I'm stripping down for my first of many sweats in that sauna in five, four, three, two—"

Vayl slammed the door on Cole's laughter and together we closed ourselves into the room we'd shared since we'd gotten back from Marrakech.

It reminded me of its owner. Large, masculine, with a preference for life's luxuries. The walls, papered in ivory with a hunter green stripe, each held a single memento from his past that, I hoped, someday he'd feel comfortable explaining. On one hung a glass case that displayed a British heavy cavalry saber that I dated to around 1800. On another hung a framed program and two tickets to *Don Giovanni*. The third wall held a black-and-white photograph of two men, one of whom was Vayl, standing arm in arm in front of Saint Basil's Cathedral in Moscow. The fourth I had demanded an explanation for, because preserved behind a long glass frame was a beautifully tailored wedding dress that had gone yellow with age. The moment I'd seen it, the fact that I carried my dead fiancé's engagement ring around in my pocket didn't matter a damn. Vayl was gonna fork over a reasonable explanation or I was out the door.

He'd touched a finger to the frame with a tenderness that nearly broke my heart. Then he'd said, "Helena wore it when she married John Litton." And I'd wrapped my arms around his waist. I didn't care how pretty that dress was, if I'd had a long-dead adopted daughter, anything that reminded me of her would've had to be buried in a trunk and stored in the attic. But Vayl had preserved this piece of her happiness so he could always remember those few years when they were a family.

I felt her now, like an old friend at my shoulder, as I walked to the dresser and looked down at the items I'd arranged there. In a strange way she was responsible for their presence. If Vayl hadn't discovered her back in 1770—an eleven-year-old orphan cowering in a deserted mansion about to be attacked by Roldan—that same Were would never have tried to give him permanent amnesia. Because Roldan had become obsessed with her, and the fact that Vayl had saved her from him made them bitter enemies. And if they hadn't been enemies, we might never have discovered that Roldan's pack was guarding the Rocenz, which sat on the dresser, a silver hammer magically glued to a chisel, looking like nothing more than an extra-fancy paperweight.

Next to it lay the map we'd stolen, which had led us to its hiding spot in Marrakech. We'd kept the dusty old leather because on it was written a clue related to separating the hammer from the chisel. Naturally it wasn't in English, but the translation read, "Who holds the hammer still must find the keys to the triple-locked door."

I picked up the map and curled up on the couch while I watched Vayl prepare his room for the coming day. He pressed a button beside the balcony doors that activated light blockers within the window glass, turning them pitch-black. But Bergman, whose middle name was probably Redundancy Plan, had also installed a massive canopy above Vayl's bed that was made out of the same black material as the traveling tent that he slept in when we went out of town. It could descend from the ceiling and spread over the intricately turned wooden frame that towered feet above the gold silk bedspread. During the night Vayl kept the canopy raised almost to the top of the frame so it looked like a regular bed. Now he flipped a switch on the wall and the curtain lowered to the floor.

I hadn't been able to bring myself to crawl under that enclosure with him yet. For a kinda-claustrophobic like me it all seemed a little too cave-like. So when I finally decided to hit the sack I'd scooch the curtain toward him until I literally tucked him in, flip the covers back, and settle in. Kinda weird, I know, but so far it had worked okay. And I loved waking up beside an emerald-eyed vampire who couldn't wait to see what I'd decided to wear to bed that morning.

Vayl sat down beside me to shuck off his shoes. "Have your researchers had any luck deciphering the clues?" he asked as he nodded to the map in my hand.

"Nothing new," I told him. "You know, when Cassandra called and said she'd found a reference to the triple-locked door I thought my hair was actually standing on end. But it's been a whole week and I still can't figure out what it means."

"Well, at least you know that the triple-locked door is, literally, the Rocenz. That is progress," Vayl said comfortingly. He balled up his socks and threw them in the corner right next to a rattan hamper. Sometimes he was such a guy.

I hid a smile and said, "Yeah, Bergman should probably get a medal for discovering that little nugget in the archives. But it's what Cassandra dug up, you know? What am I supposed to make of the phrase 'Cryrise cries bane'? Okay, I know Cryrise was a dragon. And the hammer was forged from his leg bone. But I've been running that info around in my head every waking moment and the only conclusion I come to is that Cryrise is a pussy."

Vayl laughed.

"I'm not kidding!" I insisted. "What kind of respectable dragon goes and gets himself killed by a demon in the first place?"

"Perhaps it was not that simple," Vayl suggested as he undid his shirt, slow, the way he knew I liked it.

"Jasmine?" he murmured as he leaned forward to slip his shirt off, his shoulder muscles and biceps bunching and releasing with fascinating results.

"Uh?"

"Are you panting?"

I licked my lips. Realized my breath had started coming a lot quicker. I put my hand to his chest, sliding my fingers into the thick curls that covered it as I threw my leg over his hips and sat facing him. "I like this couch," I told him.

"You do?" His fingers, free of the responsibility of his own buttons, had begun toying with mine.

"Yeah." I brushed my cheek against his as I leaned forward to nibble on his earlobe and say, "It's got great handgrips." I reached past his arms and buried my fingers in the soft leather cushions of the back.

And then neither of us talked anymore for a long, long time.

Chapter Nine

Wednesday, June 13, 8:00 p.m.

I woke up beside Vayl in his huge, comfy bed the night after Aaron's attempted assassination, amazed I'd slept the day through as I picked up the curtain to wish him a good evening.

"What's up?" I asked. "You look like somebody just called off your birthday."

"The Rogue has left our territory," he said. "Now we have no evidence to plant on Aaron." He held up a hand. "And before you try to comfort me, just imagine if we sent him in with faked remains. His description last night was not far off. Roldan could injure or even kill him before we were able to intervene. We must save him. You know he cannot do it himself."

"He's a dead man and you know it," I said bluntly. "That Were never had any intention of leaving either boy alive once he figured out they were connected to you. Not after they'd served his purpose anyway. Now quit being so emotional—" I stopped. What a weird thing to have to say to the man whose expressions had to be read with a magnifying glass. But by now I knew that under that tightly wired exterior boiled passions that could leap out and destroy whole cities. I said, "Okay, that's not fair. Just, you know, try to back off and think. That's what's going to help the most here, and you know it."

He took a deep breath. "All right. We can eliminate a Rogue vampire after we make the flight. It would have been difficult to explain a bag full of remains to airport security at any rate."

I nodded. Not impossible, because we still carried our department IDs, but since our status was officially inactive it could've still been problematic. So we spent the rest of the night trying to get more information from Aaron about his contacts, shuttling Cassandra, Dave, and later on Bergman from the airport to Vayl's house and preparing for our psychic's reading. Which failed on nearly every front.

All she got from Junior was more of his dad's tortured pleas. And when she touched Vayl she couldn't see the other son. Not his face. Not his location. All she sensed was audio. A revving engine and the horrifying sound of crumpling metal. Afterward she sat back in her chair, swept her long black braids from her regal face, her big brown eyes so full of sympathy I nearly cried myself as she embraced Vayl with her gaze. "I'm so sorry," she told him. "Definitely Hanzi is here, I can feel that. But the sense of violence and impending death is so strong it interferes with every other image." She smoothed the skirt of her bright orange sundress, her elegant black hands hesitating at her stomach a moment longer than was necessary, making me wonder if the reading had left her nauseous.

Then Dave stepped up with his amazing admission.

"I think I can find him."

We were sitting in the coziest room in the house. Tucked at the back behind the billiard room within easy reach of the kitchen, it seemed to reflect more of the Vayl-who-was than the ass-kicking Vampere he'd become. I'd seen his den before we'd become a couple, but then I hadn't been in the mood to take in much more than the country-gentleman squares of gleaming brown paneling that gave the area a warmth that was backed up by the chocolaty leather couch, matching love seat, and two burgundy wing chairs with matching footstools. They huddled around a sturdy square coffee table that looked like it had been crafted from railroad ties and ceramic tile painted with the most colorful horse-drawn wagon I'd ever seen. Usually books covered the design, but since I'd come Vayl had gotten better about putting them back onto one of the three black floor-to-ceiling shelves against the walls.

Most of Vayl's rugs had been imported from the Middle East. Beautiful Persian designs that seemed to reveal a new picture every time your eye fell on a different section. Underneath the rugs the floors were well-maintained, deeply stained pine. But in the den he'd chosen a hand-woven rag rug in all the colors of the rainbow that stretched nearly the length and width of the room. The colors were muted just enough that they lifted the spirit when you walked in, rather than making you want to bang your head against the wall.

The rug stopped at the black marble fireplace. Covering the opening was an iron grate in the shape of a dancing woman, her skirt twirling and her hair flying as she spun in front of the flames. One night he'd confessed that she reminded him of his mother. Not that he'd ever seen her. Just the picture he'd built in his mind, gathered from watching his grandma and his aunts working through the day. But at night they always seemed to have the energy for at least one dance. That was when I'd asked him about the wagon on his table.

"I painted it," he'd told me. "It was my first home." And that was all he'd say. But I spent every moment I could spare staring at it, memorizing the red mini-caboose shape of it that was highlighted by gold-painted slats, a four-square window, and a green roof, all of which rode on ridiculously spindly tires with red spokes. Every time I saw it I thought I understood a little better the motherless boy who'd traveled so far inside that tiny, beautiful rig.

I'd been gazing at that wagon when my twin had said, "I think I can find him," had risen from the love seat, and left his fiancé's side to stand beside the mantel. He'd really caught my attention when he grabbed the mantel with both hands, like he needed the help to keep from falling.

"Dave?" I asked.

He stared at the single white earthenware pitcher Vayl had set above his fireplace, like if he eyeballed the wedding party marching across it long enough he might be able to make the flower girls dance right off the container. When he turned around everyone in the room went still.

My brother is a commander. That alone causes people to sit straight and shut up. But as I looked around the room, at Vayl and Cole on the couch beside me, at Bergman and Raoul in the wing chairs and Cassandra on the love seat, at Aaron uneasy in a chair brought in from the dining room, even at the animals curled up beside the cold fireplace, I knew they shared my dread. It wasn't just the fading scar on Dave's throat, an unwelcome reminder of the fact that he'd spent time in the service of a necromancer. It wasn't only the no-bullshit gleam in his piercing green eyes, or the fact that his time in the desert had hardened him into a lean, muscular warrior worthy of the utmost respect. It was also the haunted look in his eyes, and the way his lips pulled against his teeth, like he could barely stand the taste of his thoughts.

Cassandra stretched her arm over the back of the love seat, her gold bracelets clinking musically as she reached for him. He nodded to her. *I'm okay.* Then he said, "If I have to talk about this I only want to say it once. So listen up." I watched his broad chest rise with the breath he scooped into his lungs. "Ever since I was a zombie—"

Cassandra jerked toward him, every one of her ten pairs of earrings shivering in alarm, but he held up his hand. "No. I'm not gonna put pretty words on it. My soul might not've been allowed to move on, and that's why Jaz and Raoul could ultimately save me"—he stopped and bored his eyes into each of us, like he could bury his gratitude so deep we'd feel it every time we woke up—"but basically I was just a slave with skills. Anyway, ever since then, some weird things have been happening."

Suddenly he couldn't look at any of us. His eyes skirted the room and finally landed on the window, where Vayl had used a couple of bright red shawls in place of curtains. He went on. "I talked to Raoul about it, and he told me it's a function of my Sensitivity. How, when people agree to serve the Eldhayr, the circumstances of their deaths burn themselves into their psyches. And that they often develop special talents related to that."

I thought about some of my own abilities—to sense violent emotion, to cause sudden and deadly fires—and immediately understood his point.

He went on. "During my last mission we were tracking an imam who'd reemerged from hiding after fifteen years and was, yet again, recruiting suicide bombers. We had a pretty good source in the area, but when we went to him he told us the guy was dead. We said that was impossible. Our psychics insisted that he'd been active as recently as the previous month. So he showed us a picture of the body. He even said he could take us to where it was buried, because it had become a local shrine. So we went."

Dave realized his hands had started to shake, so he clasped them behind his back. At that moment I realized how much he resembled our father, Colonel Albert Parks, the ultimate marine. Strong. Determined. And wounded. Why is it you never recognize the pain in your parents until it's too late?

I wanted to call my dad. And, more urgently, go to my brother. Lend him a shoulder. But I knew he needed to stand on his own. Just speaking, knowing I heard without judging, would push him closer to healing than anything else I could do at this moment. So I sat without blinking as he said, "The grave had the right name, and the date of death lined up with when we'd last lost contact. But our psychics are the best in the country. So we dug for proof. Halfway to the body I started to feel sick. Because the corpse was *talking* to me. Whispering foul suggestions from inside its rotting skull. It patted my head and kissed my cheeks like a loving father, and then told me how if I killed all the men in my unit I'd live forever in heaven with seventy virgins at my service. At the same time I felt like the sound was coming from outside the corpse. So I followed it, you know, mentally. I traveled through every dead donkey and half-eaten carcass I could find along the path it took until I saw a fifteen-year-old boy preaching in this imam's name."

"Instant reintegration of the soul into a new body," Raoul murmured. "That never happens. Unless the dying imam called upon some powerfully foul magicks."

"I have no doubt about it," Dave replied. "This kid *knew* he was the reincarnation of the old imam. He was able to access this guy's wisdom and direct his evil plans without admitting it to anyone. You wouldn't think older guys would listen to him, but his charisma was already off the charts." Dave nodded. "I've convinced my superiors to let us go after him next."

Cassandra's hand clenched into a fist. An instant of intense worry aged her face by twenty years. Then it passed and she smiled up at him proudly as he said, "I think I can do the same sort of thing for you, Vayl. If we visit your son's grave and I can reach down to his body, I'll be able to communicate with what's left there. It should be able to lead me to its new form."

Bergman spoke up. He'd maintained a stoic silence since arriving to find Astral displaying a new symptom at the edge of the front lawn. He'd given her the ability to transform so that she looked like a little black blob. That way she could slide under doors and into air vents when the situation called for extreme secrecy. Except now she'd begun morphing randomly, sliding into molehills and snake holes, killing the inhabitants and piling up her prizes at the front door like UPS packages from Stephen King's nightmares.

Now he said, "I'm not sure it'll be that easy, Dave. I mean, I'm sorry to bring up a painful subject, Vayl, but when were your sons killed?"

"Seventeen fifty-one," he said shortly.

"Nearly two hundred and sixty years ago," Bergman said, doing the mental calculations so quickly I'd have wondered if he'd inserted a computer chip in his brain if I hadn't heard him whine about wanting one on a regular basis since college. "Plus we aren't generally aware of our connections to our past lives. That would make Dave's search even harder."

"Dude, you have a way of crushing a whole room and then promising us Disney World," said Cole.

Bergman raised a finger. "But there's an unless."

"Unless what?" Dave asked.

Our theorist started playing with the hem of his sweater, stretching it nearly to his knees (which, I realized, might be why he was the only guy in America who wore sweaters in mid-June) as he said, "Well, I'm just throwing this out there, okay?"

"Go on," said Vayl.

"You said Astral had organized every scene she could access that involved a fall, or someone flying through the air, right?"

"Pretty much," I said.

"She's overloading, probably getting excess stimulation somewhere in her temporal lobe."

"Wait a second." I realized I'd raised both hands. "You gave the robokitty a brain? With lobes?"

Bergman grimaced. "It's so close there's no point in splitting hairs. Or, in this case, subatomic particles. Which would lead to a really beautiful but destructive explosion. Which is kind of what I think will happen with Dave. Too much information at such a speed that he'll never be able to process it. So what I suggest is that I program Astral to act as his filter. Her Enkyklios contains Vayl's file. What if I tinkered with that? Made it into more of a sound barrier that Dave could listen through. Hopefully it would muffle all the lives Hanzi has lived in the years since his death as Vayl's son, and Dave won't get lost in all the decades that he's lived between then and now."

"That's not possible. Is it?" It was Aaron, leaning forward, looking from Bergman to Dave and back again like they'd just thrown off their disguises and revealed their superhero costumes.

Bergman's face took on that pinched look that meant he didn't want to explain anything, including why he continued to wear extra-large sweaters and ripped jeans when he was easily pulling in a six-figure income. But for once, maybe because of the mix of cynicism and hope in Aaron's voice, he bent his cardinal rule. "The Enkyklios is more than a library. The Sisters of the Second Sight are born with special powers, and when they record the stories, they can't help but imbue those records with bits of their own essence. Combine those with a catastrophic event like blowing Astral's head off, and you end up with something unique. So much so that calling her a robot would be like referring to the pyramids as a collection of stone coffins. So yeah." He turned his concentration to Dave now. "I think you might be able to use her. Especially if—" He stopped now, every drop of color draining from his face as his eyes darted to Vayl and then dropped to the floor.

My little buddy had built himself an actual spine over the past few months. But I'd seen psychopaths grovel at Vayl's feet, and all he'd had to do was take one menacing step forward. "What is it you want of me?" he asked.

Bergman's words came out strained, like he'd just gotten over a bad case of laryngitis. "It would help if you filled in the blanks in your file where Hanzi is concerned. Just, you know, talk about what was important to him. What he enjoyed. Also what scared him and even what he hated. Strong emotions are the most likely to follow us through our lives. And..." Bergman licked his lips. "I don't know if it's in there. But you should talk about how he died. I understand it was violent, and from what I hear, those are the memories that come back to haunt us most."

Vayl sat back so slowly it became obvious that he was forcing himself not to leap out of his seat and turn the coffee table on its side. I realized I must've been the only one in the room who knew that his sons had been shot by a farmer while they were returning a wagon they'd stolen from him.

I watched the memories leap behind his eyes, as new and raw as if they'd happened that morning, and said, "Vayl." I put my hand on his arm. His muscles were so tightly coiled I could feel every ridge and outline. "It's over." His eyes, the black of a funeral carriage, met mine and understood that I knew his pain, because sometimes I still walked that path reliving Matt's death. I nodded to Aaron. "I know how hard it must be for you to turn the corner after spending most of your life running toward the same goal. But you're here. You made it. Now it's about him." I pointed to Astral. "And it's about Hanzi, whoever he's become. These are innocent people caught up in our disaster because a couple hundred years ago they happened to know you. We've gotta dig them out."

Vayl looked at Aaron like he'd never seen him before. "I will do everything I can for you."

Junior sat back, his hands falling away from each other like he wanted to beg for an explanation but knew he wouldn't understand. Still he said, "But. You're a vampire. Who I just tried to kill."

Cole sat forward and slapped him on the knee. "Don't feel too bad about your big fail, dude. People try to kill Vayl all the time. It's kind of a cult project that nobody's ever been able to complete. I hear they've designed a patch for the winner and everything." He grinned at Vayl, who responded with a smile that made Aaron's eyes pop.

Raoul nodded toward me as he told Vayl, "Just because we prevented Aaron from following through doesn't mean you'll head off the next assassin. Which means you'll need good people around you until this whole issue is resolved. I think I should stay until this story has spun itself out."

Vayl raised his eyebrows so high that his eyes actually widened as he gazed at my Spirit Guide. "You—want to help me?"

Raoul shrugged a shoulder. "You've earned it."

That was all. But coming from an Eldhayr it meant more than a thousand words because it pointed so directly at one: "Redemption." Vayl reached across the table and leaned forward enough for Raoul to meet him halfway and give him a powerful handshake that was as much an affirmation of Vayl's future as it was a contract.

Raoul sat back, relaxing into a smile as he added, "Besides. I'm probably in so much trouble already that by the time I get back they'll have demoted me to a desk piled with charts and raw data."

"Is it that bad?" I asked.

He shook his head, but he said, "There's a reason some of the Eminent call me an interfering old hen." He held up his hand when I started to apologize. After all, I was the one who kept demanding that he get his ass front and center before my world swirled back into the crapper. "I'm a big boy, Jasmine. I make my own choices, and I stand by every one of them."

"Then I hope you enjoy flying." Everyone stared at Vayl. Especially Jack, who'd rather spend the day getting rabies shots than take another ride on one of those gigantic birds whose wings never ever flapped.

Vayl nodded decisively. "We must go to Romania. That is where the bodies of my boys are buried. Once we are there, David will try to reach the soul of Hanzi."

"What about me?" Aaron had leaped to his feet, his arms outstretched in one of those how-dare-you-forget-me gestures that always made me want to kick people in the ribs.

Vayl's eyes glittered so brightly that Junior immediately dropped his hands as his former father said, "I have a plan for you as well."

Chapter Ten

Saturday, June 16, 8:45 p.m.

We are expert travelers. Together Vayl and I have hit so many different countries our passports look like a little girl's sticker book. We've flown over oceans, deserts, mountains, and swamps. You'd think a little trip to Romania would pull itself together in a matter of hours. Um, no.

Romania is not so simple to reach from America. You've gotta fly into a much more popular destination first. Say London or Paris. Then there's the train. And, after that, even more transportation to arrange, since not everybody would fit into my shiny black 1963 Ford Galaxie. And I was damned if I was going to leave my baby home after Vayl had promised me I'd never have to drive a shit-sucking rental again.

Also we had a huge group to deal with. I felt like a damn travel agent keeping track of Dave and Cassandra, who needed privacy whenever possible, and Bergman, who demanded special dispensation for his electronics. Cole and Raoul were easygoing enough, but Aaron flipped out at the idea of eating "foreign" food, which was when we learned of his *long* list of dislikes. This seemed to include everything but peanut butter and chocolate. No wonder he looked like somebody had stuck an air pump under his skin and inflated him to double his natural size. And then there were the animals, who absolutely refused to travel in cargo. Vayl finally gave up, chartered his own plane, arranged for a tour bus to meet us in Bucharest, and shipped the Galaxie via some top secret transport the details of which none of us were privy to because that's how shit gets done in DC.

Although Raoul made Jack jealous by doting on Astral, Bergman accidentally caught Dave and Cassandra in the sauna, which grossed him out so much that he threatened to go home, and Cole made Aaron scream like a little girl by slipping his clanking vamp teeth into his shower, Vayl finally herded us all onto the plane two nights later. And after traveling so long that I considered shooting every single member of my party, including those I loved the most, we finally arrived in the brightly lit city that had once sparkled like a gem among the mountains and hills that surrounded it.

Bucharest had style, it just couldn't decide what kind. An eclectic mix of classic French architecture, modern skyscrapers, and decrepit old hulks ready to tumble into the street during the next big earthquake, it couldn't seem to shake the shadow of Communism that had tried to hammer it senseless for so many years. And yet I loved the place. Because it, and its people, had figured out how to survive. And more, because they'd finally stood up to their twisted government and yelled, "Bullshit!" So whenever I saw a couple holding hands or a family sauntering down the sidewalk, I waved respectfully as I drove down wide black boulevards that reminded me bizarrely of streets I'd navigated in St. Louis. That is, except for the metal fence that marched down the median. And the sad lack of shapely automobiles to keep mine company. (Note to European automakers: Square sucks. Pass it on.)

Vayl sat in the front of the car with me, listening to the Galaxie's engine thrum like the bass of our favorite song. Cole and Bergman lounged in the back with Jack draped across their laps as if he'd decided they might get cold without his kind assistance. Their heads were bent over Astral, whose fur was split from neck to ears so Bergman could see better as he tinkered, using the miniature tool set he stored in his front pocket. None of us discussed the sights as we headed out of the city, north toward Peles Castle and the woods surrounding. Because we knew that somewhere inside the trees on the distant horizon, Vayl had buried his sons. And how do you make small talk about a minaret-roofed museum with that thought dangling at the front of your mind?

Eventually I'd be there for Vayl. Maybe even figure a way to talk to him about it. But for now I had to concentrate on getting my old girl through traffic that didn't seem to include a single trained driver who cared if he or she survived to get to the dance club. Except, maybe, for Dave, who was piloting the monstrosity behind us.

I touched the tiny plastic receiver stuck just inside my ear. I'd be able to hear anything going on in the vehicle behind us because Bergman had provided enough of the Party Line sets to go around the whole group. The microphones, which looked like beauty marks, rested on different parts of our faces. Mine was just to the right of my upper lip. Vayl said it made him want to nibble on me, so I had sworn never to wear it anywhere else. The rest of the crew wore theirs near their mouths as well, except for Cole, who insisted that his should rest on the inner curve of his nose until he could find a nymph to pierce it, and then it could become part of the nose ring. Nymph-piercings, he'd said, were lucky, but I hadn't been able to ask him why at the time. And now didn't seem quite the moment either, so I put it off again. But I suddenly realized that somebody needed to say something. The silence was diving too deep.

I glanced at Vayl, wondering if he understood that, as in every other mission with potentially dire consequences, we needed this downtime to unclench if we were going to operate on all cylinders when it mattered most. He'd lived a long time. Surely he understood why people needed to banter, tease, and, yeah, laugh. Sometimes even when they were at wakes.

As he had so often in the past, Vayl touched his eyes to mine, sensed the direction of my thoughts, and turned slightly so my brother could see his half-smile as he said, "David? The quiet is disturbing in that children-are-up-to-no-good sort of way. Is everything going all right back there?"

"So far so good," my brother replied. "Except I think Raoul is chafing. We may have to stop for baby powder."

"I don't need powder!" Raoul exclaimed.

I looked in the rearview mirror at the vehicle following us and shook my head yet again. Where Vayl had scrounged the 1968 Volkswagen bus I didn't dare ask. But I did make a mental note never to let him near the Internet again. It had come equipped with a microphone because it actually had been a touring vehicle. Which worked for our cover. So we'd dressed Raoul in a PARTY BIG IN LITTLE PARIS T-shirt and stiff new blue jeans and informed him he was our guide. Then we'd had to tell him to at least try to look relaxed. For his sake I regretted the necessity of asking him to shuck his uniform, but it's kind of tough to pull off the whole tour group disguise when the guy who's supposed to be showing you around Romania is dressed like a commando.

Despite the difficulty of steering the hefty vehicle through streets as busy as midtown Chicago, Dave managed the time to say, "Relax, Raoul! You look fabulous." He switched to the fashionista voice he used when he really wanted to make Albert crazy. "Those pants make your tush look like two ripe cantaloupes. Just so squeezable you're gonna make all the boys swoon."

I grinned as Cole broke into peals of laughter behind me. I heard a clunk, which I imagined was Raoul dropping his head against the window as he moaned, "You people are insane. Even you, Cassandra. No, don't sit there trying to look innocent. I know sooner or later you're going to open up that giant bag of yours—what is it made of, Christmas beads?—and something alien is going to pop out that you're going to expect me to kill."

Cassandra chuckled. "Well, I have noticed things seem to be moving around in there on their own." Squeaky sound as she moved in her seat. "What do you think, Aaron? Is my lovely beaded purse haunted?"

"If it's not now, it probably will be before this is all over." Gah. Leave it to Junior to spread dread all over the happy moment.

"That's not necessarily true," said Cassandra. Her voice, calm and smooth as a lake at sunrise, soothed me even from this distance.

But Aaron said, "Don't touch me! I know you're a psychic—hey! I thought you said you were engaged. That's a wedding ring on your finger!"

Silence. The kind you get after you've stood next to the speakers at a rock concert. Ear-ringing, head-shaking silence.

Now, I know I'm supposed to be supah-spy. Damn near invincible because nothing gets past my eagle eyes. But I'm giving myself a pass on this one. I'd been a little distracted with Aaron's assassination attempt, Cole's big news, and the arrival of my entire crew within the following twenty-four hours. Plus, Cassandra wore jewelry like at any minute she might be asked to trade it for food. Gold studs lined her ears, followed by hoops so huge that small bunnies could use them for collars. So many chains hung from her neck that I couldn't imagine how she kept them from tangling into a huge gold coil. And each finger held at least two rings. Sometimes three.

So I instantly forgave myself that I hadn't noticed before as I said, "What the hell? Cassandra? Is Aaron right? Are you wearing a wedding ring?"

I wished I could look into her eyes. Her skin is so dark I can never tell if she's blushing, but by damn, if she'd ducked her head so that her braids fell across her fine, high cheekbones I'd have known the score. When she didn't instantly reply I snapped, "Daz, you tell me the truth, dammit!"

Using my old nickname on Dave worked. My twin said, "We were going to tell everybody when we came north. You know, throw a little party? But every time we see you you're in the middle of some crisis." His voice dropped. "Seriously, Jaz, you need to consider reprioritizing your life. You know, before you can't outrun the fire anymore."

"Hey! Don't try to deflect this on me. You got married and didn't tell me!" I paused. "Or invite me!"

Cassandra said, "Oh, Jasmine, I'm so sorry." I could hear her tears even from this distance. Which was kinda weird. Usually she had better control of her emotions. I looked at Vayl, who nodded, and I suddenly realized how much my opinion of her mattered. *What the fuck? She's, like, 975 years older than me!*

Doesn't matter, said Granny May, as she flipped over her project and took a step back to admire how it looked lying there all nicely framed on her dining room table. I was so shook I barely glanced at the tapestry she'd been sewing for the past several weeks. *You saved her from Kyphas. She's in love with your brother. She respects you. So quit acting like a douche before you break her heart!*

Gran, stop talking like Teen Me. I mean it. It's just disturbing when you say words like "douche."

I wondered if all granddaughters had to put up with this kind of shit as my granny, still cackling, hung the tapestry on the wall above her gleaming mahogany buffet. And then I forgave her everything.

Gran?

She glanced at me over her shoulder, her eyes gleaming with the wisdom that only seems to come with age and daily doses of Geritol. *What?*

We both looked up at her needlework, a project so detailed I could pick out the shadowy form of the earthbane that the cowboy Zell Culver had vanquished reflected in his clear brown eyes. She'd added details I hadn't picked up the first time I'd seen him as a hologram playing from Astral's projector. Then he'd been part of a report detailing everything she knew about the Rocenz.

Now he wore a tooled leather band around the rim of his broad-brimmed hat, a plain brown long-sleeved shirt, and worn leather chaps over dark brown work pants stained with blood. Blood spattered his worn work boots, but they looked comfortable rather than ratty. His plain silver buckle closed on a gunfighter's rig, but the holsters hanging from its belt were empty. His hands hung at his sides, each one holding half of the tool that had destroyed his monster and would, I hoped, someday kill mine. I suddenly felt like a tool myself.

Gran, I whispered, mentally pointing at the picture. *Zell Culver knows how to separate the pieces.*

Yes, she said. *I know.*

But Astral said he was taken back to hell the day after he won.

How convenient that you have to go there to beat Brude anyway.

Silence. Not golden. But at least, finally, hopeful. Because now we didn't have to force information from Roldan that he would never, even on pain of death, reveal. We had a source. A man who would, no doubt, happily share what he knew—if we could just find him.

When I tuned back into Dave and my new sister, I didn't have to fake the happiness in my voice as I said, "I'm just giving you guys a hard time because it's so easy to do. Seriously, I just wish I had a big fat present to lay on you. Because we should be celebrating right now. And it sucks that I can't do more than tell you how the rest of my life will be happier because you two are together now."

Now I could really hear Cassandra sobbing, and Dave telling her to get up here so he could give her a hug, and Raoul demanding that they both take care because these old buses didn't drive themselves.

Bergman leaned over to Cole. "Is she going to cry this whole trip?"

"I heard that, Miles," Cassandra warned him.

"Sorry. I was just wondering. Because it upsets me when you cry. In fact, I liked it better when you were yelling at me all the time."

Cassandra laughed. "Then that's how I'll deal with my stress from now on."

"Good."

Vayl spoke up. "Now that we have that settled, we must attend to another problem. We are less than thirty minutes from our ultimate destination and we have not decided yet how the team is to be divided."

Another silence, this time more thoughtful than freaked.

Raoul spoke up. "I think that's because no one is perfectly clear on the details. All we know is that Dave is supposed to try to find Hanzi through contact with his remains. And you have a plan for Aaron that requires us to split up temporarily."

"Yes," said Vayl. "I have thought this out carefully and discussed it at length with Jasmine. We believe one group of us can rescue Aaron Senior from the Thin while the other half accompanies David on his mission. Because we know time is of the essence now, for Hanzi's sake, we can imagine no better way to do it."

I cleared my throat. "I think they want to know exactly how we mean to get it done."

Vayl turned clear blue eyes on mine. "We need at least one more person to join us in the Thin."

"We?" Raoul sounded slightly pissed. "What makes you think *you* can travel beyond?"

Vayl said, "I already have." His silence gave Raoul the chance to recall the time he'd allowed Vayl to enter into his realm. But even before that he'd come into the Thin with me. He'd gotten there through my dream, pulled by my will the same way I had been yanked there by Brude in the first place.

I said, "Raoul? Can you send us there?"

He said, "No. It's not as easy as going through a plane portal. We always need scouts in place to help us find the holes to enter where we won't be caught and instantly annihilated. It takes time and people, neither of which we have."

"So we go in guns blazing," I suggested.

He made a familiar sound, one that let me know he'd raised his hands to his head and shoved his walnut-tinged crew cut even more upright than usual. "I will go with you. But you have to believe it would be suicide to enter that way. We need to find another route. And, of course..." He paused so long that I realized he was trying to send me a silent message.

"What?" I asked.

"You shouldn't go. Brude is trapped inside your head right now. What happens when you take him back to his base? *I* would expect him to gain strength. Maybe even enough to break free."

I considered the alternative. Let this part of the plan ride until after we'd found Hanzi and figured out how to extricate Aaron without any risk to me. Which meant, I had no doubt, that he'd try to kill Vayl again. Because there was something about the way his eyes shifted from his former father's when they were together that told me he hadn't revealed his whole story. He kept trying to distance himself from Vayl, and us, because he still believed the vampire needed to die.

I said, "I have to go." And not only because of that. Vayl and I knew one more detail about the Thin we hadn't shared with the rest of the crew. One truth Brude had let slip during his incarceration in my mind that I didn't even think he realized I'd latched on to, because only recently had I realized its significance. Besides his little fiefdom there were twenty-three other realms in the Thin ruled by strong-willed souls such as himself. None of them had yet made plans to build their rulings into mini-hells and eventually dethrone Lucifer. Most of them, in fact, preferred to keep their nasties to themselves. But a few had already figured out Brude's plans, those close enough to observe the growing menace that could only mean the eventual demise of their own kingdoms. And they had begun to fight him.

I figured that's why somebody upstairs had kept pounding the number twenty-three into my head. Because they were my potential allies, not only in this plan, but in ways I couldn't yet fathom. Unfortunately, of those twenty-three, the ruler who was most accessible to us right now might also be the least likely to help us.

Still studiously ignoring Vayl, Aaron asked, "If you rescue my dad—"

"Make that a 'we,' Junior," I said sharply. "You want this to happen, you're taking the trip too."

To give him credit, he didn't shy from the news. Just nodded and wiped the sweat off his brow as he finished his question. "Say we break him out of the Thin. What happens to him then?"

Raoul said, "If you can rescue Aaron Senior, he'll fly free." Which should've been a relief to Aaron. So why could I sense his anxiety like it was a black and wriggling disease in his belly?

Because I didn't want him to catch on that I was catching on to him, I moved my attention back to my Spirit Guide. "Okay, so you have no scouts in the Thin. And it's obvious you don't want to drop in blind. So how the hell—"

Vayl said, "Do not worry, Jasmine. Raoul will know exactly what to do when the time comes. Now, I believe our friends were asking for a detailed plan. Shall we let them know what we have decided?" When I nodded reluctantly, he held up a brochure. On the front was a picture of a palace that looked like it had been influenced by a German architect.

"Pelisor Castle is situated quite close to Peles." He turned the brochure over and displayed a map that Cole and Bergman managed to catch a glimpse of by leaning forward and holding on to Jack so he wouldn't flop to the floor. "One of its former residents returns, from time to time, to remind its caretakers whom it really belongs to despite the fact that she has been dead for nearly seventy years. Jasmine and I are hopeful that she will help us find Aaron Senior."

"Assuming she spends time in the Thin at all," Bergman said doubtfully. "How do you know she hasn't hooked up with Brude?"

Even Miles could detect Vayl's smile when he replied. "This ghost was once the queen of Romania. A politically brilliant woman, Marie will not have lost her desire to rule. We believe she will have found in Brude an opponent, not an ally. In fact, we are quite certain of it."

"And you think she'll want to help us?" asked Cole.

Even Vayl couldn't put one hundred percent certainty into his voice when he said, "If we can convince her it is in her best interest, yes, we believe so."

Dave spoke up. "So the four of you are going to jump into the Thin. That is, if Raoul can figure out a travel plan that won't get you killed en route. Beautiful. And at the same time Bergman, Cole, Cassandra, and I are supposed to go ahead with plan B. You really want us to do that without you, Vayl?"

My *sverhamin* stared at his clasped hands. "I believe it would be for the best." Which meant, while he was all for Dave's attempt, he wasn't sure he could stand idly by while my brother defiled a sacred spot, even though his intentions were pure. Best for Vayl to make sure he never knew exactly how that scene had gone down.

Dave got it too. I could tell by the way his voice had roughened when he said, "Good enough. You don't even have to give us an exact location. All you have to do is get us close and—" He paused, and I heard Cassandra whisper something in a comforting tone. "Yeah," he went on, more definitely. "I can find the grave sites. I seem to have a way of homing in on cemeteries now."

I thought Dave was done then. He'd spoken words that were so hard for both Vayl and himself to hear that I wouldn't have been surprised to hear nothing but his breathing the rest of the way to Pelisor. Then he said, "You're sitting very still inside that car, Vayl. Do you trust us to do the right thing?"

Vayl's hands tightened around each other. Then he turned so he could see my twin, driving remarkably well behind us despite the fact that minis kept insisting on darting between us. He said, "You are the brother of my heart."

If I'd tried a line like that Cole would've slumped to the floor, passed out from laughing so hard, leaving Jack flustered and confused as Bergman rolled his eyes in disgust and Dave tried desperately not to wreck the bus from his own inability to control his hysterical response. But since it came from the vampire, everybody understood. He'd just handed over half of his life's quest to Dave because he considered him family. And that's what brothers do.

Dave held his fist up and pushed it toward Vayl. "We'll find your boy," he vowed.

"We'll find him," confirmed Cole as he steadily scratched Jack's head. "But where exactly are we starting?" He glanced away from Bergman's tinkering with Astral to peer down the rutted asphalt road, which was now far enough from the city for only sporadic traffic, all of which seemed to be passing us.

"We will stop at Peles Castle first. Your group will begin its mission from there," said Vayl. "The castle was not yet built when my family and I traveled this area, but it works as a fine landmark. Walk into the forest directly north of the tallest spire. The pines are quite dense around the castle, so it will not be easy to find the path, but I was here a month ago and cleared it myself. So once you find it, rest assured it will lead you to the spot."

"You can count on us," said Dave.

Vayl inclined his head slightly as he said, "Just be careful. I would hate for this entire mission to fail because someone"—he raised his eyebrow a bit at Cole—"decided to see how the local security detail felt about chattering vampire teeth."

Cole crossed his heart solemnly as he said, "I will keep my fake fangs in my pocket until the deed is done." He wiggled his eyebrows at Vayl. "Now *you* try to do the same, okeydokey, sweetie pie?"

I'd never thought I would see the day when Vayl rolled his eyes like an irate ninth grader, but then Cole manages to bring out the juvie in all of us sooner or later. Which was probably why we were all still relatively sane. Cassandra rescued the conversation by asking, "What will you be doing while we're trying to find Hanzi?"

Vayl explained how he and I, plus Aaron and Raoul, would be driving my Galaxie back to Peles Castle. He looked like he wanted to say more, but he sat back and let his arm fall into his lap. "Best of luck to all of us. And please remember, I am trying to save my children. I would be eternally grateful if, this time, you helped me succeed."

Chapter Eleven

Saturday, June 16, 10:30 p.m.

After doing another Party Line sound check at Bergman's insistence, we separated at the car park of Peles Castle. Since security would come to investigate us within two to three minutes, we pulled out of the lot together, but Dave parked on the shoulder of the road just outside of Peles, turned on his emergency blinkers, and left the bus open in case somebody decided to investigate.

I drove the Galaxie to Pelisor so quickly I barely had time to wonder what the rest of our crew was doing, or why Astral wasn't feeding me any video. Then I realized she was, she just happened to be looking at the grass as she walked, because every once in a while I could see one of her paws step into the picture. Then a huge pink tongue slurped across her nose. *Way to go, Jack! Keep that robokitty on her toes—not to mention all the humans who sometimes need to be reminded that the most important things in life are big, wet kisses.*

I glanced at Vayl, wondering if I should lay one on him. *Definitely soon*, I decided, as I brought my car to rest in a small park where, during the daytime, visitors might stop and have lunch before returning to the nearest city, which called itself Sinaia and catered to skiers, hikers, rock climbers, and people who'd convinced themselves the mineral springs were actually the Fountain of Youth.

Tourists got a huge kick out of the castles, of course, and in the daytime Pelisor's little nook of Romania looked like it had been peeled off a painting, with bright green grass and dark green pines forming a small break in the endless roll of the Carpathian Mountains. Pelisor itself was kinda homey for a castle, which had been the intent of its first owner, King Carol I. The main reason, I decided, was the hodgepodge of materials that had been used to build the place.

The foundation was formed from traditional gray castle stone. It was topped by German-cottage-style gables, with medieval church archways and turrets that looked pink in some lights and sandy brown in others pinched between. Topped by so many russet-colored roofs that it seemed as if the place had been built in sections and superglued together, it confused the hell out of my white-siding senses. And yet it worked.

I almost regretted getting past the caretaker so easily. Despite Raoul's tour-guide costume, the slope-shouldered old gent hadn't fallen for our American-VIPs story at first. Then Vayl had laid a gentle arm around his shoulder, looked deep into his eyes, and spoken to him in his own tongue while shoving hypnotic suggestions down his throat. He'd instantly dropped a handful of castle maps into our hands and shuffled away, twitching like he was trying to shake a persistent mosquito. I found myself wishing he'd fought Vayl's push a little harder. Then I wouldn't have had to face the gilding so soon.

"Oh. My. God." I stopped three steps into the Gold Room, where Queen Marie's ghost appeared the most, forcing Aaron to backpedal so he wouldn't slam into me. His curse drew itself out when he got a load of our new surroundings.

"Shee-it!" he said, sliding past me to wander around the room's edge, slowly, like he had to get his bearings or he just might get lost amid the glitter. Raoul had stationed himself near the center by a chaise longue draped with black lace. It was in startling contrast to the rest of the space, which shone with the color of power. Not purple. Nuh-uh. I've-got-a-Golden-Ticket gold.

Gilded thistles covered the walls and ceiling of the room, the center of which held a Celtic cross framed by four golden lights. I immediately looked to Vayl to see how he'd be affected by the holy sign. He'd noticed it right away too, and was checking the backs of his hands for signs of smoke.

"Don't worry," Raoul told him as he nodded toward the cross. "You're under my protection here."

Vayl stuck his hands in his pockets. "Thank you," he said. He went to the opposite side of the room, where a door flanked by two arched stained glass windows would let beautiful light in during the day. I tried to gauge his mood by the way his shoulders strained against his suit coat, but it was too hard to tell while his back was turned. So I let my eyes wander to the Tiffany lamp on the heavy rectangular table that sat between the chaise and the bank of windows, which gave the room an unearthly glow. Stately square chairs sat at each end of the table. At a diagonal behind one of them a double throne—I couldn't think of it in any other terms—waited for its owner's return. Behind the other a golden cabinet held some of Marie's most treasured possessions. A book of poetry written in her own hand. A pair of giant pearl earrings surrounded by diamonds. A blue velvet hat trimmed with white fur. A statue of her daughter, Elisabeth, lifting her face to a refreshing breeze, her long hair and ruffled skirts flying behind her.

Vayl turned, the dimple on his right cheek appearing briefly as he asked, "Jasmine? Is this what you would call over-the-top?"

I said, "Vayl? This freaking room is the reason royals should be wired with an off switch."

Aaron said, "Holy shitsky, this guy's got a gold dick!" He was pointing at a statue that stood beside the flower-painted doorway we'd entered. The artist seemed to be into helmets and swords but little else in the way of armor.

"Shitsky?" I asked, raising my eyebrows. "Where are you from, Aaron? Sheboygan?"

"Close," he said. "My mom was from Madison and I grew up in St. Paul."

I crossed my arms. "Nice boys from Wisconsin do not go around killing people. Even after they've turned into vampires."

He blew his breath out his nose. "That is exactly something my mom would've said."

"I know. My Granny May was from the Midwest."

"Is she in the Thin?" he asked hopefully.

I laughed out loud. "Hell no! She's probably in God's left ear right now, informing him that maybe he should change his gemstone polish, because the pearly gates aren't looking quite as shiny as they should."

Aaron's smile suddenly made the whole room look dull by comparison. "Mom was just like that!"

"How about your dad?" I asked.

Instant sorrow. "Not so much. Dad knew two things. How to brew beer. And how to say yes to Mom. I was fifteen when she died, and then it became my job to tell him what to do."

Now I understood how Aaron's dad had been caught.

Raoul said, "Your father would have been easy prey, then. A wavering soul is a vulnerable one."

The kid dropped his head. "I've thought about that. But he's a good guy."

"I know." Raoul gestured down to the chaise. "According to the plaque, this is the spot where Queen Marie died in 1938. This will be where she returns when I call her."

"So that's what you're going to do?" I asked.

I came over to stand by him, staring down at the last cradle of a country's ruler. It did feel different to me, as if I'd sidled up to the emotional firewall of a woman's entire life. But I knew that I could reach through if I wanted to. That I could touch the sliver of soul that she'd left behind, that continued to call her back. And it would burn to be so close to such raw humanity.

I clasped my hands behind my back as Raoul said, "If I invited her back to a place where she habitually walked anyway, we'd all be less likely to become ghost kebabs. You could talk, hopefully make the deal, and then take it from there. If she even—"

I held my hand up to head off his doubts before he polluted the room with his negative energy. I said, "I've sensed it in Brude. She spends most of her time in the Thin. This is the only place that calls her back."

Raoul stared down at the plaque mounted on a gold-painted post. "All right, I'll buy that. But only because you two are the types who make it your job to know. Did you also know that when she shows up to haunt the place, she heralds her entrance with the scent of her favorite perfume?"

"Which is?" I asked.

"Violets," Raoul said.

"Nope, we missed that. But we're not surprised. Are we, Vayl?" I asked as my *sverhamin* came over to join us.

Vayl came over to stand by us. "Nothing the queen did would raise my eyebrows," he told us.

"Good," replied Raoul. "Because I'm about to bring her here, and I suspect she'd see that as a sign of weakness."

"What happened to opening a doorway?" Vayl asked, his voice deepening with frustration.

"The queen will take you through if you talk fast enough," said Raoul. He eyed Vayl. "You look frightening enough to curdle milk. I suggest you let Jaz take this one." Before Vayl could reply he went on. "Marie is a queen, so she'll probably travel with a retinue. I have no idea how many she'll bring with her, but they'll be hungry." His eyes wandered to Aaron as he finished. "I suggest you stay inside the room until the meeting's over."

"Why would we leave?" asked Aaron.

"You could be forced out," Raoul said. "And for my protection to work at maximum strength right now it can't extend beyond these four walls." He gestured at the wallpaper as Aaron began looking for something sturdy to hang on to. Then he said, "As soon as she's accepted your deal, you'll be all right. But until then, be vigilant."

"I was a Boy Scout," Aaron offered. "Is that anything like 'Be prepared'?"

I crossed my arms. "That all depends. What are you preparing to do?"

He shrugged. I said, "Well whatever it is, just don't touch the ghosts. Nothing enrages them more than to be touched by the living. They'll morph from gracious conversationalists into parasitic bloodsuckers right before your eyes. I've known them to slice arteries with rage alone. So, you know, if you can't figure out how to be prepared. At least be polite."

Chapter Twelve

Saturday, June 16, 10:40 p.m.

While we set up for the queen's visit, the other (better?) half of our crew took the short hike to Pelisor's older and oh-baby-grander brother, Peles.

Astral's video combined with the Party Line and vivid descriptions by members of what later came to be called the "Bergman Got Balls Expedition" revealed that security around a museum full of priceless artifacts just oozing stories related to Romania's colorful history is as tight as a miser at Christmas. Which was why they didn't bother knocking. They parked just off of Str. Pelesului and hit the tree line. Dave and Jack took the lead. Cassandra followed with Astral at her heels, Bergman at her shoulder, and Cole at her back, his gun drawn but hanging at his side.

"Is that really going to be necessary?" hissed Bergman, his eyes darting nervously from Cole's nine-millimeter Beretta Storm to the moonlit pines surrounding them and beyond, to Peles Castle, which sat in its valley to their right, sparkling like an amulet full of diamonds.

"Absolutely," Cole whispered. "Because you never know when we might be attacked by a horde of Vlad's impalers. Just imagine it, Miles. Three hundred screaming warriors on horseback, their faces painted with the blood of their enemies, their lances set to pin us against these trees here like a couple of scarecrows."

"That's just...Would you stop with the ridiculousness? That's not even how it happened back then."

Cole shrugged. "Like I'd know. I spent my entire History class trying to convince the teacher that my dad actually found Hitler while he was still alive and that he was the one who shot him. And that my mom was really Eva Braun. Almost had him convinced too. Then he saw the three of us together at a wrestling tournament, figured out my folks weren't even alive during World War Two and the whole game collapsed." Cole sighed. "It was fun while it lasted, though."

"Shut up back there," Dave said. "We're supposed to be skirting security, and it's gonna be kind of tough to pull off stealth mode while we're all laughing."

Cole grinned as Bergman gave him a dirty look, which seemed especially to be aimed at his Beretta.

"It's just a precaution," Cole reassured him. "I promise if I have to, I'll shoot the guns out of their hands just like in the old Westerns."

"And then will you sing to them like Roy Rogers used to do?" whispered Cassandra.

"Only if you buy me a white shirt with fringe *and* sequins."

Cassandra said, "Done," just as Astral made a matter-of-fact suggestion: "Mammas Don't Let Your Babies Grow Up to Be Cowboys."

They all stopped and stared down at Bergman's robokitty, who had paused when she noticed Cassandra do the same. She looked up at them and said, "Ghost Riders in the Sky."

"What does that even mean?" asked Cole as he peered off into the dark, cupping his shooting hand with his free one and pulling the Beretta up to shoulder height. He went still, raising his nose as if sniffing the air.

Dave motioned for them to stand perfectly still. Moments later he and Jack had disappeared into the pines.

"Wow," whispered Bergman. "He's good."

"He'd better be back soon," Cole finally whispered.

"What is it?" Cassandra asked.

"Something's here."

Bergman slapped his hands against his cheeks like he was trying to wake himself up from a bad dream. "How can you tell?"

Cole rolled his shoulders as if he suddenly felt the need to stay loose. "It's hard to describe. It's like the back of my brain itches. Sometimes, just by the way it's irritated, I can tell what's set me off. Like a vampire. Or a fairy. But this time"—he shook his head—"I'm not quite sure."

Bergman stepped to his side. "But maybe you could be sensing something innocent. Hunters do that. And you're kind of a hunter. So maybe it's a raccoon. Or a frog." He squinted into the woods. "Ribbit?" he ventured hopefully.

Cassandra had also closed ranks. But she'd turned so that she could detect movement behind them. "Is your gun going to be effective against whatever you're sensing?" she asked Cole.

Cole shrugged. "It's loaded with holy silver. So it'll slow down a vamp or kill a Were. It's just that this thing doesn't *smell* like that."

Dave and Jack rejoined the group so quietly that even Bergman forgot to jump. "I found the grave site," Dave said. "But it's being guarded."

"By what?" Cole asked.

Dave rubbed his jaw, which made Cassandra start to play nervously with her rings. Already, like a good poker player, or a loving wife, she'd begun to pick up on Dave's stress tells. He said, "It's a Rider."

Cole swore under his breath, another sign of bad mojo. Only Bergman still hadn't fully caught on to their predicament. He asked, "What's a Rider?"

Neither Dave nor Cole acted like he wanted to answer, so Cassandra clasped her hands together, her eyes so luminous she might have been channeling her inner oracle as she told him, "It's a big, hulking brute that latches on to its victim, digs in, and then sucks out all the thought and emotion, until there's nothing left but a staring, slobbering husk."

"So it's a vampire?" asked Bergman.

Cole turned to him. "Think of it as the first vampire. In the same way that scientists consider Neanderthals the first salsa dancers. Not quite, but without that link you'd never have Vayl."

"So..." Bergman struggled to stay in the classroom part of his brain. "It's, what, less evolved?"

Dave nodded. "It doesn't turn its victims. It tortures them. Gets into their blood and melds their minds into truth machines. Tell me something, Miles. Have you ever seen a person take a good look at himself in the mirror?"

Bergman shook his head.

Dave said, "I did once. Friend of mine, ended up punching the glass so hard he needed twenty stitches to put his hand back together." He leaned in closer, trying to explain a creature whose power even he had only heard whispers of. "Most of us spend our whole lives tucking our weakness under the mattress, hiding our fears inside the closet, pretending we're not miserable shits to our spouses and kids. Not because they deserve it. Because that's just who we are. Riders turn people into horses, jerking the reins so they have to face their own miserable bitchiness, prejudice, and petty crap. The more you fight, the harder those spurs dig in until you're literally bleeding all over the carpet. Feeding the monster on your back. If you don't give in, pretty soon you're dead. But if you can face the horror, walk through your own nightmare without flinching too much, you can buck that Rider and cut his fucking throat."

Dave pulled a knife from a sheath he'd hidden inside the pocket of his cargo pants. "So which one of you thinks you can pull that off?"

Chapter Thirteen

Saturday, June 16, 10:45 p.m.

I'd heard all the talk in Cole's camp and it had made me half crazy. It was my job to go decimate the Rider, not hear that one of my crew was about to risk his or her life in my place. Especially since the creature couldn't have picked that particular cemetery to guard randomly. It had been sent by Roldan and Brude in another attempt to destroy us. I hated that we couldn't deal with the Rider directly, and that the pain of watching one of our dearest friends fight, and possibly die, in our place would make those two bastards crow.

Plus I knew Astral's mutterings about cowboys weren't random at all, but another push to find Zell Culver. And *soon*. I wasn't sure who'd been pulling her strings, and while I appreciated the direction, I also hated the fact that I couldn't follow it right this minute. But here I was, stuck in rock-around-the-clock mode, circling the lace-draped chaise where Queen Marie had taken her last breath along with Vayl, Raoul, and Aaron like we'd started a game of musical chairs only, damn, somebody had forgotten the props. So we just kept cakewalking while Raoul tried to conjure the stubborn old monarch to the site of her last human breath.

I could almost see her lying there, surrounded by her children and loyal servants. Mourned aloud even as they silently divided her loot among themselves. That alone would've given me reason enough to return. I'd have haunted those bastards to the fifth generation. And I kinda hoped she still scared the shit out of them on a daily basis.

"So what are we doing?" whispered Aaron. "Is this like a séance?" He held his hands in ours delicately, as if he thought Raoul and I were still pissed enough to break a couple of fingers.

I said, "I've never seen a séance yet that wasn't three parts stage show and one part bullshit. Real Raisers use an inborn power called the Lure to pull spirits from the Thin. From what I understand it makes them smell extra good to the dead, especially when they're dancing. It's like a gazelle flirting with the danger zone of a lion pride. The pride's fascinated, right? Glued to the picture. But if they've already eaten, they just watch. Raisers have a similar ability to convince the spirits they're stuffed. Since none of us were born with that power, we're going with this simpler, less entertaining technique."

We finally stopped, which must have meant Raoul had coiled our energies around the spot to a satisfactory degree. Aaron's arms crossed over his chest as he watched my Spirit Guide pull a silver dagger from the sheath hanging at his side. He'd looked so relieved to be able to strap it back on when we were pulling our weapons out of the trunk of the Galaxie that I'd felt a fresh spurt of guilt for making him ditch his uniform. Sometimes you just need your familiars around you. Aaron didn't see that, maybe because the dagger was glinting like a razor as Raoul put it into motion. "What're you going to do?" he asked.

"Sacrifice," I said.

Vayl grimaced at me. "Must you taunt the boy?" he asked.

I considered the pudgy youth who still refused to dump his country's fear of *others* despite everything he'd seen so far. "Yup."

Raoul stepped forward. "Hold your arms over the chaise," he commanded, just like he'd dropped back into the field and we were his loyal troops. We did as we were told, even Aaron, and Raoul made a small slash above each of our wrists one after another, including his own. Following his lead, we turned our arms so the blood could fall on the lace coverlet, watching the black cloth dampen as the droplets hit and soaked in.

Raoul said, "Queen Marie Alexandra Victoria of Romania. We beg an audience."

He waited. We all did while Aaron looked up, down, and around like he figured a gang of skeletons was going to jump out of a hidden doorway any second now. He whispered, "That's it? Ring-around-the-rosy, blood, and begging, and you think the ghost of a dead queen is just going to drop in on you like you're her favorite cousins? I should've *known* you guys were a bunch of posers—"

"Aaron." One word from Vayl accompanied by a look that could freeze erupting volcanoes, and our tagalong shut the hell up. Just in time for the scent of violets to waft through the room.

"Do you…?" I raised my eyebrows at Vayl and Raoul. They nodded to show that they'd detected the odor too, stronger now, centering on the chaise under our noses. A rumble shook the room, or maybe it was the whole castle, because we could hear the distant shrieks of a terrified woman. A shiver ran across my shoulder blades and I turned toward the flower-painted door just in time to see two soldiers wearing uniforms I dated to World War II lead a majestic creature through the entryway as if it had been opened and the room prepared for them. She held her head high, as if the spiked platinum crown resting on her rich brown hair weighed nothing more than its gumball machine knockoff. Her blue gown looked vivid against the gold walls I could still see glowing through it, providing a surreal backdrop to the light golden cape she wore over it. Two long ropes of pearls swayed back and forth across her breasts as she walked toward us, followed closely by the rest of her party, two ladies wearing pale pink-and-white lace scarves over their dark ringlets and two more cavalrymen in knee boots over tan trousers and hip-length tunics set off with gleaming buttons and shining swords.

I was impressed. And chilled.

Because Queen Marie had chosen to stay in the Thin rather than move on. That meant she'd sacrificed her soul's salvation in exchange for power, manipulation, greed, and the random cannibalization of her fellow spirits. And she looked well fed.

I curtsied just the way they'd taught us to in spy school and said, "Queen Marie, my name is Jasmine Parks. It's a true honor to meet you."

She raised her hand up to me, palm out, which seemed to be a signal to the guards. They glanced back at their ruler expectantly. She gored me with her pitiless blue eyes and said, "Kill her."

Chapter Fourteen

Saturday, June 16, 10:50 p.m.

The woods beside Pelisor Castle seemed to fall as silent as the grave-searching half of our crew as they tried to figure out what the odds were of any one of them successfully overcoming a creature so ancient even vampires gave it a wide berth. While Cassandra, Bergman, and Cole debated the wisdom of fighting a battle that was really Vayl's, Astral and Jack stared at each other until Astral said, "Bad Moon Rising" in a low, even tone. Jack huffed. Cole told me later he suspected my malamute was in full agreement.

Dave murmured a couple of lines from Creedence Clearwater Revival's hit: "Don't go 'round tonight./Well it's bound to take your life." He looked around the circle at the others. "But we have to. Vayl's depending on us." He shook his head. "No, I'm his brother. Or as close as he's ever going to get. I'm the one who has to do this."

Cassandra's gasp had barely cleared her mouth before Bergman grabbed the knife out of her husband's hand. Luckily my twin had lightning reflexes or Miles might've stabbed them both in the exchange. As it was Dave backed off fast, leaving our tech guru to stand in the middle of the circle holding Dave's survival knife, looking down at its doubly lethal edges, one serrated, one sharp as a razor.

"Are you sure about this?" Cole asked him. "I think that blade is thicker around the middle than you are."

Bergman dropped his arm. "You can't do it. Even when you don't have horns you're a hell-raiser," he said.

Cole's nod admitted that his brush with demon-kind minimized his chances of winning a battle with a beast like the Rider. Bergman went on. "Dave has to find out where Vayl's kid ended up, so he's out. And Cassandra's pregnant, so—"

A chorus of shocked denials and surprised gasps from his group along with distracted confusion from mine at his announcement. "Well, crap, don't any of you have even the tiniest shred of observational skills? She keeps rubbing her stomach, which she's never done before. She's been kind of nauseous. And she married Dave without telling Jaz, when we all know she would've loved to have her and Evie there, and probably even that horrifying old colonel they grew up with. They had to do a quickie wedding so they could fake the kid into thinking he was legit. Which"—Bergman glared at the expectant parents—"if it has half a brain, you're so not getting away with."

Cassandra put her hand to her mouth as Dave pulled her close. "We didn't want anyone to know until we were sure..." She took a shuddering breath. "I have lost babies early on before. I'm still not out of danger."

"What did the doctor say?" asked Bergman.

"That I'm fine."

He waved his hand at her. "Then relax. As long as you don't let this Rider jump you, I'm thinking you'll be changing really disgusting-smelling diapers in another six months. Which, as I said, leaves me to deal with..." He trailed off, biting his lip. "I can do this," he whispered.

She held out her hand, realized the last thing he probably wanted right now was for a psychic to touch him, and pulled it back. "I'll pray for you."

"No offense," he replied. "But how is your new relationship to the gnome-god going to help me?"

She shrugged. Among her many talents, she'd recently rediscovered her original gift just in time to pull off a last-minute save during our mission to kick some fanatical gnome ass in Australia. However, Bergman did have a point. As the oracle to Ufran, she probably didn't have a whole lotta pull in the human arena. Still, she said, "You're very thin. Maybe he'll take a liking to you."

"Great. I'm about to attempt the bravest thing I've ever done in my life, and you want to make me an honorary gnome." He squared his shoulders and turned to Dave. "What do I do?" he asked.

Dave looked him hard in the eyes. "Fight. Look, Miles, Cassandra's right in a way. You are thinner than my mom's chicken noodle soup, but I know you. When you sink your teeth in, you don't let go until you get what you want. Go to that place in your head, face your personal demons, and then make the Rider battle you there. You will win. At which point"—he nodded to the knife—"that should come in handy."

Bergman looked down at the blade. "I have to kill it."

"Hopefully we'll be able to help. But because of where it rides, you'll be the only one who can reach its heart. Stab it there and it dies," said Dave.

"Okay." Bergman stared off into the forest, his face set in firm lines. They could see the man he would look like in twenty years if he survived this night. And they quietly honored him for offering himself that future.

Cole wrapped Jack's leash around his wrist and Cassandra gathered Astral into her arms.

"What do I do?" asked Bergman.

Dave pointed. "The cemetery is about twenty yards in that direction. You won't see him, maybe won't even sense him until he's on your back." He hesitated, then said, "As soon as he's on you, we'll move past and get to work. We wouldn't do this if Vayl didn't think his kid's life was in danger. And if it wasn't pretty much the dream come true for him. You know that, right?"

Bergman swallowed and nodded. He raised the knife in front of him, almost like it was a lantern that could light his way, and strode off into the trees.

Chapter Fifteen

Saturday, June 16, 10:50 p.m.

As Queen Marie's personal guards strode toward me, not even bothering to pull their swords as they came, I couldn't help but smile. Finally. Enemies I knew how to fight. And, like most men I encountered, ones that had sorely underestimated the pale, undernourished redhead they knew they could easily overcome.

I pulled the bolo from my pocket. Once, in Scotland, I had watched Brude's ghost army decimate a coven of Scidairan witches. But the girls had gutted more than one of his mercenaries using forged steel anointed with a red powder I'd learned later was made mainly from the ground bones of the unjustly executed. It was astonishingly easy to find, even if a tablespoon of the stuff did cost more than a month's rent.

Since I'd sprinkled my entire supply into the sheath that my seamstress had tailored into my jeans, my bolo came out thoroughly coated and ready for spectral action.

The first guard spoke to me in Romanian. "What did he say?" I asked Vayl, who'd come around the end of the chaise to stand by my side. Raoul took his place at my other shoulder while Aaron hovered behind us, watching the action like a hummingbird who wants to dive in and fight, but is sorely undertrained and outmaneuvered.

"He says you are unfit to sully his queen's presence with your foul stench."

Vayl began to reply, the rage in his tone a flaming counterpoint to the ice of his power, rising like a glacier just birthed from the arctic circle.

Raoul said, "Jasmine, wait!" but I ignored him, riding the electric line of Vayl's reaction right into the face of the soldier who'd insulted me.

I slashed at his eyes before he could think of pulling a weapon and he jumped back, the shock on his gaping mouth pulling a delighted laugh from mine. Even more so as I learned that I would, once again, be able to look forward to becoming an aunt. Something else to live for. Cool, that was just what I needed.

I lunged again just as the second guard finally moved his blade into a useful position. My knife sank deep into the first guard's sternum. He crumpled as the women behind him screamed in furious protest. But then the ladies-in-waiting fell to their knees. I knew what happened next. I'd seen it in Brude's dungeon, hadn't I? They'd tear his chest open at the wound, pull out his lungs, and sink their teeth into them before the rest of his body began to melt away as the powder residue my knife had left worked its magic.

"Enough!" bellowed the queen.

Her servants pulled back. The guard rolled his eyes up at Marie as she leaned over him. Almost kindly she said, "It is your choice, my boy, as always. You may serve your queen. Or you may be free."

"You, my liege," he croaked from a throat already fading into mist.

She laid her hand on him, and presto-change-o, he began to solidify.

My opinion of the queen faltered. She didn't allow her subjects to gnaw on each other like a bunch of alley rats, so maybe she wasn't as cold-blooded and calculating as I'd thought. But then, she'd just ordered my execution.

As if she could read my mind she turned to me and said, "Rumors run rife about you, Jasmine Parks. They say King Brude has possessed your soul."

Something about the way she said his name tipped me off. They'd been close once. Cozy enough that it was easy for her to hate him now. Of the twenty-three other rulers in the Thin, had she been his *closest* neighbor? I said, "They're wrong. He's in here." I tapped my forehead. "But *I'm* in charge of the castle."

"What do you intend to do with your tenant?" she inquired.

"Kill the bastard."

"Then I apologize for the misunderstanding. I assumed the Upstart was in command of your senses."

"No, Your Highness. He tried. He failed."

Her approving nod contained all the grace of royal training. Yet that wasn't her only skill, otherwise the ghosts under her command would never willingly fall to heel like they had. Which meant she must have legendary charisma and the ability to connive with the most twisted of politicians. Dammit, I was beginning to like her. Even more when she gestured to the second guard and said, "Perhaps you would be so kind as to call off your vampire? Toma is the only one of my retinue who can play a challenging game of chess."

"Oh!" I turned to Vayl, who seemed to have forgotten that he carried ghost-powdered steel of his own. He'd grabbed the second guard by the neck, no small feat for a man whose enemy has only partly entered into his world. He'd managed it by dropping the temperature so radically that even I was shivering like I'd just spent the past hour sitting in the coroner's corpse-fridge keeping the stiffs company. The beyond-the-grave chill had brought the guard farther into the physical world, allowing Vayl to crank his head sideways and bury his fangs in the guy's neck.

There's no blood, whispered Teen Me from behind the gap-fingered mask she'd made of her hands. *What's going down Vayl's throat?*

I wasn't sure, but I could see him swallow, view the glow through his skin as whatever passed through his esophagus dropped into his stomach. *That can't be good. Can it?*

I said, "Vayl? It's all good now. The queen's cool with us staying alive."

Usually speaking is enough to break the spell vamps seem to fall under when they feed. But this ghost must've been yummylicious, because Vayl didn't even act like he knew I was in the same room.

The guard began to shriek, the sound so loud and shrill I had to cover my ears. Queen Marie stepped forward and peered over the terrified spirit's shoulder. She searched Vayl's face, taking in the sweep of his dark lashes as they closed over his ebony eyes, and the pitch-black curls cut so close to his head they could've been molded on.

"You are a gypsy," she said, her voice echoing eerily in the room, like it came from unsynched speakers. She reached out to touch him, hesitated, and then let her arm fall. "A vampire gypsy. I have never seen the like."

Vayl dropped the guard, who started to melt into the floorboards like furniture polish.

"My queen, I serve only you!" he cried. She sighed, like she was really tired of dropping things and having to pick them up again, as she leaned over and touched her hand to his forehead. He gained color and form so quickly it was almost like he'd never been gone.

Vayl watched the trick through half-interested eyes as he licked his lips. Then, as if a switch had clicked on in his brain, he remembered who she was and what we needed, and bowed so low his head nearly touched her knee. "I am Vasil Nicu Brâncoveanu," he said, straightening and nodding again with that extra-formal attitude he gets when he's about to make an important deal. "I am Rom."

She blinked. Message received—she knew that "gypsy" wasn't considered a nice name by those who'd been forced to wear it. So when she said, "I have been fascinated by the Rom all my life," he knew she'd offered him an apology for the slip. She went on. "But I understand they have intense superstitions against the Vampere. How is it, then, that you fell into eternity?"

His smile, almost as ghostly as the queen herself, spoke volumes to anyone who knew how to interpret it. But all he said was, "My thirst for revenge outweighed my better judgment."

She sighed. "So true for so many of us. Is that why you summoned me? Are you here to beg my aid in a personal vendetta?"

"No, Your Highness. Though I believe you would be a staunch ally in any cause, we have come to seek your help in leading us to the spirit of Aaron's father. We know that Brude, and a werewolf named Roldan, have trapped him in the Thin. However we cannot reach the location without you."

"Which one of you is this Aaron child?" asked Marie as she looked over our tiny crew. I pointed to Junior, who was leaning over with his hands on his knees, probably so he wouldn't pass out, if the paleness of his face was any clue.

Since nobody seemed willing to take the ball, I kept it going. "It's a long story, but the bottom line is that if you help us save the dad, Brude will suffer. And, ultimately, it will be easier for me to vanquish him."

Her finely sculpted eyebrows jumped at that. "Vanquish?" she repeated.

"I said what I meant," I replied. And then I stopped, because I wasn't sure what more I should share. But Raoul seemed to think she should know.

"Jasmine has the Rocenz. She plans to carve his name on the gates of hell."

New respect in those icy eyes. "I like women who travel where they are not welcome," she said. She glanced at Vayl. "And so, it seems, you will be the one who secures *my* revenge." Her fingers went to her throat, which was bare now. But I thought that once she'd worn a torque just like the ones Brude's loyal soldiers had. Only she'd been a lot more than that to him. And he'd gone and blown it.

She said, "Follow me." And then, as if she assumed we'd just trot right after her, she turned and walked back through the door.

Chapter Sixteen

Saturday, June 16, 10:55 p.m.

Cole told me later that he'd never felt as proud of Bergman as he did when the tech genius emerged from the shelter of the huge, fragrant pines and first set his eyes on the Rider. It blocked the entrance to the small, fenced cemetery, a bat-shaped shadow hovering across the entrance like a visible disease. And our Miles walked right toward it. So what if his shoulders shook a little and his hands were clenched into white-knuckled fists, the one that held the knife physically swaying as if moved by a breeze? He held his head high. And we heard him say quietly, "This is for you, Jaz."

Though I had Astral's recording to prove otherwise, I nearly cried when Cole told me that Bergman seemed to get thinner as the Rider stretched its wings, revealing a wasp-shaped body banded with rib-like bones outside its rubbery skin that ran from upper chest to lower thigh. As Bergman approached the bones creaked, pulling away from the body as if to welcome him into their embrace. Even when razor-sharp needles shot from the end of each bone, Bergman didn't hesitate. He just said, "Hop on, you son of a bitch."

It flew at him with the sound of a million bats escaping their cave for the night. He flinched and took a step back, but it was the impact that drove him to his knees.

Cole lunged forward as Jack strained at his leash, both of them growling incoherently as instinct overrode intellect in their need to save the man who had now totally disappeared beneath the Rider's wings. Dave's hand, steel around Cole's forearm, stopped them both. Pulled them past the writhing bodies, held them tight when they heard Bergman scream. Cassandra, clutching Astral so close that entire chunks of her memory record were simply the back of our psychic's arm and the sound of her small gulping sobs, slipped her hand around Dave's wrist. And together, linked like three scared kids with their unwilling pets in tow, they walked into the graveyard.

Chapter Seventeen

Saturday, June 16, 11:00 p.m.

The last time I'd visited the Thin hadn't been a voluntary drop-in. Even so, I'd realized the drop zone had been a pure creation of its most powerful spirit. Which meant Brude's land had been both as beautiful as he remembered his native Scotland to be, and as terrible as he'd remade it to be considering he wanted to rule a lawless and chaotic realm. So, knowing Queen Marie had been a big fan of the arts and quite the interior decorator (not to mention a girl who "got around" as evidenced by the fact that historians named at least two and sometimes three different dads for her six kids), I'd figured on transitioning into the ethereal version of a commune. However, when we followed her out the door of Pelisor, what we stepped into was an armed camp.

Unlike Brude's mishmash of mercenaries from every era, Marie had recruited only Romanian soldiers from World War II and, by God, they hadn't forgotten their uniforms or their discipline. Lines of well-armed men marched past neat rows of barracks while fields made for target practice or hand-to-hand combat held groups of fierce, serious foes who seemed sure that battle was only an order away.

Marie led us down the dirt paths, nodding graciously when men stopped to bow and then peer at us sideways. At the northern edge of the camp was a thatch-roofed cottage surrounded by well-tended gardens and a roughly hewn fence. The arched red door opened when we got to the arbor gate, and a wrinkled, balding gentleman wearing a butler's uniform tottered down the path to let us in.

"My queen," he said, bowing deeply enough that I wondered if he'd fall on his head before he was able to right himself. Then I saw he had a firm grip on the gate and relaxed.

"We have guests, Stanislov," she said as she breezed past. "Make sure the dogs don't get loose, will you? I don't want them eaten before they've fulfilled their potential."

"Very good, madam."

I suddenly wished I'd brought Jack. He would never let another dog eat me. I glanced over my shoulder. Nope. Nothing even close to canine. Although the soldiers did look a lot hungrier than you'd generally expect in such a well-run camp. Probably Marie didn't let them feast on each other. And then it hit me.

"Your queenishness?" I asked. "What do you call your soldiers?"

As she sailed toward the open door of her cottage, Marie said, "I thought you knew, darling. Those troops are none other than the Dogs of War. They are leashed tightly here. But I am training them to tear the throat from Brude's army." Under her breath she added, "Even if they have to do so without the aid of my squeamish neighbors to the south." Realizing she was thinking out loud, she finished with a flourishy sort of punch to the air, saying, "When the time comes, they will rage, my dear, they will rage."

She glanced over her shoulder at me, the smile in her eyes so sly and calculating that I shivered. Vayl put his arm across my shoulders. "We have the key to destroying Brude. All we need is your cooperation and you could win this war."

"I *will* win this war," she corrected him imperiously. "And when I do this little universe will step to *my* tune. *I* will force order onto this bedlam." She sighed. "What a shame it was that Brude never shared my vision." Her laugh, so bitter, was clearly aimed at herself. "Leave it to me to involve myself with the most ambitious and least loyal of Satan's elite guardsmen." She shook her head. "I have such terrible taste in lovers." Her eyes rested on mine, and for a moment she looked at me as an equal. "What about you?" she asked. "Are you satisfied with him?" She nodded toward Vayl like he was a piece of sculpture that she might, at some point, consider stealing.

"He's mine," I told her, keeping most, but not all, of the warning growl from my voice.

"Why?"

I looked at him steadily for a while before I answered, "Because it could never be any other way."

"I thought that about Brude once," she said, her voice dropping into melancholy.

"What changed?" I asked her.

"I came face to face with the real *domytr* one day," she said. "And I couldn't fool myself any longer." She narrowed her eyes at me. "Have you truly faced your vampire?"

I glanced at Vayl. "He's a killer," I told her. "But then again, so am I. Which is why we're such a good fit. Aren't you lucky you found us?"

Chapter Eighteen

Saturday, June 16, 11:00 p.m.

I had never visited the site where Vayl had buried his two sons. It was like he wanted to keep that part of his past completely separate. And I respected that. But I saw enough of Astral's feed, and Cassandra described the emotions of those moments so clearly, that I could always visualize it as if I'd been there myself, locked inside the weather-treated steel fence with the two black marble stones Vayl had bought to replace the broken pieces of the white, unreadable originals. They still lay at the bases of the new monuments, like offerings to the bodies that lay beneath the rich, needle-blanketed sod, so precious to their surviving family member that he had etched A FATHER'S LOVE IS FOREVER into each of the stones. It was in Romanian, but Cassandra had asked Cole to translate, and felt her throat close at the catch in his voice when he'd done as she asked.

Dave said, "We can't let Vayl down now." They nodded, Cassandra and then Cole sneakily wiping away a tear as David continued. "This could get scary." They looked over their shoulders at Bergman and his Rider, whose positions hadn't changed. Then they looked back at him. "I know what you're thinking," he said. "I mean worse than that."

Big swallows. Nods. "Let's get this done," said Cole, leaning over to pet Jack, who kept prancing sideways and glancing toward

Bergman, as if he knew something should be done and he was falling down on the job.

"The sooner the better," Cassandra agreed. She handed Astral to Dave as she said, "I want that Rider off Miles *now*."

He nodded and said, "All right, cat. Let's see how good you really are." He knelt between the graves of Hanzi and Badu Brâncoveanu. He took off his backpack and from it pulled two steel rods that had been folded multiple times, the same way tent poles are broken down after a camping trip. Assembled, they were at least ten feet long, with the last section of each tipped like a spear. He carefully shoved each of them into the ground as far as he could. Tapping his shoulder, he waited until Astral had taken her place, perching beside his ear like he was just another mantelpiece to add to her collection. And then, wrapping a hand around each pole, he closed his eyes and began to chant.

Cole and Cassandra took their places, each standing at one corner of Hanzi's grave.

Cole whispered, "I still don't understand what we're supposed to be doing."

"We're like landmarks," Cassandra explained. "Dave is traveling a long way in his head. He needs to be able to find his way back. Even with Astral acting as a filter, he could get lost. You and I, standing right here along his route, can actually be seen and latched on to when he tries to find his way back."

Cole glanced back over his shoulder, wincing as Bergman groaned. "How long?"

Cassandra nodded. "I know what you're thinking. We have to be here until he comes all the way back."

"Both of us, though? I mean, we're standing three feet apart!"

"In this world. But in that one we might be hundreds of miles away from each other, we don't know. Which is why we have to stay. But only just until Dave is done. Then"—she pointed at Bergman—"we run for him."

Dave cracked open his left eye. "People? I'm trying to home in on a traveling soul while a robot tries to take root in my collarbone and you guys are gabbing like a couple of beauty shop regulars. Could we concentrate here? That would help a lot."

Cole and Cassandra traded guilty looks. "Sorry," said Cole. "I talk when I'm nervous. Sometimes I have to pee. Like right now, I could whiz clear over that fence, bounce it off that tree, and sink it into that hollow stump, that's how bad I have to go."

A laugh, so dry and cracked it could've been confused for a smoker's cough, interrupted them. Except it had come from Bergman, so everyone knew what it meant. *Don't stop. That was funny, and because it made me feel better, I can fight a little longer. So while you're just standing there like a couple of lumps, how about you goddamn goofballs make. Me. Laugh.*

Chapter Nineteen

Saturday, June 16, 11:10 p.m.

In the end, Queen Marie had to admit we'd come up with a plan that might just work. So she called in a couple of her best Dogs and demanded that they switch their uniforms for something a little less bow-wow and a little more Brude-rocks. While they turned the camp upside down looking for a couple of outfits that didn't scream trained cavalryman, the queen took us behind her house to a fine brick patio surrounded by blooms. In the center sat a birdbath whose water looked like it hadn't been changed for at least a millennium. My nose, still physically intact thanks to Raoul's ability to transport us all in the flesh, wrinkled as I walked past it and stood next to Vayl under an arched trellis covered with yellow roses.

"I didn't know water could turn that shade of brown and still stay liquid," I said.

"I think you are being generous in referring to it as water," he replied.

I had to agree when the center of it bubbled up, stretching the edges toward it as if the entire surface were made of rubber. When it popped I had to cover my mouth; the stench was so oily that it felt like it was trying to crawl down my throat and nest in my stomach.

Aaron, who'd chosen that moment to walk past it, moaned, "Oh,

God," and ran to some bushes to his right, where he spent the next few minutes gagging and spitting. Raoul, still standing at the entrance to the garden, stared first at the birdbath, and then at the queen, who sat comfortably between him and us on an intricately tooled metal bench while her ladies-in-waiting arranged the skirts of her dress as if they were flowers that had just been added to the garden.

She waved the women away when Raoul said, "Well disguised," as he gestured to the infested water. "The last one I saw was in the Eminent Museum of Enlightenment."

"It is a classic piece," she agreed. "However it has its advantages, even now. For instance, it can transport entire regiments of my men into areas of the Thin that are not currently guarded by Brude's hordes. We like to call them avoidance jumps. Or it can shoot a single person directly to the site he wishes to visit." She rose, reached into the birdbath, and completely grossed me out when she pulled free a gerbil-sized handful of shit-colored goo that smelled like a neglected zoo. When she threw it at Raoul he sidestepped, and I thought he was going to let it fall into the bushes behind him. But he caught it between his fingertips, his lips turning down at the corners when the impact let loose a fresh barrage of odor. He let go of the sphere with one hand, and I was pretty sure he was going to throw it down with disgust when the queen ripped into him.

"Hold on to that!" she snapped, the command in her voice automatically straightening his spine.

He renewed his grip on the slippery ball as I asked, "What's the idea?" afraid that whatever Raoul had touched might foul him permanently. When he tried to protest I waved him off. "I should have that. Or Vayl."

"No." Her reply felt more like the passing of a law than conversation. "Raoul is the senior Eldhayr here. He has the sense that the Sniffer"—she nodded to the ball—"needs in order for it to find Brude's realm. You didn't think it stayed in one place, did you? If it had, I would have razed his castle and fed his minions to my

Dogs ages ago. Speaking of which." She nodded to Aaron. "Were you planning on leaving this one as payment for your guards and the Sniffer?"

"Luscious!" "Juicy!" screamed her ladies.

I hadn't seen Aaron so pale since he thought he'd committed vampicide. He looked around wildly, not, I noted proudly, for help. But for something heavy to defend himself with. Unfortunately the only weapon he could find was the fountain, and he didn't dare get any closer to it. Which meant he actually looked grateful when Vayl stepped up to face the queen.

He said, "In all the years I have lived, I have learned that nothing is truly required to exist. As a result, I am the best killer in the world and the Whence. Shall we try for the Thin as well?" The queen's smile never wavered at the threat on her life. Maybe she understood what a hard time Vayl would have actually snuffing it out here, on her turf. But her eyes, shifting slightly to the left and then to the right, admitted that he meant what he said, and she would probably find herself in a world of hurt before the deed was done, no matter what the outcome.

Raoul stepped forward. "No, Vayl. Aaron may be your son, but this place is more my territory than yours." He looked steadfastly at the queen. "Your skill at bartering nearly equals your political finesse, Majesty. But you need, and will receive, nothing more from us than Brude's destruction, if we succeed. You should remember, as well, that if you threaten any of mine, you threaten me." He paused. "And all the Eldhayr."

The queen smiled happily. "Just as I'd hoped. Barring the boy, every one of you is as fierce as a Romanian infantryman. *Now* I am sure of your plan. *Now* I can send my Dogs with you in confidence. They will guard you while the Sniffer jumps you into Brude's land. After that I feel sure the strategy you have outlined will gain you entrance into his castle." She pierced every one of us with a meaningful look. "Remember also that while you have your own agenda, you also fight for Queen Marie. My people follow me, and my laws, because their souls need structure in order to rest and mend and, perhaps someday, even move on. Be noble in this noble cause."

Wow. All this time she'd been testing us. Suckage. And yet maybe a true leader needs to do those things if she's going to ask her people to risk their lives on a venture as dangerous as the one we'd proposed. Which made me admire Marie all the more. As if I needed another reason to decimate Brude. But if I could destroy him, at least Marie's little realm would become a place where lost souls could shelter, safe from torture and violence, until they found themselves again. What a cool concept.

Chapter Twenty

Saturday, June 16, 11:05 p.m.

Dave felt like he'd spent hours kneeling between the graves of Vayl's sons, bearing Astral's weight like it wasn't trying to cave his shoulder joint while he held tight to his spiritual divining rods and kept an eye on his "landmarks," Cole and Cassandra, so that he'd be able to find his way back. He'd entered into serious chant mode now, barely pausing to breathe between lines that sounded so much alike that sometimes only the last vowel of the last word changed. *"O ma evetale râ. O ma evetale ré."*

At least that was how it sounded to Cole and Cassandra. When they had three seconds to listen. Which wasn't often because they too were busy. Doing improv. For Bergman.

The one-liners had dried up fairly quickly, though they had allowed Bergman to peel back the wings that enfolded him. Which meant they could see his hand still gripping Dave's knife and his lips turned up in appreciation when he heard Cole say, "Cassandra, you know why I got into this business, right?"

"To meet women?"

"Nope. For the dental plan." He opened wide and stuck his finger way back into his mouth so he kinda sounded like a sinus-infected cowboy with a speech impediment when he said, "See this gold fiwwing, heyah? I got fwom a mobster I offed back in New Yowack."

"You did not!"

Cole pulled out his finger and wiped it on his jeans. "Okay. Maybe he was the mobster's dentist who I paid for some information and he was so grateful to get free of the guy he threw in the filling for free. But look at the dentures he gave me for when the fillings fall out!"

Cole opened up his other hand and his wind-up vampire fangs began their teeth-chattering, shoe-stomping dance.

Cassandra giggled as Bergman gasped, his chest heaving up and down with the effort of his fight with the Rider. But also, if his grin was any clue, with big gulps of muted laughter.

Their first sign that the atmosphere had changed was Jack, whose fur stood on end as he began to bark, pointing his nose at Dave, Astral, the grave markers, and occasionally Bergman's Rider. Cole tugged on his leash, reminding him that he had no business with the Rider, just as Dave's chanting stopped. The spirit-rods, which had been thrumming in his hands like a couple of guitar strings, began to whine. He jumped to his feet and held them tight while Astral balanced on his shoulder, her ears twitching in circles as they always did when she was processing mounds of information.

Cassandra and Cole weren't sure where to look. The muscles in Dave's forearms, biceps, and back bunched with the effort it took to keep the rods from whipping so wildly that they sliced off an arm or leg, or even decapitated him. At the same time Bergman had dropped his chin nearly to his chest, his face twisted in an awful grin as he launched into a series of full-body spasms.

Dave looked up, as if for help from the invisible Beings who sometimes decided it might be okay to intercede in the paltry affairs of men. But his Spirit Guide had already thrown in with his twin. And nobody else seemed interested in picking up the slack. His jaw clenched, the veins in his neck cording with ultimate effort as the energy from the graves passed into his body and began to make him shiver.

Cassandra reached out to Cole, a worried wife in need of support. And, understanding she might See something that would make him miserable in the future, he still took her hand, held it tight, so that she didn't have to watch her husband's struggle all alone. But it wasn't just him. When Dave's effort felt like too much to bear, they only had to turn their heads and there was Bergman, clenching the knife he'd been given and slowly turning it toward himself. Cassandra hugged her free arm around her unborn child as the knife crept closer to his heart. "No, Miles," she whispered. "It's not for you."

Cole swayed, gripping Jack's leash as the malamute growled their mutual frustration. But they couldn't desert Dave, leave him lost in the spiritworld forever. "Hang on, dude," he said. "Just a little longer, and I'll be there. I promise you, I'll be right there."

"Hanziiiii!" Dave yelled, his voice echoing through the forest like that of an ancient shaman summoning a spirit to purify one of his sick patients, as Astral crouched down as if preparing to leap on a mouse.

"Monique, where…I can't *see* you!" Bergman panted, the knife inching closer and closer to his chest.

"Miles!" Cole yelled. "For Chrissake, Jaz is gonna be so pissed if you screw this up!"

The stick to Dave's left stopped moving. He held on to it a moment longer to be sure, and then he moved that hand to the remaining stick. Which began to wobble so hard it looked like Dave was causing the movement. Until you checked out his holding-on-for-dear-life expression.

Cole asked, loudly and somewhat desperately, "Yo, Cassandra? What happens when that spirit-rod of Dave's starts whipping him around in circles like an Olympic gymnast?"

"It should be all right," Cassandra replied in a falsely cheerful voice. "I think he's wearing his maximum-support tights tonight."

Bergman laughed fully, from the belly. The knife retreated as he climbed to his feet.

Dave wasn't amused, especially when the rod finally won, jerking him off his feet and throwing him against the fence like a pissed-off stallion. Astral jumped ship just before he hit, landing gracefully beside him as if she'd practiced the trick a thousand times. She stared at him as he lay still, trying to decide whether or not he'd ever be able to put his experience in the W column. Then he did an allover body check, probing his head, ribs, and leg bones delicately to make sure nothing was broken.

"Honey?" Cassandra asked as she came to lean over him. "Are you all right?"

He moaned. Sat up and dusted off his jacket.

"Is he back?" asked Cole. She turned to him and nodded. Which was all the signal he needed. He spun around, cocking his Beretta as he moved to face Bergman and the Rider fully. He yelled, "Anyone who's seen *Star Wars* more than twenty times, including the digitally remastered edition, *and* who owns an original Stormtrooper costume raise your hand!" His fingers shot toward the sky, followed closely by Bergman's as Cole said over his shoulder, "We just went to Jedi-Con together. My God, you should've seen all the Leias! Best thing about the Stormtrooper costume? Tinted eyeholes. You can let your eyes go upsy-downsy and the girls never get a clue."

As Cassandra's jaw dropped and Bergman laughed louder than ever before, Cole leaped toward the Rider, yelling, "Time to dump the neandervamp, Miles! Think happy thoughts!"

Chapter Twenty-One

Saturday, June 16, 11:15 p.m.

Two of Queen Marie's Dogs joined us in her garden soon after she'd given Raoul what I now mentally referred to as the Shit Sniffer. The soldiers had, between them, managed to find one T-shirt, one button-down shirt, a pair of riding breeches, a pair of precursors to sweatpants with leather bands instead of drawstrings, two flat red caps, and two pairs of pointy-toed shoes that made them look like they'd just come from the bowling lanes.

I looked them up and down, turned to Vayl, who sat next to me on a backless bench, and whispered, "These are our guards? I wouldn't be scared of them if they came running at me with bazookas."

His left eyebrow twitched, along with the entire right side of his mouth. "You and I both know the queen is only sending them so they can report back to her. She may even be able to see through their eyes."

"Wow. Talk about the perfect spies."

He tilted his head. "Should we go that far? As you pointed out, they did seem to misunderstand the concept of going in undercover."

However, when we mentioned the Dogs' bizarre costumes to the queen she waved off our concerns with a limp hand. Taking a sip of lemonade from a crystal glass as she enjoyed the scents of her flowers

(*Damn, they get the details pretty good here in the Thin!*) she said, "As long as they are out of my uniform, they will not be questioned." The way she said the word "questioned" made me think of spiked clubs and flesh-packed molars.

Sitting on my other side, Aaron audibly gulped. Vayl touched him with his eyes. "This ordeal is not going to get any easier," he said evenly. His raised eyebrows asked, *Can you cope?*

I compared his quiet buck-up-and-be-a-man approach to my dad's. Albert would've taken one look at Aaron's shaking hands, his twitching shoulders, and said, "Oh for shit's sake, ya pansy! Screw your balls on tight and let's tuck this brick-shitter under the pillowcase!" I never quite understood what that last part meant. And, having been born without the formerly mentioned appendages, I never thought that demand applied very well to me. But somehow it worked every time. My dad might be a gnarly son of a bitch. But he's a stellar motivator.

Aaron said, "I'm fine. I'll be fine."

"Oh, we believe you," I told him as my inner girls laughed somewhat hysterically. "Two things, though."

"Okay."

I held up my fingers so he could follow my points, because my high school speech teacher had passionately believed in visual aids, and I never forgot that. "Number one," I said, pointing to the first finger. "Walk on the edge of the group so that if you puke you can direct the spew away from the rest of us. Number two"—I pointed to my flip-off finger and enjoyed the fact that he realized I might be sending him a double message—"If you pass out?" I waited until he nodded his understanding. "We're leaving you. Here. In the Thin."

Queen Marie's ladies squealed and clapped their hands. And the Dogs' laughter sounded so much like barking I was beginning to have a hard time thinking of them as ever having been human. Together they did a good job of freaking Aaron out just exactly to the extent that I wanted. Satisfied that the lawyer-to-be wouldn't be slowing us down, I looked at Raoul, who stood in his original spot, holding the Sniffer like he wished it would disappear already. "Are we set?"

He shrugged. "Believe it or not, I'm always ready for battle."

I smacked myself on the chest proudly. "That's why you like me, isn't it?" When he started to smile, sheepishly, like I'd caught him stealing cookies from the save-these-for-grandma's-visit plate, I snapped my fingers. "I knew it! We actually have something in common!"

The rap of Vayl's cane on the bricks distracted us. "I assume we can trust your Eldhayr to control your berserker tendencies until we have at least freed Aaron's father from his current situation?"

"Which is… what?" asked Aaron. "How do we even know where to go, much less how to find him?"

He hadn't been allowed to overhear the negotiations because we kinda thought he'd spaz and run, which is not a good idea for a human in full body and soul surrounded by spirits whose wild hunger is tamed only by their loyalty to a tightly stretched queen. So all Vayl said was, "It is not easy to imprison something as ethereal as a spirit. Queen Marie has given us an artifact that will detect the one place in the Thin where that is possible. Her Dogs will accompany us there. After we arrive, we will free your father and return to the world."

Aaron looked at Vayl doubtfully. "How?"

Vayl smiled. As his fangs gleamed, for the first time I saw respect for the power of a vampire dawn in his son's wide eyes.

Chapter Twenty-Two

Saturday, June 16, 11:15 p.m.

Cassandra witnessed the entire Rider battle. So Astral combined her impressions along with the men's memories of the fight into a remarkably complete video that we reviewed closely later on through her Enkyklios.

Cole charged toward the giant parasite, yelling like a Celtic warrior, his hair flying out behind him, his gun gripped so firmly in his hand it seemed like an extension of his arm. Bergman's glasses had flown off sometime during his ordeal, so he couldn't quite get the details. But, in general, he knew it might be time to panic.

"Cole!" he yelled. "What are you doing?"

"Dave made it back, so I'm free to save you!"

He peered at Cole's hand. "With a remote control?"

"Bergman! For once, could you stop thinking and just duck?"

Miles bent over, the Rider nearly toppling him onto his head as his balance shifted. For a second they resembled a couple of kids playing Superman. And then the Rider looked up. Cole said later that only his inertia kept him moving forward in the face of those eyes. Deep pink pupils surrounded by lighter pink irises bored into Cole's face like a couple of ice picks. He had a few seconds to realize the grinning mask was full of flat, broad teeth, none of which could've pierced Bergman's delicate veins. And then he understood. The

Rider's needle-tipped ribs were also its teeth, every one of which had pierced Bergman's sides so cleanly that barely a drop of blood had stained his old brown sweater.

Now those teeth throbbed as they attempted to draw out his very essence. Bergman's chest heaved as he fought against the attack. Spit bubbled on his lips. His eyes rolled, following Cole into the mix.

Our sniper, normally lethal at five hundred feet, closed in on the Rider, yelling, "Long live the Bemonts!" like some crazed Scottish Highlander as he emptied his clip into the Rider's face. It jumped and howled with each shot, making Bergman dance like a Broadway star. But after the last shot had been fired, not even a single rib had detached.

Which was when Cassandra said to Dave, "This may not end well." Jack's low growl echoed her sentiment. She'd grabbed his lead when Cole dropped it, and was now rubbing his head, though which of them was more comforted by the touch she couldn't have said.

Dave nodded and pulled yet another knife from a sheath he'd strapped across his back. Kissing her on the cheek, he said, "Don't watch if this is going to change your mind about me."

She snorted. "I've seen gladiators shove their hands inside their enemies' rib cages. I think I can handle a little knife fight."

He looked down at her admiringly. "You're such a rocket in the sack I keep forgetting you could've been the model for a Spanish doubloon."

"Who says I wasn't?"

"Tease."

"Oh? So you've seen the new miniskirt I bought?"

Dave huffed. "That's it. I'm killing this sumbitch in record time." He whirled away, calling, "Move over, Cole! I've got plans for the next hour and they don't include getting my ass kicked!"

Cassandra, having already met Albert, knew that his methods of motivation might meet with occasional success. But with his son, her approach worked every time. And best of all? It gave him an excellent reason to make sure he survived. Which was why she took credit for Dave's extra burst of speed, the one that allowed him to catch up with Cole, so that the sniper's gun-butt bludgeoning coincided with her husband's slice-and-dice as if they'd practiced on a Rider-shaped dummy in Vayl's backyard.

The Rider screamed in pain as Cole's improvised club and Dave's blade battered the soft skin between its tusks. But so, unfortunately, did Bergman.

"No, Mom!" he shouted. "I'm not going to your goddamn protest!"

Cole spoke urgently into his ear. "Miles! Come on, buddy, you know these suck-you-till-you-sag types. The sadder, the more violent, you feel, the sweeter you taste. So flood your head with good stuff. Your first peek at a *Playboy*. The invention that's going to win you the Nobel Prize. The time Jaz and I had to ride those ridiculous mopeds all around Corpus Christi. Like that."

At first Bergman didn't answer. Cole, struggling to yank one of the teeth out of Miles's side, had finally decided Bergman hadn't heard when Bergman giggled, "Monique! It's the middle of the day!"

The fang came free with a sucking whoosh that Cole expected to be followed by a rush of blood. But the incision-like wound was already closing, the saliva stretching from the Rider's tooth to Miles's skin quickly drying into a bio-bandage. "That's handy," said Cole. "Also kinda sick. Bergman is not gonna be happy."

Dave pulled a fang out from the other side and sliced it off at the Rider's body, causing it to scream and convulse even as Bergman blushed and murmured, "Sweetheart, I'm not sure that's legal in this country!"

"Who is Monique and what the hell does she see in this brain-on-a-stick?" demanded Dave as he and Cole continued defanging their tech guru, covering him, the Rider, and themselves with a startlingly rancid combination of saliva, blood, and bile.

"She's Bergman's girlfriend," said Cassandra, who'd come closer to lend moral support. "He met her when we were in Marrakech."

"She's a little older than him," Cole said. He added, "Watch out, Cassandra. I think this Rider's about to hurl."

It was shaking and heaving like Bergman's blood hadn't agreed with it after all. Cassandra stepped aside just as it puked up the contents of its stomach over Bergman's left shoulder. They hit the pine needles with a wet, splatting sound that made her nose wrinkle. "This job is so nasty. They should, at the very least, send you off with your own personal bottle of Germex."

"I agree." Bergman sighed. Dave and Cole had nearly torn the Rider from his back. But the final connection, a pair of knitting-needle-sized ribs that seemed to shoot straight into Bergman's back and out his chest, would not yield.

"We've done all we can," Dave told him grimly. "Like I told you before, it's still up to you."

Bergman nodded, his head winding around in a circle like he was too tired to make a precise up-and-down motion anymore. He sighed again. Dave and Cole shared a look of round-eyed worry with Cassandra. She stepped forward to urge Bergman on to greatness, but before she could say her piece, Astral had hopped over to the open spot at his feet. Jumping up so her paws rested on his shins she said, "Learning to fly, but I ain't got wings."

"Tom Petty was right when he wrote 'Learning to Fly,'" whispered Miles, his eyes so tightly shut his lashes had nearly disappeared. "And that was why Astral kept scrolling through all those disaster videos. To show us how to reach for the sky, even though it feels like we keep crashing."

Everyone was nodding, even Jack, though he was probably only doing it to be polite. Cole said, "Exactly! Never give up, baby! Not even when your glider dives straight into the Pacific!"

Bergman's eyes snapped open. He threw his knife into the air, caught it so that the blade now faced the Rider, performed a neat one-two side-step, and stuck that sucker so hard that they both fell to the ground.

The last pair of ribs withdrew from Bergman's chest. He cried out, rolling off the Rider as it freed him. But he was back in an instant, shoving his knife into the parasite's heart, once, twice, a third time until he was sure it would never twitch again.

For long, quiet moments everyone just stared at the corpse. Then Bergman stood up, swayed, and sat back down. "I feel like a Chinese noodle. Seriously. If you want me to move, you're going to have to use chopsticks. And a stretcher."

"You're so thin we *could* pick you up with chopsticks," Cassandra told him. "Why won't you ever eat anything? You might be able to get through ordeals like this much easier!"

He dropped his head like it was just too heavy for his neck to support at that moment, and wagged it back and forth. "Food's annoying."

"Not as much as dead scientists!" she snapped.

Dave found Bergman's glasses and set them back on his nose. Miles peered at Cassandra over the tops of the lenses. "You are such a nag." He looked up at Dave. "You know what you're getting into with this one, right?"

Dave patted him on the shoulder. "You wouldn't believe what kind of reward your life is worth to her, buddy. Believe me, I'm golden."

Bergman looked at his hands, lying limp between his knees. "So, did you get what you wanted?"

Cole came to stand beside them, wiping the blood off the butt of his Beretta as he moved. "Yeah, dude. Tell us poor Miles didn't sacrifice his vamp cherry in vain."

As Miles huffed in embarrassment Dave said, "I made the connection. Hanzi's in Spain."

Cassandra was the first to pick up on the hesitation in his tone. "What did you see?" she asked.

"He was riding a motorcycle. Wearing a helmet, so that was good. Except that I saw him racing toward a parked semi. And there was no way, going as fast as he was driving, that he could've stopped in time."

Can a group of friends collectively shiver? Probably not mine, but they did share a moment of frozen silence. Then Cassandra said, "Did you feel like it was happening as you saw it? Or was it a future scene—you know, just potential that you pulled from the stratus?"

Dave shrugged. "Hey, I'm new at this. Plus I was kind of in the middle of a tornado."

"You're a Special Ops commander," Cassandra drawled. "Give it your best bet."

He leaned forward and touched his forehead to hers. "You don't let me get away with anything, do you?"

She kissed him and purred, "Only when you deserve to."

Cole said, "No smoochies when the rest of us only have animals to cuddle with." Jack and Astral looked up. And if my dog looked slightly concerned, it's only because he understands every word people say. "Don't worry," Cole told him. "You're not my type. But you—" He wiggled his eyebrows at Astral, who sat down and began to lick her paws, as if she felt a bath might be in order, considering.

Dave got to his feet and helped Cassandra stand while Bergman grabbed Cole's leg and climbed up far enough on his own that our sniper finally took pity and gave him a hand. "Why do you love messing with my inventions?" he asked.

"Jealous, I guess," Cole replied. "Jaz is practically swimming in cool gadgets. I save your life and what do I get?" He motioned to his gore-covered khakis and hunting shirt.

"I'll buy you new ones," said Bergman.

"Or..." Cole began.

Bergman's eyebrows lifted in sudden comprehension. Maybe he could be forgiven for not understanding right away. After all, he'd just fought a Rider and won. His wounds, while closing quickly under the strange healing qualities of the parasite's weblike saliva, still hurt like a mother. And, no matter what Dave and Cole had done to help, he never would've survived the first leg of that journey without depending on his own strength. Which, he'd finally learned, was hefty—but not unlimited. Even so, he said, "I could invent you something marvelous. Both of you," he added, catching Dave's eye.

Dave waved him off. "Don't bother with me, Miles. I'm comfortable using the tools I've been trained with." Having cleaned off both his knives, he resheathed them and led the cemetery crew back toward the tour bus thinking that, considering he was about to become a dad and he'd like to be around a lot more than Albert had been, maybe soon he wouldn't even need those anymore.

Chapter Twenty-Three

Saturday, June 16, 11:20 p.m.

One of the easiest ways to infiltrate an enemy base is to let a patrol catch you and then demand that they take you to their leader. Of course, then you're depending on the patrollers to have some sense of honor and military discipline. This couldn't be the case with any member of Brude's army. Which was why, once the Shit Sniffer had led us to an enemy patrol, we'd decided to put a slight twist on that plan.

The unit we targeted was made up of Brude's finest and most diverse fighters. They came to him from every age of Earth's history—their uniforms ranging from barely scraped animal skins to medal-plastered dress blues. As expected, their weapons ran the gamut too. Except, since firearms didn't function in the Thin, they'd all hung on to their favorite blades. Some had remembered them long and glittering, engraved with the runes of their personal gods. Others carried daggers so dull only the violent double-fisted shove of heavily muscled biceps would prove them fatal.

Counting Aaron, our numbers matched almost evenly. And considering we had Vayl, Raoul, and two Dogs fighting on our side (not to mention me, with a sword from Raoul's armory that felt like it had been forged to my hand) I figured our odds wouldn't bring huge winnings on a two-dollar bet. And then *he* stepped out from behind the tree line that had separated us.

We'd been hiding behind a long line of scrub interrupted by piles of fallen trees and mounds of ivy-strangled branches that'd all flame like a hairspray-soaked wig the second somebody thought to bring a match to the game. Still, good cover, until I got my first real look at the blemuth lumbering toward us. And then I reminded myself to write thank-you notes to every one of my trainers, who'd once again done such a good job that despite the shock of seeing a creature I had been sure never existed outside Sandy's Bar (where the stories always outsize the hangovers), I managed not to give away our position with the gasp of awe that had shot up from my quaking stomach. I didn't even break the twig sitting right next to my foot, despite the fact that my knees had begun to shake so badly that my pants would probably have ridden right down my thighs if I hadn't been wearing a decent belt.

I rolled my eyes toward Vayl, who'd thoughtfully clapped his hand across Aaron's mouth and wrapped another steel-muscled arm across his chest before he could accidentally betray us.

Can't be, I mouthed. He nodded. Which was as close as he'd ever get to *Can too, Jasmine. Now wrap your mind around this before all your moving parts freeze permanently*.

I closed my eyes and concentrated on breathing, feeling the air of a rarified plane slide in and out of my nostrils as I accepted the inevitable. I'd just seen one of the most twisted creatures ever created. According to legend the first blemuth had begun life as a dragon's egg, but once the sorcerer Aliré had shoved his wand and a huge glob of ogre slime into the guts of the poor thing's DNA, it had very little chance of hatching into anything but what it became: A war machine, programmed to decimate every living thing it encountered. What surprised me was that it had enough soul left to get itself trapped in any sort of afterlife. Most creatures like the blemuth managed to incinerate themselves completely when their time came. The fact that this one had remained to rampage through the Thin worried me more than I liked to let on.

I caught Vayl's attention and mimed shivering and then breaking spaghetti between my hands. He understood that I wanted to know if he could freeze the blemuth long enough for us to attempt to hamstring it. When he shrugged, I understood we'd be winging this one. Vayl might be überexperienced, but even he'd never had to face a creature with the reputation for being resistant to attack. As in every. Single. Kind.

I wondered how keen the Dogs were to complete their mission now they'd seen how much tougher the blemuth was going to make it. They didn't leave me curious for long. Pointing to each other and then making huge circles with their hands, they let us know that they wanted to be the ones to tackle the creature.

Hey, the dumbasses wanna be heroes. That's so damn sexy, said my Inner Bimbo. She spun around on her bar stool, singing, "I think I'm in love, and my life's lookin' up."

She should let Eddie Money do his own songs. She's just butchering the hell out of that piece, Granny May murmured. What she really wanted to say was that Bimbetta was sick and twisted, so that was the issue I addressed.

I said, *If not for you it could've been worse.*

So true. Granny looked at me, then she pointed to the needlepoint of the cowboy, Zell Culver. *Once you've unchained Aaron Senior, don't let him go until you ask him about the cowboy.*

Wow, that was kinda out of the blue, Gran, but okay.

Sometimes it pays to listen to the voices in your head. Sometimes you end up looking like a complete loon. Soon I'd get to see which category I'd be playing for. But for now I watched the Dogs get into position to take down the blemuth. It wasn't pretty. Later I figured their lack of good judgment was caused by the fact that they'd been forced to leave their uniforms behind. Some people just don't think well in civvies. Like the Dogs. Who stood up. Barked. And charged.

"Why does it always seem like our team is heavily seeded with dumbshits?" I yelled to Vayl as I followed him into the melee.

He grinned over his shoulder at me. "You are only saying that because we are outnumbered, outsized, and outviciouse."

I felt my lips draw back from my teeth, the pre-battle smile brought to life by my lover's excitement. "Vayl! Did you just make up a word?"

"Perhaps I did at that."

And then we were too surrounded to talk.

Vayl and I stood back-to-back with Raoul and Aaron just to our right. Brude's mercenaries came at us randomly, their attacks as disordered and chaotic as the realm they defended. It worked to our advantage. A foe who fights out of pure emotion leaves plenty of openings for the clear-minded defender to exploit.

I'm not saying it was easy. Their blades were just as sharp and deadly as ours. But raised too high, or held too far away from the body, they did nothing to protect the most vulnerable spots, the places we'd been taught to target since our rookie days in the field. The moment my sword sliced through a former Nazi's jugular, I knew we were going to clean up.

Grunting. The sound of whistling blades, the scream of dying spirits, and I was right. We were winning. I could feel the tide turn before I saw it. Brude's mercenaries fell at our feet like dead leaves. They hadn't even managed to cut one of us, so that the smell of our blood would bring more spirits screaming down on our heads. And then the blemuth stepped into the center of our ring, one screaming Dog clutched in each taloned fist.

It slapped them together like a couple of cymbals and spirit residue fell on our heads like bloody rain. Before the Dogs could melt into the ethos, the blemuth stuffed them into his giant, gap-fanged mouth, crunching them up like fresh celery sticks.

"Shit!" I yelled, wiping sweat and Dog remains out of my eyes.

My Spirit Guide skewered two of his foes like they were a couple of chickens headed to the barbecue. Nobody stepped up to take their places right away, which gave him time to yell over to me, "Save yours for later!"

I said, "Okay!" My opponent, a former member of the Republican Guard, made a stupid move, raising his sword over his head with both hands. I took the advantage and split him like a ripe melon, amazed that the sound of skin tearing and blood spurting still worked here, where so many of the world's rules had been shattered. I looked over at Raoul guiltily. "That was just too easy. You saw."

"Can't you do one thing without putting *your* signature on it?" Raoul bellowed.

Vayl snorted. And although he didn't say anything, I got the picture. Jaz had forgotten how to be a team player. Probably sometime during childhood, when all Evie wanted to do was play Barbies, and Dave couldn't be distracted from his G.I. Joe's imaginary missions to, of all places, Pennsylvania.

Well, fine. If Raoul wanted a prisoner I could probably round one up for him. In fact...the stench of rotten flesh brought my attention to the blemuth. Who was picking pieces of Dog out of his teeth with a bloody talon and, in the brain-scrambled way of his kind, just now deciding what to do next. Something I'd heard years ago swam to the top of my head. A way to tame these huge beasts so that they were forced to obey every command. I couldn't remember which of my college professors had done the field research, but I decided now was the time to put it to the test.

I ran toward the blemuth. The closer I got the more I decided the yellow gunk caked under its thick black toenails was probably old, rotten cheese. Wishing for a bandana to tie over my nose, or even a horrible cold, I charged toward the opening between the pads of the blemuth's first toe and the one right next door.

Wanting badly to look away, knowing I couldn't even squeeze my eyes shut, I shoved my sword into the gap between pads, gagging as the smell of foul feet and new blood mixed with the air my body needed for survival. It got even worse when the blemuth bellowed in pain and jerked his foot back, pulling me and the sword I clutched with him.

"Jasmine!" I heard Vayl call behind me. "What are you doing?"

"Taking a prisoner!" I yelled back. "Just give me a—" A dry heave stopped me as a big chunk of toenail trash came loose and flew past my head. Knowing I could only dangle from my sword for so long before I was either smashed by the blemuth's descending foot or so revolted that I willingly jumped to my death, I scrambled to the top of the foot. Which was when I realized the creature was made of more than wisps of soul and cosmos dust. Somehow Brude had managed to import a real live soul-crusher into his realm.

I knew I was right when the king's tinny laughter echoed off the insides of my head, leaving spikes of pain every time it bounced off one of the walls that kept it contained. I felt a wetness beneath my nose, pressed it into my shoulder, and knew without looking that blood stained my sleeve. More laughter from Satan's most dangerous adversary.

Go ahead and laugh, you fucker. You're still my prisoner. And soon you'll be staring down your own execution.

Silence, sweet and pure as a mountain stream, inside my mind. It allowed me to climb the blemuth's blue-scaled foreleg with the ease of a kid on a jungle gym. I kept moving up until I'd reached the top of its plated shoulder. I found the joint where a pathetic sort of chicken wing grew out of its upper back, a reminder of what could've been if Aliré hadn't mutilated Mother Nature. Balancing myself on that spot, I drew my knife and shoved it into the blemuth's scale-covered earlobe. It pinched just enough that he yelped. "Listen up, train wreck. You feel that pain in your foot?"

He nodded. One fat tear rolled down his snout and plopped so close to Aaron that his pants were soaked from calf to ankle. He jumped and swore, looking up to find the source of the attack. When a snot bubble quickly followed, he dove for cover.

I might've felt sorry for the blemuth. After all, the worst pains often seem to be the smallest. I was gored by a Kyron and shed not a single tear, but paper cuts have made me cry. And he was obviously hurting. Except that part of a Dog's disguise had gotten caught in his lower tooth and was still dangling out of his mouth. So, yeah, no sympathy for the spirit-eater.

Instead I said, "I'm the thorn in your paw." Suddenly I realized.

Oh crap. I'm basing this entire idea, not on years of professorial research, but on some kid's story Granny May read to us that I thought was bogus then*! We are so screwed.*

But it was way too late to back out now. So I talked fast, hoping this blemuth's brains were more scrambled than breakfast eggs at Denny's. "When you've done everything I ask, I'll stop the pain for good. Do you understand?"

He nodded. Blinked. A few more tears plopped to the ground. Raoul and Vayl, who were far too self-respecting to run for cover, chose the next best course and ascended the blemuth like a couple of seasoned mountaineers. I kept talking while they climbed, hoping he wouldn't notice all the "fleas" he'd suddenly attracted.

"What's your name?" I asked.

"Daisy."

I coughed. "Wh-huh?" My eyes took another roam over the blemuth's reptilian body. "You want me to call you Daisy?"

He nodded. "I'm Daisy."

I blew out my breath. I'd just temporarily enslaved a gigantic, Dog-eating blemuth named Daisy who, if everything went right, would help us save a trapped spirit. Even Granny May didn't dare tell me that stranger things had happened. This one broke the scale.

I called down to Aaron. "Climb up here, ya quivering sack of pudding! We're taking the express to Brude's place!"

Aaron peered up at us, briefly weighed his options, and then shook his head.

"Another patrol will find you," Vayl told him. "They are just as capable of eating you alive as this blemuth."

Raoul, who'd settled on Daisy's other wing joint, sat forward to frown at Vayl and me. I shrugged and held up my hands. "I didn't say anything."

Still, Raoul told Vayl, "Your fatherly advice is about as helpful as a case of smallpox."

"I was simply telling him the truth."

Raoul called down to Aaron, "Why don't you want to come?"

"I'm afraid of heights!"

My Spirit Guide's frown deepened as he looked over at us. "I don't suppose either one of you thought to bring rope."

"One of our Dogs was carrying some," I said. "Should we assume it got eaten?"

"Blech," said the blemuth.

"I'll take that as a no." I leaned over until I could see the acrophobe. "Yo, Aaron! Look around for the Dog's pack! It had rope in it!"

While he searched I said, "Vayl, do you trust me?"

"Implicitly," he replied.

"Then will you let me handle this situation? I think it needs a woman's touch."

He lifted my hand and kissed it, his lips lingering just long enough to remind me that we hadn't had any *us* time in so long that my body had started to ache in all the special places only he could touch. "As you like, my love. Only be quick. I sense another patrol approaching."

I licked my lips to keep them from pressing against his and climbed down as fast as I could. Yanking Aaron from cover and whispering fiercely, "Quit being a big pussy just when your dad needs you the most," I pulled the pack from the bush where it had landed when the straps had broken, and jerked the rope out of it. As I unwound it I said, "I'm going to tie this around you. Then I'm going to climb back up there and tie it around the blemuth's wing. There will be no way you can fall because Raoul and Vayl will also be holding on to the rope and together they're about as strong as a construction crane. So all you have to do is climb. Got it? Good. How the hell long is this sucker? Shit, we could probably summit Mount Rainier after we're done here. Come on, turn around."

After I knotted Aaron in, I also cut myself a good length and secured it to the pommel of the sword that was still securely jammed between the blemuth's toes. Taking the ends of both ropes, I wrapped them around my wrist a few times, tucked the raw ends under, and made my climb, all the time saying, "See how easy this is? A monkey could do it. In fact monkeys do it all the time."

"Monkeys have tails!" Aaron called.

"They are also often being chased by bigger monkeys," Vayl told him. "In your case, that would be another group of Brude's fighters, closing in on our position more quickly than I anticipated. Is someone bleeding?"

We all checked ourselves, found no cuts or bruises. Then I realized. "It's the blemuth. He's as real as we are. They've got to be smelling his injury."

Raoul called down, "Aaron! You have about thirty seconds before we're surrounded again! Get your ass up here!"

I glanced at Vayl and whispered, "Raoul said 'ass.'"

Vayl's head descended a notch, his version of a nod. "He seems to be quite excited. I think he may be enjoying this adventure of ours."

"And you're not?"

"I am with the woman I love and one of my sons. My life has never been so complete."

I glanced down. "So how long are we going to let him dangle there before we start pulling him up?"

"Give him a few more seconds. His character could use some polishing."

"You really do love him, don't you?"

Vayl sighed down at Junior, who was making the ascension about fifty times more difficult than it had to be. "I love him more than life itself. However I do not like him much yet. I am hoping that will change as we spend more time together."

"Aaah!" Aaron looked down, flipped out, lost his grip and slipped a total of twelve inches. Vayl nodded to Raoul, who came over to our side to help haul the kid up. "He's something next to useless," Raoul growled.

"Not everyone was meant to save the world," Vayl said. He looked down at Aaron fondly. "But the fact that he is trying to rescue his father, despite the fear that hounds him, continues to draw my admiration."

I wasn't sure how impressed Vayl was when Aaron finally joined us at the blemuth's shoulder, accidentally caught sight of the ground, and passed out. But, having spent some anxious moments inside elevators and, once, a very small closet, I could admit that we've all had better moments. Maybe Junior's were still ahead of him.

Vayl didn't seem quite as hopeful. He leaned over his son and brushed his hair back from his forehead. When he looked up the concern made deep furrows between his eyes. "Tell me, does it look to you as if he is fading?"

He did look pale. I held my hands in front of my face. No sign yet that our extended absence from the world had affected me physically. Maybe I was building up some kind of resistance from previous "vacations." But the fact was that we didn't belong here and our bodies knew it. If they failed before our mission was accomplished, we could well be stuck in Brude's horror show for eternity. I yanked on Daisy's ear and got a low, rumbling growl to let me know he was paying attention.

"Take us back to the castle."

Daisy began to lope, like a horse who's been working all day and suddenly catches a whiff of his trough full of oats. Surreal, the feeling of riding on a giant creature's shoulders. I told myself it was just like galloping through the fields on the back of my grandpa's old gelding. Except supersized. With a fairy-tale element that I'd thought was rarer than platinum until I'd hit high school and found a brownie hiding under my desk because he didn't want his wife to discover he'd been out drinking all night. Which was when I realized how much humans silently agreed not to see or discuss so that they could live happy, comfortable lives. And when I knew that I could no longer be one of them.

So I acknowledged how weird it was to feel the wind of the Thin blow the hair back from my face as I rode toward the absent king's torture chamber, while the king himself, or at least the most important part of him, remained imprisoned inside my own skull.

Beyond walking the length and width of his cell, Brude had been quiet since his last outburst. Too quiet. Which let me know that he knew the score. Maybe he could smell his castle, coming closer with every giant step of his spirit-crusher, the scent of despair coming to him through my own nostrils. I knew the stillness within my brain wouldn't last forever. He'd know when we reached his base. He'd try like hell to escape. And it was entirely possible that nothing I could do would hold him back.

Chapter Twenty-Four

Saturday, June 16, 11:45 p.m.

I'll give blemuths this much, when they want to cover ground, they can *move*. We crossed fields, forded creeks, waded through dark forests that should've taken days to negotiate. I wasn't happy about the hanging bridge that creaked and swung like something from a neglected playground, or the raft that kept threatening to capsize every time the ferryman stuck his pole into the grimy green water below it. But at least he accepted our story that we were new recruits, just come from the world to lead Brude's armies to victory.

All around us I felt the soft wisps of passing spirits, most of them moving too quickly to be caught in the net of the Thin. They made the air feel hotly humid, as if the exhaust of their flight influenced the climate of the place Brude wanted to fashion into New Hell. Had that been the reason he'd chosen it? For the heat? Or because every once in a while some poor schmo did get caught, and then we found them dangling in the tops of the trees or slumped against a boulder, exhausted from the fall?

Then the blemuth would set them on their feet and motion for them to follow. Like a fluteless Pied Piper, all he had to do was crook his gore-caked talon and they stepped in line behind him. By the time we reached the gray stone castle that Brude had built on a plain of salted ground we had a parade of fifteen spirits trailing us.

I glanced over at Vayl. "This has got to be the most *obvious* jailbreak attempt in the history of mankind. Ever."

He grinned at me again, possibly breaking his record for most fang revealed in a single day. And reminding me, once again, that parts of him were pure predator. "*We* know it is a jailbreak. For all *they* know, the blemuth has captured a great many humans for the kitchen fire. Let us see how long we can make that illusion last, shall we?"

He sprang to his feet and pinched the blemuth's neck. "Do you want the stinger out of your foot?" The blemuth moaned in agreement. "Then take us inside and pretend we are your prisoners. Straight to the dungeon with you."

Which was when I felt Brude stir inside my head, his movements coinciding with the first pangs of a headache. "He knows we're here," I whispered.

Vayl brushed his hand over mine and the pain in my head receded. "Can you handle him?"

"I think so. But if it gets bad, you may need to…do something."

"All right." We stared at each other. Neither of us quite knew what that would be. We were just hoping we'd be able to figure it out if the situation came to that.

Vayl leaned forward so he could see Raoul and Aaron. "Soon," he told them. "Will you be ready?"

Raoul nodded and dragged Aaron to his feet. I heard him tell Junior, "There's nowhere to run that won't get you into worse trouble here, understand? These spirits can sense weakness, and as soon as they do, they attack. So you need to at least pretend to be tough."

"When I've never been more scared in all my life?" Aaron asked.

"Do you want to see your own intestines today?" Raoul said.

"No."

"Then find a way."

Aaron swallowed hard and pressed his hand against his stomach, like he was promising his entire digestive system he would do everything in his power to ensure it remained intact. He kept it there the entire trip through the castle, while the spirits of Brude's army howled at the blemuth, demanding news of the patrol, information about us, and above all else a taste of our delectable flesh. A couple of reminder pinches to the ear forced him to ignore them all and even smash a few of the more persistent ones against the mold-covered walls.

Those walls were lit, as I'd remembered from my first visit to Brude's castle, with stacks of burning skulls set in wall brackets. It didn't seem like they should give us that clear a view as we wound our way to the lower levels. But we had no problem picking out members of the king's personal guard lounging against the walls, throwing dice, playing find-the-wench's-giggly-spots, or tearing out each other's hearts over a minor disagreement regarding the bloodline of the hound lapping up the fluids dripping from their ever-widening wounds.

I heard Aaron whisper, "I think I'm going to be sick," and Raoul reply, "Are you ready to die so soon?" before the blemuth reached the bottom of the winding stairs.

The halls had been built wide enough to hold a Sherman tank, tall enough to make a herd of elephants feel comfortably cozy. The blemuth still had to squeeze to get through to the dungeon, but he didn't seem to mind. In fact, I suspected that twinkle in his flat yellow eyes was pure glee as he viewed the havoc Brude's forces had wrought among the realms of the Thin and, occasionally, Brude's own people.

In hell, spirits are forced back into physical form. This in itself is torture for a soul that has, at least for a while, experienced pure freedom. It also aids in further tortures as the various demons and devices of hell become inspired with increasingly malicious ideas. Brude had followed his master's lead to a degree. But rather than pushing his prisoners' spirits completely back into the flesh form, he'd gone in the opposite direction. So the straps of the rack on which one of Queen Marie's Dogs was currently being broken were made from the skin of another human's wrists and legs. This both held him firm, and burned him through, because it wasn't his flesh. Clever.

Diabolical. Inside my mind Brude laughed and, true to pattern, the headache began.

Unfortunately it wasn't blinding, so I clearly saw the spirits hanging like psychopathic artwork on the bloodstained walls, dangling from manacles made of human flesh. Elsewhere they writhed on beds of nails carved from human bone and half-drowned in repeated dousings of human excrement. Having already been to hell, I thought I was hardened to the worst that evil could shove in front of my eyes. But my stomach clenched when I saw the cage.

I knew it was important by the way it hung suspended in midair by heavy chains anchored to the ceiling and the floor. But that was where my mind stuttered, begging me not to process what it was made of. The sharp pain behind my right eye, accompanied by Aaron's gasped, "No! Raoul, tell me I'm not seeing that!" confirmed the worst. The four-foot-by-five-foot rectangle was made of human skin, stitched together by dried intestines, stretched over a large collection of leg and arm bones.

"Jesus." It was the closest I'd gotten to a prayer in a while.

"They had to confine him," Vayl said, his voice so sad and low I only caught it because I was used to listening for it. "His spirit was too important to leave to chance." He nodded to the prisoners moaning their misery all around us.

"So." I nodded at the cage. "It's a trap?"

"I am sure that if we breach that cage, all of Brude's home guard will be alerted to our presence. In fact, he and his allies are counting on just that."

"But it's my dad!" Aaron cried. "We can't just leave him there!"

As if to underscore his point, an unearthly wail came pouring out of the cage, its anguish so acute I felt my heart break a little to hear it. Still...

I said, "Aaron, we can't risk it. So far we've been able to fight Brude's forces. But I guarantee whatever trap he's laid has been heavily tipped in his favor. I'm not saying we're giving up for good. Just for now. Until we can figure out—"

"I have an idea," said Raoul.

At the exact same moment Vayl and Aaron asked, "What is it?"

Inside my head Brude yelled in protest. I fought to keep my hands from clamping at my temples. No sense in worrying the men just yet. It was only pain, right?

Raoul said, "The doors. The ones that allow us to move from plane to plane—they follow Jaz closely, almost like Jack and Astral."

I looked around. "That's true, but I don't see one here."

He nodded. "I think you can call them. In fact, I suspect you do subconsciously. It's part of who you are as an Eldhayr. Part of what you call your Sensitivity. You've never been able to control it because you didn't know you could. But now you have to. Call us one that would fit a plane hangar."

"Sure, no problem, Raoul, like I'm gonna be able to make an interplanar doorway that burns around its rim appear just like that!" I snapped my fingers. And a door appeared. In the air. Right next to the hanging cage. "Holy shit!"

Vayl frowned at me. "Your language has deteriorated remarkably quickly in the past few weeks."

"I'm willing to give her a break on this one," Raoul said. He turned to me. "Can you make it bigger? And then—"

But I was way ahead of him. Drawing lines in the air. Stretching the parameters of the door in my head. Feeling it widen and lengthen, and watching it cooperate in this particular reality as if it were no more than one of Astral's holographic images. Finally it seemed more than big enough to hold its cargo.

But it wasn't easy. I might have snapped my fingers, but the moment the door appeared I felt like the fire lighting its frame was burning me up inside. No fever had ever worked on me the way this heat did. Sweat dripped down my face as the pain in my head built to new heights. I felt sure that if we didn't wind this up soon, the heat would melt my eyeballs from the inside out.

"Everybody off the blemuth," I muttered. Raoul and Aaron began to scramble down while Vayl held my wrist, staying with me as I delivered Daisy's final instructions. The blemuth grunted that he understood.

"What about the thorn?" he asked plaintively.

"Just as soon as you deliver," I promised.

He nodded his understanding as Vayl and I descended. My palms were so wet with sweat that I slipped and nearly fell, but Vayl caught me before I could hit the floor.

"You are burning up," he whispered.

"It's the door."

"Your nose is bleeding as well."

"Brude," I muttered.

"You cannot contain it all," he said as we made our way to the filthy stones beneath the blemuth's paws.

"What else am I supposed to do?"

"Perhaps you should light a small fire of your own?"

"No." One of the talents that had risen in me after I donated blood to a dying Were named Trayton was the ability to start fires. First they'd just appeared as an extension of my extreme emotions. Then I'd figured out how to control them just in time to save precious lives, including my own. But I'd learned that the flames I shot out from my Spirit Eye also burned a part of me. And I couldn't trudge through life hoping bits of my soul would grow back before I watched my niece walk down the aisle. So I held back, keeping the burn in check even when I was at my most furious. Then Vayl said, "Perhaps this is why you were given the power in the first place. Not to destroy those who would harm you. But to protect yourself from the fires that are sent against you."

Inside my head a chorus of girls went, *Aha!* Everyone needs a shield. Brude had his tattoos. Vayl could once call up armor made entirely of ice. I'd fought reavers who were so thoroughly protected that hitting them felt like pounding your fists into a brick wall. So why shouldn't I get some sort of defense? Especially when I kept having to fight hellspawn?

"Okay," I told him. "I'll try." But for the moment I had to concentrate on the rope that I still held in my hand, the one tied to the "thorn" in Daisy's paw. I made sure it couldn't get looped around anything. I checked that Raoul and Aaron had found places to perch among the links of the skin-cell's chain. "It's going to be a bumpy ride," I warned them. "You may not be able to hold on by pure strength." Aaron unbuckled his belt and used it to strap himself around the link he'd chosen. Raoul had already done the same with his sword belt.

When Vayl and I had tied ourselves in to our satisfaction we nodded to each other. "Okay!" I yelled to the blemuth. "Upsy Daisy!" Then I snorted, because I'd always wanted to say that, and damned if this wasn't the perfect time!

The blemuth grabbed the ceiling-bound chain of Aaron Sr.'s cell between its teeth and yanked. Debris began to fall. The torturing crew finally looked up from their grisly business and realized the blemuth wasn't in it for the fun, like they'd assumed. They screamed as more of the ceiling fell, crushing them and a few of their victims alike.

When a slab of rock the size of my Corvette landed right next to me I said to Vayl, "Maybe this wasn't such a great idea."

"It was better than any of the alternatives. How are you feeling?"

"Why?"

"You are bleeding from both nostrils." He touched the back of his hand to my forehead. "If we were in the world, I would take you straight to an emergency room. Brude is attacking you from the inside. He knows this is his last chance to escape before we take him to hell. And that door—" He nodded up to the portal, whose flames had turned a startling shade of magenta. "Its power is immense. I can feel it pulling at you. Trying to suck you dry. Where is your fire, Jasmine? Where is the heat of your resistance?"

I felt the blood drip from my nose down to my chin. The pounding in my head had gone so far past migraine I was seeing pink. The *domytr* had begun raking at the walls of my mind with his fingernails, pounding them with his fists and feet, leaving rivulets of blood and bruises in his wake. And the portal, I could sense it, just like Vayl had said. Eager for my power. Lapping at the energy that had called it despite the fact that it could stand on its own.

Suddenly I was so tired. I wanted to fall to my knees, bury my head in my hands, and cry until somebody came to save me. And Vayl would try. But he couldn't fight invisible demons. All he could do was stand beside me, hold me up, and hope I was strong enough to battle through to the end.

I reached inside for the rage that never seemed to stop burning, even during my happiest moments. It leaped to my hand like a long-lost pet. And I welcomed it. Knew it was the reason I was strong and, after everything, still vibrantly alive.

I pulled it around me like a Kevlar cloak. And then I pushed it outward like the shell of an exploding bomb, driving Brude into a howling retreat as he beat at the flames that singed his hair, his skin, and his beard. The flames of the portal billowed and shot straight upward, burning the pieces of debris as Daisy shook them out of the ceiling. They tried to reach for me as well, but my fire was bigger, hotter, and it burned them back to where they belonged.

And then I felt myself lifted into the air. Daisy had broken our anchor from the ground. The ceiling anchor had come free as well. Just in time, too, because Brude's guards had come howling into the chamber, waving their weapons over their heads as if we should be intimidated by their noise and motion alone.

"Now, Daisy!" Vayl yelled. "Into the gateway with us!"

The blemuth swung us into the portal, and as we flew through, I yanked on the rope, pulling my sword free of the monster's foot, gaining myself a roar of thanks as we hurtled out of the Thin.

Chapter Twenty-Five

Sunday, June 17, 12:15 a.m.

No other motion feels quite as exhilarating as flying, whether you're parachuting from a Cessna Caravan at thirteen thousand feet or hang gliding off the cliffs at Mission Beach. However, in those cases you know that you have at least a decent chance of landing softly enough to maintain the integrity of your skeletal structure. Not so much when a blemuth has tossed you high into the cosmos and you're not even sure your landing site is solid. So, while part of me grooved on defying gravity to the point that I felt like I was thumbing my nose at Mother Nature, the rest was trying desperately to figure out what I was hurtling toward.

I ruled out hot lava, just because our landing site wasn't particularly glowing. I couldn't hear surf, so we probably wouldn't be swimming for it. Which left sharp, spiky rocks that could impale us in the most ghastly, gut-wrenching ways. Or some guy's roof, in which case only a couple of us would have to worry about taking a furnace chimney up the ass while the rest of us could enjoy more typical crash-related injuries. Or—

"Trees!" Raoul called out. "Get ready for a beating!"

Oh. Goody.

They were pines. So besides the abuse we took from smashing through at least half a dozen treetops whose branches tried their hardest to whip us off our perches, we also sustained slashes, cuts, and bruises that would take days to heal. But we didn't die. I decided that was a plus.

When we finally dropped to the ground we lay there for a few minutes, gasping and sore, trying to convince ourselves we'd survived. Vayl was the first to decide he should ask the rest of us just to be sure.

"Jasmine." He reached out to touch my bare shoulder where a piece of my shirt had ripped away. I shivered, laughed lightly. Only he could get a rise out of me after I'd nearly been stoned to death by a falling ceiling and then thrashed soundly by a forest. "Are you all right?" he asked.

"Yuh," I answered. I touched my tongue, which was so sore it hadn't wanted to make the S sound so I could reply to Vayl with a "Yes." It was bleeding and slightly swollen. I must've bitten it during the landing.

Vayl sighed with relief. Then he said, "Aaron? Raoul? Did you make it?"

"We're fine," said Raoul.

"I need a knife!" Aaron replied. He'd already made it to his feet and was scouting for rips in his father's cell. Though some of the bones that formed its structure had broken in the fall, the membrane itself remained horribly intact.

"Let us do this," Vayl said as he helped me to my feet.

When Aaron started to protest I added, "We're pretty handy with weapons. It would be a shame if you sliced half of your fingers off and bled to death at your moment of triumph, now, wouldn't it?" First, however—"I've gotta talk to Aaron Senior."

Vayl held out his hand. "Let us free him and see if he is in the mood to converse then, shall we?" I nodded, pulling my bolo and giving it to him as we approached the corner of the cell where Raoul and Aaron were already standing.

Aaron went into a crouch and said gently, "We're gonna get you out, Dad. Just go to the other side of the cell for a second, okay?"

In the moonlight that shone down through the broken treetops we saw the shadow inside the box move to its opposite end. Vayl made three quick cuts and a flap the size of a doggy door fell down inside the horror room.

The smell that wafted out gagged us, backing us all off a step or two. Then Aaron Junior's dad came rocketing out of that place so fast that I could see the air flowing off his shoulders just as if he were a race car barreling down the track.

"Get back here right this minute, you ungrateful bastard!" I yelled.

He swooped down and hovered in front of me, his grin showing a huge gap between his front teeth. "Forgive me. You can't imagine how awful it's been being cooped up in there all this time."

"Well, you're about to be free forever," Raoul told him.

"Except," I added. Everyone paused to look at me. "The cowboy, Zell Culver. Did you know him? I mean, did you meet him in the Thin or anything?"

Aaron Senior shook his bald head. "I didn't meet any cowboys. Not anybody at all, really, after they had the cell assembled. Except"—he nodded toward our group—"you people, the one time I was allowed out."

I pulled the Rocenz from my belt. "Does this look familiar?"

"No."

I crossed my arms and tapped my foot. I was missing something. Senior was important, or Granny May wouldn't have made her suggestion in the first place. And then I had a thought. "Does the number twenty-three mean anything to you?"

He shrugged. "That's the mystery tattoo."

"What do you mean?"

"Well." He jerked his head back toward his cell. "Lots of those walls came from parts of people that had been tattooed. To keep myself from going crazy I numbered them. Number twenty-three never made sense to me, so I always thought of it as the mystery tattoo."

I glanced at Vayl, whose eyes reflected the same excitement I felt building in my gut. "Show us," he demanded.

Senior led us into the horror chamber and obediently pointed out a stretched bit of yellowed leathery skin covered with the words THE SOUL SPLITS, with a ragged tear and nothing after the comma. "See?" he said. "The soul splits. Whatever follows that last S looks to have been cut off and left," he sighed, "with the rest of the body."

I just stared, because when Senior had said "The soul splits," the Rocenz had warmed in my hand like cheese in a microwave. "Vayl, we—" I swallowed, grossed out by my next words before I had to say them. "We need that tattoo."

He cut the piece away from its anchors, the ripping sound the knife made as it freed its second prisoner of the day making me wince. When he was done he folded the patch neatly inside his handkerchief. And then handed it to me.

Ugh. I bolted out of the chamber, followed closely by Vayl. Senior had left the minute he knew he was no longer needed. He was hovering beside Junior, talking quietly to his namesake as Raoul watched them with a look of regret that spelled out just how long they had left together. As I moved toward my Spirit Guide I rebelted the Rocenz and tucked the tattoo inside my jacket pocket. The one that zipped, so I wouldn't lose it. Or worse, accidentally stick my hand in there and feel it. By the time I'd stowed everything safely I'd moved within earshot of Aaron Junior and his dad.

"You're going to be free now," Aaron was saying. "Don't get caught in the Thin again. Go straight toward, I don't know, I've heard there's a light or something."

Senior had started to shake. "Don't worry. I'll fly like a rocket ship. I won't even look back. Or down. Or to the side, because there are scary things in the dark with eyes that glow a sort of purply red—"

Raoul cleared his throat. "You'll see the Path clearly as soon as the Way opens for you. Stay on it. It's that easy."

Now Senior looked like he wanted to hug everyone. "Oh! Thank you all so much!"

Junior brushed tears from his eyes. "Be careful, Dad."

"Of course!"

"And say hi to Grandpa for me."

"That too." Senior gave his kid a kindly look. "Make sure you walk on the lit side of the street at night. And don't think, just because you don't have a fever, that you should skip going to the doctor when you feel sick. People die that way, you know."

"Yeah, Dad. I know."

"All right, then. If you can figure out a way to that won't send her screaming to her psychiatrist, tell your mom I love her."

"Okay."

Vayl slipped his hand around mine, his signal to stop eavesdropping on the family convo. We backed off as Raoul signaled Senior that it was time to stand, or rather hover, front and center.

"Keep watch," Raoul muttered quietly.

He meant for anything that might come through the opening he was about to make. Anything undirected and entirely neutral, with the ability to slither through the cracks before we could catch it.

I said, "Okay." I held my bolo as Vayl lifted the tip of his cane from the ground and rested the shaft over his shoulder, casually, as if he weren't primed to spring the shaft off the sword that rested inside and skewer the first monster that crossed his path.

Casting a frightened look at his son, Senior had moved to stand in front of Raoul. Raoul clasped his hands together, making a small circle with his own body, and began to chant. I always felt Vayl's powers, like a slow simmer that usually gave me the kind of comfort you get from locked doors and well-trained dogs. Raoul's were never evident until he blasted them at you like a well-aimed rocket. Now the tips of my curls wound tighter as they emerged, full and pure as a Brazilian waterfall. Falling over Aaron Senior, they began to reveal him as he truly was, a scared and wounded soul desperate for redemption. As the seconds ticked past he stopped resembling a pale echo of an overworked beer bottler, and instead took on the glittering beauty of a gem-laced spirit full of the colors his life had laid on him, most of them the sweet pastels of spring.

As Senior took his true form, the words of Raoul's chant blew from his lips fully formed, wisps of silver coated in the cold fog of his breath. And I realized my *sverhamin*'s powers had risen, as if summoned by Raoul's. Mine, also, had sharpened. How else could I be seeing so clearly? Vayl's fingers tightened on mine and suddenly, without his even opening a vein, his magic coursed through me. I jerked my head back, shouting to the skies as I pushed my Sight into Vayl's glittering green eyes, and *knew* that he shared it completely.

Aaron Senior gasped, tears running down his face as he rose into a whirlwind composed of pine needles, snowflakes, and billowing clouds so purely white I finally knew the color of peace. Another minute and he was gone. Vayl and I fell silent, though we couldn't let each other go. We just stood there, lost in one another's eyes, the rapture of entanglement so complete I knew we'd never feel alone again.

Then Junior sniffed. And said, "Does anyone have a handkerchief? I hate rubbing snot on my shirtsleeves."

I looked over at him. Tears were streaming down his face. And, yup, his nose was trying to add to the river. I sighed. Then I looked at Vayl. "I'll bet they don't have boogers in heaven."

"No. And, most likely, your underwear never gets stuck up your crack just when you are required to meet important people like, oh, the President of the United States."

I dropped his hands. "How did you know about that?"

His lips twitched. "Sometimes you talk in your sleep."

"Great. Just great. My most embarrassing moments are a hit parade for you the second I start snoring!"

He pulled me into his arms. "You are quite adorable. And I know you have always wanted to meet Abraham Lincoln. So I am simply assuring you that when the time comes, you can calm yourself in the knowledge that your panties will remain securely in place."

Raoul cleared his throat. "I'm uncomfortable now!"

Vayl laid a soft kiss on my cheekbone, a caress completely innocent to witness but highly erotic to receive from lips so warm and promising, before he smiled over the top of my head at my Spirit Guide and said, "Then let us rejoin the rest of our crew, shall we? I believe I have another son to account for."

Chapter Twenty-Six

Sunday, June 17, 3:30 a.m.

Vayl's positive mood lasted until Dave's report. After which he snapped that since our trip to hell was still on hold, we might as well be driving in the direction of Hanzi's rescue as staring balefully at one another like a bunch of grave diggers. Then he dropped into the passenger seat of the Galaxie and began to brood. He spent long tracts of time staring out the window as we headed toward Spain, where Dave was sure he'd seen Hanzi in dire straits. He interrupted his thoughts only to throw a barrage of questions at my brother, who'd given his tour bus responsibilities to Cole so he could report on what Cassandra called his "Spiritwalk" directly to Vayl. Our psychic sat in the backseat beside him to help fill in the blanks, though his memory never failed, possibly because he'd reviewed Astral's holographic recording of the event three times before leaving the cat with Bergman. (Yeah, it would've helped to have her in on the review as well, but our tech guru had said he wanted to tinker with her some more to make sure she didn't have another funky falling-people episode. I thought he just wanted something to take his mind off his near-death experience. Hey, no judgments from my corner. If it worked for him I was going to try it the next chance I got.)

We'd been driving for three hours when Vayl twisted in his seat.

Cassandra poked Dave to wake him just before my *sverhamin* leaned toward him. "Tell me again where you saw him."

"Vayl, we've been over this," Dave said. "It was some kind of accident waiting to happen. Your kid on a collision course with a semi."

"No, I do not mean the specifics of the vision. I mean the periphery." Vayl shook his head with frustration. "A Sister of the Second Sight told me that I would meet my sons in America. It was why I moved there over eighty years ago. And I did encounter Badu, pardon me, Aaron," he said, nodding toward the tour bus behind us, where Junior was snoring loud enough to be heard over Bergman's Party Line, "in Ohio. So it makes no sense to me that we should be heading toward Andalusia."

"Your kid's in southern Spain," Dave insisted. "That at least I could figure out from the writing on the side of the truck." I recognized the tone in his voice. He was starting to get pissed. Which meant he'd dug in his heels. But Vayl had spent enough time with me to know how to handle Parks stubbornness.

"All right, then," Vayl said, so calmly that Dave blinked and pulled in his just-try-to-change-my-mind attitude. "My firstborn is riding a motorcycle toward a semi truck in the southernmost region of Spain. Can he see the truck or is it blocked from his view?"

"He's looking right at it."

"Is he on a blind curve?"

"No. It's a—well." Dave's pause brought Vayl up in his seat. "It's so wide it doesn't even seem like a road. More like a runway."

"Can you see the edges?" asked Vayl. "Are there planes? Do you see more semi trucks?"

"People," Dave finally answered after a lot of thought. "Temporary viewing stands full of people. And some of them are in uniform." His face suddenly lit up like he'd been granted his dearest wish. "I know the place! It's our air base in Morón!"

"US soil," Vayl murmured. "Hanzi is on US soil. But I still do not understand what you have seen."

"Me either. Maybe your kid's demonstrating some new military weapon or something. Doesn't matter. We've gotta get there before he turns himself into Hanzi-sauce."

"Well said." Vayl tapped at his earpiece. "Cole, Jasmine's car will do one hundred and eighty miles an hour without even a shimmy. Surely you could get your contraption to move somewhat faster than sixty?"

Our bus driver had been humming an old Alabama tune called "Dixieland Delight," belting out the lyrics when he wasn't blowing bubbles and popping them into our receivers. At the moment he was singing, "Hold her up tight, make a little lovin'/A little turtledovin' on a Mason-Dixon night." He cleared his throat and pronounced, with a Bill Cosby–esque twang in his voice, "Fathers should all be regularly tranquilized the minute their children turn thirteen. And what I mean by that is, if I go any faster, I'm pretty sure the chassis of this old bug will disintegrate, at which time Bergman will go flying out the back like a paper napkin."

Cole sang another couple of bars from his chosen tune. Then he stopped to say, "So tell us, Vayl, since you're old enough to have legitimately turtledoved, and the guys in Alabama seem pretty psyched about the idea, is it everything it's cracked up to be? Also, can you turtledove just any girl? Or does she have to have a certain, shall we say, generously mounded upper quadrant?"

Despite the shade Vayl's face had reddened to, Dave chuckled. "Wouldn't quadrant be referring to four boobs? That's kinda sci-fi, Cole, even for you."

Cole said, "I would totally go there. For my country's sake, of course."

Vayl blew an irritated breath out his nose. It was so close to the snort a pissed-off bull makes just before he charges that I was amazed Cole kept the tour bus moving in a straight line. I figured even he was smart enough to change the subject while our leader was so anxious about Hanzi's safety, but before he could do anything that smart, Vayl sat back, his entire posture relaxing as he looked at me like he'd only just seen me for the first time that day. It was like he suddenly realized that Cole wasn't trying to piss him off at all, that he just wanted to help him get through the trip so that by the end he still possessed at least a shred of sanity.

He said, "I cannot imagine anyone of your temperament taking the time to turtledove a lady. However, if you ever manage to slow down long enough to enjoy the finer moments of seduction, remember that a woman's body is like fine art, to be taken in by all the senses until she is enveloped in them so completely that she is no longer separate from you."

Because holding Vayl's eyes would probably lead to a fatal accident, I was that distracted, I glanced in the rearview and noticed Dave sitting in rapt attention, taking mental notes with his sharp little brain pencil because he knew the master rarely spoke, and he'd better not blow this chance to file away a few precious pointers. Given his attitude and the total lack of comment by Cole, Bergman, Raoul, and Aaron, I figured all of them felt pretty much the same about this moment. Which made me want to sit up straight, tap the back of the seat, and announce, "Gentlemen, there will be a test later. Try not to muff it." But then they'd all giggle at my terrible pun and forget everything they'd learned in the past thirty seconds. And I just couldn't do that to the women in their lives. So I kept my mouth shut and basked in the glow that was part of being Vayl's lucky girl.

Cole said, "Vayl, I bow to you. Look over your shoulder. See? My forehead's touching the steering wheel. As for moving faster? At this rate we'll make our destination in, like, thirty-nine hours. Maybe more, because Jack has told me he'll have to stop to pee at some point. *I* will just crank open a window when the urge strikes—you're welcome, by the way. Bottom line? I suggest you settle in."

Vayl turned back to Dave. "That will not do."

"We could fly," Dave said. "That would cut our time to about eight hours, but when you count ticket-buying time, security checkpoints, stopovers, that kind of thing, it would expand to twice that. Plus we have the animals and gear that would have to be dealt with so it's kind of a wash."

Vayl spun to me. "Jasmine, we need another door."

"What do I look like, some kind of genie? Holy crap, the last one practically fried my eyebrows from the inside!"

When he simply looked at me, not pouting, not pleading, just waiting for me to put myself in his shoes and understand his need, I sighed. "I can take you to another plane, like Raoul's apartment, maybe. But then when you step back out of the door, it's going to drop you pretty much where you started. That's been the way they've worked ever since I could see the damned things."

Vayl touched his ear again, a gesture I was beginning to find charming in a *Star Trek*–ian kind of way. He said, "Raoul, you could do it. You could take us to your penthouse, and from there you can descend to any spot on Earth. You could drop us right into the path of Hanzi's motorcycle."

Raoul had been sitting quietly beside his window in the bus, staring out at the darkened countryside of what I was pretty sure was now northern Croatia. Later Cole told me that Astral had curled up in Raoul's lap and he'd been petting her as if she were his own cat. Apparently they'd bonded during the time I'd loaned her to him as a prop to help him net a date. Now his voice seemed to come from the bottom of a lake, dark and mysterious as the creatures that swam there as he said, "I could, but I won't. This is one event I cannot interfere with."

"So you know what's going to happen?" I asked.

No answer.

"Then I'll take that as a yes."

Still nothing. Vayl and I shared narrowed eyes. What the hell kind of truth did he have access to?

Bergman, who'd been so silent that I'd almost decided he was sleeping off his nightmare tangle with the Rider, spoke up. Perkily, as if he hadn't just been mentally and physically gnawed on by an evolutionary throwback. He asked, "Raoul, are you some kind of prophet? Should we be writing everything you say down?" And then, "Jaz. Astral's recording everything he says, right?"

"That seems like an invasion of privacy, Bergman. Why don't you just stalk him instead?" Cole began to snicker and Astral, apparently feeling she should have some say in the matter, began to speak. "Metamorphosis in five seconds. Four, three, two..."

"Bergman, now look what you've done," said Raoul. "She's turned into a pancake!"

"That's not supposed to happen," said Bergman. "Don't let her jump... Raoul! I wanted to test her timing system!"

I glanced back and saw Aaron rise in his seat so he could see farther forward. "What's the cat doing to the dog?" he asked curiously.

"Somebody let me in on the action," I demanded.

"Yeah!" Cole seconded me. "I can't see them from up here!"

Aaron had moved into the aisle for a better view. "The cat's sliding over to where the dog is lying under the front seat."

"The dog is Jack; the cat is Astral," I reminded him. "If you're going to be traveling with us for the next couple of days, it would be nice if you memorized a few names. You know, in case you get lost and have to ask the Walmart lady to page us over the intercom."

Ignoring me, Aaron said, "Jack's twitching in his sleep. What does a dog of yours dream about, Ms. Parks?"

I said, "I always figured Jack was chasing bad guys across endless fields of clover. Not sure he ever catches them, but he has a fabulous time trying."

"O-kay then... well, I think he's going to be in for a surprise. Because the cat, Astral, I mean, has positioned herself between his paws. She looks like a warped Frisbee. But at least now all his twitching makes sense."

Realizing how badly she was going to freak him out when she popped back into her full form, I said, "Whoever is closest to her needs to lean over, snap their fingers, and order her back to normal."

Aaron said, "Okay, I can—"

Loud, brash music blared from the floor of the tour bus.

"What's happening?" I demanded as Dave and Cassandra both turned in the backseat to see if they could get a better view.

"It's Astral!" Aaron yelled. "She's playing that AC/DC song. You know which one I mean?"

"We can all hear 'Back in Black,' Aaron," Cole drawled. "In fact, I think the first three lines are now imprinted on my eardrums."

Aaron laughed. "Oh my God, it was great! Jack jumped completely off the floor. He looked like a grizzly bear that's just been stung in the butt by a bumblebee! That's a smart dog of yours, Ms. Parks. It only took him, like, two seconds to figure out that Astral was screwing with him. Oh, man!"

"What's he doing now?" asked Cassandra.

"He's sitting down on the floor in front of her," reported Aaron. "He's looking at her kind of sideways."

"Uh-oh," I said.

My brother and sister-in-law turned toward me. "What does *that* mean?" asked Dave.

"He's planning something," I predicted, wishing I were on the bus so I could prevent whatever catastrophe was about to occur to what had to be a multimillion-dollar piece of technology and, even better, keep Bergman from experiencing his first heart attack.

"You're right!" Aaron said. "He's leaning over, real slow. Like he's afraid he's going to spook her. And now, wow, he's really being gentle! He's clamping her head in his jaws, just enough so he can give it a quarter of a turn to the right. Now he's letting go. He's coming down the aisle, and now he's hopped into Bergman's lap."

As if the sudden groan from Bergman wasn't an even better clue.

"What was that all about?" Aaron asked me.

"Jack was sending Astral a message she'd understand. He was telling her, *Remember that time I accidentally blew your head off? Well, I'm not above doing it again, this time on purpose*. And now he's planted himself on top of the one man who can fix her if anything goes wrong. My guess? She'll behave herself for at least the next twelve hours."

Murmurs of wonder and pride from the rest of the crew as they settled into what was fast becoming the longest marathon drive of my life. And then Vayl said, "Stop the car."

Such a quiet command, but it would've easily halted a battalion of tanks. I pulled over, Cole lined up behind me, and we all gathered onto the shoulder of the road, which I thought was a good thing for several reasons. I needed a break from dodging potholes the size of my hubcaps. I was tired of following oxcarts full of mystery plants that were bigger and scarier than corn, and passing when I felt like the next pothole might be deep enough to lead into an entirely new dimension. Plus Jack needed some exercise. So I was feeling pretty positive about this new turn of events until Vayl stepped into Raoul's personal space, his cane nearly impaling my Spirit Guide's foot as he stood nose-to-nose with the Eldhayr who'd saved my life.

Even Jack cut his relief time to a minimum and came back to stand at my side as the atmosphere spiked into the same realm of intensity that must have been felt inside the boardroom during the last postwar peace treaty negotiations.

"Your attempt to distract me from your remarkable lack of interest in a human's impending death has failed, Raoul." Vayl spoke so slowly that even my Spirit Guide could tell he was reaching hard for tact because the predator in him was swimming hard toward the surface. "Tell me. From what are you *not* protecting my son?"

Raoul's face took on that frozen look that so often preceded a barked recitation of name, rank, and serial number followed by stony silence. Then his lips pursed, and his loyalty to the Trust he'd become part of without even meaning to won out. He said, "Hanzi's fate has come to a crossroads. It's not for me to make his choices now." He nailed Vayl with a hard look. "Or you."

My ears started to tingle. I said, "What the fuck does that mean? Speak plain, Raoul. We're not into riddles, especially not this late in the game."

Raoul squeezed his eyes shut. The international sign for *I have paddled so far up Shit Creek I will never smell good again*. He said, "Hanzi's soul hasn't evolved a great deal in the lives he's led since he was Vayl's son."

"I got that feeling during my Spiritwalk," Dave muttered to Cassandra. "But how do you tell a guy his son's been pretty much a jerkoff for the past three centuries?"

A slight turn of Vayl's head acknowledged he'd heard the whisper, but he let the comment go because he was so fixated on Raoul. "Give me a bottom line, Raoul. I have time for little else today."

Raoul's shoulders tightened. Vayl's were already so stiff they could've doubled as car jacks. Raoul said, "Hanzi may very well die today. A crew of demons is waiting to take him if he does. If the humans at the event where it is to happen can resuscitate him, the Eminent hope that he will make the choice to change his life. In that case he would be a fine addition to our circle. But, because of how he has lived to this point, they've ordered us not to interfere." He stared hard at Vayl. "This is one place where *I* can't help you." Vayl nodded, understanding as clearly as I did that if we got there in time, Raoul wouldn't interfere with any plan *we* might come up with.

He rammed his cane into the road so hard I was surprised it didn't shatter. In his most controlled, and therefore dangerous, voice he grated, "We must reach Andalusia as quickly as possible."

My Spirit Guide looked up, like the clouds held a map only he could see. "We'll make it in time," he said. He looked at Vayl and said cryptically, "Just be ready for a few more surprises from your firstborn. I haven't told you everything because, well, for you I think some things have to be seen to be believed."

Chapter Twenty-Seven

Sunday, June 17, 3:50 a.m.

Since it was nearly four in the morning, giving us only ninety minutes until dawn, we decided to find ourselves a place to shower, grab a meal, and set Vayl up inside his sleeping tent before jumping back onto the road, where we'd take shifts sleeping on the bus. Having already left Bucharest far behind us, we gathered in the bus and broke out the maps and laptops. Bergman, Aaron, and Cassandra searched for hotels while Dave, Vayl, Raoul, Cole, and I plotted our next big move.

"I can't imagine it happening," I told Cole.

"Come on," he whined. "We're right on the border of Slovenia. I can practically see the guards waving leis at us from here. This is our big chance to experience true Slovenian culture."

Vayl shook his head. "I am certain the lei is a Hawaiian tradition. And I do not see how dressing up in leopard-print uniforms and racing llamas around the city square while we shout 'Long live General Maister!' has anything to do with being Slovenian."

"Trust me, it does. I should know, my grandma married a guy who could answer all the crossword puzzle questions that made any reference to Eastern Europe." He clapped a hand on Vayl's shoulder. "I'm telling you, buddy, you'll feel so Slavic when you're done you may just get the urge to talk out of the back of your throat for the rest of your life."

"I've never ridden a llama," said Raoul. "Are they comfortable?"

"They're covered in wool!" Cole said. "It's like sitting on a pile of sweaters!"

Dave snorted. "Sweaters with teeth, maybe."

I know, I know. We should've shut him down the minute Cole uttered the words "llama saddle." But those of us who hadn't been in the room when our wizard friend Sterling brought his soul back from the brink of Spawn City had heard the story enough times to know that these moments, above all others, were the ones that Cole needed to help him maintain his humanity. So we indulged him until Bergman hooted in triumph.

"I found something! It's a place called the Flibbino Inn. Oh wait, the reviews are pretty scary. There's no indoor plumbing, and this one lady says they give you a toilet lid to take outside with you when you have to go, otherwise the neighbor kids steal them for their own outhouses."

"I wonder if they're the squishy kind," Cole said.

"Is that really going to make a difference in your decision?" Cassandra asked him.

He thought a minute. "That depends on the reading material that goes along with the lid," he decided.

"I'm beat," Dave said. "As long as nobody mentions bedbugs, I'm willing to put up with primitive conditions for one night."

I glanced at Aaron expecting, at the very least, the look of lawyerly disdain he'd probably practiced in the mirror for the day he finally passed the bar. He said, "I was a Boy Scout. I can sleep on the floor if I have to."

As I shared a look of dawning respect with Vayl, Bergman tapped at his keys a few times. "No bugs here," he said. "Although one reviewer felt the rooster was kind of a pest."

"Am I to understand this inn is situated on a farm?" Vayl asked.

"Yeah, I think so."

"Pass," I said. "The last thing I need is to be squatting in an outhouse on an unattached lid when some big-and-ugly jumps down from the haymow because, guess what? it's my time to die."

Among a general chorus of agreement, during which somebody mentioned that Bergman might even accidentally slip down the hole in such a situation, Cassandra came up with plan B. "How about this place?" she asked. "Its name is translated as The Stopover."

She passed around the laptop so we could all study three muzzy shots of the trucker-type hotel situated between a major highway and what looked to be a well-traveled goat track lined with beech trees. The Stopover stood two stories tall, a square brown edifice that drooped at the corners, making it resemble a pile of giant poo. In front sat a line of three gas pumps, one of which was servicing a car so ancient even I couldn't tell in what year it had pulled out of the factory lot.

The lobby could've doubled as a convenience store. Who knows, maybe it did. And the rooms looked like they'd been decorated by depressed nuns. Behind the hotel stood a second building whose purpose remained a mystery. Bergman pointed to it. "That's probably where they hide the bodies until it's dark enough to dispose of them."

Cassandra laughed. "Miles! It's not that bad! Believe me, I've slept in dives that make this place look like the Ritz!"

Bergman shook his head. "I hate to disagree with you. Well, actually, it doesn't bother me at all to disagree with you. But it seemed like a nice way to start out saying you're full of crap. This is totally a Norman Bates hotel. I'll bet the owner has a furnace in the basement just like Sweeney Todd."

Dave held up his hand. "You can't mix movie slashers with musical villains. It's just wrong, Bergman. I thought you knew that."

"I don't know," said Cole. "I could happily spend the next half hour discussing which of those guys is the most twisted."

"Definitely Sweeney Todd," Aaron offered. "The guy ate his victims after all."

"Did he eat them, or did he sell them to other people to eat?" asked Cole.

"Does it matter?" asked Cassandra.

"I'm not sure there's a line that fine," I said. The last word came out as a grunt, mostly because Jack had, once again, stepped on a major organ in his attempt to pass himself off as a Pomeranian. I was trying to decide if a paw could actually fit between my pancreas and liver when Vayl found that ticklish spot underneath my earlobe and began to circle it with his thumb. I blanked on everyone else in the bus as my mind centered on Vayl's touch. Such a little thing, and yet I nearly gasped out loud when his fingers, which had been folded and resting against my neck, uncurled. His fingertips, hidden by my hair, brushed toward my spine, making me shiver with anticipation.

"Jasmine?"

"Huh?"

"What do you think?"

"Uh-huh."

"About the hotel," Vayl clarified, amusement threading through his voice now.

"We need to stop somewhere," I said.

I saw a quick glint of fang and then his hand went still. Mine rushed to cover it, a silent protest I hoped the others wouldn't notice. He murmured, "You must think for everyone, not just us. It will not be a pleasant day, Bergman's reviews have assured us of that."

I dropped my hand to Jack's head and rubbed at his soft fur. Reality came flooding into my mind so fast that it felt like somewhere a water main had exploded. "We're going to hell tomorrow," I murmured. "It seems right that we should take our first step in this world."

"Perhaps the hotel's owners would not appreciate such a comparison?"

I shrugged. "Then they shouldn't have painted their place the color of shit."

Chapter Twenty-Eight

Sunday, June 17, 4:25 a.m.

Thirty-five minutes after discovering The Stopover hotel on our laptops, we pulled into its garbage-strewn parking lot. Not a single light provided extra security, or the ability to see where to walk Jack for his pee break so he wouldn't tread on broken glass. Since Vayl could navigate the dark better than any of us, he took my dog's lead while the rest of us got shower gear and clean clothes out of our overnight bags. I hated to leave my Galaxie in a lot where there were more hubcaps than cars, but I'd made my choice, and an hour from dawn was no time to back out. So I locked the doors and hoped that the thieves were into VW buses as I looked down at the cat standing beside me.

"Okay, Astral," I told the kittybot. "No talking in front of strangers."

She looked up at me innocently, as if she was offended I would think she was capable of such rudeness. I pointed my finger at her. "No freaking out the dog. And definitely no home movies of people falling off mountains. You got me?"

She stared down at the asphalt, paying close attention to her trotting paws as she followed me toward the front entrance. But I thought I heard her say, "Dammit" in a small metallic voice that still managed to express disappointment.

Suddenly every light in the place flipped on. The ones above the gas pumps came to life too, bright neon white spotlighting us like a bunch of military targets. I knew Dave was thinking the same thing when he yelled, "Take cover!"

He wrapped his arm around Cassandra's waist and pulled her into the alcove between the front door and the building's outer wall.

I pulled Grief and shot out the gas pump lights, backing toward the tour bus with Astral at my heels. Vayl and Jack met us there. Bergman, Aaron, and Raoul had clambered back inside the vehicle, abandoning their bags halfway between the building and the bus. Cole had taken shelter against the only other automobile in the parking lot, a black sedan so covered with grime it couldn't have been washed since the country's last election.

The door to the inn flew open. "Don't shoot! Please don't shoot!" A skinny old Indian man with a thin mustache, wearing a brown vest and blue pants, walked into the parking lot with his hands held high above his head. "She said you would come here. She is the one playing with the lights, not us. Please, those bulbs are expensive!"

I lowered my gun as Vayl demanded, "*Who* said we would come?"

"The woman in black. She has taken over our entire establishment. She has been just waiting, waiting for you to arrive. Please, please talk to her now so she will leave us alone." He clasped his hands together, really begging, truly scared of whoever was waiting for us inside.

As Cole left cover and Raoul opened the bus door for Bergman and Aaron, the owner of The Stopover, whose name badge said we could call him Sanji, motioned for us to join him. Dave, still holding Cassandra safe behind him, remained in the shadows. With my arms still at my sides, I lifted my palm to him, silently encouraging him to keep it that way. We held our weapons out where Sanji could see them as we approached him and the front door. "Please," he said again. "She said she would go as soon as she spoke to you."

"Did she give you her name?" Vayl asked.

"Bemont," he said. "When she checked in she said her name was Mrs. Bemont."

Even Aaron knew better than to gape at Cole. But we all felt the shock that shot through him at hearing that whoever had anticipated a move we'd only just decided to make was posing as his wife. I reminded myself, once again, to create a whole new vocabulary for our line of work, because "creepy" just didn't cover it.

When we didn't show any signs of movement, Sanji asked, "Are you ready now? Mrs. Bemont is not a patient woman. You should hear the yelling if we are late with her breakfast."

Vayl held up his hand. "In a moment. Cole." Our sniper stepped forward. In his hand he held a duffel full of clean clothes and a second padded bag containing his rifle, a Heckler & Koch PSG1 that was nearly new but had already seen action (translation: Saved our asses) in Marrakech. Vayl said, "Find the back way in. Clear it if necessary. Then cover Mrs. Bemont's room. But before you go, give Raoul your pistol."

Cole reached into his shoulder holster and pulled out his Beretta. Handing it to my Spirit Guide he said, "I know it's been a while. Do you need a refresher course so I don't have to worry about you shooting off your big toe?"

Raoul took the gun with a well-practiced hand, making sure to keep the business end pointed away from the rest of us. "I haven't forgotten."

Vayl said, "I suppose I shall need something as well. Sanji, give me your gun."

"I-I have nothing of the sort!" blustered the manager. "I'm a peaceful man—"

"I beg to differ," Vayl replied, his voice so mild Sanji had no idea how close he was to getting his head slammed against the wall. "You run a rotten hotel in a neighborhood infested with criminals. Where do you keep it, behind the counter? If not, I will be happy to tear this place apart until I locate it."

"No! No, that won't be necessary." Sanji rushed into his office and came out carrying a sawed-off shotgun.

I said, "Now I'm having weapon envy."

My *sverhamin* smirked at me. "You are just saying that because you know how much I would rather use my cane." He turned to Sanji. "Where is Mrs. Bemont staying?"

"She's in the honeymoon suite."

We stared up at the sagging building. "You have a honeymoon suite?" It was the first time Aaron had spoken since he left the bus. And I was sure these words had been ripped out of him by pure disbelief.

Sanji shrugged. "It's the biggest room in the establishment, really two rooms put together. Up there, on the corner of the second floor." He pointed to the windows, the curtains of which were closed tight. Vayl nodded to Cole, who left so swiftly that Sanji didn't even notice. He just kept blabbing in the way of lonely innkeepers, "I think they forgot to put the wall up in between them when they raised the building, so now it's the honeymoon suite. It has a wonderful view of the river."

"How does Mrs. Bemont like the view?" I asked.

"I don't think she ever looks. She just complains about no running water and makes us haul buckets up to fill the tub we had to buy for her. She bathes quite often. 'Cleanliness is next to godliness,' she says, and then she cackles in that awful way she has, as if she's got razor blades stuck in her throat."

We all nodded sympathetically until Vayl was finally satisfied that we were set to meet Cole's fake wife. He'd made sure that I still carried Grief and that I was armed both with the holy water I carried on my right wrist and the bolo sheathed in my pocket. He'd also checked to see that Raoul still carried his holy blade, it was just hidden beneath the back of his jacket at the moment. Bergman, as usual, hadn't thought to arm himself, and Aaron was without weaponry as well.

Vayl handed Bergman his cane, saying, "I noticed you turned

your ankle slightly while you were debarking the bus earlier this evening. Here, please feel free to use this to aid you for the rest of the evening."

Bergman received the cane as if he were being given the care of a kingdom's crown. His reverence nearly brought me out of the intense concentration I'd thrown myself into the moment the lights came on. Aaron's whine, "What about me?" did the rest of the job.

"You'd manage to kill one of us with a butter knife," I snapped. "Stay out of the way until further notice."

He looked to Vayl for support, which amused me. Like some kid running to Daddy for permission after Mommy's barred him from the cookie jar. The twinkle in Vayl's eyes let me know his mind had fallen into the same track. He said, "Jasmine is right. If you would like to be trained so you know what to do in these situations in the future, I will be happy to accommodate you. But for now your life, and ours, depend on your staying safely out of the way."

I smiled inwardly as Aaron bobbed his head. Finally a little respect from the would-be killer. And all it had taken was major risk to his own hide. As soon as he fell to the back of the line I allowed myself to refocus. This deal, whatever it was, smacked of foul spells and demoncraft. I'd need to be on my toes if I wanted to bring everybody back from this one. And oh God, did I ever want everybody to survive. One more second to recognize the crack in my shell, to realize nearly everyone I loved was in this place at this time. And then I shoved that sucker together, sealed it with superglue, and got on with my job.

Which, at the moment, was to follow Vayl and Sanji into a building I'd never scouted before, knowing full well it could be booby-trapped, packed with enemy forces, or just plain bad for the sinuses. I whispered down to Astral, "You go ahead of us. Let me know if you see hostiles."

She trotted ahead, slipping through the doorway as soon as Sanji opened it, and disappearing into the recesses of the building long before we reached its lobby.

I'd taken Jack's lead from Vayl and wrapped it around my left wrist. But since I needed both hands to shoot straight, now I knotted it through my belt loop. "Be calm, boy," I told my malamute, whose ears were perky enough to say he was enjoying this outing, but whose sleepy eyes thought I was way overreacting to a few surprise neons and what quite possibly was just a bitchy ex-girlfriend.

"Oh, I would be so pissed off if that was the case," I whispered down to my dog. "Do you think he would actually date somebody that crazy? Don't answer that. I already know."

Followed closely by Bergman, Raoul, and Aaron, Vayl and I trailed Sanji into the lobby, which held several shelves full of snack foods as well as necessities like toothpaste and small bottles of Tylenol. Across from these shelves stood the counter where, presumably, you could either pay for your gas, buy munchables, or rent a room. We walked past this area into a short hallway that turned sharply right, giving us the choice of taking the elevator or the stairs to the second floor. I told myself that I chose stairs because Jack needed the exercise. No, it wasn't at all because I'd rather eat raw slugs than pile into an elevator with more than, say, one short, skinny, ideally under-the-age-of-three person. That is, after all, the only time there's enough room in an elevator. Strike that. Because, truthfully, there's never enough room in an elevator. If there were, they'd call it a mobile home.

Jack and I were halfway to the second floor, which Astral had already shown me consisted of a typical hallway lined with faded green carpeting and diarrhea-brown doors, when I realized everyone had followed my lead. When Vayl stood beside me once more at the top he said, "I presume you feel better."

I nodded. So did Jack, because he's just that supportive. "Aerobically speaking, we are now completely warmed up and ready to roll."

His dimple made a brief appearance. "Then I take it you are looking forward to our next confrontation?"

I took Grief's safety off and made it ready to fire. "You could say that."

"Would you do me a favor, then?"

His suddenly serious look caught me off guard. "Of course."

He stepped into me until our thighs aligned. When his arm went around my waist and lifted, our hips locked like they'd been made in the same factory. "Make sure Raoul is not merely here to take you away from me forever."

He let the words loose carelessly, but I heard the desperation behind them. *Don't die tonight, Jasmine, you're all I've got.* That's what his purple eyes told me. The message had been significant in earlier times, when that had been true. But now that he'd found Aaron, now that he was closing in on Hanzi, they stirred my heart like never before.

"I'll be careful," I promised him.

He nodded. "Good."

A kiss, the brush of lips that sent tingles racing straight to my toes, sealed the deal. And then we were leading Raoul, Bergman, and Aaron down the hallway toward an ugly brown door onto which a scratched brown plaque had been glued. I didn't know Slovenian, but there was no mistaking the message. This was the honeymoon suite. Astral sat at the base of the door, as if she'd known right where I needed her to go. Fuh-reaky.

"Cole, are you in place?" asked Vayl.

"I'm in the attic above the suite's bathroom. Luckily somebody here's a big pervert, because there's a camera system all set up, with predrilled holes for the naughty boy to peep into the shower anytime he can get away from the front desk. Jaz, when you get a chance, you may want to kick old Sanji there right in the gonadiphones."

"Will do," I said.

Raoul tapped me on the shoulder. "It might not be him, you know."

"I'm willing to give him the benefit of the doubt. But you'd better not be holding me back if we find him drooling over sex tapes after this is all said and done."

"That's a deal."

We stopped outside the door. I handed Aaron Jack's lead and scooped Astral into his free arm. He nodded over what he understood was an enormous responsibility, especially after I pointed to him, then to the animals, and made my if-anything-happens-to-them-I'll-kill-you face.

Bergman whispered, "Should we knock?"

I glanced at him. He was pale, but not nearly as shaky as the old Miles I'd known, who would've found five perfectly logical reasons to wait for us in the bus. I said, "She knew we were coming before we did. I imagine she's got cookies and milk waiting on the table for us, don't you?"

He shrugged, then nodded, then shrugged again. "I'm new at this," he finally said, in an effort to explain his indecision.

Vayl said, "You will be fine, Bergman. All you have to do is open the door and get out of the way. I expect it to be unlocked. If it is not, just move out of my line of fire. Can you do that?"

Bergman swallowed so hard that for a second it looked like he had a chicken bone stuck in his throat. Then he held up the cane and shook it a couple of times to express his certainty.

"Excellent." Vayl looked to one side, like he could see Dave and Cassandra through the walls of the inn. To them as much as to our inside backup he said, "We are going in. Be on your toes, please. Our lives may be in your hands."

"Yes sir," Cole replied.

Dave maintained Party Line silence. The fact that he'd chosen to go into pure stealth mode, combined with Vayl's refusal to mention him by name, gave me an odd sense of comfort. No telling how long ago "Mrs. Bemont" had predicted this meeting. But Dave and Cassandra had been last-minute additions to our crew. So if luck was on our side, and none of us blew their cover, my brother and his lovely, magical wife could turn out to be our secret weapons.

We lined up on the latch side of the door, just like we were in kindergarten and it was time for recess. Only this time we were required to keep contact, my hand on Vayl's shoulder, Raoul's on mine.

Vayl and I knew our responsibilities once we were inside. I'd already told Raoul what part of the room to cover. Bergman would enter after we'd cleared the room, and Aaron had been instructed to stay in the hall unless he deemed it safer to slip into the room behind us.

Which left it to Vayl to begin. On his nod, I waited for Raoul to squeeze my shoulder. When I got his I'm-ready message I squeezed Vayl's shoulder and he motioned to Bergman to open the door and step out of the way.

The door wasn't heavy, like you'd expect in an American hotel. Miles could've swung it open with his pinky. Instead he jerked the latch down and shoved it wide, causing it to bang against the wall as we rushed into the room.

We stayed tight so we wouldn't stray into each other's line of fire. Vayl moved directly to his right, covering that corner of the room. I took the center and Raoul, stepping in directly behind me, covered the left corner. I could feel Bergman's breath, hot against my neck, as he shadowed me, Vayl's cane tapping nervously against the dingy wooden floor. I didn't bother tracking Aaron. Some people are just born with a well-defined sense of self-preservation. He, Jack, and Astral would be fine.

We all spoke at the same time.

"Clear," Vayl said.

"Clear," Raoul echoed.

"Don't move or I'll shoot," I snapped.

Chapter Twenty-Nine

Sunday, June 17, 4:45 a.m.

The creature lounging in the middle of the unmade bed looked, and smelled, like it hadn't stirred from that spot in days. Covered in black from head to toe, it seemed more like a pile of funeral laundry than a living being. Until it turned its head.

"Holy shit!" I jerked back, immediately pulling my finger off the trigger because I was afraid I'd twitch again and shoot it accidentally.

Sometime in the creature's recent past it must've stood in the middle of a bonfire. Nothing else could've caused the scars I tried not to see as I winced at the massive damage that had made it cease to seem human. I assumed it had survived the burning because of the otherworldly power I felt seeping out of it like pus from an infected wound. And even then I could tell that it had only barely escaped. The skin of its face had a red, puckered texture as if it had been gone over with a cheese grater. Its nose had melted to half its normal size, and its lips had been incinerated, leaving only a line of thin white skin to mark the barrier between face and teeth. No eyebrows or lashes gave evidence of masculinity or femininity. Just misery. That was what oozed from the creature. Wave after wave of pain-laced despair.

It had covered itself with a chador, the black tent-dress we had seen women wear so often during our trip to Iran. Over its head it had draped a black shawl nearly as long as the dress, under which it huddled so successfully that I couldn't see a hint of any other skin. No jewelry gave us a clue as to who the creature might be, so Vayl decided to go at it with a directness that surprised me.

"You cannot be Mrs. Bemont," he said. "We have seen pictures of Cole's mother, and she looks nothing like you."

The creature's awful pink tongue darted out and licked a bead of sweat off what now passed for its upper lip. "Is that how you greet an old friend, Vayl?" It nodded toward me. "You've been spending too much time with Little Miss Mannerless over there."

I felt my brows come together. The voice, raspy as it was, still sounded eerily familiar. Where had I heard it before?

Before I could think of a legit question that would force the creature to speak again, Raoul began to shift from one foot to another as he plucked at the buttons of his shirt like they'd been heated over a stove. When he backed off to where Aaron stood beside the door, holding the handle with the hand that also prevented Jack from leaping to my side while he clutched Astral to his chest with the other, Raoul visibly relaxed. The fact that he'd drawn his sword didn't hurt his demeanor either.

"What is it?" I asked him.

He nodded toward the bed. "That is an abomination."

My stomach fell, hard, like it had just slipped on a trail of bacon grease. Raoul had worked around unholy types before. He'd taken me on a field trip to hell, for Pete's sake! And he'd never reacted like this. I slipped my finger back onto the trigger.

"Whatcha got going on under all that material, Mrs. Bemont?" I asked the creature as I stepped toward it.

"Oh, I'll show you soon enough," it assured me. "But first, I made a promise to you not so long ago. Do you remember, Jasmine? Standing in the rubble you made when you blew the seal off the entrance to Satan's canal, watching me steal the Rocenz from right under your nose? I told you then that if you got it back I would meet you at the gates of hell to help you defeat Brude." The creature motioned with one black-draped arm to the gleaming silver tool at my belt. "You have it back. And I am sitting at one of the gates even as we speak."

"How can that be?" whispered Bergman. He'd stayed so close to my shoulder that if someone had turned on a bright light he'd have blotted out my shadow.

"I don't know," I told him. "It's not one of your physics problems you can work out with a little thought and a great calculator, Miles. Some things just don't make sense."

"And yet…" Raoul cocked his head. He came forward and yanked off the black blanket that covered both the bed and the creature's lower half, and we all jumped back. It wasn't sitting on a bed at all. It was dangling. Impaled on a spike that reached down into a fog that writhed with tortured souls.

The creature's smile turned ghastly as blood welled up from its throat and coated its teeth. And that was the easiest sight to handle. Because its spike didn't stand alone. In the space the bed should've taken up, standing as if in a cavern created from another universe, more posts carved to evil points at their tips rose from a surface that smelled like a slowly burning landfill. Every post was stuck through a body. And every single body twitched or moaned in its turn, assuring us that no creature who rode a roughly hewn spear had been blessed with death.

Finally I found my voice. And the knowledge that had been scratching at my brain for the past few minutes. "Kyphas? Is that you? We thought…" I glanced at Vayl. "We were sure you'd died."

Even without her lips, the demon whose beauty had once raised a desire in me that had made me grateful I liked guys managed a sneer. "Since when have you played pretty with your words, Jasmine?" She compounded the insult by pronouncing my name as only Vayl did, *Yaz-mee-na*, hoping, I was sure, that the next time he whispered it in my ear, my shiver would be as far from one of ecstasy as it was possible to get.

She said, "Speak it plain, or by all that's evil I will break my vow and suffer torments stacked on those I've already brought on myself just for the satisfaction of seeing you pout."

I briefly considered shooting her through the head. The only reason I decided against it was that it would only cause her more pain. Instead I said, "Miles and I saw you sucked through that planar door." Bergman had hugged against my back the moment he realized we were facing the demon who'd nearly dragged him into hell with her. I could literally feel him nod in agreement. I went on. "We also saw Vayl and Astral jump through to fight you. And when they came back, all they brought with them was your severed hands."

"What? You mean these?" She raised her arms and the material fell back.

"Jeeezus," whispered Bergman, who'd never felt the need to call on any deities in person until this moment and who, I was pretty sure, had been raised Jewish. I would've joined him, but I was too busy watching all my inner girls fall to their knees in panicked prayer.

Even now, three weeks later, Kyphas's wrists were still leaking black gouts of blood and gore. But they didn't end in stumps as we'd expected. The same villain who'd burned her face into an unrecognizable mask and shoved her on a stick like some sick puppeteer had welded a three-headed hydra to each of her wrists. Each head was taking turns sinking its fangs into her wounds, causing her to shake like a malaria victim as it drank its fill.

"What happened to you?" Vayl asked, his shoulders tightening into steel plates at the sight of Kyphas's snakes. "You are the daughter of a Lord of Hell. Where is your father? Why did he allow this?"

"I gave up my heartstone," she said. "Or have you forgotten? Leonard has turned his back on me."

"Oh, don't act like it was some great act of charity," I snapped, using my resentment to cover my horror at her pain and my surprise at her lineage. Her father was the Lord of Black Magic and Sorcery. I couldn't believe he hadn't tried to pull some strings to give her at least some relief. "You were trying to turn Cole into a demon. If you hadn't given your heartstone to us he'd be trolling Satan's playground for cute babes to skin alive even as we speak."

"I broke the Second Law," Kyphas informed me.

Even though I'd never warmed to Kyphas, I was beginning to believe she really had wrapped her arms around this fate for Cole's sake. Demons took all kinds of crap for letting souls slip through their fingers, but they never experienced true punishments for the failure, because it was so hard to snag them in the first place. Only when someone like Cole was allowed to escape on purpose, breaking Satan's Second Law, did demons burn. Which meant she'd acted out of real love. Damn.

I cleared my throat. "How long…" I couldn't finish, couldn't imagine the pain she must be enduring.

She said, "I am to be punished for the next half-century for my crime. And yet my vow supersedes even my jailer's power. So I've come to give you the last bit of help that I'm required to."

"How did you know we were coming?" I asked, knowing that as soon as she fulfilled her vow she'd disappear again. And that even this small break was helping her push back the agony.

She pointed down at one of the women writhing beneath her, the snakes on her right wrist coiling up her arm at the sudden movement. "Lesia is a prophet. Ironically, the more they burn her, the clearer her visions become. Which is why I know that my beloved has crept through the attic access in the bathroom and is waiting just outside the door for your signal." She sighed. Then she said, loud enough for her voice to carry across the room, "Cole. Mercy or revenge. Either way you think of it, your bullets can't kill me."

The bathroom door swung open and Cole stepped in. He regarded Kyphas for a long time, his face so still that none of us could figure out what emotions were moving behind his clear blue eyes. Finally he said, "Tell Jasmine why you came and then go back to hell where you belong, Kyphas. We'll follow you when the time's right."

He glanced at my belt, where the Rocenz hung heavier than ever. When he looked back at Kyphas some silent communication passed between them, because they both nodded and, despite her immense suffering, she seemed almost…relieved.

She nodded to me. "That lovely piece of artwork you carry in your pocket is obviously incomplete."

I nearly put my hand against the hanky-wrapped skin, but kept it steady under the butt of my gun instead. "I noticed."

"The rest is still on the cowboy, Zell Culver. He'll come if you call him. Stand by the gate, give it your blood, knock three times, and shout his full name."

"Thank you, Kyphas," Vayl said. "Your promise to us is fulfilled."

She barely acknowledged his words. Her eyes, the only bright and shining parts of her soul left unshattered, kept a steady watch on Cole. "You look fine," she said. "I'm glad of that."

He nodded. "My friends brought me back." His stare, full of dark memories and nightmares, wouldn't give her an inch. This was the Cole that stayed hidden, the man I knew least and liked best. "I'll never forgive you for what you did. You should know that."

"I'm sorry," she said.

What she said made perfect sense. She should feel apologetic for what she'd done to Cole, even if she had paid in skin and blood. But the prickling between my shoulders told me she wasn't talking about Marrakech. I spun around as Aaron shrieked. Miles, still hanging at my shoulders like a badly organized backpack, hampered my movements and my line of sight. For a second all I could see were two blurs leaping through the doorway.

"Vayl!" I yelled, relying on my Spirit Eye to guide me until the rest of my senses could come into play. "Hellspawn!"

Bergman ducked, I thought to get out of my way until I realized he was rolling up his jeans. Hoping whatever he'd built into his boots wasn't another one of his unreliable prototypes, I triggered the holy water strapped to my wrist, filling my palm with an attack-ready syringe even as I knocked the first demon back with a barrage of gunfire that wouldn't kill it in this world. But judging by the squeal, it hurt a lot more than beanbags. That, and the flying steel from

Vayl's shotgun as well as Cole's rifle, gave me a few seconds to assess our situation.

As I'd thought, we only faced two opponents, but they were a couple of the baddest fighters hell had ever puked forth. Called *Ichoks* by those who'd encountered them and survived, these creatures could throw so much nasty into one blow it felt like you were facing five well-trained enemies. Part of that was because they were ambidextrous, wielding their katanas equally well with either hand and with such speed that people were left staring at the stumps of arms and the gaping wounds from which their intestines had begun to snake out without even having felt the blows. *Ichoks* could also deal a potentially fatal strike with what I called their spit glands. Located in a specialized pouch tucked inside the lining of their bloated, gill-covered cheeks, the glands could be emptied with force, usually into an opponent's eyes. Blindness was the first result, after which the *Ichok* could finish you off at its leisure. But if something distracted it, you'd eventually die from the poison as it worked its way through your system, paralyzing major organs along the way.

They preferred to fight in a crouch, which left a much smaller target to aim for. And, like most hellspawn, they came shielded, though their armor was easy to see, even to Unsensitized eyes like Bergman's.

"What's that chest plate made of?" he whispered to me as I reloaded. "It looks like..."

Knowing he'd never be able to finish the sentence, I did it for him. "Skulls, Miles, those are human skulls. The top, cap part, to be exact. Hundreds of them cut to fit into neat little rows and linked together with bits of silver chain. What a great Halloween costume that would make, huh?"

He caught my bitterness and seemed about to respond, but he couldn't look away from the armor. "All those people," he whispered.

"If you don't want to become one of them, you need to give me a little more room," I told him.

He backed off, moving to stand next to Aaron, who'd tipped an armchair over in the corner and hustled Jack and Astral behind it.

Beside me Vayl had also reloaded and gone another round, blowing his *Ichok* back into the wall. But even before that his most effective weapon had already swung into full motion. In fact, the second the demons had entered the room I felt Vayl's power working at my hands, which were cold enough that I worried they wouldn't squeeze the trigger in time. And in my nose, which had begun to run. Even in my breath, which poofed out gray and frost-laden. I realized this might be the biggest storm Vayl had ever called.

I glanced at Miles and Aaron. "You might want to bundle up."

Already their teeth were beginning to chatter. Still, Bergman kept struggling with his boot. I couldn't see the hilt of a knife, so what the hell? "Did Vayl have to be a Wraith?" he complained. "I hear *lethryls* are a lot warmer."

"They also require a lot more blood to heat up the place, which usually means a couple of full-time suppliers working the entourage angle. Do you want to be some *lethryl*'s bitch?"

"Point taken." He gave up on the boot. "I'm freezing. And my VEB is stuck. Feel free to start without me."

Wondering what a VEB was and if I should've taken out insurance against being disintegrated by one, I emptied my clip into Cole's *Ichok*. Its armor had kept its chest from turning to dog food, although blood trickled down its arms and legs in a steady stream, and our combined rounds had thrown it to its knees. But still it was roaring and spitting, warning us that soon we'd be wishing for more powerful weapons.

I reached for the sword Raoul had lent me. As I pulled it, I realized my Spirit Guide was not waiting patiently for us to finish with the long-range fighting so he could wade in with his own weapon. He was standing just outside the door, fully engaged with a third *Ichok* who stood at least a head taller than the two we were holding off. His blade arched and slashed so quickly it was just a blur, but so were the *Ichok*'s weapons, and I swallowed a spurt of fear as I saw that his uniform was ripped in several places where blood had darkened it to black.

Then, like the warning had been ripped from the middle of her chest, Kyphas cried, "Watch out, Cole!" and I had to turn back to our fight.

He'd had to throw himself to the floor to avoid a spit-patch of poison that now dripped from the wall behind him. Worse yet, the blows from our bullets had begun to ping off the skulls of the *Ichoks*, as if the armor had *learned* how to deflect them in the time we'd been shooting.

Cole's hellspawn had risen and begun to twirl its double katanas like saw blades, and all he had was a now-ineffective sniper rifle and a sheathed sword that he'd never be able to compete with in a fair fight.

By now my blade was in hand as I stood beside him. "Draw steel," I ordered, although I didn't hold out much hope for our survival.

Next to us Vayl had centered the cold of the grave he'd never entered on the hellspawn whose realm was full of the burning dead. In one massive cloud of air that looked like a perfect coil, Vayl surrounded the *Ichok* with tiny, razor-sharp shards of sleet. And then he drove them into it. The boom of sound that accompanied the strike shook the floor, making us all stagger backward as Vayl's opponent shattered into a million pieces.

Cole and I pressed our advantage, swinging our blades at our unbalanced adversary as he leaned toward the wall. Unfortunately he recovered quickly, and soon we were both on the defensive, fighting for our lives against blades that seemed to be everywhere at once. Of course, this was giving Vayl a chance to move around behind the creature, but given the speed of this attack nothing was going to save us in time.

I glanced over my shoulder at Raoul. Nope, he couldn't wade in beside us, because his hands were full as well.

Then I saw Dave and Cassandra running down the hall. Dave had drawn his knife. The sheen of its blade matched the edge of steel in his eyes, making me glad I was fighting on his side. Suddenly I felt sorry for the *Ichok* who was about to die. But only a little.

I turned back to my own fate. Cole, back on his feet and fighting more fiercely than I'd ever seen him, raised his sword just in time to parry a blow meant to separate my arm from my shoulder. And then Bergman yelled from behind us, "Okay, I'm ready, guys! Duck!"

Cole and I traded a single look. And dropped to the floor like we'd just heard the whistle of a bomb zeroing in on our coordinates.

The *Ichok*, seeing its prey do the don't-slice-me dance, leaned over us with a leer on its butt-ugly face and roared. I saw its throat work and realized, "Cole. It's going to spit on us. Cover your eyes!"

And then I forgot my own advice, because Bergman whooped like a cheerleader whose team has just won the playoffs. "It's gonna work, guys! Watch this!"

We all turned to where Bergman stood, holding his boot in front of him like it was his very first twelve-gauge, the toe tucked under his arm for support, the empty leg pointed toward our foe. Only it wasn't quite empty, as we could tell from the blue spiral of smoke curling out of it. My guess? Bergman had just lit a fuse.

He said, "So long, mo-fo," growly, like he was just recovering from a bout of laryngitis. And then the back blew off the boot, smashing into the wall behind him, shattering a mirror that had been hanging there. He glanced over his shoulder, frowning. "That wasn't supposed to happen. Maybe I have the power-boost too—"

He never finished his sentence, because out of the opening his leg had so recently filled shot a series of cannonballs so small they looked like marbles. Except they hit like vats of acid, leaving smoking holes that ate at the skin, growing larger with each second, making the *Ichok* scream and writhe with pain.

"Bed," Cole panted.

I nodded, and without another word we charged. I fended off the *Ichok*'s weak attempts at defense as Cole drove it toward the narrowing gap between worlds, a door closing quickly behind Kyphas and the other sufferers like it was a living thing that knew we wanted to use it to our advantage.

Who knows? came the random thought, *maybe it is. Maybe all the doors are*. And that's when I knew, as surely as I knew my dad would never stop bitching at me because that was the only way he could tell me he loved me. I'd stood at the threshold of such a door at each moment of my death, my soul about to shatter into thousands of diamond-like shards that would travel the universe, settling into my family, my friends, and other destinations I could only imagine. I'd communed with the creature that provided pathways into worlds beyond worlds. Felt her fire caress the gemlike skin of my being. And promised her, one day, that I'd return so she could fly me home. So now she was always near, letting me know the trail was clear, no matter which turn I chose to take.

With this thought fresh in my mind I snapped, "Open up," at Kyphas's door. "Or I swear I'll put a hole in you so big cement trucks will be able to drive through it."

The door hesitated. Then slowly reversed course as Cole continued harrying the *Ichok* toward the bed, slamming it with slicing blows that left it looking like the victim of an old-time British Navy whipping. I slammed my heel into its knee, cracking it so soundly that my ears rang. It screamed and fell into the pit just as Cole swung his sword, cleanly decapitating the hellspawn just before it hurtled out of reach.

We turned to help Raoul, Dave, and Cassandra just in time to see Raoul shove his sword deep into the *Ichok*'s side while Dave's lightning knife strike left the creature's right arm limp and hanging.

"He's going to spit!" Cassandra cried, but neither one of the men was in any position to prevent the strike. So she stepped in and dumped her enormous, beaded bag over its head just as it let go. We could heard it scream as its venom hit falling tubes of lipstick, a paperback book, and a bright green cosmetics bag, not to mention a smaller purse full of necessities and at least one full bottle of Febreze. Some of its spit also dripped down onto its neck, where it began to eat into its skin like a plague of carnivorous beetles.

Dave caught a pair of handcuffs as they fell from the bag and locked them around the handles.

"Oh, baby," murmured Cole. "I gotta know the story behind those puppies."

"Shut up," I said as I cranked my elbow into his ribs. "For all you know Cassandra's a deputy sheriff."

"Ha!" Cole's laugh was cut short by another elbow. This one to his gut. One guess who threw it.

Now Dave and Raoul hefted the *Ichok* between them, shuffled it to the portal, and, after a three-count that allowed them to swing the creature into a nicely rhythmic arc, threw it into the pit. I don't know if they aimed or it was just dumb luck, but the demon hit an empty stake about halfway down and impaled itself on it. The last thing I heard before the door closed was its screams.

Cole leaned over the abyss and yelled to Kyphas, "Looks like your prophets were wrong, demon. In fact, you can just tell them they can kiss my ass!"

Her smile, ghastly as it was, still seemed to approve. "Even they can be blind sometimes," she said. "It all depends on how they *look* at things." She emphasized the word so clearly that I knew she was trying to send him a message. And then she threw her head back and screamed. I looked to see if one of the hydras had taken a fresh bite out of her arm, but she'd covered herself up again. What I saw instead was that the fog was rising. Or maybe she was being swallowed within it.

"This door is closing," Raoul said. "We need to leave the room in case something reaches through it at the last minute and manages to trap us inside it."

"Could that really happen?" Aaron asked me nervously.

"Just the fact that you can ask that question shows what a rookie you are," I said. "Now, see how Bergman has hustled his butt to the hallway? There's a guy who knows how to take physical threats seriously. You should follow his lead."

"Except when it comes to raiding old cemeteries, right, buddy?" said Cole, slapping Bergman on the back as he joined him outside the room.

"Huh," was Bergman's pale-faced response. Thank goodness Astral had witnessed that event or we might never have known the extent of his heroics. "What about the bed?" he asked Raoul as he, Vayl, and I joined him in the hall.

Raoul said, "By morning very little will be left to show that the room was once a gate to hell."

We looked around at each other. Raoul seemed the worse off for injuries, having been cut deeply in a couple of places. Cole and I had each taken minor wounds to the arms that we hadn't even felt until this moment. Vayl's two chest wounds were already closing. Dave, Cassandra, and Bergman hadn't been touched. We'd been lucky, we knew that. Hell wouldn't be so kind the next time.

Vayl wondered aloud, "Will we be safe here or should we move on immediately?"

"I can make us safe for at least an hour," Raoul replied. "It wasn't like we were going to tackle that gate anyway. Our scouts will find us a much less well-traveled route."

Cole snorted. "Which the prophets have already seen."

Cassandra said, "Kyphas was trying to tell you something about that. I think there's a way to cloud their vision."

"I agree," Raoul said.

"Then I need to consult my Enkyklios. And Astral," she added. "If there's a way, I'll find it."

Vayl nodded. "Do that. Everyone else must eat, and think. If you have any ideas of how to improve this mission, now is the time to come up with them. Because as soon as we find a way to rescue Hanzi, Jasmine, Raoul, and I must leave for hell."

Chapter Thirty

Sunday, June 17, 5:00 a.m.

Raoul's idea of protecting the hotel from further invasion was simply to bless it. He took my holy water, scattered it at the four corners, and prayed as he walked around the building. It seemed like such a simple solution. And yet, as I watched the part I could see from the room Vayl and I had temporarily claimed on the ground floor, it seemed to me like if I turned my head just right I could see Raoul, transformed by the ceremony and his place in it into his true self. The shining white beacon whose slightest whisper could blast my brain to jelly if he wasn't careful.

It wasn't that he shone with an inner light or that I could see his skeleton glowing through his skin. It was that I could glimpse, just for a second or two, the rare and beautiful creature he'd become moving just behind the physical form he'd taken in order to walk with us. And I had to wonder—was this what Granny May had become? When Matt had chosen paradise over me…had he known this perfect grace, this wisdom wrapped in white fire, was waiting for him?

I felt Vayl before I heard him, his fingers moving gently up and around my shoulders, his chest pressing against my back as I dropped the curtain. "Does it hurt you?" I asked. "Standing inside a blessed building?"

"Yes," he admitted. "But Raoul gave me this. It shields me from the worst of it." He turned me around so I could see the amulet hanging from his neck. Made of gold, the pendant looked like a reverse question mark in which the circle had nearly been closed. Inside the circle, held there by fine golden lines that reminded me of Queen Marie's favorite palace room, was a second nearly complete circle whose opening was at the exact same space as the first. Filling those spaces was a golden arrow so intricately made that I could see the fine lines of its feathers had been hammered in by some meticulous craftsman.

I wanted to touch it, but settled for laying my hand against the soft shirt below it. "So." I looked into his eyes, trying to gauge his mood. They were brown. Leave it to him to be totally relaxed before the biggest mission of our lives. "Hanzi. And then hell," I said.

"Yes." He caught my other hand in his and brought it to his lips. "We have had so little time together of late. And now." He pressed his lips into my skin and I closed my eyes, concentrating on the feel of him, his hips crowding closer to mine. His tongue tracing a path to my wrist. Had the air just thickened? As I took a deeper breath, I thought maybe so.

I raised my eyelids and smiled as I watched his eyes brighten to hazel and then to the emerald green that always felt like a celebration to me. "What do you say we leave them in the future where they belong?"

He glanced toward the window. "Dawn approaches. Already tomorrow is nearly here."

"How much time do we have?"

"Perhaps an hour."

"Then let's make the most of it."

Even now that our deadline loomed like a factory boss in our heads, yelling at us to get to work fast because every second counted, we undressed each other slowly. Savored each new bit of skin an unbuttoning revealed with lips and tongues and softly worded murmurs.

The bed creaked like its box springs had been sitting at the bottom of a river for the past twenty years, so we moved the bedding to the floor and lay in each other's arms as comfortably as if we'd been testing out a Tempur-Pedic mattress.

Vayl wrapped his arms around me and pulled me close, my breasts flattening against his chest as he whispered in my ear, "Tomorrow may be our last day together. I try to banish the thought, and yet it keeps tearing through my mind."

I shuddered, holding him tight. "Listen, I'm not letting you go. No matter what happens to us, I'll find you. Somehow, I'll come for you. Okay?"

He buried his mouth in my hair, muttered something I didn't understand, and then kissed me so fiercely that I couldn't have formed a single coherent thought for fifteen minutes after that.

We made love with a desperation I'd never experienced before, a love so immense I realized my cheeks were wet, and then knew that I was weeping. But it was all right, somehow. Our rhythm was the rhythm of the universe, and it sang out that we were meant to be. That we would always find one another, because music like ours was timeless…eternal. Afterward we lay in each other's arms until another rush of fear, of need, of desire pushed us forward again, to that place where only we could go together.

I must've dozed off, because my eyes felt heavy and my concentration dim when Vayl finally said, "Dawn is breaking. I need…" He trailed off. I'd never seen him go into the daysleep before. But now I'd looked into his face just in time to see his eyes flutter shut, his expression relax. I slapped my hand against my heart. *He's not dead. He didn't just die. Chill, Jaz. He'll be up again at dusk. If you can make sure no light hits him in the meantime.*

I went to our luggage and dug out the sleeping tent. Since there was no way I'd be able to lug him onto the bed, I set it up right next to our spot. When it was done I levered Vayl into it, using angles and his weight, more than my muscles, to get the job done. Once I'd zipped the door closed I sat down beside him and cried. Because the past hour had been one of the best we'd ever spent together. And despite what I'd said, I wasn't sure we'd ever get the chance to repeat it. Then I jumped into the shower. Because everybody should face their fate with clean hair, a full stomach, and at least an hour's worth of lovemaking behind them.

Chapter Thirty-One

Sunday, June 17, 6:20 a.m.

What is it about the shower? Water hitting your head in just the right pattern? I don't know, but I get some of my best ideas while rubbing suds into my hair. This time it helped a lot that Jack chose that moment to poke his head in and give me that doleful look that meant he had digested every morsel in his massive gut and I had neglected him shamefully by not feeding him in the past two hours.

I raised my eyebrows at him. "Seriously, dude. I have a feeling you wouldn't be my buddy like you are today if I didn't have the key to the chow cabinet."

And that made me think of doorways. And my sense that the portals following me around the planet were somehow alive.

I finished showering in record time despite the fact that I had to fend off another nosebleed, dressed, fed the mutt, and ran for Raoul's room.

"How long?" I asked as I burst inside without even knocking. With any other guy I'd have worried about interrupting something a little bent but, as expected, I found my Spirit Guide reading the latest issue of *Model Railroader* and chowing down on peanuts.

He sat up like he wasn't that surprised to see me. "Until what?" he asked.

"What's our window until it's too late for Hanzi? Do I need to try to wake Vayl up somehow, or will it hold until sundown? Can you at least tell me that?"

He shook his head and looked toward the window. Whose curtains were closed. Which was when I realized he hadn't been reading the magazine or eating the peanuts when I'd burst into the room. He'd been staring at those ugly beige window treatments.

"What?" I demanded.

"I was about to come see you," he admitted. He stood so straight I felt like an officer about to begin inspection. "I just got word from our scout. He's discovered a route to one of the most far-flung gates in Lucifer's domain. We have a very narrow window until the fence guardians catch his scent and come to investigate. As soon as Vayl rises we're leaving." He'd muttered most of this information over my right shoulder, like a TV crew was maybe standing behind me. Now he dropped his eyes to mine. "I'm sorry, Jasmine. There's no time to help Hanzi. It's all about you now."

I wrapped both my hands around the despair threatening to choke the breath out of me and said, "Look. We can do both. What if we grabbed Hanzi before the accident and took him into hell with us? What better way to show him his potential future than to sink him straight to the pit with a couple of pitiless assassins and an Eldhayr warrior who can show him the best way out?"

As Raoul hesitated I rushed on. "You know his chances of survival there are slim to none anyway; it's not like we'd be vacationing in the Wine Country or something. At least this way there's a better chance he'll choose the good fight. Plus Vayl gets to save his kid. *And* I don't have to spend the rest of my life walking under a thundercloud of guilt for denying him that chance. What do you say?"

I realized I was clasping my hands in front of me like a little kid begging for a double dip of chocolate/vanilla twist before the ice cream van passes her by.

Raoul nodded. "I need to check with a few people. But I believe that could work."

"Yes! I would make you do cheerleader kicks with me, but I can tell you'd pull a hamstring or something." So I hugged him which, as soon as I was done, I realized he'd dealt with about as suavely as a sixth grader. As I watched the blush fade from his cheeks I made a mental note, which my inner librarian dutifully filed away: *Next time…do the kicks*. I said, "Okay, do me a favor then. Tell the crew there's been a change of plan. We're camping out here until further notice."

He sat up straighter. "What are you going to do?"

"I've figured out how to get me and Vayl to Hanzi without driving."

His eyes gleamed. "I hoped you would. Do you want some company?"

I shook my head. "Your hands are pretty tied on this one, Raoul. I don't want to take you to a place where you'll be too tempted to break the Eminent's edict. Especially when you're already in hot water over us." As his face fell I said, "You guard the troops, okay? No telling what kind of trouble they'll manage to get themselves into if left to their own devices. As soon as Vayl and I get back with Hanzi, we're jumping to hell. Then I'm gonna need you like crazy."

He nodded resolutely. "This is true. I'll see you when the kid is safe, then. Be careful. And remember, some surprises are nice ones."

I tilted my head at him, but when he didn't elaborate I said, "Okay," as I backed out of his room.

With a whole day ahead of me and zero sleep behind, I skipped back to the room for some shut-eye. Jack had gobbled his breakfast and settled into one of the chairs for his morning nap.

"Seriously?" I asked him. When he nodded I said, "Okay, but wake me up if you need to take a dump. We don't want another fiasco like we had in that Motel 6."

I made a few more preparations for the night ahead. And when I was satisfied I'd done all I could I shed my clothes, curled up under the covers beside Vayl's tent, and snoozed until his whoop of indrawn breath brought me to my feet. I might've been stark naked, but I held Grief in one hand and my bolo in the other, so I *felt* at least half dressed. I also could've kicked myself for reacting so violently to the sound of him waking to life for yet another evening. I should be used to it by now. I had been, back at his house. Which proved how much this mission had frayed my last nerve. Not a comforting way to start out what could be the most important night of your life.

Especially when I looked down. Shit! Another nosebleed had left my chin, my neck, and the front third of my torso caked in half-dried flakes of blood. I supposed I should be grateful that I hadn't ruined one of my favorite T-shirts. But I just felt...tired. I touched my nostrils. Still damp from Brude's latest onslaught. *Go ahead, you fucker. Try me. I'm not going down without a fight.*

I considered throwing my weapons on the bed while I cleaned up, but Jack had decided that if Vayl and I weren't going to sleep there it was fair game for him. He'd spread out across the middle of the dingy mattress and was blinking up at me sleepily while Astral stared at both of us from the perch she'd found on the ancient TV set. So I set the lethals on the dresser and, before I hit the bathroom, took one more minute to set up supper for the bottomless pit.

"How hungry is the poopmeister?" I asked Jack as I dug into our luggage for his food supply. He bounced to his feet, making the bed creak so alarmingly I wondered if I was going to have to rescue him from the rubble of its collapse. But it held up at least long enough for him to leap to the floor and claim his food, which he chomped happily, pausing only to smile up at Vayl after he'd emerged from his tent and come to give me a good-evening hug. Which he delayed when he saw the state I'd risen in. He shook his head.

"I hope, more than anything, that tonight sees an end to your pain," he said as he pulled me into his arms, dried blood and all. When I thought about it, that was really saying something.

"That was very cool of you to say, considering," I replied. I shivered inside his arms. "You're cold."

"I have not yet eaten."

"Mmmm." I led him to the shower, underneath the spray, let him rub my skin to its usual pasty paleness. And all the while his lips brushed my neck, nipped at my skin. Eventually my shivers had nothing to do with temperature.

I said, "What you said earlier, about eating. Maybe it's not such a bad idea for you to take from me once in a while after all. I mean, the last time we joined we didn't even trade fluids. It was just—emotional."

"I know." He set the soap in the dispenser and pulled me in until it felt as if every inch of my skin was touching every bit of his. "I have a feeling our journey toward a new *otherness* cannot be derailed, but only delayed. And even that may not continue for as long as we had hoped."

"Then we might as well enjoy the ride," I murmured as I stroked his broad, muscular back. "I was just wondering, though. If this all works out, I'm definitely going to want a shower after we get back. What do you think about three in twenty-four hours? Too much?"

He considered the question as his hands drew erotic circles down my sides to my hips and back up again. Finally he said, "Well, they do say that cleanliness is next to godliness. And, considering our vocations, that cannot hurt."

"You're just saying that because you like to get wet with me."

His grin made my heart go pit-a-pat just like in romance novels. Or so I've heard. He said, "That, also, is quite true."

I turned in his arms, waiting until he'd clasped his hands across my stomach before I said, "We've got to exploit every advantage. Especially since I've got a big night planned for you. So give me that soap and let's get dirty, uh, I mean clean."

We used up most of the soap. All of the hot water. And every bit of strength in our legs. By the time we left the shower our kneecaps were no firmer than spaghetti noodles. We helped each other dress in colors so dark we'd have lost each other inside a movie theater, and then collapsed on our homemade bed for five minutes of recovery time.

At which point I told him about our change in plans. He leaped off the bed. "What are we doing here, then? We should have left the moment I rose!"

"About that," I said. "I figured out a way for us to get to Hanzi. I even tried it out to make sure it would all work earlier today. I'll show you soon. The point is, your kid isn't going to be at that location or on that motorcycle for another"—I checked my watch—"forty-five minutes. We don't have time, no. But we have to take it. Raoul told me that, for some reason, the only time it's okay to grab the kid is right before the accident. He's got to see something happen there before we take him to hell, or the deal is null and void. So 'patience' is the word of the day, okay?"

Vayl kissed me so thoroughly I almost forgot we had important items on our to-do list. When he lifted his head he said, "You are a wonder."

"I try." My lopsided smile told him to cut out the silly compliments, they were just too far over the top.

He touched the spot where I'd taped a piece of gauze underneath my right breast. I checked to make sure it didn't show through the thick cotton of my front-pocket pullover as he asked, "Did I hurt you?"

I brushed my palm against his cheek. "A little. It's teeth in skin, babe. You know it's got to. But the pleasure is so intense. I can still feel the tingle in my toes. And the bubbles are still popping in my brain. You get me high in a way that leaves me permanently powerful. Even after the crash. How does it feel for you?"

He caressed my lips, studying them so closely I would've thought his next step was to re-create the image on canvas if he hadn't started talking again. He said, "When I taste you, when I am inside of you, and you surround me, then I am no longer alone." He stopped. Stared into my eyes. And I suddenly understood the significance behind the looks he'd been giving me since before I realized how he felt for me. He'd been trying to tell me how lonely he'd been. All those years, searching for his sons. It hadn't mattered who he'd touched, whose blood he'd swallowed. He'd never truly connected with anyone in all that time. He'd been isolated, like a TB carrier stuck in quarantine, until he'd met me. And now he was about to risk losing that forever.

I wrapped myself around him until my arms and legs ached. Only then did I say, "I know a little bit about these things, Vayl. People have choices, even after death. I promise, I will always choose you."

He pulled back so he could look into my face. "Not Matt? He may be waiting for you in paradise, you know. He may be standing behind the pearly gates holding a beach umbrella in one hand and a margarita in the other."

I jumped to my feet. "I was really going to do this later. Afterward? But no, now really seems..." I rushed to my suitcase. It didn't take much digging. I knew right where I'd packed the box because I'd checked on it every day since to make sure it hadn't disappeared.

I came back to Vayl, who looked like a male model the way he sat in front of his sleeping tent, one leg stretched out in front of him, the other bent at the knee so it could prop up his arm. I said, "God, you're gorgeous. Have I ever told you that? Don't let it go to your head. Egotistical vampires are the worst. Here." I shoved the box into his free hand. "This is for you."

Which was such a stupid thing to say, but I was suddenly, incredibly nervous.

I sat on my knees in front of him, trying not to twirl my curls nervously as he unwrapped the classy blue paper and pulled out the black velvet box. When he opened it he went all Vampere on me and I couldn't tell at all what he was thinking behind his still-as-death features. So I began to babble.

"You said I could give you a ring. Remember? In Marrakech? So I asked Sterling to make me one for you, to sort of match Cirilai, which is why it's gold. I went for a semi-plain band because you don't seem the gemmy type to me. I mean, when I met you, you were wearing Cirilai around your neck, so...did I guess right?" When he didn't answer I rushed on. "The runes on both sides are, well, he wouldn't explain exactly how he did it. But my blood is in there. Not literally. That seemed a little too Angelina Jolie/Billy Bob Thornton–esque to me. But it was part of the spell that burned the runes into the band, inside and out, see? Which was how he said that some of my essence melded with the ring. When you wear it I'll be literally wrapped around you. Does that make sense to you? Are you ever going to speak, or am I just going to keep yapping like one of those annoying diva dogs? Vayl?" By now my voice had risen about three octaves, Stewie Griffin style.

When he finally looked up, Vayl's eyes had gone the honey gold I associated with his deepest feelings for me. The amber flecks mixed with green sparks to steal my breath, so that for a second I felt that time had stopped, and nothing existed beyond the love showering me from those wide, wondering eyes. "I have never before held such a treasure," he said, his voice so low I had to lean forward to make sure I didn't miss a word.

I sighed and felt the lurch as my world decided to keep spinning. "That was such the right thing to say." I took the ring from his square-tipped fingers and slipped it onto his left hand, watching his face as he registered the fact that I'd mimicked the same moves a bride would've made. He watched the ring slide over his knuckle and snug into the space just above his palm, made a fist to assure himself it fit well, then looked up at me again.

"You have made me a gloriously happy man today, my *pretera*."

I leaned forward and kissed him, tasting him fully, the way he'd taught me to, breathing in his scent, his maleness, his rising desire. I murmured, "That's my job, you know. The assassin thing is just a sideline."

"But you do it so well." He ran his lips down the side of my neck and I shivered. But I'd learned a few tricks since our first encounter, and when I slid the tip of my tongue down the edge of his ear he grabbed me with both hands, pulling me forward until I was straddling his lap.

"I do other things well too," I pointed out, just in case he hadn't noticed, as I feathered a dozen kisses down the line of his jaw.

"Ung."

Oh baby, what can be better for the ego than rendering your mega-experienced Vampere lover speechless? I felt like I'd just gained a bra size and learned how to walk in stilettos without appearing bowlegged all in one swoop! And then? Just because I wanted a little icing on the cake, I said, "We should go. I'm sure they're waiting on us. Vayl!"

He'd wrapped both arms around me and swung me to the floor, managing to land on top without bruising either of us. I kinda wanted to see the instant replay, but he already had his lips buried between my breasts, who I guess he thought should hear the news first. "Our crew can wait. You just gave me the best gift I have ever received in my *extremely* long life. I must thank you appropriately. Like this."

He did something with his lips that made me giggle uncontrollably. "Vayl! What did you—okay, you can totally do that again."

Which, thankfully, he did.

Chapter Thirty-Two

Sunday, June 17, 7:00 p.m.

We met the rest of our crew in Raoul's room an hour after sundown. I don't know if it was kindness to us or reluctance to start the last leg of the mission that had kept them from pounding on our door, but they'd left us alone, allowing us to join them when we finally decided we were ready to go.

We were pretty crowded in there, with Bergman and Cole sitting crosslegged on one bed while Raoul took up most of the other, though Astral had sprawled out beside him with her legs stretched in either direction as if she'd suddenly gone boneless. Aaron took up the single chair by the rickety old table. Each crew member held a double-edged blade that he was buffing to a shine that would send arcs of pain through your eyeballs similar to a camera flash if you looked at it just wrong.

Astral peered at us from her perch for a moment, then she said, "The devil's in the detailsssss," drawing the S out so that she sounded like a hissing snake.

Bergman looked up apologetically. "She's stopped running random videos, but I can't figure out yet where the funky audio links are coming from. The wiring's pretty intricate, and my best diagnostics equipment is in my lab."

I nodded. "It's okay. We should let her talk." Especially since I suspected she was trying to help. I sat down beside her and patted my lap. She took my meaning and hopped on, putting her paws on my chest so she could whisper into my ear, "Hello."

"You've got the hell right," I murmured back to her.

Vayl had moved over to stand by Aaron. "What is this, a cleanser?" he asked, pointing to the goop that wetted his son's rag.

Aaron glanced up. "Raoul says it has powerful properties of its own. Here it just looks like albino Turtle Wax. Down there it'll make the weapon feel a little lighter so it'll move through the air—and other things—cleaner. And then there's the writing." He pointed to an ancient script that had been carved into the blade. "Raoul says it's Hebrew."

Cole said, "Raoul's right. I've only been able to read a few words because I just started learning the language. But it seems to me like these swords are loaded for bear. I wouldn't be surprised if they grew legs and a tail and carried you down to the gate on their pommels like some sort of sword/horse breed known only to Disney cartoonists and Eldhayr fanatics like Raoul over here."

"I am not a fanatic!" Raoul replied, pretty quickly and kinda loud for somebody who shouldn't care what a bunch of Earth-dwellers thought.

"Well, you are wearing a uniform," Aaron said.

Bergman piped up. "And a couple of hours ago you freely admitted to liking Kool-Aid."

I grinned at my little buddy, who was not only developing some pure brass cojones, but a stellar sense of humor to match. Raoul thundered, "I am not some sort of cultist!" just as Cassandra threw open the door.

"Of course you are, Raoul," she said cheerfully. "And we love you for it. Everyone should be so passionately committed to one thing that they have no other life whatsoever, at least for a while." While Raoul tried to figure out exactly what she meant, she came over to me and scratched Astral under the chin. The cat's eyes closed and she began her mechanical imitation of a purr. Geez, could Bergman pull off the robotics or what?

I said, "I thought you were going to be closeted with the infomercial here all day long." I nodded to the cat on my shoulder.

Cassandra cocked her head at us. Something seemed different to me. I stepped back to try to figure it out. Was she actually dancing in place? Yeah, her ruffled yellow skirt was definitely swaying back and forth in time with some rhythm that also occasionally sent her shoulders bobbing and the beads on her freshly cleaned and patched purse clicking.

"Cassandra? Are you all right?" I asked. Then I saw Dave grinning in the hall behind her and knew it couldn't be all that bad.

"More than that," she said. "But really it's no thanks to your cat. I think we need to upgrade her databases or something. She had no information about hell's prophets anywhere in them."

"Well, of course not. I don't think anybody on Earth has ever even seen one and lived to tell about it. The Great Taker seems to keep them even more secret than Apple does their next-generation gadgets."

"True," Cassandra allowed. "But they have been felt. I've even had a glimpse or two." Her mood quickly dropped off. "It's like rubbing up against a wall of slime. But once you get past the ick factor, you can manipulate them."

Everybody in the room sat a little straighter as she explained. "These prophets who've been trailing Jaz and Vayl know they're coming. They even think they know by which gate. See, they're tapping the future, the same way a vintner taps a keg. Shoving their psyches into the fabric of time and forcing its juices to reveal pictures of what is to come. But they're bound by the same laws as I am."

"Meaning what?" Dave asked.

"Meaning they need something of Jaz's or Vayl's to drive that spigot in correctly. Preferably something they can touch. If we gave them something new, they'd be ecstatic. They'd feel like they had an even better feel for where you'll be going and when you'll get there, so they can set up an ambush and drive you right into it." She paused, grinning at Vayl. "After you snatch Hanzi, of course."

He nodded at her, giving silent thanks for her optimism.

Raoul was rubbing his forehead. "And how do we turn that to our favor?"

"We feed the wrong story into the item. Well." She looked at the floor bashfully. "Actually I would do that. It takes pretty immense psychic power to pull that off and, since most of you know how long I've been around by now, I think I should volunteer."

"Now, wait a minute," said Dave. "I may not know a lot about what you do, but I know it takes energy, sometimes so much that you're exhausted by the end of the day. How are you supposed to pull off something this big without hurting yourself and the baby?"

She nodded. "I've already thought of that. I need your energy. All of you," she added, looking around the room. "I need to feed off it so this transfer doesn't kill me or..." She reached out to Dave, who grasped her hand in both of his, bowed over it, and pretended not to cry.

"You are going to need a personal item of ours as well, correct?" asked Vayl.

Cassandra said, "Yes, like a piece of jewelry." She looked at me hopefully and I realized almost instantly what she wanted. *Which is fine*, I told myself. *It's not like I didn't know this day would come.* But it was hard, it hurt to pull the ring Matt had put so much thought into, the one he'd slipped on my finger the night he'd asked me to marry him and I'd said yes, it was so much tougher than I'd imagined to lay it in Cassandra's hand and say, "Here. This has been with me through the best and worst times of my life. It should work."

She closed her fingers around it and smiled gently. "It's for the good of the Trust," she said.

"Yes," Vayl's agreeable voice sounded booming next to my whisper. I stared around the room with its rotting bedspread, peeling wallpaper, and chipped dressers, feeling the loss, waiting for the moment when it would be okay again. Then Jack was there, shoving his nose into the backs of my calves, which was his way of saying he'd had enough snacks for one day, it was time for dinner. *And oh, by the way? I love you, Jaz.*

I knelt down. *I love you too, buddy. And we both love Vayl, who's waiting as patiently as he can. But, look at him. He's terrified that Hanzi will die in that wreck just like Dave foresaw. Isn't it about time we shoved that monkey off his back?*

I looked around the room. "Thanks for making such great preparations, guys. It looks like you'll be set when we get back."

Sudden silence as my friends faced the fact that we might not return. Even Aaron managed to look concerned. I took Vayl's hand. "There's no room in here," I said. Then I smiled, my eyes twinkling up into his as I said, "We have a lot of luck with showers. Let's try in there."

His lips quirking, he said, "I bow to your vast experience in this area," and followed me into the room, which was covered with faded pink tile, its grout so dingy that it almost looked black. Since he hadn't been told to stay, Jack followed us, watching with interest as I slid the ivory shower curtain to one side and then leaned against the sink. Vayl buried one hand in the scruff of Jack's neck fur as I thought about summoning the door, just like I had in Brude's dungeon. Only this time I considered it more like a phone call to a dear old friend. *Come on, girl. Pick up the line.*

The portal shimmered into being inside the tub like it had always been there, but I'd only now gained the visual acuity to see it. Framed by blue-and-orange flames, it stood at ceiling height and took up the entire length of the tub. It was the biggest door I'd seen, discounting the one I'd called to transport Aaron Senior's cell.

I leaned over, placing one hand on the tub's edge, keeping the other firmly on the comforting reality of Jack. "I know who you are," I whispered.

The flames danced merrily.

"You and Raoul," I went on. "You're the only beings who've ever really seen my soul. The fact that neither of you ran screaming—I appreciate that."

Another leap and twirl of flame. I began to associate it with joyous laughter.

"I understand now that you were helping me before, when you chose a familiar battleground where I could fight the Magistrate with sort of a home-field advantage. And when you appeared in Brude's territory so we could escape—that couldn't have been easy or safe for you. Now I'm ready for that favor I was telling you about before."

As I spoke the flames banked and rose, as if every thought and breath of the creature who appeared to us all as a plane portal was communicated through that movement. When I felt she understood, I motioned for Vayl to come forward beside me.

I whispered, "She's willing to help."

"She?"

"Um, yeah. I think you'd call her, like, a guardian angel. Only she's more about movement than destination, so there's probably a neutral word that works better. It's just that I don't know her language so I couldn't tell you what it is. My Sensitivity is wide open since you took my blood, so I'm feeling her pretty strongly. I can tell you she was once a spectacular human being. But she hasn't had a body like we know them for thousands of years."

"What is she going to do?" Vayl asked.

"Jump us to Spain. Pull us back."

"Why?"

I shrugged. "As near as I can tell? It's who she is. All I had to do was stop limiting her, start seeing her possibilities, and now infinite travel destinations are open to us."

His eyes began to glow. "We could go anywhere. Safe from your people and mine."

I nodded. "But we could come back to visit. Because my family is still mine. And I won't abandon them."

"Nor I."

"Speaking of which." I motioned to the portal. "Let's go get that crazy kid of yours."

Vayl's smile lit up my entire heart. "Indeed."

He took my hand, I grabbed Jack's collar, and together we stepped into the hotel tub, through my guardian's doorway, into the loudest damn arena I'd crashed since Dave and I had sneaked into the monster truck rally during our junior year of high school and nearly gotten thrown out when we'd found one idling backstage and decided to take it for a spin. Literally. Lucky for us we're really fast runners.

Chapter Thirty-Three

Sunday, June 17, 7:15 p.m.

I'll give this to my portal, she had a sense of humor. She'd set us down at the back of a temporarily fenced-in tract of watered-down dirt that looked like it was normally used as a range for long-distance target practice. Near the horizon I could see the hulks of bombed tanks and trucks. Closer to hand, set in a semicircle around the fence, mobile spectator stands had been erected. In them GIs and their families cheered on the stuntmen who were currently putting on an engine-revving, tire-spinning show for them in the cool of the Andalusian evening. At the moment three bright yellow racing-striped cars were taking turns running up to a ramp and hitting it with their front and back wheels, which levered them up into the air. Then they competed to see how long they could run around the ring before falling back to their natural state.

"Your son is a nutbag," I murmured to Vayl.

"Hanzi always was the adventurous one," he replied.

"Uh-huh. So how do we find him before— Oh, I see."

Lined up down the middle of the track were five semi trucks with their trailers attached. A ramp led up to the first one and another led down from the last. Hanzi must have intended to jump these, probably at the end of the show, since the hoops at the tops of the ramps looked flammable and it would, no doubt, promise to be the team's most spectacular stunt.

"Well, I guess we know which truck Dave saw Hanzi slamming into now," I said.

"What if I drove off in the last one?" Vayl asked. "Hanzi could hardly do the stunt then."

"Do you remember how to hotwire a car?" I asked.

"All right, then, you do it. But I am coming with you."

"Of course. Who else is going to make me invisible to all those yelling soldiers?"

So Vayl raised his powers, camouflaging us both so successfully that only our footprints in the dirt showed signs of our passage. We carefully walked up to the last truck in line. I eased open the door. And then carefully shut it again.

"We're outta here," I said, grabbing Vayl by the arm and pulling him backward.

"What happened?"

I grimaced with effort, yanking desperately and having no luck in budging my *sverhamin* whatsoever.

"The truck is rigged with explosives. I'm assuming it's supposed to blow during Hanzi's big performance. I imagine that's what he's supposed to see right before we grab him."

"Who would want to kill my son?"

"It's a military base, Vayl. Who wouldn't want to kill an American stunt crew on an American base in Spain?"

"Point taken."

The sound of a motorcycle revving turned our attention to the dirt oval at the edge of which the stands had been set. The crowd went wild as Hanzi, dressed just as Dave had described in black riding leathers and a tinted helmet, came tearing into the arena, popping such a big wheelie I was amazed he didn't flip completely over.

I elbowed Vayl and pointed. At the edge of one of the spectator stands stood a group of five men dressed in private's uniforms. They wouldn't have looked so out of place to the casual observer. It was just that I'd gotten demonic vibes from them in such strong waves that I figured they'd been sent in hungry. I suddenly doubted that much of Hanzi's soul was meant to make it to the pit intact.

I directed my attention back to the rider. Once he'd completed his circuit of the crowd he came back, this time balancing on the back of the bike like it was a circus pony.

In the meantime, two stagehands had lit the rings at the tops of the ramps.

"Vayl. We're out of time."

He was staring hard at the rider whose soul had once inhabited his son's body. "Look at the bomb again," he told me. "Does it have a timer?"

I bit my lip to keep the obscenities from spilling over my lips as I eased the door open and took more time to study the future Dave had foreseen for Hanzi. "No," I said finally. "Somebody in this crowd is holding the detonator."

"Cassandra?" he suggested.

"No, Dave would never be okay with that," I said, trying to imagine her pressing her hand to all that C4 in order to get a vision of the culprit, if we'd even had that kind of time. Besides. "Remember, Hanzi's got to see the explosion. I figure we have to grab him close to the edge of the jump."

"I agree," said Vayl.

"Okay then, let's grab ourselves a couple of motorcycles."

Here's the thing about being willing to do anything for the love of your life. It turns out—you really will do anything. While Hanzi continued to wow the crowd with his way-cool bike tricks, I ran to the trailer parked at the side of the track, Vayl galloping smoothly at my side. We knocked out a couple of perfectly innocent guys who would wake without ever knowing a skinny redheaded chick and a brooding vampire had punched them so hard their brains shut down for a few seconds. And then we stole their precious vehicles. Sometimes we just suck.

We drove back to where we'd left Jack, who jumped onto the front of my bike like he'd been riding since puppyhood. "Hold on, boy," I told him. "We're going airborne." He tilted his head up so the air could brush back his fur, then he looked straight up so he could see me over the top of his head. And he grinned.

"You are truly the best dog ever," I told him fondly as we revved our engines.

"Time?" Vayl yelled over our noise.

"Yeah!" I shouted. He nodded and we drove, hard, to where Hanzi had now decided the only way the crowd could be happier was to see him drive on a tightrope made especially for cycles. Riding twenty feet off the ground on a modified rope with no net made Hanzi seem especially suited for one of the straitjackets I'd seen displayed recently in the Museum of Torture in Prague. Then I had no more time for thought.

Hanzi had made it across. Driven down the tightrope ramp and gunned it for the final stunt. The flaming hoops had been lit. We were driving to catch up and the crowd was screaming wildly, thinking it was all set up for them, a surprise three-cycle jump over a damn long distance.

"Hanzi!" Vayl bellowed.

I yelled, "Vayl! That's not his name now!"

Ten more seconds and we'd caught up to the stunt driver. Who looked from Vayl to me and back again with surprise so immense we could feel it, we could even see it despite the tinted visor.

"Change of plan, kiddo!" I yelled.

"What?"

"Aim for the big door in the sky!"

"What?"

Vayl put every ounce of hypnotic power in his voice when he bellowed, "Aim for the big door in the sky!"

Now we'd rounded the curve and I could see the soul-rippers who'd been sent to fetch Hanzi running toward us. They, at least, had figured out that all was not copacetic in Andalusia this fine evening. But, stuck in human form, they couldn't make their little legs pump any harder than was standard, and it was clear they'd never catch up to us in time to stop the bullet train we'd set in motion.

We accompanied Hanzi back to the starting point of the run, gunned our engines, and nailed our throttles, pushing the motorcycles hard toward the ramp. As we rushed toward the temporary wooden structure, which had only been made to hold the weight of a single rider, I prayed that the builders had supported it a little extra for today's stunt, and then I concentrated on my newest friend, my portal to anywhere.

Sitting in front of me, his fur flying back from his face and chest, his tongue hanging free like a thick pink necklace, Jack barked joyfully as the doorway appeared in the air just ahead of us. But shit! The flaming hoop wasn't big enough for all three of us!

I glanced at Vayl.

"One at a time!" he yelled.

We quickly formed a line, with Hanzi in the lead, him in the middle, and Jack and me following. Hanzi leaped first, taking to the air like a rocket, the motorcycle falling away from his body slightly as gravity did its deed. He made it through the natural flames of his crew's hoop, and my portal's flames had just begun to reach out to him when the semi exploded.

He looked down, panicking as the world beneath him vanished in a ball of flame and flying metal. An instant later he'd disappeared through the portal.

Vayl, already airborne, twisted as the force of the explosion hit his cycle. He controlled it masterfully, flying through the door just before a twisted hunk of door flew past the back of his head.

The concussion flipped Jack and me in a complete circle, making the crowd yell with excitement at what they assumed was our amazing trick as I struggled to keep the machine from tumbling sideways in the air and Jack scrabbled to stay on board, his nails scoring the gas tank as he pushed back into me. I wrapped my left arm around him, praying that I was strong enough to keep the handlebars straight with one arm when it came time to land the sucker, as we punched through the door. He yelped and I whispered stupid, soothing remarks into his flat-backed ears like, "When we get home I'll buy you that new Frisbee you've been eyeing. And I'll never offer you another leftover taco again. Just hang on, okay?"

As we flew through my portal I realized it had led us right back to The Stopover's crossroads. Only we were shockingly close to the goat track, flying much lower than expected to the pitted road, which was more dirt than gravel, not to mention the towering trees beside it. We were so close to landing I had no time to prepare for impact. Which was nice in a way. At least I didn't have to worry about whether it would hurt more to break my neck on the road or crush my skull against a tree trunk.

"Shit!"

I tightened my arm around Jack. Made sure the other was strong on the handlebars but ready to bend if adjustments were necessary. I tightened my thighs around the cycle and leaned forward, pressing against Jack to give him more security when we dropped. And it came so fast. Suddenly our wheels were on the ground. We were going too fast, I knew that, but for a couple of seconds I still thought we were going to make it.

As I began to brake, out of the corner of my eye I noticed that Vayl and Hanzi had pulled off to the side and leaned their cycles against a couple of beeches, like they'd decided to have a little picnic and enjoy the scenery. Something about the kid seemed off, even in that brief a glance, but by then my hands were too full to figure out what it was. I'd hit a trench, probably dug by a wagon wheel after the last big rain, and my speed, combined with the fact that I only had one arm to maneuver with, wouldn't allow me to ride through it smoothly. The wheel tracked sideways just enough to catch and throw the entire bike off balance. I tried to pull it back, but the handlebar torqued out of my palm like it had been pinched and twisted by a bulldozer. I felt the roll begin and automatically relaxed. Wishing I could advise Jack to do the same, I grabbed him around the middle with both arms.

"Sorry, sweetie. This is gonna hurt."

They teach you all kinds of skills in spy school. How to shoot a terrorist through the eyeball at five hundred yards. How to withstand hours of torture. Even how to wreck a motorcycle. Resistance, as they often say, is futile. Seize up and you tend to bruise and break a lot more necessary parts. This is why alcoholics can fall down so many flights of stairs and total so many cars without sustaining much more than a scratch. It's all in the muscle relaxant. Which was why all I did was make sure we were headed down the road rather than into trees before I let the momentum spin me into the ground and roll me like a doughnut in powdered sugar. My only concern was Jack, folding his legs under my body so they wouldn't break, cupping his head close to mine so it wouldn't flail during the fall.

Which lasted forever.

We hurtled across the scarred and granite-strewn trail like a couple of off-road racers who've lost their taste for machinery. As our course took us closer to the shoulder, I heard Jack yelp, his pain shooting through me like it was my own. I barely felt the rock that sliced such a gash in my thigh Raoul later told me it was a miracle my bone held firm.

Finally we stopped. I knelt over Jack, the blood from my wound spilling down my leg as I checked him over. He lay panting, his eyes half-closed, an arm-long branch that had fallen from one of the beeches protruding from his side.

"Vayl!" I yelled without looking up. "Vayl!" He was there before I could call again, crouching beside me, gently pulling back the fur beside the wound, trying to see how deep the stick had stabbed into our boy. When he looked at me with troubled eyes I began to cry. "Oh, no. Oh, no you don't!" I stumbled to my feet, pointing a shaking finger at him. "We saved your fucking son!"

I shoved my finger at Hanzi, who'd taken off his helmet to reveal a mane of shoulder-length hair and the features of a beautiful young—woman? Well, at this moment I didn't give a shit if she was a Smurf! I was going to get my way, goddammit! I said, "You pick up my dog, and you take him into that hotel, and you figure out how to make him better! Or by fuck I will never, ever forgive you!" I glared at the girl for good measure. "Or you!" I roared.

I didn't mean it. Vayl told me later that he knew that, and I hoped he was telling the truth. But just then my heart was breaking in two, and this heart of mine…it just doesn't have that much flexibility left in it.

He said, "Jasmine. He needs your peace now, and your love. Shall we get him to a softer bed?"

I nodded wordlessly and clutched my arms around my waist as Vayl lifted my 120-pound malamute like he weighed nothing, carrying him back to our room as gently as if he were his own child.

"I'm sorry," I whispered the moment he put Jack on the bed. "I didn't mean…I shouldn't have said—"

"Hush," Vayl told me, turning and taking me into his arms. "Raoul will know what to do. You should get him."

So I ran for my Spirit Guide, who showed such concern that I forgave him every petty irritation I had ever felt or would ever experience about him again.

"What happened?" asked Cole, running close behind us as we headed for the sickroom. As I explained, Bergman, David, Cassandra, and Aaron strained to hear, asking inane questions that I either ignored or snapped answers to until Cole put a hand to my shoulder and said, "Dude. Imagine sitting in a cramped hotel room wondering if your best friend, your sister, is going to die tonight. And then imagine her coming back hysterical talking about her half-dead dog and Vayl's son who's actually his daughter. Can't you cut us some slack?"

As Raoul entered my room I turned in the doorway, my eyes gathering in the friends who had saved my life in so many ways. And Aaron, who at least hadn't done anything to make it worse in the past few hours. I took a deep breath. "I'm sorry. Yeah, we saved Hanzi. Who isn't a boy anymore. Which is so weird, but neither of us have had any time to deal, because on the way back through the portal I wrecked my motorcycle—"

"Where did you get a motorcycle?" asked Aaron in a voice so lost and confused that I started back at the beginning, speaking as slowly as I could bear considering I wanted to burst back into my room and, what? Provide miraculous medical assistance when I, in fact, knew zilch about veterinary care?

In the end it was Cole who opened the door and ushered me through. Raoul was leaning over the bed. Vayl stood beside him. The girl, his beautiful new daughter, sat in the chair by the window, her feet propped up on the table... *smoking a cigar*.

I stomped up to her, tore the tobacco from her hands, ignoring her angry, "Hey!" since it just made me want to slam her against the wall even harder.

I handed the foul item to Cole, who proceeded to flush it down the toilet, and said, "If you ever smoke around me or mine again I will choke you to death. Do we understand each other?" She started to laugh. Then she looked around the room and realized nobody else was amused.

"What the hell?" she asked.

Cole answered her. "That explosion that just nearly blew you to bits? Demon-laid. Because, guess what? You're a flaming jerkoff and the world is tired of your crap. But I wouldn't feel relieved to have escaped the firestorm just yet. Because you've been rescued by two of the baddest assassins on earth. And one of them"—he pointed to me—"is highly pissed. Which means she'd feel so much better if she could kill something." He pointed to her. "If I were you, I'd spend the next few hours making sure that something wasn't me."

She showed at least some of her father's brilliance by settling back into her chair. So I turned to check on my dog. "Raoul?" I asked as I moved to stand between him and Vayl. They'd covered the wound with rags torn from one of Vayl's shirts. "How is he?"

Raoul said, "He feels very sick to me. I think we need to get him some help, quickly." He turned to Bergman. "You have access to all kinds of technology, right?" Bergman nodded, pulling his personal computer out of his shirt pocket expectantly. "Find us a veterinarian and get him here as quickly as possible." He glanced at me and then back at Miles. "I know this sounds strange, but this may be the most important thing you have ever done for Jasmine in your life."

I felt tears begin to roll down my face as Miles said, "I'm on it," and wheeled out of the room. I leaned over Jack, rubbing my face against the fur of his cheek, listening to him pant and, every fifteen seconds or so, moan softly into my ear.

"It'll be all right, buddy. I'm right here. I'll be right here."

"But, Jaz," Raoul said, as he knelt beside me. "You can't stay. You have to go now. You gave me your word."

I turned to look at my Spirit Guide, his face blurring in and out of focus as the tears continued to roll down my cheeks. And in that moment, I didn't hate him. Because I'd made my choice long ago. But I knew, now, that I needed to turn another corner. That I couldn't keep leaving people I loved like this. Jack was the final straw. He didn't understand, wouldn't know why his Jaz was deserting him when he needed her gentle touch and loving voice the most. But the rest of them, they'd known.

When Bergman had been bleeding onto the bricks in Marrakech, telling me to go and kill werewolves, he'd understood. He hadn't complained, and yet he should've. When Evie had been nearly ready to give birth, and she needed me there because our mom and Granny were dead, she'd understood that I had a job to do. She hadn't complained about all my traveling. But she should've. Because family, friends, the people I adored who'd pulled me through the nightmare days and nights of my life...they mattered more even than the monsters I'd destroyed to protect them. And it was time to show them that. The shit of it was, I could never do that, I'd die before I had the chance, if I didn't leave my poor Jack one last time.

Raoul said, "Jaz? What is it?"

"This is the end," I whispered. "I'm done fighting after Brude is vanquished. Do you understand?"

He nodded gravely. "Yes. I do."

Cole came forward, tapping Raoul frantically on the shoulder. "Will she die, then? Like, there are no instant dropsies in the contract, are there?"

"No. She's earned her right to live in peace."

Vayl ran his hand down my arm and pulled me to my feet. "Then it is time. Come, Raoul. Before we change our minds. Let us gather our weapons and challenge the gates of hell."

Chapter Thirty-Four

Sunday, June 17, 7:30 p.m.

Suiting up for hell took less time than expected. Holy water on the right wrist. Gauntlet to protect against biting creatures on the left. Raoul's specially crafted sword in its sheath on my back. Bolo in the right pocket. Grief in its shoulder holster despite the fact that I only carried it for reassurance. Bullets wouldn't do harm in the netherworld.

Vayl paid a visit to Miles to recover his cane and check on his progress. He'd found a good veterinarian twenty miles away and had already left to pick him up. There was no question in my mind that he would be coming back with him.

Raoul returned from his room carrying his sword and a shield that covered most of his left arm. He also carried his dagger, which he offered to the girl, along with an introduction that Cole, David, and Cassandra listened to with rapt attention. "My name is Raoul," he said, almost shyly. "You are somewhat famous among my kind. Do you still call yourself Lotus?"

"Yup," she answered, giving him as much of a going over as the weapon she took from his hand. "Why am I so famous?" she asked. "Are your people into stunt shows?"

"You possess immense skills," he said.

She snorted. "You could say that." She spun the dagger in her hand and threw it across the room. It stuck into the head of the portrait Sanji, the innkeeper, had so carefully hung on the wall. Then she licked her lips, winked at him, and leaned over so far Raoul couldn't help but notice her boobs practically springing from her dark blue T-shirt. "I have all kinds of skills."

Raoul's expression never changed. "You also hate yourself more than any other woman I have ever known."

She sat back so fast it was like he'd slapped her. I said, "Where we're going, you're gonna want that dagger." I nodded to the weapon and then looked at her hard, letting her know she'd better get her ass out of the chair before it came to a confrontation.

Lotus tucked a strand of hair behind her ear, revealing a row of silver earrings, including one that looked like a straight pin had been shoved through the ear's top curve in two separate places. Ugh. Hey, I've got a belly ring. My best friend has more earrings than a fully stocked Claire's. But that one just looked like she'd taken a bad fall into a nest of nail guns. Which was why it was an effort not to shudder with sympathy pains as I studied her eyes. They were such a vivid blue that I hoped they didn't change the way Vayl's did. It would be a shame to see that color fade. Her heart-shaped face escaped being described as cute only because of the way her jaw jutted when she talked, like she was warning you ahead of time you'd have to be tough to deal with her.

Her eyes crawled to Raoul's as she got up and rescued his dagger. On the way back to her chair Lotus said slowly, "This vampire says he's connected with me. Him and the marshmallow over there." She gestured carelessly toward Aaron, who'd backed into a corner and made us all forget he was there. Quite a trick, I suddenly realized. How many times had he done that when I wasn't looking? I didn't have time to ponder because she'd gone on. "What's that about? I've never met them before."

"But you have," Vayl said, unable to hold himself back any longer. "We are your family, from the time you were born to me as a baby boy named Hanzi in a beautiful wooded area where we had camped just outside of Bucharest." He pointed to Aaron. "This man was your little brother then. We called him Badu." Aaron nodded awkwardly. His expression said, *Hello, sister who used to be my brother. You are one scary dudette. Do not approach without warning me at least five minutes in advance.*

Lotus laughed. "Well, I'll be damned. Talk about the weirdest family reunion ever." She looked up at Vayl. "You do realize I don't believe a word of this shit, right? I mean, I'm a stunt driver. I spend most of my time traveling around the world doing motorcycle tricks. And when that gets boring, I find...other ways...to fill my time. Most of them illegal. Or, at least, immoral. It's how I roll."

Vayl shook his head. "We were always so different, you and I. Never understanding one another, never able to come to a meeting of the minds. Now I believe I see why. And I wish it were not so." He crouched before her, his expression full of the earnest desire of a daddy trying to figure out what his little girl really wants for Christmas. "I wish to know you better. Is that all right?"

She sat back, her cheeks hollowing like she'd just discovered a lemon seed stuck in her molar. Then she said, "Nope. I'm outta here." She lunged to her feet only to find Raoul's blade at her throat.

"No, you aren't," he said, his voice rimmed with the thunder that had often brought me to the edge of consciousness. "Your destiny has lost patience with you, and selfish pride is now a choice with consequences you must face. You will join us. Now."

Finally, something other than sarcastic prickishness crossed that lovely face. Was it bad that I enjoyed seeing real fear? I glanced at Vayl and was reassured that he felt the same. Sometimes that's the sign—that inside the actor there's still a real soul that can be saved. We had to hope it was true for Vayl's firstborn.

She whispered, "Join you? Where?"

Raoul said, "The demons who tried to kill you today meant to land you in hell. We do too. It's up to you to decide whether or not you stay there."

He nodded to me. I leaned over Jack and whispered in his ear.

"Okay buddy, if you ever understood anything I said, now's the time. I have to go. It's only so I can come back for good. So rest easy. Miles is getting a doctor to make you better and I'm coming back as soon as I can." I stroked his head just like he liked it. "Love you, poopmeister." Then I turned and strode into the bathroom, not looking back because if I did, no way would I be able to take another step away from my family and toward the potential end of my life.

I was leaning on the tub, waiting for the portal to appear, listening to Raoul, Vayl, and Lotus breathe behind me. I knew the rest of my crew was huddled in the doorway, with the exception of Miles—and Astral, of course. She had decided to sit between my feet. I couldn't speak, not to any of them. The moment was too big, the potential for disaster too real. What do you say to people you will probably never see again? I had no words.

Then Dave cleared his throat. "We were talking. Remember, before? About Kyphas and her prophets and how they knew you might be coming?"

I nodded as Vayl said, "Yes. Cassandra thought there might be a way to set them onto a false trail."

"It's too late," I muttered.

Cassandra sat on the tub beside me and leaned until she could look into my eyes. "Never," she said so adamantly that I felt a little shock run through me. "I have lived forever, as far as I'm concerned. I've been married and widowed and seen my children die before they were born. I've been a slave and a priestess and everything in between. And I'll tell you this, girl. It's only too late when you're dead. You"—she circled her finger at me like I was three and she was trying to make me giggle—"are still kicking."

I stood up, the flames from the portal coming to life like a frame around my body. Hell's citizens suddenly appeared in my peripheral vision as they walked their endless hike of pain, and I wondered if the gate stood that close to my original landing zone, or if the portal had only opened that pathway because it was so strong in my memory from the last time I was there. With no answers to that question readily available, I asked one that could be answered: "Cassandra, what the hell does that mean?"

She pulled a handkerchief out of her pocket and unwrapped it enough to show me that inside sat my engagement ring. Her smile, so delighted, made my lips twitch. "We did it!" she said.

"It's ready!" Dave echoed her, like he'd been the one toiling over it for the past hour. "My wife is a genius! You should all bow down to her!"

"Or not," Cassandra said, though her smile hinted that she kind of missed those days. "I've imbued Jaz's ring with a spell that makes all the emotions it's absorbed over time more vivid. The prophets who are looking for her will find it first." She held it up to me. "All you need to do is get somebody in hell to put it on and wander around with it while you run the other way."

"Or, more practically, force them," said Dave. "I was thinking if we shove it down their throat, we probably have a good twelve hours before the prophets clear their heads."

"Too risky," said Cole, leaning against the door frame and shining his clicky vamp teeth against his shirtsleeve like they were covered in jelly stains as he spoke. "Half of you could be dead before you get within ten miles of the gate." He cocked his head to one side and grinned as he set the teeth on the floor, aiming them toward Aaron, who stood just behind him and jumped satisfactorily as they came trundling toward his feet. Cole said, "I have a better idea." Before we could stop him he lunged forward, grabbed the ring from Cassandra's hand, slipped it on his pinky, and waved happily at us as he leaped through the portal, calling, "See you on the flip side!"

"Shit!" I reached for him, but Vayl grabbed me before I could step through. "Cole! You son of a bitch! Don't you dare—!" But he had. And the portal had suddenly gone black.

"Open it up, Raoul," I said grimly.

He spoke the words that cleared the door. Cole was not on the other side. In fact, the section of hell had changed completely. Now we were viewing the oceanic part that Kyphas had landed in during our fight in Marrakech. "This isn't helping," I said, trying to keep my voice level, sticking my hands in my pockets before they punched something.

Raoul inspected the portal's frame, watching how the flames jumped and what colors they turned when. He said, "Hell does not want us to know where Cole dropped. But I can contact the Eminent. We have scouts everywhere."

I looked over my shoulder at Vayl. He said, "Cole made a choice. For you. Do not let it be in vain."

I squeezed my eyes shut, trying not to feel as if everyone I cared about was falling away from me. That next I would have to watch Raoul bleed his last drop into hell's river, or see Vayl's spirit waft away into its fiery skies. I said, "Okay. Raoul, quickly contact your guys. And then, for God's sake, let's get this over with."

I felt Raoul's hand, hard on my shoulder. "Consider it done. And remember, it's a massive domain. Plenty of room for our scouts, and Cole, to sneak around in. We've got a good chance of finding him before any hellspawn do."

Vayl turned to David. "You will guard our return? We may come fast and accompanied by the worst hell has to offer."

Dave nodded. "I'll make sure nothing blocks this door for you."

They gripped hands as Raoul began to chant and the scenery, once again, began to change. I realized the next time it landed I would be facing what could be my final destination. I looked at Lotus. She was purely fascinated by this whole exchange. Soon she'd feel differently.

"We are ready then," said Vayl.

"What about me?" asked Aaron.

"You..." Vayl sighed. "Make sure you do not die again before I have a chance to know you better."

Vayl stared at the three people he was asking to stay behind. "Please also attempt to contact Cole via the Party Line and any other contraption Bergman has left lying around his room, remembering that he adores combustible traps. We will do the same from our location. Try to find out where he has gone. Astral may be of help in that area."

The cat, hearing her name for the first time in a while, perked up her ears and said, "Hello. Hell-o Hell's o-ver your shoulder." She turned and looked at me, without blinking, and added in her purring kitty voice, "Don't look over your shoulder, Jazzy, no matter what you do."

The chill that had clamped to my spine now tried to climb right up into my brain and explode out the top of my head. It left me with chattering teeth and the feeling that icicles were growing inside my eyeballs.

"We have to go," I whispered.

The cat responded by lifting one forepaw and delicately licking it. I took that as permission, picked up the robokitty, and boogied my ass straight into hell.

Chapter Thirty-Five

Sunday, June 17, 8:00 p.m.

Here's what happens when you walk into hell without your sword drawn, with your robokitty in ass-grenade mode, and without letting your Spirit Guide go first.

You get sucker punched by a pint-sized demon with skull spikes that resemble rotten bananas.

I dropped the cat and doubled over. Pain shot up my chest and down my legs as I stared straight into the hellspawn's bloodshot eyes. Then I grinned. "You little shit," I said. "How could you tell I was spoiling for a fight?"

I planted my fist into his face so hard that he flipped head over heels and landed on his butt in a puddle of steaming glop that smelled like burned cow manure. When he tried to scurry off I caught him by the high collar of his green sequined jumpsuit and said, "Oh no you don't. You're coming with me."

I turned around to find the rest of my party had arrived and was observing the fight from a narrow path beside the field I'd fallen in. Clear of weeds, or any greenery for that matter, its stark sun-blanched furrows were planted in body parts. Arms, legs, and torsos stuck out of the nuked soil like crops grown by Jeffrey Dahmer in his FFA phase. I pushed the demon toward them. Vayl caught him, holding him at arm's length like a piece of dirty laundry, and paying about as much attention to him, because Lotus had already begun to bug out on us.

"What the fuck?" she demanded. "No!" she said, slapping away Vayl's arm when he tried to keep her from prancing around in circles like she badly needed to pee and nobody would tell her where the bathroom was located. "Seriously! Who *are* you people? I mean, I'm up for adventure and all? I figured you for mega-millionares who recognized a fellow thrill-seeker when you saw one. But this?"

She was screeching now, jumping in place and shaking her fists at the mutilated bodies that would never have moved in her world, but in this one *would not keep still.*

Raoul strode up to her and grabbed her by the arms. "You are a brilliant young woman. Wrap your mind around this right now, Lotus. You nearly died today. You probably will anyway, but at least now the choice is yours. This"—he gestured at the ghastly landscape—"is where you were going to end up. Satan's field was your final destination because of how you chose to live life above."

She was looking around, her eyes wide and terrified. But seeing now, understanding as Raoul spoke. The greenish tinge to her face made me think he maybe shouldn't be standing right in front of her, though.

He went on. "Vayl and Jasmine made a deal for your life. And this is it. You must walk through hell with us. The choices you make here will determine your future." His arm swept in a full circle, making her see every horror around her. "You can still save yourself. As Cassandra said before, it's never too late." He leaned forward and whispered in her ear. I only heard because I had the Party Line tapped into mine. Unfortunately, so did Vayl. His eyes dropped to the ground as he heard my Spirit Guide tell his daughter, "Personally, I think you're too high on adrenaline and too afraid to see what's under the stunt costume to bother. Take my word for it. You'll be planted in this field before Jasmine takes her first hit at the gate."

Leaving Lotus to stew on that piece of news, he strode forward and swept Astral into one arm. "Are we moving yet?" he asked.

"Not in a straight line," said Vayl. He motioned to the hellspawn, who was putting up a little fight, trying to kick Vayl in the shins when he wasn't digging in his heels. He also made an attempt to head-butt Vayl, which would've been painful had one of those spikes impaled him, because they looked to be leaking some sort of greenish acid.

Vayl lifted his adversary completely off the ground. "I am sure Jasmine thought you might be helpful to us. Certainly newcomers to hell's shores need all the friends they can get. However, I find you quite rude."

The demon shoved his head toward Vayl's thigh like some sort of miniature bull. But the Vampere are particular about etiquette, and they react violently to being gored. Which was partially why Vayl jerked the demon's head backward and buried his fangs in its neck. He drank deeply, spat on the ground, leaving a tiny, smoking crater as he murmured, "Agh, it is like drinking vinegar." But I understood his motives when his reddish black eyes bored into mine and he confessed, "I have missed the powers I lost, my Jasmine. Would you begrudge me this chance to regain something of what was taken from me?"

I stared at him for a moment, making myself truly see him. His fangs and lips crimson with blood. His eyes bright and hungry, hands gripping his prey so tightly that the demon showed no more signs of resistance than the occasional twitch. This was the same creature who had chased me merrily through his house a few days before, shucking clothes and trading kisses until neither one of us could quite see straight. And I realized I loved them both equally.

I said, "Take what you need."

He drank again, deeply, like a desert hiker who's just realized he doesn't need to ration his water anymore. And then he snapped the demon's neck like a chicken bone.

Raoul was already pulling a garbage bag out of one of his jacket pockets. "Here," he said, "put the body in this. We may need it later."

I cleared my throat as Vayl followed his suggestion and he closed the top of the bag with a cheerful red-and-white-striped twist tie. "Do you always carry garbage bags for this reason?" I asked Raoul.

"Yes," he said matter-of-factly. "Almost everything here feeds on flesh. It's nice to have extra around so your skin isn't the first target the monsters go for."

"Oh."

Vayl flung the sack over his back and set his cane to the path, and I tried hard not to think about horror-movie Santa Claus similarities as we headed onward, Raoul leading him while Lotus followed and I pulled rear guard.

Now that I'd gotten over the first shock of brawling with a demon my training kicked in. Despite the fact that my eyes wanted to jump from horror to horror, never resting until they found a friendly face to ease the pain, I saw that the trail was built on a bed of human bones mired in salted earth and red clay. The appendage fields ran as far as I could see in either direction. And each body part imprisoned a diamond-shaped, multi-hued soul that was straining, and failing, to fly free. Without a complete physical form to make it whole again, the soul battered against the body part, flailing helplessly like a tethered eagle. And above them all, just like I'd remembered, a sky so full of fire I couldn't look at it long without imagining that the whole thing was going to drop down and incinerate us all.

"If we had a map, what would this particular region be called?" I asked Raoul.

"You have probably heard it referred to as Limbo," he said. "It is, in fact, right outside of hell's easternmost gate, of which there are thirteen. It is a place where souls are stored until they decide what they want out of the afterlife."

"That sounds a little crazy," I said. "I mean, to hear you talk before it sounded like souls could be kidnapped into hell, and that you and the other Eldhayr regularly tried to rescue them. Or that they came here because this was where they belonged."

"Yes," said Raoul. "But some are here because they want it. They've done something hideous in life that they were never punished for, and they feel they deserve to be here. Those are the ones Satan admits personally."

"Oh. And uh." I hesitated. Did I really want to know? Yes. Because we'd been to hell together before. And to have shared this horror once meant we had more of a stake in getting it right the second time. "What are you seeing?" I asked.

He glanced around, his face more pale under his natural tan than I'd seen it in months. At first he stared at me, like he couldn't believe I'd asked. But then I could tell he understood. And he said, "It's a great clearing in the jungle. Fires have been set everywhere around it, and on them are big boiling cauldrons."

I almost asked him to stop there, but I could tell he had to finish now. So I clenched my teeth together as he said, "Inside the cauldrons are the bobbing heads of those who can't decide what to do. Their eyes are rolling, Jaz. They're still, somehow, alive. It may be the worst thing I've ever seen. And I have seen so very much."

I reached my hand forward past Lotus and Vayl and squeezed Raoul's hand, tightly, for just a second. And then let go.

I glanced at Lotus. She'd gotten the shakes sometime during our march. After Raoul's description I didn't want to know what she saw. But I could tell, even if she'd started out in deep denial, she'd been unable to keep it up. She was seeing her future and it scared the shit out of her.

We walked on.

As we traveled among the undecided dead, Raoul, Vayl, Lotus, and I watched their souls fight. Some of them, I thought, really must have wanted to be free. But they couldn't get past whatever they'd done in life. They knew time must be served. Maybe even forever. But others reminded me of moths battering themselves against a porch light. It seemed to me, after a while, that all they wanted was to cause themselves pain. And I imagined that even here, outside one of the most remote of his gates, I could hear the Great Taker laughing.

Only once did Lotus turn to me. Her eyes, wide with horror,

begged me to make it stop. I said, "This is hell's suburb, kid. Think of what it's like inside."

She whispered, "I always knew I had to be punished. I just figured—"

I said, "When you were sixteen and Vayl's son, you got your brother killed. That was over two hundred years ago. How have things been since then?"

She fell silent, a single tear rolling down her cheek as she turned back to the path.

Finally, after forty-five minutes of watching and walking, we came to the end of the fields and the edge of the great river that surrounded Satan's domain. It had gone by lots of names over time, the most recent of which was the Moat. Sure I'd read about it. How you get across. Ways to pay the Ferryman. How the Ferryman, who also had lots of names, was one of Satan's bosom buddies, which was why he'd landed such a swank job in the first place. Fight beside a guy long enough and, yeah, you're going to get rewarded. Even in a shithole like hell.

This being sort of the back way in, we didn't see him. Which meant we'd have to find our own way across water that, in some places, was rumored to be deeper than the Mariana Trench, containing whirlpools, undertows, and creatures so terrifying even catching sight of a fin or claw had been known to drive the dead mad.

I said, "Looks like it's gonna be self-serve."

Raoul nodded his agreement. "Just keep in mind what happens when we get to the other side."

To this point I hadn't let my eyes or my conscious thought go to that spot, looming like a haunted house on the opposite bank. A gate fashioned to resemble a mastiff's head, its snarling face daring us to enter uninvited, stood closed against us, taller at its apex than a three-story building. Blood, fountains of it, dripped from a trough that ran along the top of the fence that bordered the gate, emptying out of the dog's eyes, nose, and mouth and rolling into the Moat, where it was quickly absorbed by the current.

The fence itself was built to crush the spirit, its black posts sprouting razor-sharp spikes at random intervals and angles so that any thought of trying to climb them was immediately followed by images of self-crucifixion. It ran so far to either side of the gate that I couldn't see to the end of it. And, even though this had been part of the report Astral had played for us when we wanted to know more about the Rocenz, I still felt my heart drop at seeing the entrance to hell and knowing that what lay beyond it would come for me sooner or later. The worst part was that I still didn't know how to carve Brude's name on the black metal face that growled at me like it was alive. And hungry.

Get it together, Jazzy. Granny May's warm voice had never been so welcome in my head. I saw her standing on her front porch, hands on her hips, the way she did every time I got ready to leave. Now I understood that she'd always despised those moments the same way she hated this one. But she'd get me through it, just like she'd helped me go back to a home full of raised voices and mistrust. Because I needed her to.

I turned to Raoul. "I don't suppose you've got an inflatable raft tucked into a secret compartment of your belt or anything?"

"No," he said. "But I have this." He pulled out his sword, banged it against the ground, and *voila*! It became a long staff that would be the envy of every one of Robin Hood's men.

"Did you learn that trick from what's-her-face?" I whispered, referring to Kyphas's old habit of transforming a regular human item like a scarf into a locally made and lethally sharp weapon.

He blushed. "A good idea is a good idea," he muttered.

"Okay. But I don't get yours."

He sighed. "And you ran track in college!"

"Wait." I held up my hands. "You want us to pole-vault over this river?"

"Not this stretch," he said, waving at the wide water before us. "But my scout said that it narrows radically down there." He pointed to our left.

I looked at Vayl, expecting a slew of logical and valid objections. He stared at me quietly, waiting for me to see the brilliance in my Spirit Guide's plan. At which point I grabbed the pole and stomped off in the direction Raoul had pointed, suddenly, unaccountably, furious. At some point Astral had jumped from her perch on Raoul's arm, and now she trotted beside me, flicking her ears toward me as if she wanted to catch every word.

"He thinks we're just going to gracefully vault over the water, like we're Olympic gymnasts or something. Can you believe that? I'm trying to save my damn mind and I don't even get the respect of a boat ride for my final mission. Because you know what's going to happen, don't you, Astral? My pole is going to get stuck in the mud. And if it doesn't sling me straight down into the waiting jaws of a sharkogator, I'll just end up stuck there, Jaz-on-a-stick, until I finally lose my grip and slowly slide down into the muck, which is probably worse than quicksand, at which point I will drown. Dumb damn Eldhayr." And yet I still strode on, because I couldn't think of a better plan, and part of me thought it'd be great fun. Especially if none of us were eaten alive.

Which led to Astral's dilemma. "Can you pole-vault?" I asked my robokitty. She shook her head. "I didn't think so. Okay, I guess you'll have to ride. But if you dig in those claws, I will have them chopped off. Just remember that. Now where the—oh. I see."

The bank pinched in on itself before me as if it were trying to bite into a particularly luscious piece of pie. Made, no doubt, of four and twenty blackbirds just like in that craptacular nursery rhyme my mom insisted on chanting to us right before lunch every damn day until we finally screamed at her to stop.

I halted at the narrowest spot, probed the water, and found it satisfyingly shallow while I waited for the rest of our merry band to catch up with me. Vayl came to stand beside me, brushing his shoulder against mine in the way he knew would instantly soothe me. I looked up at him. "I can't tell you how much this is sucking. Brude is tap dancing across my frontal lobe like he's wearing steel-soled work boots. I have no idea if we're going to be able to open up the Rocenz, so my stomach has shrunk to the size of a walnut. And yet my intestines have shifted into full gear, so if I don't shit myself before this is all said and done it'll be a goddamn miracle."

He smiled at me. "I adore you."

"Likewise."

"I have no idea how this will all end."

"Me neither."

"But we have been through other hells and survived. I believe that raises our odds somewhat astronomically. And as long as we are together, I think we can triumph over nearly anything."

Even death? I wanted to ask as I gazed into his eyes. And then I decided. *Damn straight! Nothing's stopped us yet. Why should I suppose hell itself could stand in our way?*

I handed him the pole. "You first, twinkletoes."

"I never told you I was considered something of an athlete in my day."

I looked his broad, muscular body up and down. And then took another, slower tour. My mouth had started to water. I licked my lips so the drool wouldn't escape as I said, "I'm not surprised."

Another quirk of the lips to let me know he knew what I was thinking and felt I should think it some more at a later date, out loud, when he could react in a more physically pleasing manner. Then he backed away from the bank, ran at the sucker like he meant to overpower it with his bare hands, landed the pole in the middle of the water and vaulted himself to the other side without even a grunt to show that he'd exerted himself in the process. He pulled the pole out and threw it across to me.

"That was a good spot I found," he called to us. "Do you think you can set it down in the same place?"

"Absolutely!" Lotus was the one who'd replied. She grabbed the pole from my hand, so happy to have discovered her niche in the netherworld that she'd leaped across the river before any of us could give her a serious lecture about how she should approach this jump.

Raoul caught the pole when Vayl sailed it across the next time. He tried to hand it to me but I said, "You go next. I've got to get Astral zipped into my jacket just right. Plus, with you three over there to catch, I'm pretty sure I'll have something soft to land on."

With a small grin and a nod he took the leap. Leaving me and the metal cat to consider our immediate future.

"You got an appropriate song ready for this one?" I asked her.

She poked her head out of the top of my jacket, pulled her lips back, and said, "Metamorphosis in five, four, three, two, one." Suddenly she went flat enough to slip down and curl around my belt.

"Oh, great, thanks for the vote of confidence. Now if I squish you, you're already only an inch high. Smart move, genius."

Maybe it was just my imagination, but I really thought I heard a round of tinny laughter accompany me as I walked to where Vayl had begun his run. Then I gave myself ten extra yards, which put me beside an arm whose hand gently waved in the breeze caused by its captured soul. I stared at it for a second. Then my sick sense of humor got the better of me. "I'd ask you to clap for me, but I can see that's out of your grasp. Maybe if you just snapped your fingers?"

When the hand slowly lifted its middle finger I began to laugh. The feeling lifted my feet into the fastest run I'd managed since a satyr named Lillyzitch had chased me through the Mall of America. I knew my speed was perfect when I hit the bank. I had my eye on just the spot Vayl had picked and Lotus and Raoul had followed. I'd aimed the pole true. Then a monster the size of a half-ton pickup rose out of the water, blocking the pole's path.

"Shit!" I yelled as Lotus, Raoul, and Vayl howled my name.

I rammed the pole into the hellspawn, whose slime-covered belly had rolled toward me during its ascent from the water. It punctured skin and muscle, throwing blood so high into the air that I felt the spatter blanket my skin as I flew over the top of it.

I landed in the water twenty feet from shore, still holding the pole since I knew Raoul would need it as his sword later.

"Change this pole into something I can use, Eldhayr!" I cried out, and the pole immediately transformed into a, well, a scarf. Damn. Didn't that guy have any imagination? I tied it around my neck and began to swim toward shore.

Vayl began yelling, "Fin to your left! Swim, Jasmine, swim!"

He ran to the bank, his cane sword unsheathed, as Raoul and Lotus slapped their hands on the water twenty yards to his left, trying to convince the creature they tasted better even though they were harder to catch. I put all my energy into carving my arms through the water as if it were a solid mass I could push myself through and paddling my legs like twin boat motors.

"It is gaining on you!" Vayl called. "Faster now!"

But I was already pulling top speed. Every muscle in my body was burning. I could sense the creature, hungry for my flesh, zeroing in on the section of meat it would tear away first. I began to wonder how bad it would hurt. Or if, maybe, my brain would be kind and send me straight into adrenaline overload and shock. I thought not.

Suddenly something splashed right next to me, startling me so much that I frog-jumped at least a foot forward. It was the body of the demon who'd sucker punched me. Vayl had hurled it into the path of the water monster. I risked a look as I moved back into escape rhythm and saw a maw full of jagged white teeth open wide and then sink into the corpse floating beside me.

That sight was enough to propel me into Vayl's arms. He held me tight, lifting me out of the water and pulling me so far ashore that my feet didn't hit land until we stood right next to the fence. I felt him shudder. Heard him whisper, "You are all right. Yes. You are just fine," and realized he was comforting himself as much as me. Then Raoul and Lotus were there, and Lotus was jumping up and down, slapping me on the shoulder. Raoul was hugging me so hard I couldn't breathe anymore. And Astral spoke loudly from somewhere around my belly button, announcing, "Metamorphosis in five, four, three..."

"Aaahhh! I gotta get her outta my pants before they rip to shreds!" I reached inside my belt and pulled the dripping robokitty from her pole-vaulting position just as she reinflated. It felt so bizarre to be holding her, like it might feel to hold a bag of popcorn as the kernels zapped into fluffly edible nuggets of goodness.

Finally I found enough breath to say, "Thanks for saving—" *What's left of my life? Let's not go there, okay?* "Yeah. I'm good. In fact—" I smiled up at Vayl, reclaiming Cassandra's positive attitude as I said, "When we get back we should probably get a pool and throw a shark or two in it to chase us around just to make sure we're getting a good cardio workout every day." When he chuckled I knew we were back in business.

He pulled me toward the gate to our right, Astral trotting between us, Raoul, and Lotus as he said, "Come. Let us finish this before we discover that hell's swimmers have grown shore legs."

I didn't quite yip, but I did nod and grab his hand tightly in mine as we hustled toward our ultimate goal.

I'll say this about journeys so important that old-fashioned dudes in armor called them quests. Somehow they always end too soon. Standing at the back entrance to hell, I wanted nothing more than to be a thousand miles away from it, still trying desperately to reach it. Because now that I was here, with Brude banging against the walls of my mind like his fists had transformed into ice picks while Vayl stood tall and grim beside me, reminding me of the price of failure, I'd never been so terrified in my entire life.

I squeezed his hand, feeling the ring I'd given him brush against my fingers, reminding me of the fact that I finally had a future worth fighting for. I'd even allowed myself to picture it in my mind, a dazzling piece of art built on remembered pain and new hope. As I stared at Satan's bloody gate, I decided I was damned if I was going to let some megalomaniac slash my dream to ribbons.

I said, "Vayl. I keep getting nosebleeds just like the mutt on this gate."

He replied, "This is true."

"Brude is slamming my synapses like he's found a damn drum set that he's just learning to play. And I've had it."

Vayl turned me toward him. Looked deep into my eyes. And kissed me, gently, as if we had all the time in the universe. He whispered, "I suppose, then, that is a sign that it is time?"

"I'm thinking so."

"I love you, Jasmine." He'd said it before. A lot. And maybe someday I'd get used to the words. But, oh, how they sang off his tongue like a soul-felt melody, wrapping around my heart and pulling it so close to his that I was sure they beat with the same rhythm.

I slid my hands around his waist, up his strong back, pulling his chest to mine until my breasts heaved into his. "I love you too, Vayl." I rose to my tiptoes and touched my lips to his, savoring the everlasting dance of soft skin and wet tongues as we sealed our own bargain. When I realized I'd gone breathless I dropped my heels back to earth. "What do you say we summon that cowboy?" I asked, managing a smile despite the pain behind my eyes and the fear in my gut.

"I like that plan."

I nodded, recalling the directions Kyphas had given me: *Stand by the gate, give it your blood, knock three times, and shout his full name.*

I looked up at my lover. Cleared the sudden blockage from my throat. I said, "Are we ready?"

He glanced over his shoulder at Lotus, Raoul, and Astral, who'd turned their backs to us to guard against attack. I was beginning to think it wasn't likely, this side of the river. Then a howl, so far off we'd probably only heard the echo, made them swing in that direction. Raoul looked over his shoulder. "Hurry," he whispered, as if the creature could hear us, even from that distance.

I nodded, drew my bolo, and sliced into the soft skin above my wrist. I made sure I had a generous supply of blood on my fingers before I swung around to the gate, drew a double slash across the mastiff's jaw, and then rubbed my offering into it. The metal trembled at my touch, soaking up the blood so quickly that within seconds I couldn't tell where I'd left my mark. Which I thought was weird, considering the generous portions flooding its face. But, of course, that was probably coming from hell's citizens. As an outsider's, mine probably tasted a whole lot better.

I knocked three times and yelled out, "Zell Culver! This is your summons! Come out and be questioned!"

On the other side of the gate a man ran out of the mist. He was sprinting across the rock-strewn ground with that look of abject fear you often see on the faces of those who are at the front of a mob of Black Friday Walmart shoppers. He wore a tattered brown shirt that he still kept tucked into the waistband of his darker brown trousers. Which were held up with an empty gun belt. Hmmm.

"Zell? Zell!" I yelled. He glanced my way. I peered into the fog behind him. I couldn't see or hear anything huffing, spitting, or galloping within half a mile of him. Good. That meant I'd only called the cowboy, not whatever had been chasing him. "Dude! You've escaped! Get over here, will you? I don't have that much blood to spare!"

He shot a look over his shoulder. The expressions that crossed his face—confusion, then relief, then even deeper bewilderment—would've been comical in any other situation. But the howling on our side had been joined by a joyful sort of hooting. And they'd both gotten closer. I began wondering if their makers could swim.

I said, "You're Zell Culver, right? The guy who destroyed the earthbane with the Rocenz?"

He jogged over to us, carefully wrapped his hands around the bars of the fence next to the gate, and said, "Only for a day." He grinned, showing a dimple on each cheek and another on his chin. "Sometimes I still think it was worth it, though." He tipped his hat to me, a wide-brimmed ancestor to the Stetson with a tall black band and battered flat top that looked like it had been used to beat off mosquitoes the size of his fists. However, perched back on his well-shaped head, setting off eyes that managed to twinkle even in these circumstances, it looked as comfortable as his scuffed old boots. "I don't believe I've had the honor to make your acquaintance."

I will only admit this because if I didn't Vayl would probably take out an ad in *The New York Times* calling me out. Zell's old-fashioned gallantry went straight to my head. My hand went all floppy like I'd suddenly been airlifted into the 1850s, where women routinely lost all muscle tension in their extremities. My limp fingertips raised to my neck, where they brushed my collarbone in an I-do-declare reaction to his chivalrous manners. And I said (yes, dammit, in a slight Southern accent), "Mah name is Jayaz."

Then I heard myself. Also Raoul snickering behind my back and Lotus muttering, "What the fuck?" while Vayl literally bit his lip to keep from laughing. I dropped my hand, thumping my fist into my thigh as I added, "I called you here for a reason. You're the only one we know of, besides an unhelpful demon, who's ever managed to separate the pieces of this tool." I pulled the Rocenz out of my belt. "It's imperative that you teach us how to do that." I jerked my head around as the sounds of hunting animals grew louder.

Zell shook his head sadly. "I'm sorry, I can't remember." He slowly rolled up his left shirtsleeve. What I saw crawled my fingers right around my neck. The place where his captors had carved away his tattoo had never healed. His entire forearm from inner elbow to wrist was covered with oozing sores and stank of gangrene.

Schooling my expression into carelessness, I reached into my jacket pocket and pulled out the piece of skin that had been cut from him. I unfolded it and showed it to him. "We recovered this recently," I said. "If we give it back to you, do you think you'll remember how the separation spell works then?"

He nodded. "There could be no other reason for them skinning me. It should work. Yes. I'm sure of it." He was still nodding when he said, "But first you have to promise to get me out."

"I promise," I said quickly before anybody else in the party could think of any objections.

He nodded. "Give me that knife."

Without question I handed him the hilt. He sliced into his bicep, grabbed the blood, smacked it into the back of the gate. Vayl and I barely had time to trade looks of dread before he'd knocked three times and yelled a name we both knew. She appeared as he had, running for her life, her ragged white dress flying out behind her like last decade's kite.

I stared as she went through the same emotions Zell had as she realized she'd been miraculously saved. It gave me time to gather my wits as well. Then I finally found the words I needed to say. "Vayl. Is there anything you want to tell me?"

Chapter Thirty-Six

Sunday, June 17, 9:00 p.m.

If people hang around me long enough, they learn that I don't appreciate surprises. Because in my case they rarely turn out to be pleasant ones. Take the time my darling sister decided to pay me a surprise visit in college. She walked in on a huge breakup scene and caught a flying vase in the middle of the forehead. I had to haul the poor kid to the emergency room and explain to the doctor why he was stitching up a wound meant for my "Sorry, Jaz, I just realized that I like guys" boyfriend.

So when I turned to my lover, he knew immediately that I was prepared to hurl objects large and small, probably starting with the robokitty, if he didn't come up with a reasonable explanation as to why a woman who looked exactly like my mother had joined Zell Culver on the opposite side of Satan's fence.

He cleared his throat. It was the first time I could remember seeing him sweat. And so he should. Because that wasn't the only problem I had with this amazing coincidence. The name Zell had uttered was *Helena*. The same name Bergman had labored under during our mission to Marrakech, when Vayl had been convinced we were all members of his household from 1777. Bergman had argued that he suffered the most, because Vayl had thought he was a girl—his adopted daughter. Which had all been fine and good then. When I didn't know what she looked like.

But I'd seen her before. Right here in hell. At the time I'd actually believed she was my mother, Stella. Mainly because she looked and talked just like her. But *she'd* helped save me from a bunch of howling demons, something Stella never would have done. At the time I'd convinced myself even a mother like mine would sometimes find a small store of generosity and love to act upon. Now I knew better.

You shoulda figured it out back then, scoffed my Inner Bimbo. She spoke to me from a tub full of steaming water and white bubbles. Stretching one long white leg out of the bathwater and idly watching her red-painted toenails point toward the showerhead she said, *Stella would never have helped you escape from hell. Shit, Jaz, she'd have clapped you in irons and arranged for some rank torture if it would've meant freeing that first husband of hers.*

At my core I knew that. But I'd wanted her, just once, to be a real mom so badly that I'd bought my own fairy tale. And I'd even had evidence to make me believe Helena was my mother. Because only someone of my bloodline could've left her mark on me, the curl of white hair that proved I'd been touched by a family member in hell. Which meant—

I grabbed Vayl's arm, as if he wasn't already tuning in to me so completely that the only reflection I could see in his eyes was my own. I said, "Your adopted daughter, Helena, is my ancestress." I didn't mean to sound accusing, but it sure came out that way. "You've been following my family's line since 1770!"

His eyes, a distant, steely blue, gave nothing away. "Yes, I have," was all he said.

Helena, smiling gently at us through the bars, said, "It's good to see you again, Jasmine, although I would choose happier circumstances." She looked up at Vayl. "And you, Father? Has Lucifer finally caught you?" Her voice broke a little, tears filling her eyes at the question, though she still kept hold of that angelic smile.

His brows crunched together as he turned to the girl he'd raised from the age of eleven. "My darling. What happened? How did you end up here?"

Helena had been standing in the circle of Zell's good arm. Now she slipped her slender fingers through the cracks in the fence. "Life was so good in America, just as you had promised us it would be," she began. I remembered, then, how Vayl had told me that she'd married a man named John Litton. That they'd moved to the States and that, a couple of years later, she'd died after giving birth to twins.

She continued. "We thought we had escaped Roldan. But we were wrong. He came into my room after my daughters were born. He and that monstrous gorgon that rides him killed me and tossed my soul into the pit. But I remembered everything you taught me," she told him proudly. "I fight here. Zell and I have organized a little pocket of resistance. It isn't much, I suppose. But it is what we need to survive."

Zell and I, I thought. *What a strange coincidence that you two found each other.* I looked at Vayl, waiting for him to find it odd as well, but he'd stopped thinking straight as soon as he saw his daughter behind the bars that he was now trying to shake with white-knuckled fingers. "We are getting you out. Both of you. Now!" he said, his voice as hard as the metal that stood between us and them.

"You already promised," Zell reminded him, the practical cowboy in him finding this display a little overwhelming and somewhat unnecessary.

"Yes, we did." Vayl spun to face me. "Jasmine, get that infernal demon out of your head. We have innocent souls to save."

I glanced at Raoul, wondering what his reaction might be, but he and Lotus were still scanning the horizon. Okay, mostly him. She was starting to jump every time the water bubbled or the wind sighed. So far she'd stepped on Astral's tail and nicked Raoul. I thought if she managed not to faint before a demon cut her to bits we'd be doing very well for ourselves.

I looked back at Vayl, who certainly hadn't included my soul among the innocents. *Huh. Well, okay, it might have a few black streaks.* But I suddenly felt relegated to the bottom shelf with last season's shoes and that old pile of *National Geographic*s that subscribers always feel too guilty to dump. Then he grabbed me by both arms and planted the most passionate kiss on my lips that either of us had experienced in at least an hour. When he was done I stood blinking at him, my mouth gaping like one of those fat goldfish at the botanical gardens that just keeps begging for food pellets despite the fact that one more will probably instantly transform it into eight boxes of McNuggets. His smile, scary enough to give kids nightmares, made me feel warm all under as he said, "My *avhar*, we are almost home."

I nodded as I worked my hand through the bars and offered the missing part of Zell's arm to him. He gave it to Helena, who unfolded it like it was no more problematic than a lace-trimmed hanky. Vayl and I traded intense looks. I could see his thoughts as clearly as he could read mine.

My darling Helena! What has she seen here? What has she been through these past 220 and more years? He didn't want to ask more than that, but I'd already given him the answer.

Your adopted daughter has walked through horror the same way you and I hike through your woods at night. Torture, maiming, pain, and battle are her life. She's not the girl you knew. But she's managed to survive this awful existence without losing the ability to love a cowboy or help a descendant being chased by demons. And that was because of what you taught her all those years ago. So you were a good father after all.

He reached for my hand, and I grasped his as tightly as I could manage while we peered through the bars at the two people who mattered most to us at this moment. "Look, Jasmine," he whispered. "It is as if Zell's skin was spelled to return to its former position!"

And, of course, it probably was. That's what happens when you tattoo a rune onto your forearm. Zell, being an English speaker, had translated it for himself. Slowly, as the edges of his existing tattoo melded with the severed portion and the dying tissue underneath began to heal, the words revealed themselves until I could read the entire phrase.

I pulled the Rocenz clear of my belt and held it in front of me as

I repeated the words now glowing a vivid red on Zell Culver's arm. "The soul splits, pairs and destroys, until it is one again."

The silver tool heated so quickly I was afraid I'd have to drop it. I was about to grab the hem of my shirt to use as a buffer when it reached maximum temperature and began to separate, a crack appearing right up the side of the handle of the hammer where it met the chisel. I grabbed the edges with both hands, not pulling, just holding each side firmly as a sound as loud as a rifle shot came from the tool and it tried to jump out of my hands. Again with the popping sound, four more times as the two parts of the Rocenz released one another. And, finally, I stood before the gates of hell holding Cryrise's hammer in my right hand and Frempreyn's chisel in my left.

I laughed out loud as Brude screamed inside my head and blood poured out of both my nostrils. "Go ahead, you fucker," I whispered to the *domytr*. "Throw the biggest tantrum you can manage. At the end of the day I'm still gonna rip you out of my head and smash you against this gate until there's nothing left of you but a moaning pile of mud."

Chapter Thirty-Seven

Sunday, June 17, 9:45 p.m.

I set the chisel that had been carved from the rail who'd failed to beat Lucifer at his own game against the bloody maw of the mastiff and hauled the hammer back for my first true blow against Brude since he'd invaded my head four weeks before.

"Wait!" Raoul's warning, bellowed from three feet away, nearly put me on my knees. "Remember the warning on the map that led us to the Rocenz in the first place!"

I turned to look at him, my eyes scanning the horizon for the source of the howls that still split the air intermittently as he pulled the rolled leather out of his pocket and unfolded it. Zell cleared his throat. In fact, he seemed to be on the verge of saying something a couple of times, but then he pressed his lips together and stared at the toes of his boots.

As soon as Raoul held the map so we could see it, he said, "The message at the bottom. It's clear, yes? 'Who holds the hammer still must find the keys to the triple-locked door.' That has to refer to Zell. We needed him. We needed his skin. And we needed the spell on his skin."

I didn't mention that the first key to Zell had been my Granny May. Or that the last key had been a demon. Neither one seemed like a comfortable subject to bring up at the moment. And since they had worked, it seemed doubly unnecessary.

Zell opened his mouth, but Helena put a hand on his newly healed arm and murmured something. Since her lips were partially hidden by the fence, I could only read the last part, which was, "for themselves." What did we need for ourselves? Before I could waste time guessing Vayl said, "I will agree with that assumption."

Raoul went on. "But the phrase at the top of the map must be just as important. More so, because it's mentioned first. 'Cursed and thrice cursed be ye who raise the Rocenz without offering proper dues or sacrifice. For Cryrise's hammer and Frempreyn's chisel may spell your salvation, or your doom,'" he read. He stared hard at us. "I hate to ask for theories on that meaning, because I know what kinds of ideas I'm having. I've only known demons' minds to track one way when they start talking sacrifice." His eyes went from Lotus to Astral to Vayl to me. Then he included Helena and Zell in his concern before he said, "I think this tool has to have blood before it will work properly. In fact"—he stopped, shook his head, forced himself to go on—"I think it needs death."

I shook my head. "I don't know. Back in Marrakech, Kyphas only had to rub her blood on it and chant a few words before she separated the parts. She was already working her heartstone when I found her."

Raoul held up his fingers as he ticked off his objections. "She's a demon. They can use the tool differently. She told you that herself."

"True," I admitted. I looked at Zell. "You got anything to add?" I asked.

He shrugged. "Nothing that will not make my tongue turn to ash inside my mouth the moment I say it. I can only confirm what you deduce on your own."

Vayl stepped forward. "Is that why you are here, Zell? Did they capture you and bring you to hell because you know all the secrets of this tool, and it is so valuable that they cannot risk allowing your soul to fly free?"

Zell nodded. "You hit that one on the head."

"And this last secret?" Vayl continued. "Are we on the right track?" Zell just stared. Vayl's smile looked a lot more triumphant than I felt. "I will take your silence as a positive sign." He turned to Raoul. "Let us assume Kyphas managed the death this tool requires and we never discovered that detail—"

"I say we give it what it wants." We all looked at Lotus, whose face had paled so drastically she looked like a mannequin before the makeup's gone on. The starkness of her expression, her absolute certainty amid all our doubt, made her seem more Vayl's progeny than anything else she'd done so far. "Then we can go, right? Then this whole nightmare will be over?"

I said, "Not necessarily for you, snookums." I kept my voice gentle as I pointed to Helena and said, "She was a good, honorable woman. And she's trapped inside, still being righteous, still fighting on the side she chose when she was just a girl. You, on the other hand, are still trying to turn your back on the pile of bullshit you've made out of your life when you're actually buried under it." I pointed to the souls that had chosen maiming and torture. "That's you if you don't start digging." I made a fist. "And I'm not helping you make it worse by killing someone in this crew."

Astral had been sitting quietly beside Raoul all this time. Now she stood up, looked over at me intently, and then stared at Lotus. "Grenade?" she offered politely, as if she knew exactly how I was feeling and had already figured out a quick way to rid myself of the unwanted company.

"Not at the moment, thank you," I told her.

"Maybe later, though," Raoul said.

We all looked at him. "What if we invite the noisemakers"—he jerked his head toward the howls we'd been monitoring since our arrival at the gate—"a little closer?"

"Are you sure you want to do that?" asked Zell. "Normally spiderhounds aren't creatures you fight. They're ones you hope you can outrun."

I stared him straight in the eyes. "I have to put this name on the gate, Zell. You, of all people, should understand why."

He nodded. "I have another idea. If it works, it might even get us out of here. But you have to trust me."

"No problem," I said. "Anybody else have any issues with trusting the cowboy?" I asked. Then before they could answer I did it for them. "Nope, we're all for your plan. Don't even bother filling us in. Just throw it in motion and we'll learn as we go."

Zell nodded and began stomping. It was hypnotically rhythmical, like the precursor to every stage show that had ever involved drums and heel taps. Helena joined him, linking her arm in his and adding a double stomp every fourth beat. Sometimes she would pause and grind her toe into the chalky soil, leaving a crescent moon–shaped indentation that, combined with all the others, began to look a lot like some of the spells I'd seen scrawled across pieces of ancient parchment.

While Zell and Helena performed their bizarre dance, my comrades pulled every blade they'd brought with them. Since my job was to bloody the Rocenz with its sacrifice, I gave Vayl my bolo. He held it in his left hand while his right continued to grip his cane sword, its sheath still lying at the foot of the gate, waiting for the final outcome.

Raoul held his shining weapon with both hands while Lotus gripped the dagger he'd lent her. They both stared off into the horizon thinking such different thoughts that it was a wonder to me that they could stand next to one another without small lightning bolts zapping into their brain stems until one of them finally blew a gasket.

I didn't see any weapons on Zell or Helena, though I sensed they were both carrying. Maybe it didn't pay to display, especially when you were basically walking around inside a huge prison all day long.

Astral, perhaps sensing the rising tension, paced restlessly among the four of us as if we'd caged her. Most often her nose pointed toward the source of the howls and a new, deeper rumbling that signaled many more than two or three creatures heading our way. It seemed like she already knew Zell's plan and her place in it. Especially when she leaped into my arms and said, "Hello!"

Suddenly the ground under my feet tilted. I grabbed Vayl's arm as Astral anchored her claws into the soft meat of my shoulder. Vayl wrapped his arms around my waist as another rumble of unstable ground moved us into an awkward fighting-for-upright dance.

Zell and Helena intensified their movements on the other side of the gate, barely acknowledging the dead earth beneath their feet groaning like an arthritic old man trying to get out of bed in the morning.

"Guys," Astral hooted.

"What?" I turned my head so my ear was next to her mouth. "What do the guys need to do?"

"Geyser coming!" she shouted just as a fountain of boiling-hot water shot out of the ground on Zell's and Helena's side of the fence, its perimeter inside the perfect circle I could now see that Zell and Helena had made with their boot, toe, and heel marks.

"Do you see how we did it?" Zell called.

"Yes," said Vayl.

"We're gonna need at least three or four on each side of the fence before the durgoyles will smell the water and come to drink." He didn't have to explain further. Durgoyles were hell's livestock, herds of four-leggers inhabited by the souls of those who had plodded through life with rings through their noses, allowing everyone from gangbangers to dictators to lead them into evil as if they were as docile and dumb as cattle. Bigger and meaner than full-grown moose, they fed on scavenged meat and spent most of their waking hours thinking up new ways to maim each other. If we could attract a herd, one of them could be sacrificed to the Rocenz. Unfortunately, where there were durgoyles, you could usually count on at least a couple of spiderhounds as well. Somewhat ironically, even death's realm had a circle of life, and the spiderhounds had managed to climb the food chain faster than the durgoyles. What a crazy flipping world.

What Zell had surmised was that we'd been hearing spiderhounds following a herd somewhere south of us. Now he wanted to turn the durgoyles our way. Which was an excellent plan since we didn't want to sacrifice any humans to the Rocenz. But none of us discussed the possibility that we'd probably have to fight their natural predators if we meant to get back to our world alive. Instead we paired up and joined Zell and Helena, copying their moves until every one of us, Vayl included, had become an expert at the watering hole dance. One by one geysers shot into the air, until we had to stand on the far right side of the gate in order to avoid being burned.

And still Astral continued repeating her message. "Geyser coming!"

"Okay, okay," I finally told her. "I gotcha."

"Do you think that is enough?" Vayl asked as we watched seven fountains stink up the atmosphere. They smelled of sulphur and unwashed ass. I couldn't imagine any living thing sticking its face in a concoction with such an obnoxious odor, especially one designed to boil your nose off the second you came within a foot of it. But within five minutes we could hear the steady clip-clop of what Zell estimated was a herd of between forty and sixty durgoyles. And Raoul said, "I see them! Horns on the horizon and closing fast!"

They emerged from the water-induced fog like a fleet of sailing ships speeding into view, their gray skins resembling stained sails, their protruding ribs reminding me of rigging. The yips and howls continuing at the back of the herd explained their speed. I don't know where they thought they were headed, but the plan definitely seemed to involve escaping the spiderhounds snapping at their hooves.

The doomed animals' horns grew straight out from their heads and then curled back in, so that the tips were constantly rubbing against their necks, leaving a steady trickle of blood that turned their forelegs a permanent rusty color. Flies pursued them relentlessly, buzzing in and out of their ears, forcing them to slap their hindquarters with whiplike tails that left bloody slashes, opening sores for the insects to lay eggs in, many of which had hatched and flourished, transforming the sores into oozing pits full of wriggling maggots.

As if they needed yet another reason to be permanently pissed.

Fights broke out at the brushing of a flank. Horns clashed almost constantly, filling the air with echoes of bone smashing against bone. At least once a day a durgoyle fell to its knees, where it was promptly trampled by the rest of the herd, which didn't moo like cows. The sound they made, and they did it with the frequency of New York car horns, squeaked through the air like dolphin calls, making me suspect my ears would also be bleeding before this episode had ended.

"I think I wanna kill them all," I said. "Is that a bad thing?"

"Just pick the one you want," Vayl told me.

"Wait," said Zell. "We need them to crash the gate first."

"And how are we supposed to do that?" I asked. "They're on the wrong side of the Moat."

Zell said, "Four of the geysers are over here. Half of them will cross just to drink this water." He nodded at Astral as a series of yips made us look beyond the herd. We still couldn't see the spiderhounds at its edge, but their calls were clearer than ever. "The durgoyles will think your cat is one of their predators. Not a spiderhound, of course, but perhaps a zenqual, who hunt in herds of sometimes twenty or more. I noted she can talk. Can she make special sounds too?"

"When she's in the right mood."

His eyebrows quirked. "Well, the zenqual often hunt silently, but many of them squeal like a hog at feeding time too. If you can get her to make that sound while you help herd them toward the gate, panic should do the rest."

I glanced over my shoulder at the huge metal edifice leering behind me. Even with the entire herd butting their heads against it at once, I doubted they could round up enough force to break open an entry that the devil himself had ordered closed until further notice. But it was worth a try. So I nodded as Raoul and Lotus went to the other side of the gate to make sure they'd be somewhat on the opposite edge of the herd once they moved into range.

The yips got louder and more frequent, assuring us that the spiderhounds had stayed on the durgoyles' tails. We became even more positive when the pace of the herd increased. When their heads came up, their ears swiveled, and they began to squeak at each other more often, we knew we'd be seeing predators sooner rather than later.

The first of the durgoyles hit the Moat without even hesitating, swimming strongly toward the geysers we'd danced out of the earth despite the depth of the river at this point. Luckily the current was slow enough that it didn't carry the creature far downstream at all. Within minutes half of the fifty head had joined it.

I pulled the cat, who'd been perching on my shoulder, into my arms. Somehow it felt important to maintain eye contact as I said, "You need to squeal like a pig as soon as the durgoyles hit shore so they'll run toward the gate. Make it seem like you're fifty cats, not just one. Can you do that?" I asked.

Her reply was a soft grunt that sounded an awful lot like contented pig. But I wasn't really sure until she headed toward the water and jumped in. As if I hadn't been impressed with Bergman's invention or the fact that he'd deigned to give it to me rather than sell it to some mega-rich country for enough dough to retire on, now I felt real affection for Astral as she emerged from beneath the water, swimming strongly against the current, and making pig squeals so authentic I could almost see the waller from here.

Unbelievably, every time she made noise, the durgoyles lunged forward as if they'd been tased. It began to be entertaining. Until we got a whiff of them.

"Whew!" exclaimed Lotus as she pinched her nostrils together. "They're in the frigging water! How come they still smell like rotting meat?"

"Because, in a way, they are," Raoul explained. "Now herd them toward the gate. Raise your arms. Yell a little. You should know a lot about that, thrillseeker."

She actually looked hurt, which amazed me. I glanced at Vayl and caught him smiling. Then the expression changed to one of intense concentration as he looked first toward Astral and then to me. "Be ready," he said. "Let us get this right the first time so you do not have to suffer any longer."

Which was why I so loved the guy. I'd tried not to complain anymore, but it had begun to feel as if my head might literally explode. Also, the rest of my body was now unaccountably sore, as if the nosebleed had reversed itself and spread, and now every organ had sprung a leak.

Astral cleared the water and ran to my side, where she paused long enough to shake all the water she hadn't yet shed onto my jeans. Vayl pointed to the nearest field and said, "There. Beside that torso wearing the Raiders sweatshirt. Do you see it?"

I did. Spiderhounds are easy to spot, mainly because their heads are covered with eyes. Thirty-two of them to be exact. Not all of them work at the same time or in the same way, which is what makes them such a dangerous enemy. But then, they are a vulnerable area on the animal, and one it pays to target. Because the hounds are also big, fanged, clawed, and vicious. If you can even partially blind them you radically increase your odds of survival.

This one, a pure white giant that made Jack look like a dachshund, was wagging its spiked tail up and down like it was about to play fetch with one of the feet that stuck out of the ground at paw level. I was about to signal the hound's location to Raoul when I realized one set of its eyes was the same shade of yellow as those I'd seen in Vayl's memories of Roldan. But in those visions his fur had also been covered with patches of black, proving this was just another coincidence. Like Zell finding Helena. I factored in the knowledge that Kyphas's eyes turned yellow when she was pissed off too, and decided that hell just preferred that color. So I shrugged it off and let Raoul know where the spiderhound was located. He quickly showed Lotus.

I leaned in to Vayl. "Do you see any other spiderhounds?" I asked.

He nodded. "The second is trotting at the back. I have only been able to see his eyes twice. They are glowing." Raoul signaled that he'd heard. And wasn't happy about it. Because it meant the alpha had come along for this hunt. Not unusual, but bad for us. Alpha spider-hounds, besides the obvious attribute of larger size, also carried sacs of poisonous spiders underneath their jowls. Not a threat from a distance, but if the alpha could put the bite on you, so could his little friends. By the tens of thousands. It was not a pretty way to die. I'd seen a couple of the corpses that had made it topside before succumbing. They'd all gone screaming.

Well, that wasn't how I planned to face my end. But if it happened here, while I was fighting beside the man I loved, nobody would hear me bitching when they found me looking up his address in the afterlife.

I tightened my hands on the Rocenz and wiped my nose on the hem of my shirt yet again. It wasn't fancy, just a black pullover, but I'd liked it once. Now the sucker was going straight to the rag pile when I got back home.

"They're coming," Zell whispered. "Get your cat ready." He and Helena were crouched beside the fence, their hands clutching the bars so tightly that the spikes had begun to cut into the edges of their fingers. To be free after all this time—I couldn't even begin to imagine what it might mean to them. Or how our failure could crush them. So I didn't try. I just crouched beside Astral, pointing out the durgoyles I wanted her to chase as soon as I gave the word.

I glanced up at Vayl, hoping for a little moral support. But his glance had crossed the Moat, where it was glued to the spiderhounds. They'd targeted an old cow that looked to be limping.

The squeals of the spiderhounds signaling their attack galvanized Zell as well. "Now, Jaz!" he yelled.

"Go get 'em, Astral!" I gave her a slight push and she took off, squealing irritably at the durgoyles as she waded into them, deftly weaving in and out of their paths, jumping clear of an irately jerked horn or kicked hoof. At first it seemed like all she was going to accomplish was to piss them off so much that they'd either find a way to stomp her into scrap or massacre each other trying. And then she sprang up and bit a big old bull in the butt. When she landed she began singing a Bloodhound Gang hit at top volume: "You and me, baby, ain't nothin' but mammals, so let's do it like they do on the Discovery Channel."

The bull had felt the double insult like it was a pitchfork thrown by the Great Taker himself. He jumped into the air so high that all four hooves cleared the ground at once, his eyes rolling whitely as he shrieked in panicked protest. Every durgoyle gate-side flinched as if it had been struck, and the air suddenly filled with high-pitched what-the-hell squeaks. Chaos broke out as mothers tried to protect their young, the young trotted in circles trying to figure out where the hell safety had gone to, older males each decided it lay in five different directions, and the biggest bull of them all trumpeted for the herd to get their heads out of their asses and follow him.

He came charging straight for Vayl. Who stood his ground like a Neanderthal determined to skewer some fresh protein for his starving tribe. My *sverhamin*, so fully channeling his inner Wraith that the tips of his curls had gathered frost, raised both hands over his head, his sword pointing straight at the fiery sky like it was a match he needed to light. The sudden gust of arctic wind whacked the bull on his brown nose, turning him directly toward the gate. His herd hesitated. Tried to turn. But Raoul and Lotus were on the other side, yelling, singing, and trying out their own version of pig squeals.

And then Vayl opened his mouth. From it issued a stream of tiny red crystals that blew off his tongue like frozen fire. And I knew it was the hellspawn's blood that he'd taken upon entering this realm, transformed into his own personal weapon, pelting the durgoyles into action. They followed the bull at a jump, thirty squeaking, flank-bashing, panicked lemmings headed straight off the cliff. Or, in this case, into the gate.

They crashed into Satan's doorway with the jaw-clenching sound of breaking bones, screaming wounded, and trampling hooves. Metal groaned. Hinges screeched. On the other side of the river the remnants of the herd milled and fought, as if they were irritated that their neighbors were making them wait to move on. The spiderhounds howled in triumph as their prey made a fatal mistake and wandered too far from her sisters. They pounced, each of them taking her at a different angle. The rest of the herd distanced themselves from her, ignoring her dying screams in the I'm-glad-it-wasn't-me way of the future victim.

On our side of the river the pile of dead and broken durgoyles grew as the herd continued its mindless assault on the gate. It didn't give in the middle, where the two doors met. Instead the bottom set of hinges on our side splintered so badly that they fell to pieces at our feet. The durgoyle who'd made the break shoved the gate aside. It swung back and smashed into the bull behind it, tangling in its horns, forcing it to its knees, where it formed a living door prop for the rest of the herd.

I eyed the spiderhounds feasting noisily on their kill. "Should we take them out next, while they're distracted?" I glanced at Raoul, then at Lotus, not sure which of them could come up with the most dastardly game plan for this particular creature.

Raoul shook his head. "If you can finish your business before they're done eating, we should be able to slip past them. In this case I agree with Zell. It's better to avoid a fight than to force one."

I glanced at Zell, momentarily forgetting that he couldn't hear our Party Line conversation. He'd been busy glancing over his shoulder. Now he had Helena by the hand and they were moving to cross over. He said, "Whatever you have to do, rush it. They'll know the gate is breached. People will come to escape. Demons will come to stop them. We're out of time now."

"I'm on it." Without wasting another second I turned one of the dying durgoyles. Feeling like an old-school biblical figure I whispered over it, "Uh, so you're the sacrifice. If you promise not to gore me, I'll make this quick and painless." It fulfilled its side of the bargain, so I did too, watching the relief flit through its brown-on-brown eyes as its blood coated the Rocenz and what remained of its hellish life slipped away.

The two parts of the tool shivered in my hands as indentations appeared beneath my fingers, giving me a better grip for the job ahead of me. I waited for Zell and Helena to slip through the opening in hell's gate. And then I set the chisel onto its surface.

Less than three weeks before I'd watched Kyphas use this same tool to mark Cole's name onto her heartstone. Until now I'd never wondered what it had felt like for her to raise the shining silver hammer and bring it down, *clang!* onto its brother. Now I understood the look of ecstasy I'd seen on her face. Though our motives were as different as heaven and hell, our feelings, as they often had, ran parallel. Power, baby. Fiery energy running up my arms and into my body until I felt like I could touch a dead heart with a single finger and jolt it into action again.

I realized I was grinning as the B took shape on Satan's gate. The *domytr* inside my head beat his fists against the walls of his cell so relentlessly that the pain behind my right eye finally shut it down. Half-blind, bleeding from my nose and both my ears now, I laughed aloud as I chiseled the R and then the U. I could feel Brude draw the tattoos that covered his arms and chest together into the armor that had protected him so well against Raoul's attack back in Scotland. Now I thought of it more as a shroud as I tapped the letter D into hell's doorway.

Behind me I heard Lotus yell, "Something strange is—watch out! The spiderhounds are…changing! Goddammit, you should never have let them get this close! Why don't any of you people have guns? Oh my God, they're not what we thought they were at all!"

Vayl said, "Lotus is right, Jasmine. The spiderhounds are slipping their skins. They may be some other form of spawn we have never seen. Whatever they are, I believe they have tricked us into taking this path in order to regain the Rocenz. Right now they are raising some sort of bridge from the bottom of the Moat."

I couldn't have spoken if I wanted to. All my inner girls were running around like disaster victims, some screaming mindlessly, some weeping. Even Granny May was pacing frantically while she bit her fingernails like she hadn't eaten for a week. I felt Vayl, Zell, Raoul, and Astral arrange themselves behind me, readying themselves for the fight, protecting me from yet another attack. Lotus was just pacing, muttering, swearing at anyone who seemed easily blamed. I didn't want her to distract me. But when she fell over the cat, I was suddenly grateful, because it reminded me of what Astral had said to me before our descent.

"Don't look!" I yelled as I continued the work. "They're not really spiderhounds. I was right! The one with yellow eyes *is* Roldan! Which means the alpha is his gorgon. So whatever you do, don't meet her eyes. If you do, you'll be destroyed!"

"Turn around!" Vayl called as Raoul bellowed, "Face the gate! The alpha's eyes are transforming into snakes!"

Believe it or not, I was relieved to hear that I was right. Gorgons have this odd code of honor. They'll kill you, oh yeah, in about three hundred different ways, starting with the whole paralyze-you-with-their-steely-vision trick. But they will not attack unless you're facing them. So I knew that as long as my people kept their nerve I could continue cutting the cords that had connected the *domytr* to me.

Only a few remained, and my inner girls—having received at least a short reprieve from certain death—hacked those free like a bunch of slayers out for a midnight run. When the final connection snapped they cheered as the locks fell from the cell that Teen Me and I had trapped Brude in. The door creaked open to reveal his ghostly form standing in the middle, head down in defeat, arms hanging loose at his sides as he faded into mist. The moment the final droplet disappeared from my mind, a shimmering form began to take shape just on the other side of the gate.

It wasn't a clean transition, like a beam-me-up-Scotty moment in which the traveler arrives even cleaner and tidier than when he left. As I worked on the E, Brude began to convulse. Wounds appeared on his chest, arms, legs, even his face. *Funny. The more he bleeds, the better I feel.*

My sight came back first. Then my headache disappeared, along with the bleeding from my ears and nostrils. As I put the final cut into the gate, I felt a satisfaction like an actual weight leaving me, though no physical burden could've been as hard or heavy to bear. On the other side of the twisted metal dog, the last image of Brude fell to his knees, so roundly defeated I wouldn't have been surprised to see him beg for mercy. But he just knelt quietly and waited the three beats it took for his fate to catch up to him.

I pulled the Rocenz away from the gate. Staring proudly at me, he said, "You could have been my queen," as his skin, his hair, even his eyeballs began to leak fluid like a faulty radiator. As the thick pink liquid flowed into the ground, small beetle-like creatures with barbed tongues and pincers at the ends of their tails scuttled out of their holes to slurp it up, and then to explore the source of their unexpected snack. They swarmed up Brude's legs while his body steadily shriveled, melting into their mouths like a finely cooked pork roast.

When the creatures reached his chest it got hard to watch. But I reminded myself of what this *domytr* had put me and mine through. What he'd tried to pull on the Great Taker himself. And what that might've meant to the Balance if he'd managed to succeed. I didn't even blink when the muscles in his jaw failed, his mouth dropped open, and the skin-suckers scurried inside. He didn't scream long.

I waited until nothing was left of Brude but the elements his body had been made from. Then I reached out to Vayl. "He's gone," I whispered.

His hand tightened on mine nearly to the point of pain, clear communication of the depth of his relief. "You are free."

"Not quite," said Raoul. "I've been watching the gorgon out of the corners of my eyes. She's raised a bridge."

Lotus sounded close to hyperventilation when she said, "It's made out of scum-covered skeletons. Oh my God, oh my God, oh my—" I put my hand on her arm, squeezing hard enough to make her stand still.

I said, "Skeletons with souls trapped inside, Lotus. The souls of people who'd made themselves into doormats in the world just so they could manipulate the strong into doing their dirty work for them. Now they've discovered how eternity feels about those who let others trample them just so their families and friends will be forced to shoulder the load."

She drew a sobbing breath. "I don't want this."

"No."

"It's not too late?"

"Lotus, you deserve better than this, don't you think?"

"Yes."

"Then act like it!"

She dropped her face into her hands, and I thought she was crying until she began to report on what she was seeing from the corners of her eyes, "The bridge is wide enough for a couple of cars to pass, but the footing will be iffy. It could work to our advantage. Or not. My guess is that as soon as it's completely clear of the Moat, the gorgon and her slave will start their crossing."

"Her slave is a werewolf that hasn't yet changed," Raoul told her. "He's moving so slowly you'd almost think he likes his man form better. Also, just so you won't be surprised, Jaz, the alpha's nest of spiders is now the gorgon's necklace of scorpions."

Zell turned to Helena and sighed. "I've never fought a gorgon before, have you, dear?"

"No, but you've told me how to kill scorpions and snakes. And surely they can't be any tougher than strangling a krait."

"You got yourself a point there. We will just think of her as a nest of nasties and fight her that way."

Nice to know the cowboy and his immigrant bride had a plan. As for me and my vampire? He smiled down at me. "It looks as if our training is about to pay off, my dear. Shall we make the CIA proud?"

I pulled my sword, so high on my new freedom that I didn't care if it sounded obnoxious as I said, "It's a good thing Astral's here to record this. Now we can put on a show the rookies will be studying for years to come."

Vayl's dimple appeared as Zell asked, "Then what are we waiting for?" He glanced at Helena as he pulled a roughly made weapon from the seam of his homespun pants. It looked less like a dagger than like an extra-long bolt with a handle on one end and a hand-sharpened point on the other. She smiled at him, flipped up the skirt of her dress just long enough to give her access to the bowie knife she had stowed there, then dropped it back down again.

"Why Granny H," I murmured, gaining raised eyebrows from Vayl and a broad smile from her. "What a big knife you have there."

She nodded once. "I took it off of the carcass of my first kill. I had to smash his head in with a rock." She grimaced. "Awful business, that. I wouldn't recommend it to the easily nauseated." I caught just a hint of her former accent. Once strongly British, it also had nearly surrendered to the onslaught of hell's eternal attack. And yet, when she smiled at Zell with that glow of love in her eyes, I couldn't help but admire her for hanging on to what really mattered.

Granny May had fallen into her front porch chair and found a hand fan from church emblazoned with the words GOD BE PRAISED, and in smaller print, SHOP YOUR HOMETOWN GROCER, which she was using to give herself more air as she openly admired our forebear. *Well, that explains where we get it from. I guess you can't beat heredity after all.* She stared at the cheap paper set into a balsa wood handle, watching its almost hypnotic back-and-forth movement as she said, almost to herself, *Even when your mother spends her whole life trying. I wonder what she couldn't face. Hmm. I really should look her up sometime. After being dead all these years, maybe she'd finally feel free to tell me.*

Raoul's voice interrupted my inner monologue. "I'm thinking that as soon as the gorgon and her pet are halfway across the bridge we should turn and attack. It's a fairly wide crossing so that if a couple of us can get behind them, considering that we've got them well outnumbered and most of us are skilled fighters, hopefully they'll see reason and surrender quickly. Is everyone happy with that idea?"

"I'm scared of snakes," Lotus said in a wavery voice. "But I've been in my share of bar fights. In fact, I once shoved a stiletto through a guy's eye. Purely out of self-defense, I'd like you to know. Just saying—I can hold my own out there."

I glanced up at Vayl, realizing instantly that he had no idea how to digest this new information about his daughter. Finally he said, "I do not care for snakes either." And when they traded small grins, he was happy that was the route he'd chosen.

At a nod from him we raised our weapons and spun, steeling ourselves for the battle that lay ahead of us. Among the six of us, seven counting Astral, we must've seen it all. And yet we still froze, stunned into paralysis by the scene that lay before us.

Chapter Thirty-Eight

Sunday, June 17, 11:45 p.m.

Gorgons are, first and foremost, death-eaters. They haunt battlefields and burn wards. Nursing homes—not so much. Because they love riding their victims through time, sucking up the soul's reluctance to move on, like kids at a candy counter. And young souls work so much harder to beat death than old ones. They say gorgons can survive for centuries on the backs of seven-year-olds. The fuckers.

You can't see them in the world unless they're about to make a deal. But you might get hints. Maybe you'll catch them in a stray expression that doesn't quite fit your husband's face, or a disturbing personality quirk in your sister that appears suddenly after a nearly tragic accident that the doctors explain as the result of brain damage. It's not dead brain matter, it's a gorgon. Sliding up against your sweetheart's back like the strumpet she was born to be, clutching him so tight he can only breathe when she inhales for them both.

But in hell? Yeah, we could've seen her clearly if we'd wanted to spend the rest of eternity as statues. But since we all enjoyed mobility, we caught her in darting glances as she advanced across the bridge, pulling her all-you-can-eat-buffet behind her on a delicate silver chain that must've been hidden in his fur when he'd been masquerading as a spiderhound.

Roldan, I thought as I exchanged a shocked glance with Vayl. *Oh, how the mighty have fallen.*

In the world, with the gorgon riding him like a shadow, he'd held himself like the most-wanted villain he was. Gawd, how long had his gaunt, hard-eyed face stared at us from the kill-'em-if-you-can bulletin board in Pete's office every time he called us in to assign a new mission? A king among cutthroats and thieves, the Sol of the Valencian Weres had gained so much status with his decimation of NASA's communication centers in California and Madrid that his following was threatening to become a worldwide cult. Not so shocking to see him touring the netherworld, considering his worst enemy (Vayl) and dearest love (Helena) had managed to find each other again. But as we watched him connected to his parasite by a single thin metal cord, we understood what he'd really become.

"No wonder he didn't want to take human form," Lotus said in a hushed whisper. "While he was still a spiderhound the gorgon kept leaning down and hissing into his ear. Slapping him on the back of his head, even flicking at his eyeballs. Nothing. Then she found that chain, yanked it a couple of times, and suddenly he stood up and became... that."

Now the man he'd been born to become, he shambled behind the gorgon aimlessly, trying to wander off the path until she jerked him back to heel, blood trickling unheeded from the spot on his neck where the collar had cut into his skin. In wolf form he was a fearsome hook-fanged creature with black claws and fur generously patched in black. That had been one scary monster. The spiderhound form had been even more fearsome. This? This was a skinny old man with sunken eyes and receding gums who kept trying to draw the number eight in the air, and then forgetting how to finish the final loop, forcing him to start all over again. Then I reminded myself. This piece of shit had been responsible for the deaths of Ethan Mreck and my old boss man, Pete. He was going. Fucking. Down.

"The old man I can take. But I've never had to battle a gorgon,"

Lotus noted nervously. "If Zell and Helena are going for the creepy-crawlies, what am I supposed to target?"

We waited for Raoul's word on the subject since it had been his plan in the first place. "Gorgons are very nearly godlike," he admitted. "The best we can hope for is to harry her until she finds us too painful to deal with and decides to go play with easier prey. So, Lotus, just try to make her bleed."

"I'm a lot better with the sword than I used to be," I said, "but damn, Raoul. Considering her defenses, that's kind of a thin plan."

"If you can think of anything heftier, speak up," he said. We were in such desperate straits he didn't even sound irritated.

Vayl said, "Why did it have to be snakes? Her hair could have been crawling with rats and I would have gladly faced her a thousand times over."

I didn't have to look at him to know his jaw was tight as a vise. I reached for his hand and gripped it. "I'll make you a deal," I whispered. "I'll protect you from those snakes if you agree to get me out of the assassination business."

He looked at me sharply. "You are finished?"

I looked at him squarely. "I risked my soul for my country. I carried a damn demon around inside me for the good old US of A. I think I've done enough, don't you?"

He squeezed my hand. "What if you find you miss it?"

"I figure Bergman can keep us busy enough to make sure we're never bored. But this way I can say no to the missions that make my skin crawl. Plus I can make time for my family whenever they need me." I raised our hands like we were about to shake. "Deal?"

"You know I would do nearly anything to avoid those serpents. But this I would have done in any case." He raised my fingers to his lips, kissed them, and said, "Deal."

Feeling about fifty pounds and ten years lighter, I said, "I don't guess anyone brought a mirror?" Silence all around. "Didn't think so. Well, that whole reflect-the-evil-eye-back-on-the-nasty-gorgon scheme probably never worked in the first place."

As the bridge continued to rise from the depths of the Moat and the gorgon led Roldan to its front edge we moved to meet them. Waiting silently at our end of the bridge, hands gripping our swords or rubbing the sweat off on our jeans and then finding a new, more comfortable position on our weapons, we watched the bridge rise to its zenith. Water poured from the jaws, femurs, and shoulder blades of flesh-picked bodies that had been interlocked so tightly that you couldn't tell where one began and another ended. What you could make out clearly were the moans and groans coming from the souls trapped inside them. And we were supposed to step on these people? Desecrate their skeletons, break their bones under our feet just so we could fight and probably die on top of them?

Hell yeah! yelled Teen Me. *Stop being so melodramatic! They sucked. Now they're paying. Just get on with it, okay? I have a life to live. It sounds like it's going to be übercool and I'm going to be so mad if you die before you're even thirty. Plus we have to pee.*

All excellent points. So when the gorgon and her pet werewolf reached mid-bridge I was ready. I didn't even flinch when Raoul yelled, "Charge!" like some damn cavalry captain. I just hauled off right along with Vayl, Zell, Helena, Astral, and Lotus, and followed his orders to the letter.

I'd never fought a gorgon on a bridge made from scum-covered skeletons. As Lotus had predicted, it's a tricky proposition. First of all, the footing sucks. Also, the footing sucks. Which is what I discovered the first, second, and third times I fell into the water.

"Fuck!" became my battle cry as I fought beside some of the toughest warriors I'd ever encountered. And for once I wasn't the biggest potty mouth in the bunch.

"Take that, you manky bitch!" cried Lotus as Raoul's sword found an opening, causing the gorgon to spin toward them. Lotus shoved her dagger at the monster's face with such hope in her eyes that I felt her disappointment in my own heart when she missed wide and nearly went all cementy before Vayl yelled a reminder at the last second for her to avert her eyes.

"Fuckaroo!" she cried. "That was too fucking close to shitsville for me!"

"Lotus!" Vayl objected as he dodged a lunging snake and spun aside to make room for Zell to move in low with a stab to the gorgon's thigh that Helena followed up with a slash at her ribs, which also connected.

"What?" Lotus demanded, backing off before the gorgon's nest of hair-snakes could reach out and turn her into a quivering blob of poison-filled organs.

I sighed as I pulled myself out of the water—again. "I think your language offends," I explained, having been on the receiving end of that tone many times myself.

She huffed. "It's how I talk! It's how I was raised, for shit's sake!" I put my hand on Vayl's arm as he twitched, all his dreams of a well-bred daughter going up in flames when Lotus added, "Speaking of which, let's take this gorgon down quick, shall we? I'm in dire need of a crapper."

"Did my child just say 'crapper'?'" he asked the world at large.

"Yeah," I told him. "But you should look at the bright side of this."

"There is a bright side?" he asked incredulously.

"Of course. At least she's potty trained."

With Roldan pretty much a no-show—he barely noticed he was surrounded and seemed to have no desire to take on his wolf form and jump into the fight—we concentrated on his mistress. While Lotus took wild pokes with her dagger that sometimes landed, the rest of us took turns making the gorgon wish she'd stayed topside chowing on the old wolf's mortality where she could digest in peace. Looking back, I have to think the battle would've gone down in history as a lot more militarily important and politically influential than it ended up being if I'd just kept my mouth shut. But, uh...

I said, "Roldan, you mangy old mutt. How on Earth did you talk yourself into rolling over for some cobra-haired bitch who wouldn't give a shit if the moon became a strip mine?"

His vacant gaze, which had been wandering across the landscape like a dreamy painter's, locked on to mine. "What did you say?" His lips drew back from his unbrushed teeth, and even from ten feet away I could smell the stench of decay blasting out of his throat. It was as much a psychic odor as a physical one, making my brain shrink for cover. And I realized, looking into eyes whose spark had nearly suffocated, that what I scented was the rot of a living soul.

Vayl explained, "Jasmine likes to needle people into a murderous rage before she kills them. Otherwise she feels it is not a fair fight and the guilt is more difficult for her to bear afterward."

Oh. Is that what I do?

Roldan's eyes widened. It wasn't the first time they'd crossed Vayl's face. But now I could tell he was seeing the vampire for the first time. "Vasil Brâncoveanu," he hissed. The snakes in the gorgon's hair echoed him. Only because I was watching closely did I see a fine shudder shake Vayl's hands in response to the gorgon's wriggly do. Then he forced himself into stillness as he lowered his head slightly in acknowledgment. Roldan's boss lady whispered into his ear, and his head turned until he could see Helena standing between Zell and Raoul, her bowie knife dripping with the gorgon's blood. He held out both hands. "My Helena."

He walked to the end of his chain but the gorgon held him back. And I realized this little jaunt to hell must've been her idea. What was she gaining from it? More juice from a soul that had shriveled to nearly nothing? The fun of torturing her longtime partner by showing him that he really hadn't punished Helena after all? Or was she really trying to give him a gift by killing us all for him? I couldn't tell.

While I tried to guess her motives, Zell put an arm around Helena's shoulders and both of them raised their weapons in response to Roldan's advance. Zell said, "Helena is mine. And I'm hers. That's how it's been for over a hundred and fifty years, and that's how it's gonna stay."

Wow, romance in hell. Who knew? My Inner Bimbo had made it back to the bar, where she'd settled in at her favorite table. Now she raised her hand. *Oh, waiter? Bring me a goddamn martini! Extra olives on those little sticky thingies!* She drew a picture in the air, holding an imaginary plastic sword with one hand while she pointed to a couple of imaginary olives with the other. How strange that the image she drew in the air was exactly like the nearly-number-eight Roldan had been tracing.

Before I could make sense of the similarity Roldan spun around, nearly tripping over the chain that bound him as he grabbed his gorgon by the shoulders. "Is this why you brought me here, Sthenno? So you could shred my heart into even smaller pieces than you do every single day?"

Raoul made a sound, soft enough that it didn't distract our foes, but loud enough to catch my attention.

"What is it?" I asked softly.

"Sthenno isn't just any gorgon," he replied. "She's one of the original three. Her list of crimes is so long there's a whole bookcase reserved for her in the Hall of Monitors. But what matters most right now is that she's the mother of Lord Torledge."

"Wait. What? The demon who made the Rocenz? *That* Lord Torledge?"

"Exactly. And he despised her, Jaz. I mean, we know of at least two separate occasions when he tried to kill her."

My brain spun into action. Lord Torledge had crafted the tool I'd defeated Brude with for demon hands, though I'd never been convinced its original purpose was to turn humans into spawn, as Kyphas had attempted with Cole. Or that Torledge had ever imagined humans would be able to reduce demons to their most basic elements with it. As with all magically imbued items, the Rocenz had shown itself to be full of unexpected surprises.

What had been predictable was the fact that the Rocenz could separate Sthenno from Roldan, and if that happened they'd both die. Especially here, where Sthenno had no other willing soul to host her. This had to have been why Torledge originally designed the tool, so that he could trap his mother and her dinner partner in hell where whoever was carrying the Rocenz at the time would be forced to vanquish her.

So all Torledge had to do was let the Rocenz be "stolen" and wait for Sthenno to hook herself up with the right partner. Once she'd made the deal with Roldan, and Torledge recognized the Were's hatred for Vayl, he knew these were finally the perfect circumstances for murder. He just needed to figure out a way to lure them both into his realm. Allowing Roldan to throw Helena into the pit must've seemed a brilliant plan, especially after he managed to hook her up with Zell, the only man on the plane who knew how to operate the Rocenz. After that, all he had to do was add Vayl to the mix, but that turned out to be more difficult than it sounded. Enter Brude, who (probably also manipulated by Torledge) formed a partnership with Roldan. Together the two of them pushed Vayl and me closer and closer to the abyss, until we finally had no other choice than to jump, bringing the Rocenz to hell's gate, Zell Culver to the exact spot where he could be of the most help, Helena between Vayl and Roldan, and Sthenno into a no-win situation. Because, despite knowing all about Lord Torledge's dirty damned dealings now, there was still no way I was going to let his mother win this battle.

"Fuck me."

"Jasmine!" This time it was Raoul objecting to my choice of words.

"Sorry, I just think, wherever I look lately, I end up deciding I'm working for the wrong damn people."

"We can make good come from it."

"You're Eldhayr. You're supposed to believe stuff like that."

"So are you."

I thought about that while I watched Roldan confront his gorgon. He'd been yelling at her for a while. Working himself into a frenzy of spittle-on-the-lip fury because she'd made him witness the love of his life with another man when all the time he'd thought she was in utter misery here. He was outraged that she'd used him so badly over the centuries, leaving his heart-sworn enemy hale and hearty while he had been reduced to little more than a bag of bones under her care.

When I dared a glance at Sthenno, it was to see her staring at him calmly, a small smile pasted across her paint-me-and-be-instantly-famous face. Finally two of her snakes sank their fangs into him, one in each shoulder. His knees buckled. She lifted the chain to keep him from falling flat on his face. Watching him shudder as his body tried to say uncle and his soul fought to stay at anchor, she finally pulled him into her embrace, pressing his head between her breasts. It would've been a loving gesture in anyone else. But for her it meant convenience, allowing her to reach down his back and claw his shirt up over his shoulders. I winced at the thousands of marks on his back, like unhealed mosquito bites, some of which had turned black and begun to leak a dark, oily fluid that looked like it should never come from a human body.

Sthenno looked down, giving me a chance to scope out her face, which (if you managed to ignore the snakes) seemed to me to be the perfect combination of high cheekbones and pouty lips that every woman dreams of but only plastic surgery pulls off. Even I felt slightly envious at those perfectly sculpted brows and thick black lashes. Until something pink and worm-like emerged from the inner corners of her meet-their-gaze-and-die eyes.

They stretched down both sides of her nostrils, over her lips, down her neck, and onto Roldan's hair. Still stretching, wriggling from her eyes, they moved as if they knew exactly where they were going. And when they reared up, revealing two small, three-fanged mouths, before they buried them in Roldan's back, I believed they did.

So this was how Sthenno ate Roldan's death. Every day she killed him, and then she chowed down. It made sense. She wouldn't want him to die naturally. What if she wasn't ready with the utensils at just the right time? Her meal could actually cross over and then she'd be in a world of hurt. Which was just where we needed to put her.

I whispered to Raoul, "Okay, so we need to use the Rocenz on her. But how? I don't figure her name on the gate is going to work the same way it did on Brude, even if we could convince Roldan to do it."

"No," said Raoul. "We need her heartstone. Remember the one Kyphas had? It will be locked inside her chest."

"Oh, that'll be easy to snatch."

Vayl spoke up. "What is that saying? I like it quite well. Jasmine?"

I wanted to stick out my bottom lip, but it seemed a little immature to pout in the middle of Satan's playground. So I just said, "There's no time like the present."

"Yes," he said with such immense satisfaction that I found myself smiling instead as I watched him blast his way in, swinging his sword right at the wormlike appendages that were just now withdrawing from Roldan's pockmarked back. But Sthenno's snakes had been keeping watch while she was busy, and their reach was much longer than he'd anticipated. He jumped back just as a cobra that was bigger around than and twice as long as my arm darted toward him, its jaws open so wide I could see the pink of its throat.

I lunged forward and hacked the snake's head off, which caused Sthenno to scream with pain and rage. She tucked her little soulsuckers back into her eyes and turned them on me, trying to transform me into Jaz-granite. But I avoided her glare as I leaped in for another shot. This time I missed, but hitting hadn't been my intention. I just wanted to distract her long enough to give Zell and Helena a chance to step up. Which they did. Zell danced past the snakes just long enough to slam his bolt-knife into Sthenno's side while Helena threw her knife so accurately that she decapitated another snake and still had time to rescue the blade before falling back to stand beside her cowboy.

We continued to hassle the gorgon, feinting, waiting for mistakes.

As a result she, and Roldan, were becoming more and more infuriated. The Were, especially, was bitching out his gorgon like they were an old married couple.

He said, "Why don't you just kill them? It's only my worst enemy and the woman I confessed to you that I could never live without. Right here! In hell! Why don't you tear them to pieces already?" he demanded.

I couldn't get past it. Even in dotty old man form this was the Sol of the Valencian Weres. Why was he just talking? Why hadn't he made a single attempt to wound one of us? Or better yet, why hadn't he changed? Even in hell I had to figure he could transform pretty much at will. So why was he stamping his feet like a three-year-old demanding a second piece of cake for dessert?

Because he wants you to win, whispered Granny May from her seat on the porch. *He's old and tired, worn to the bone from the looks of it. He's trying to distract her, throw her off her game without seeming to, so you can dig out that heartstone and chisel her name onto it.*

I stared at him thoughtfully. *No, not her name*, I told my Granny. *I don't think that would work. But the glyph that he was drawing in the air, the almost-number-eight that our Inner Bimbo was retracing when she was demanding her drink before*. I pointed to our fast-and-loose girl, who'd leaped to the stage and was now singing along with two other karaoke stars. *That, I think, will do it.*

Then what are you waiting for?

The snakes, there are so many of them, and it seems like for every one we decapitate two more grow in its place. We need, I don't know, a couple of eagles or something. They eat snakes, don't they?

Granny May nodded at me, her eyes wandering over my shoulder to let me know my attention should be moving elsewhere pronto. *Eagles I can't do. But what about those two?*

I turned my head and, though I know I should've been pissed, I can admit here at least that I'd never in my life been so glad to see Dave and Cole come darting through the field, taking cover wherever they could find it. Often that meant lying prone while a fence of forearms waved in front of their eyes. Or sliding into the shadow of a row of bodiless legs, their shredded connections screaming silently of chainsaw disasters and land mines.

"Geyser coming!" Astral said triumphantly.

"Oh!" Finally I understood her message. Dave and Cole had probably found a way to tap into one of her databases to message me that they were on their way. Only, given the circumstances with the durgoyles, I'd completely misunderstood.

I allowed myself a second to feel relieved that Cole had survived his solo stint in hell, and to be thankful that he'd given us the time we needed to get to the gate in the first place. Then I whispered the news on the Party Line, and Vayl and Raoul quickly let Lotus, Zell, and Helena in on it. Together we intensified our attacks, doubling up on Sthenno while Roldan screamed his frustration and did absolutely nothing to help.

Though we managed to avoid the snakes, the gorgon began to fight desperately enough that her claws became impossible to dodge, especially once Dave and Cole left cover. Raoul took the first hit, a slash to the skull right at his hairline that brought the blood gushing so fast he had to back out of the fight to bind it before it blinded him.

Surprised at how deeply an injury to Raoul pissed me off, I rolled under Sthenno, slicing up into her rib cage as she bent over to intercept me. I was still rolling back out of range when I saw one of the rattlers leap out of her hair. *Fuuuuck!* The angles were perfect. It would land exactly where I meant to stop. I dug my heels into the ground and reversed myself just as Vayl stepped up, holding his sword up by his ear like a big-league batter. As soon as the snake hit the sweet spot Vayl swung for the bleachers, and it dropped in two pieces by my side.

I scrambled for safety as Vayl said, "I thought I had forgotten how to do that."

"Holy crapinator, Vayl, I never realized you knew how!"

"I will have to tell you sometime." He nodded over my shoulder to where Zell and Helena were battling. Helena had just crushed a snake's head under her boot, which I found extra badass considering she'd been brought up to swoon at the sight of an earthworm, but then Zell managed to impress me even more when he punched Roldan in the face (although maybe that was just on principle because the Were was only baring his teeth), shoved his bolt-knife through the gorgon's cheek, and caught the black mamba that was preparing to strike *with his bare hand*, snapping its neck and leaving it to dangle from Sthenno's do like a greasy curl.

Cole and Dave were racing toward the gorgon and the Were at full speed, their swords held tight and low for piercing. They'd each put on a pair of reflective sunglasses for the fight, which I didn't quite see the point of until Cole whistled.

"Oh, Gorgonzola! Give us a kiss, ya big, beautiful girl you!"

She spun around. Dave and Cole had put their heads together and grinned, like they were posing for a picture one of them was taking at close range. That much charm packed into such a tight space? I couldn't resist looking. And neither could Sthenno. She stared straight into those mirrored shades behind which, I guessed, two pairs of eyes were tightly shut. Because Cole's skin remained its typical golden brown and Dave's kept all its freckles. Hers, on the other hand, began to get that leathery look you see on old gals who've sacrificed softness for tanning. Even her snakes looked a little gray around the edges.

"You think this will kill me?" she bellowed as she dragged forward a foot that had suddenly gone sand-tinted. "After generations of men, all of them more brilliant and virile than you, have tried to freeze me with my own stare?" Second foot forward. She looked like an elephant trying to reach its water bowl after a hard night of partying.

"This only slows me down!" She looked over her shoulder at us, her gaze even more venomous than the snakes waving almost drunkenly around her skull. "And makes me harder to stop."

"That works for us," Dave called. He swept his sword up one side of her head. The snakes regenerated much slower than before.

That gave Cole time to carve a ravine in her chest that should've laid her flat. But she was one of the original three, and still connected to Roldan to boot. Which meant she still had the strength to bat his sword away as if it were no more irritating to her than a kid's toy. Cole went flying, landing among a planting of hands that caught him and rolled him into the mud like he was a round of pizza dough.

Muttering so low that I couldn't catch the words, only that Vayl sounded like he was giving himself the lecture of a lifetime, my *sverhamin* rushed up behind Sthenno and shoved his hand around the front of her, into the gaping wound Cole had caused. She screamed, turning her head to sink her teeth into his shoulder. Her claws sank into his hips as he reached for her heartstone, but the snakes struggling to respawn couldn't join in the fray. They yawned their baby mouths and reached out to him like chicks in a nest, begging for regurge, and he laughed as he yanked his hand free, the blood and gore dripping from his fist unable to disguise the treasure he'd found.

"Jasmine! Here!" He tossed me the heartstone, which I caught despite the droplets of ick flying off it and the slick layer of goo that made it slippery as an ice cube. For a second, as I turned toward shore, I did lose my grip. In that nightmare moment I could see it falling through the gaps between the ulnas and skulls on the bridge into the river, where we'd never be able to recover it again. I leaped to land, ran about ten yards, and put it safely on the ground. Not even giving myself time for a sigh of relief, I steadied Sthenno's heartstone between my boots, pulled the hammer and chisel from my belt, and began my second carving of the day while Astral sat so close it was a wonder I didn't smack her on the upswing.

Visualizing the symbol that Roldan had traced repeatedly in the air and my own Inner Bimbo had copied, I tapped the pattern into the stone. Sthenno screamed again. My peripheral vision told me she was coming for me, but everyone in my crew blocked the bridge, their blades forming a barrier her claws and slow-growing asps found impossible to breach.

The rock was slippery. So was the mud underneath. This made the chiseling harder and slower than it had been with Brude. And, perversely, now that Roldan could feel his death drawing near, he'd decided to fight for every last breath. When I heard the growls of a fully changed werewolf, my heart launched into triple time.

Isn't that just like a villain? said Granny May. *Can't even hold on to the little bit of honor he's found for ten damn minutes.* She and the rest of my inner girls had all brought their lawn chairs onto her front porch for the final showdown.

Popcorn? You've decided to watch me battle for my life as if you were at a movie theater?

Not completely, said Teen Me, holding up her snack. *I have yogurt.* She took a bite and then, with her mouth full of strawberry-banana lusciousness, added, *Isn't it interesting how demons react differently to having their heartstones carved by humans? When Kyphas did hers with Cole's name he got all demony and she was all, "Mwa-ha-ha-ha-ha." But now that you're doing Sthenno's, she's acting like it's the end of the world!*

Hopefully it is for her, said Granny May. *Now, hurry up, Jazzy. Your people may be good, but the snakes are growing and Roldan is getting stronger. Finish that already!*

Luckily I work well under pressure. I chinked in the last flourish of Sthenno's glyph just as Roldan broke free of her chain and charged our line. He ran straight for Zell. And though Vayl, Cole, Dave, and Raoul all closed on him quicker than NOLA cops on a rowdy Mardi Gras tourist, he still had the head start and the speed. Zell went down under his snapping jaws and tearing claws.

Helena's scream tore at my heart as I ran to help, still holding the pieces of the Rocenz in my hands, the completed heartstone forgotten in the mud just like the slumping form of Sthenno behind us.

When the men pulled back from their attack on Roldan, his white coat was stained a dark, bloody red. Vayl, alone, tore him off Zell, the sight of whom brought another jagged cry from Helena.

He was also soaked in blood, his throat torn open so badly I thought I could see his spine shining at the back ofi t. But he'd given as good as he got, which we saw when we rolled the Were over to find his homemade dagger sticking out of Roldan's chest.

Helena leaned over Zell, weeping so desperately that her entire body shook. She clutched at his clothes and demanded for him to come back, to wake up. When I looked to Vayl to see if watching this scene was breaking his heart too, I saw two bloody tears tracking down his face.

Helena wrapped her arms around her love and cried even harder, which I hadn't thought possible. Vayl crouched down to lay a hand across her shoulder. The rest of us stood by, helpless. Behind us, a sigh. We turned. Sthenno had dropped to the ground, her snakes limp around her head, her entire chest such a bloody mess she looked like she'd just fallen off an autopsy table. But she wasn't too far gone to whisper, "Cole. You've hovered over the edge of the pit before. Remember all the delectable temptations Kyphas dangled in front of you? She could have given you everything you ever dreamed of. But I can give you more. Not just eternity. You have that now, I can see it in your eyes. Not just women, your skills are so renowned that even I have heard of them."

Her dying eyes turned to me. "I can give you Jasmine. She considered you once. She'd be easy to turn. And then you'd have a lifetime. Redheaded daughters and towheaded sons. A house on the beach and a big-screen TV to cuddle in front of on rainy nights. What do you say, Cole? All you have to do is accept me. You'll never even see me."

He looked at me, then at Vayl. "My girl is waiting for me out there. And I have a feeling she'd be überpissed if I dumped her before we even met. Plus—" He shook his head at Sthenno. "Girl, your sales pitch is just old. Kyphas tried it on me weeks ago and it worked like a salvage-yard reject."

Sthenno sighed again, closed her eyes, and crumpled in on herself like a wilting flower. Which seemed kind of appropriate given her location.

Helena had now begun the hiccup sobbing that let me know she was fast dropping into hysteria. I knelt beside her, opposite Vayl, suddenly acutely aware that this woman was probably my granny's great-great-grandmother. That she'd died giving birth to twin girls, one of whom had continued a line that Vayl had watched over until he'd finally met and fallen for me. Had I been the only one? I couldn't bear to look at him, much less ask just now. So I shook her, whispering, "Helena. Helena," until she looked up and I was staring into the clear blue eyes of my ancestress. I asked, "What are the rules here? Can he die? I mean, considering the fact that he's already dead?"

She shook her head. "I don't know."

Raoul spoke up. "He's being given a choice. He can stay in this body and continue to work with Helena. Or he can find peace. If he chooses the latter, we'll see his soul ascend within a few minutes. If he decides to stay, he's going to be in real danger. The pain will be immense, and the chance for some sort of wicked infection setting in on a wound like that is excellent. As soon as we know, we should move him."

"Then I'd better get busy."

Cole had shoved his shades back, which swept his hair away from his face as well, giving him a much more serious look than usual. He held out his hands to me. "I need that tool."

Something about the way he said it made me decide that questioning his motives was so far out of order that I might lose his friendship if I went there. So I just raised the Rocenz to him. He took the hammer and chisel in his hands, holding them so comfortably I'd have thought he'd been born to work wood, except I'd never seen him craft anything more artistic than a ham-and-cheese sandwich. He took a stone from his pocket. The same one Kyphas had used to carve his name on in Marrakech.

"Cole," said Vayl, his voice firm, warning. "Do you know what you are doing?"

Cole stared into his eyes. "I've never been so sure of anything in my life." He glanced over at me solemnly. "I have to do this." I nodded, only barely understanding. But I didn't have to. He was my friend. He needed my support. That was all I really had to know.

Steadying the rock between his feet just like I'd done with Sthenno's heartstone, Cole began to chisel letters. K. Y. P. H. A. By the time he got to the first curve of the S, the sky above us had begun to darken. We tried to ignore it, but Helena began to look worried.

"We need to get out of here," she whispered to Dave, who was bending over Zell, providing the first-aid skills he'd learned in the military.

He nodded. "I agree." He looked up at Raoul. "Can you take him to your place? He's dead so, you know, I can feel his state pretty clearly." Dave cleared his throat uncomfortably as we tried, and failed, not to gape at him. "The good news is that he's back." Helena clapped her hands to her mouth to hold back a whole series of sobs that insisted on pouring out around the edges of her fingers anyway. Dave stared at her grimly. "The bad news is that he's already infected with something, and he's not fighting it off because he's so badly hurt. It's less like a disease than a way of thinking. He's already considering giving up."

"That's not my Zell," said Helena.

Dave shook his head. "No. I think it's hell, getting into his spirit. And if we don't evacuate him soon, it'll sink into his core. I'm not saying he couldn't beat this on his own. He's got you, Helena, and that's a lot. But if what Raoul said is true about hell's atmosphere, and I'm right about this infection..."

"Then we go," said Raoul. He picked Zell up and threw him over his shoulder like he weighed only slightly more than a basket of dirty clothes. "You can handle this," he told me.

"Of course. I'll be in touch."

He smirked. "That I know." Then his lips stretched into a smile. "I'm proud of you, Jasmine." That was all he said. And I didn't know how to answer except to blink like a damn barn owl. Then Helena distracted us both, reaching out to Vayl, who took her hand, bowed over it like they were still living in eighteenth-century London, and kissed it. When he rose again, the sorrow in his eyes was so deep it threatened to swallow them both.

"My girl. Had I known you were here—"

"I know. You would've rescued me in an instant. And probably died, or worse, been captured and suffered endless tortures in the attempt." She smiled up at him. "You showed me the way to survive." She glanced at Zell. "Even to be happy. And then I found out how to continue on my own. Isn't that what good parents do?"

He shrugged. "I would not know."

She put her arms around him. "But you do. I love you, Papa. Zell and I will come visit as soon as he's better." She glanced over at me. "We have a lot of catching up to do, don't we?"

No shit, Sherlock! I glared at my Inner Bimbo, but she was belting out the wrong words to "Banana Fana Shoshana" along with her newfound backup singers between long sips from her third margarita, so I looked further. To my mental librarian, who was skidding around the stacks in her sensible pumps, pencils sticking out of her bun in five different directions as she searched wildly for something to write with. She found a crayon lying on top of a slightly dented study carrel and waved it at me as she yelled, *Helena is family? And Vayl never told you? Shouldn't we feel betrayed? Plus, what does that make him, your...guardian-in-law? Should we be grossed out? Or mad? How do I categorize this???*

I looked at Vayl, who was watching his adopted daughter help Raoul balance Zell on his shoulder. The love on his face, purely paternal, changed radically when he turned to me. *You know what, Book Lady? We're just going to let this one go.*

A sound, something between a scream and a cry of anguish, turned us both toward hell's fence. As it had with Brude, the air had begun to shimmer and then to take shape. Kyphas appeared, still enveloped in her billowing black dress with its extra-long sleeves and face-masking hood. It was pulled back to reveal her expression, shocked out of its misery as soon as she realized what Cole was doing.

She held up an arm. "No," she croaked. "I haven't paid my dues. They'll come after you if you do this."

He paused to look up at her. "In the end, you showed me a moment of true love. How could I move on without doing the same for you?"

"Cole—"

Her head jerked back as he finished her name. She screamed. And a million black moths shot out of her mouth, flapping into the sky with the sound I had always secretly thought Death would make as it sneaked up to an old man's bedside. When she dropped her chin, we gasped. Her face had re-formed, its beauty so breathtaking I found it hard to sit still beneath that brilliant golden gaze. The hood had completely fallen off, revealing her mane of blond hair. And when she raised her hands to stare at them wonderingly, they were complete, the skin back to the healthy tan that pale women like me had envied in her better days.

Love and gratitude spilled from her eyes along with her tears as she said, "Thank you. Oh, Cole, thank you." And then she closed her eyes as she began to glow, the color brightening first to bright orange, then to red. It didn't seem to hurt. Her expression remained serene as she burst into so many pieces that she resembled the sparkling residue from a high-flying fountain whose droplets cross into the sun before they drop back into their pool. Hers had direction as well, pointing themselves directly to the rock Cole had carved: They poured themselves into it until it sparkled like a gemstone. When the light show had finished, Cole dug a hole with his fingers and gently buried Kyphas's heartstone in the field. Raoul told me later that a red rosebush grew in that spot, and that occasionally Cole asked one of the hell scouts to bring him a flower from it.

I wasn't so sentimental as my old friend. But, then, I didn't have to wait nearly as long as he did for the love of my life to show. He walked beside me all the way back to the world while the rest of our crew followed at our backs. He was holding my hand as we stepped through the plane portal. And he was the one who hugged me first when Bergman rushed into the bathroom to say, "Jasmine! Jack's going to be okay!"

Chapter Thirty-Nine

Monday, June 18, 3:15 a.m.

Funny how seeing your dog attempt to wag his tail as you enter the room brightens your entire outlook on life. Even Aaron, who'd had to spend the entire mission holding a gun to the portal and hoping he didn't have to shoot it, seemed cheered by the sight.

After our battle-wind-down powwow, during which we all retold our stories, Bergman demanded to be repaid for the exorbitant vet fee, and Aaron apologized a thousand times for doubting us—because, damn, it's a little mind-shattering having to guard the only escape for a whole group of innocent people when the pregnant woman's husband informs you he'll kill you if you fail—everybody scattered. Cassandra and Dave wandered back to the honeymoon suite. Cole and Bergman waved good night and went their separate ways. Astral curled up on the bed beside Jack, who instantly began to snore. Which left Aaron and Lotus sitting at the table with Vayl and me.

He regarded his children, first his son, then his daughter, with adoring eyes. "You have turned into quite fascinating people over time," he told them. "I cannot even begin to tell you how it fills my heart to know you are well. That your souls survived and continue their journey even into today."

Lotus nodded. "I'm telling you what. This girl?" She pointed to herself with both thumbs. "Not journeying back to hell. Ever. Even if that means wearing a bra every single day."

I turned my laugh into a cough as Vayl went into the absolute stillness that occasionally substituted itself for deep embarrassment. Finally he said, "I am overjoyed to hear that." After a beat, he went on. "I shall not make a pest of myself. But if you would both allow me to check in on you from time to time, I would be grateful."

Lotus and Aaron exchanged looks that were, to give them credit, only slightly weirded out. Aaron said to Lotus, "My dad's dead. How about yours?"

She shrugged. "He's kind of a jerk. But he's the only one I have. Had." She frowned at Vayl. "Until now." She raised her eyebrows at Aaron, who nodded for her to continue. "As long as you promise not to bite us or try to turn us, we're cool with you coming to visit. But you have to call first."

"And plan on staying at a hotel," Aaron put in.

Lotus added, "Also? Don't be killing anybody in the towns where we live. We don't want to have to move every time you decide to stop by for a chat." She turned to Aaron. "Do you have anything else?"

He nodded. "Yeah." He pointed at me. "She's kinda scary. So she has to learn how to bake cookies. I was thinking anybody who knows how to bake cookies should be okay."

He wiped a band of sweat off his forehead and resolutely avoided my glare as he turned to Lotus, who said, "Actually, that makes a lot of sense. What do you think, Vayl?"

I leaned over and whispered in Vayl's ear. "How did they know I don't know how to bake cookies?"

Minute shrug. "Perhaps they can see it in your eyes?" He waited.

I humphed. "Okay. But they have to be chocolate chip."

"I do not think they care which kind you make, as long as you promise to learn."

I sat back in my chair, willing Vayl not to chuckle as he leaned forward and shook hands with his children, saying, "We have a deal," so formally he might've been sitting across from a couple of big-time CEOs.

Soon afterward Lotus and Aaron found rooms for themselves, leaving us alone with our pets, our grubby clothes, and our wildly divergent thoughts.

"It has been quite an adventure, my *pretera*," Vayl said.

"Yeah." I'd sent my inner girls on a mission to knock on all the doors of my mind. If anyone who wasn't supposed to be there answered, I just might have a nervous breakdown. But so far…no demons anywhere. I was beginning to accept the fact that Brude was gone forever.

"I found my children."

"And they are unique."

"Helena is a wonder as well."

"Yeah." I cleared my throat. "About her."

He took my hand and led me to the bathroom, where he slowly began to peel off my torn and bloody clothes. Whenever he found a scratch or bruise he paused to lay a kiss on it as he explained, "Yes. She is your ancestress. And yes, I have looked after your line ever since I adopted her. For the most part I have kept a respectful distance, so that the good fortune that has befallen your family members has seemed to be just that. And it seemed that the same would be true of you. I had never even seen you until after Matt died. But your circumstances demanded that I come closer. I felt you needed protection from something, though I could not pinpoint what that was."

"Because it was myself," I whispered, as I began to unbutton his tattered shirt.

He nodded. "The moment I saw you, everything changed for me." He wrapped his hands around mine and I looked up into his eyes. "I had never felt for a woman the way I did for you then. I loved you instantly." He raised my hands to his lips, his ring glinting in the soft glow of the single light we'd left on as he brushed them softly against each knuckle until I could feel the tingle of his touch down the backs of my thighs and into my feet. "You are part of my soul."

I waited until he had thoroughly kissed each finger, then I freed my hand so I could part the front of his shirt and slowly pull it down his arms so I could enjoy each new bit of skin and muscle it revealed. His chest, as broad and curl-covered as it had been the day he was turned, rippled under my fingers as I swept them across it and down to his flat, hard stomach. I looked up into his emerald eyes as I began to undo his belt. "I never wanted to be this close to you. But you're irresistible, you know." As I freed the leather band and dropped it to the floor, I wrapped my arm around his waist and pulled him so close I could feel already that I'd excited him in the extreme. "You're like air to me now. Without you, I couldn't breathe. I wouldn't want to."

I raised my lips. Instead of dropping his head he lifted me in his arms, holding me effortlessly while I wrapped my arms around his neck and my legs around his hips, pressing my breasts into his chest.

"I love you, Vayl," I said between multiple kisses along his jaw and neck.

"And I love you, Jasmine." Long pause while we shared a kiss so phenomenal that when it was finished I had to think for a minute before I could remember where in the world we were standing.

"Are you still cool with me spending more downtime with family? Because, you know, that would mean you'd have to hang out with them too."

He took another moment to kiss my forehead. "I relish the thought. Perhaps, one day, *you* would like to join Evie and Cassandra in motherhood?"

I regarded him seriously. "I don't know. Do you think we could pull that off?"

"Perhaps. We are becoming so…different. Also, I hear I am a wonderful father."

I threw my arms around him. "You are. Which is a good thing, because it's entirely possible I'd suck as a mother."

"I doubt it."

"You know," I whispered in his ear, "it's also entirely possible we may never find out."

"I do not care," he said earnestly. "We will be together. And think of the fun we will have trying!"

I snorted. Then I stopped. Because I *was* entertaining a couple of ideas, and it was suddenly taking all my concentration to stand upright. Then I got a whiff of myself. I said, "I hate to ruin the moment. But I stink. Plus, I think I might have gorgon blood on my bra."

Vayl chuckled. "That is more than blood."

"Eeeeewww!"

"The last one in the shower has to unwrap the hotel soap."

"Get outta my way!"

extras

orbit

meet the author

Cindy Pringle

JENNIFER RARDIN began writing at the age of twelve. She penned eight Jaz Parks novels in her life. She passed away in September 2010.

introducing

If you enjoyed
THE DEADLIEST BITE,
look out for

TEMPEST RISING

Book 1 of the Jane True series

by Nicole Peeler

Living in small town Rockabill, Maine, Jane True always knew she didn't quite fit in with so-called normal society. During her nightly, clandestine swim in the freezing winter ocean, a grisly find leads Jane to startling revelations about her heritage: she is only half-human.

Now Jane must enter a world filled with supernatural creatures that are terrifying, beautiful, and deadly—all of which perfectly describe her new "friend," Ryu, a gorgeous and powerful vampire.

It is a world where nothing can be taken for granted: a dog can heal with a lick; spirits bag your groceries; and whatever you do, never—ever—rub the genie's lamp.

I eyeballed the freezer, trying to decide what to cook for dinner that night. Such a decision was no mean feat, since a visiting stranger might assume that Martha Stewart not only lived with us but was preparing for the apocalypse. Frozen lasagnas, casseroles, pot pies, and the like filled our icebox nearly to the brim. Finally deciding on fish chowder, I took out some haddock and mussels. After a brief, internal struggle, I grabbed some salmon to make extra soup to—you guessed it—freeze. Yeah, the stockpiling was more than a little OCD, but it made me feel better. It also meant that when I actually had something to do for the entire evening, I could leave my dad by himself without feeling too guilty about it.

My dad wasn't an invalid—not exactly. But he had a bad heart and needed help taking care of things, especially with my mother gone. So I took up the slack, which I was happy to do. It's not like I had much else on my plate, what with being the village pariah and all.

It's amazing how being a pariah gives you ample amounts of free time.

After putting in the laundry and cleaning the downstairs bathroom, I went upstairs to take a shower. I would have loved to walk around all day with the sea salt on my skin, but not even in Rockabill was Eau de Brine an acceptable perfume. Like many twentysomethings, I'd woken up early that day to go exercise. Unlike most twenty-somethings, however, my morning exercise took the form of an hour or so long swim in the freezing ocean. And in one of America's deadliest whirlpools. Which is why I am so careful to keep the swimming on the DL. It might be a great cardio workout, but it probably would get me burned at the stake. This is New England, after all.

As I got dressed in my work clothes—khaki chinos and a long-sleeved pink polo-style shirt with *Read It and Weep* embroidered in navy blue over the breast pocket—I heard my father emerge from his bedroom and clomp down the stairs. His job in the morning was to make the coffee, so I took a moment to apply a little mascara, blush, and some lip gloss, before brushing out my damp black hair. I kept it cut in a much longer—and admittedly more unkempt—version of Cleopatra's style because I liked to hide my dark eyes under my long bangs. Most recently, my nemesis, Stuart Gray, had referred to them as "demon eyes." They're not as Marilyn Manson as that, thank you very much, but even I had to admit to difficulty determining where my pupil ended and my iris began.

I went back downstairs to join my dad in the kitchen, and I felt that pang in my heart that I get sometimes when I'm struck by how he's changed. He'd been a fisherman, but he'd had to retire about ten years ago, on disability, when his heart condition worsened. Once a handsome, confident, and brawny man whose presence filled any space he entered, his long illness and my mother's disappearance had diminished him in every possible way. He looked so small and gray in his faded old bathrobe, his hands trembling from the anti-arrhythmics he takes for his screwed-up heart, that it took every ounce of self-control I had not to make him sit down and rest. Even if his body didn't agree, he still felt himself to be the man he had been, and I knew I already walked a thin line between caring for him and treading on his dignity. So I put on my widest smile and bustled into the kitchen, as if we were a father and daughter in some sitcom set in the 1950s.

"Good morning, Daddy!" I beamed.

"Morning, honey. Want some coffee?" He asked me that question every morning, even though the answer had been yes since I was fifteen.

"Sure, thanks. Did you sleep all right?"

"Oh, yes. And you? How was your morning?" My dad never asked me directly about the swimming. It's a question that lay under the auspices of the "don't ask, don't tell" policy that ruled our household. For example, he didn't ask me about my swimming, I didn't ask him about my mother. He didn't ask me about Jason, I didn't ask him about my mother. He didn't ask me whether or not I was happy in Rockabill, I didn't ask him about my mother...

"Oh, I slept fine, Dad. Thanks." Of course I hadn't, really, as I only needed about four hours of sleep a night. But that's another thing we never talked about.

He asked me about my plans for the day, while I made us a breakfast of scrambled eggs on whole wheat toast. I told him that I'd be working till six, then I'd go to the grocery store on the way home. So, as usual for a Monday, I'd take the car to work. We performed pretty much the exact same routine every week, but it was nice of him to act like it was possible I might have new and exciting plans. On Mondays, I didn't have to worry about him eating lunch, as Trevor McKinley picked him up to go play a few hours of cheeky lunchtime poker with George Varga, Louis Finch, and Joe Covelli. They're all natives of Rockabill and friends since childhood, except for Joe, who moved here to Maine about twenty years ago to open up our local garage. That's how things were around Rockabill. For the winter, when the tourists were mostly absent, the town was populated by natives who grew up together and were more intimately acquainted with each other's dirty laundry than their own hampers. Some people enjoyed that intimacy. But when you were more usually the object of the whispers than the subject, intimacy had a tendency to feel like persecution.

We ate while we shared our local paper, *The Light House News*.

But because the paper mostly functioned as a vehicle for advertising things to tourists, and the tourists were gone for the season, the pickings were scarce. Yet we went through the motions anyway. For all of our sins, no one could say that the True family wasn't good at going through the motions. After breakfast, I doled out my father's copious pills and set them next to his orange juice. He flashed me his charming smile, which was the only thing left unchanged after the ravages to his health and his heart.

"Thank you, Jane," he said. And I knew he meant it, despite the fact that I'd set his pills down next to his orange juice every single morning for the past twelve years.

I gulped down a knot in my throat, since I knew that no small share of his worry and grief was due to me, and kissed him on the cheek. Then I bustled around clearing away breakfast, and bustled around getting my stuff together, and bustled out the door to get to work. In my experience, bustling is always a great way to keep from crying.

Tracy Gregory, the owner of Read It and Weep, was already hard at work when I walked in the front door. The Gregorys were an old fishing family from Rockabill, and Tracy was their prodigal daughter. She had left to work in Los Angeles, where she had apparently been a successful movie stylist. I say apparently because she never told us the names of any of the movies she'd worked on. She'd only moved back to Rockabill about five years ago to open Read It and Weep, which was our local bookstore, café, and all-around tourist trap. Since tourism replaced fishing as our major industry, Rockabill can just about support an all-year-round enterprise like Read It and Weep. But other things, like the nicer restaurant—rather unfortunately named The Pig Out Bar and Grill—close for the winter.

"Hey, girl," she said gruffly, as I locked the door behind me. We didn't open for another half hour.

"Hey, Tracy. Grizelda back?"

Grizelda was Tracy's girlfriend, and they'd caused quite a stir when they first appeared in Rockabill together. Not only were they lesbians, but they were as fabulously lesbionic as the inhabitants of a tiny village in Maine could ever imagine. Tracy carried herself like a rugby player, and dressed like one, too. But she had an easygoing charisma that got her through the initial gender panic triggered by her reentry into Rockabill society.

And if Tracy made heads turn, Grizelda practically made them spin *Exorcist* style. Grizelda was not Grizelda's real name. Nor was Dusty Nethers, the name she'd used when was a porn star. As Dusty Nethers, Grizelda had been fiery haired and as boobilicious as a *Baywatch* beauty. But in her current incarnation, as Grizelda Montague, she sported a sort of Gothic-hipster look—albeit one that was still very boobilicious. A few times a year Grizelda disappeared for weeks or a month, and upon her return home she and Tracy would complete some big project they'd been discussing, like redecorating the store or adding a sunroom onto their little house. Lord knows what she got up to on her profit-venture vacations. But whatever it was, it didn't affect her relationship with Tracy. The pair were as close as any husband and wife in Rockabill, if not closer, and seeing how much they loved each other drove home to me my own loneliness.

"Yeah, Grizzie's back. She'll be here soon. She has something for you... something scandalous, knowing my lady love."

I grinned. "Awesome. I love her gifts."

Because of Grizzie, I had a drawer full of naughty underwear, sex toys, and dirty books. Grizzie gave such presents for *every* occasion; it didn't matter if it was your high school graduation, your fiftieth wedding anniversary, or your baby's baptism. This particular predilection meant she was a prominent figure on wedding shower guest lists from Rockabill to Eastport, but made her dangerous for children's parties. Most parents didn't appreciate an "every day of the week" pack of thongs for their eleven-year-old daughter. Once she'd given me a gift certificate for a "Hollywood" bikini wax and I had to Google the term. What I discovered made me way too scared to use it, so it sat in my "dirty drawer," as I called it, as a talking point. Not that anyone ever went into my dirty drawer with me, but I talked to myself a lot, and it certainly provided amusing fodder for my own conversations.

It was also rather handy—no pun intended—to have access to one's own personal sex shop during long periods of enforced abstinence…such as the last eight years of my life.

"And," Tracy responded with a rueful shake of her head, "her gifts love you. Often quite literally."

"That's all right, somebody has to," I answered back, horrified at the bitter inflection that had crept into my voice.

But Tracy, bless her, just stroked a gentle hand over my hair that turned into a tiny one-armed hug, saying nothing.

"Hands off my woman!" crowed a hard-edged voice from the front door. Grizelda!

"Oh, sorry," I apologized, backing away from Tracy.

"I meant for Tracy to get off *you*," Grizzie said, swooping toward me to pick me up in a bodily hug, my own well-endowed chest clashing with her enormous fake bosoms. I hated being short at times like these. Even though I loved all five feet and eleven inches of Grizzie, and had more than my fair share of affection for her ta-ta-riddled hugs, I loathed being manhandled.

She set me down and grasped my hands in hers, backing away to look me over appreciatively while holding my fingers at arm's length. "Mmm, mmm," she said, shaking her head. "Girl, I could sop you up with a biscuit."

I laughed, as Tracy rolled her eyes.

"Quit sexually harassing the staff, Grizzly Bear," was her only comment.

"I'll get back to sexually harassing you in a minute, passion flower, but right now I want to appreciate our Jane." Grizelda winked at me with her florid violet eyes—she wore colored lenses—and I couldn't help but giggle like a schoolgirl.

"I've brought you a little something," she said, her voice sly.

I clapped my hands in excitement and hopped up and down in a little happy dance.

I really did love Grizzie's gifts, even if they challenged the tenuous grasp of human anatomy imparted to me by Mrs. Renault in her high school biology class.

"Happy belated birthday!" she cried as she handed me a beautifully wrapped package she pulled from her enormous handbag. I admired the shiny black paper and the sumptuous red velvet ribbon tied up into a decadent bow—Grizzie did everything with style—before tearing into it with glee. After slitting open the tape holding the box closed with my thumbnail, I was soon holding in my hands the most beautiful red satin nightgown I'd ever seen. It was a deep, bloody, blue-based red, the perfect red for my skin tone. And it was, of course, the perfect length, with a slit up the side that would rise almost to my hip. Grizzie had this magic ability to always buy people clothes that fit. The top was generously cut for its small dress size, the bodice gathered into a sort of clamshell-like tailoring that I knew would cup my boobs like those hands in that famous Janet Jackson picture. The straps were slightly thicker, to give support, and crossed over the *very* low-cut back. It was absolutely gorgeous—very adult and sophisticated—and I couldn't stop stroking the deliciously watery satin.

"Grizzie," I breathed. "It's gorgeous…but too much! This must have cost a fortune."

"You are worth a fortune, little Jane. Besides, I figured you might need something nice…since Mark's 'special deliveries' should have culminated in a date by now."

Grizzie's words trailed off as my face fell and Tracy, behind her, made a noise like Xena, Warrior Princess, charging into battle.

Before Tracy could launch into just how many ways she wanted to eviscerate our new letter carrier, I said, very calmly, "I won't be going on any dates with Mark."

"What happened?" Grizzie asked, as Tracy made another grunting declaration of war behind us.

"Well..." I started, but where should I begin? Mark was new to Rockabill, a widowed employee of the U.S. Postal Service, who had recently moved to our little corner of Maine with his two young daughters. He'd kept forgetting to deliver letters and packages, necessitating second, and sometimes third, trips to our bookstore, daily. I'd thought he was sweet, but rather dumb, until Tracy had pointed out that he only forgot stuff when I was working.

So we'd flirted and flirted and flirted over the course of a month. Until, just a few days ago, he'd asked me out. I was thrilled. He was cute; he was *new*; he'd lost someone he was close to, as well. And he "obviously" didn't judge me on my past.

You know what they say about assuming...

"We had a date set up, but he cancelled. I guess he asked me out before he knew about...everything. Then someone must have told him. He's got kids, you know."

"So?" Grizzie growled, her smoky voice already furious.

"So, he said that he didn't think I'd be a good influence. On his girls."

"That's fucking ridiculous," Grizzie snarled, just as Tracy made a series of inarticulate chittering noises behind us. She was normally the sedate, equable half of her and Grizzie's partnership, but Tracy had nearly blown a gasket when I'd called her crying after Mark bailed on me. I think she would have torn off his head, but then we wouldn't have gotten our inventory anymore.

I lowered my head and shrugged. Grizzie moved forward, having realized that Tracy already had the anger market cornered.

"I'm sorry, honey," she said, wrapping her long arms around me. "That's...such a shame."

And it was a shame. My friends wanted me to move on, my dad wanted me to move on. Hell, except for that tiny sliver of me that was still frozen in guilt, *I* wanted to move on. But the rest of Rockabill, it seems, didn't agree.

Grizzie brushed the bangs back from my eyes, and when she saw tears glittering she intervened, Grizelda-style. Dipping me like a tango dancer, she growled sexily, "Baby, I'm gonna butter yo' bread..." before burying her face in my exposed belly and giving me a resounding zerbert.

That did just the trick. I was laughing again, thanking my stars for about the zillionth time that they had brought Grizzie and Tracy back to Rockabill because I didn't know what I would have done without them. I gave Tracy her own hug for the present, and then took it to the back room with my stuff. I opened the box to give the red satin one last parting caress, and then closed it with a contented sigh.

It would look absolutely gorgeous in my dirty drawer.

We had only a few things to do to get the store ready for opening, which left much time for chitchat. About a half hour of intense gossip later, we had pretty much exhausted "what happened when you were gone" as a subject of conversation and had started in on plans for the coming week, when the little bell above the door tinkled. My heart sank when I saw it was Linda Allen, self-selected female delegate for my own personal persecution squad. She wasn't quite as bad as Stuart Gray, who hated me even more than Linda did, but she did her best to keep up with him.

Speaking of the rest of Rockabill, I thought, as Linda headed toward romance.

She didn't bother to speak to me, of course. She just gave me one of her loaded looks that she could fire off like a World War II gunship. The looks always said the same things. They spoke of the fact that I was the girl whose crazy mother had shown up in the center of town out of nowhere, *naked*, in the middle of a storm. The fact that she'd *stolen* one of the most eligible Rockabill bachelors and *ruined him for life*. The fact that she'd given birth to a baby *without being married*. The fact that I insisted on being *that child* and upping the ante by being *just as weird as my mother*. That was only the tip of the vituperative iceberg that Linda hauled into my presence whenever she had the chance.

Unfortunately, Linda read nearly as compulsively as I did, so

I saw her at least twice a month when she'd come in for a new stack of romance novels. She liked a very particular kind of plot: the sort where the pirate kidnaps some virgin damsel, rapes her into loving him, and then dispatches lots of seamen while she polishes his cutlass. Or where the Highland clan leader kidnaps some virginal English Rose, rapes her into loving him, and then kills entire armies of Sassenachs while she stuffs his haggis. Or where the Native American warrior kidnaps a virginal white settler, rapes her into loving him, and then kills a bunch of colonists while she whets his tomahawk. I hated to get Freudian on Linda, but her reading patterns suggested some interesting insights into why she was such a complete bitch.

Tracy had received a phone call while Linda was picking out her books, and Grizelda was sitting on a stool far behind the counter in a way that clearly said "I'm not actually working, thanks." But Linda pointedly ignored the fact that I was free to help her, choosing, instead, to stand in front of Tracy. Tracy gave that little eye gesture where she looked at Linda, then looked at me, as if to say, "She can help you," but Linda insisted on being oblivious to my presence. Tracy sighed and cut her telephone conversation short. I knew that Tracy would love to tell Linda to stick her attitude where the sun don't shine, but Read It and Weep couldn't afford to lose a customer who was as good at buying books as she was at being a snarky snake face. So Tracy rang up Linda's purchases and bagged them for her as politely as one can without actually being friendly and handed the bag over to Linda.

Who, right on cue, gave me her parting shot, the look I knew was coming but was never quite able to deflect.

The look that said, *There's the freak who killed her own boyfriend.*

She was wrong, of course. I hadn't actually killed Jason. I was just the reason he was dead.